T5-DHD-481

"WOULDN'T YOU DO ANYTHING TO BE ALIVE AGAIN?"

"You have been assigned a target," the old man said, "specially selected with a great deal of thought." He broke into a cough, then snapped his fingers. A little girl wearing old-fashioned buckle-on skates dashed in, carrying a plastic bag full of small envelopes. She zipped over to them and held out the bag.

Mia hesitated and Quentin rolled his eyes. Mia snatched an envelope. Holding her breath, she lifted the flap. Their lives depended on the person named within.

She stared at the typewritten letters.

She looked up at Quentin, her mouth sagging open.

He turned the plain white card around so he could read the name. Then he whistled.

CHELSEA JORDAN.

Save the soul of Chelsea Jordan, the child star who'd turned into a soft porn princess before maturing into a genuine movie star bitch?

"Think of this as a creative challenge," Quentin said.

Mia thought she'd be sick.

HEAVEN COMES HOME

NIKKI HOLIDAY

AVON BOOKS ◆ NEW YORK

HEAVEN COMES HOME is an original publication of Avon Books. This work has never before appeared in book form. This work is a novel. Any similarity to actual persons or events is purely coincidental.

AVON BOOKS
A division of
The Hearst Corporation
1350 Avenue of the Americas
New York, New York 10019

Copyright © 1996 by Nancy Wagner
Inside cover author photo by Debbi De Mont Photography
Published by arrangement with the author
Library of Congress Catalog Card Number: 96-96076
ISBN: 0-380-78456-4

First Avon Books Printing: September 1996

This book is dedicated with love to
L.J. and Maxine,
the best parents ever

1 〜

"**W**hat do you mean I'm dead?"

"Both," Mia Tortelli corrected Quentin Grandy, winner of last year's Academy Award for Best Director. "We're *both* dead."

"Impossible."

"If it's so impossible, why does the sign over this door read 'Entering Purgatory. Please take a number'?"

Quentin whipped around, scanning 360 degrees. Boisterous as ever, he shouted and waved his hands. "Okay, guys, very funny trick. Come on out and tell me how you did it. It's been a long day. Mia and I just want to go home."

Mia studied their surroundings too, knowing in her heart she wasn't looking for tricks played by clever friends and co-workers. They stood in an alley, the midnight blackness relieved only by the dim glow of the Entering Purgatory sign. Uneven bricks lined the ground beneath their feet; the arched wooden door they faced would fit nicely as a set piece for a medieval castle. In the muddy light, the number counter next to the door looked like the one in old man Merona's corner market.

She stepped closer, ignoring Quentin's shouts and antics. There, carved on the side of the battered red ticket machine, were her brother's initials. A parade of goosebumps marched up her arms and she backed away.

Mia had often been heard to say she'd follow film maker Quentin Grandy, her mentor and employer, anywhere, but she never meant to include the after-life.

"Quentin, hush." Rubbing her arms, she said, "Think back and tell me what's the last thing you remember."

As usual, her soft voice halted his tirade. Looking thoughtful, he said, "We were on the lot, for the special-effects show for the children with cancer." He paused and seemed to be playing a scene in his mind, a habit of his Mia knew well. "No, we'd just finished the show and you walked over . . ."

Mia nodded. "And then?"

His eyes widened and Mia knew he was picturing the same scene that played in her mind. A scene more vivid than the incredibly good dailies of Quentin's latest film, *DinoDaddy*.

A frown troubled his normally light-hearted countenance. Quentin, Mia often thought, was the quintessential little boy, a trait which accounted for his success in creating movies that so easily touched America's heart and spirit. He teased, he fascinated, he brought the audience to the edge of their seats and always, always, gave them the gift of believing the world a magical place.

"And then I talked you into climbing into the stunt chopper and you said only if I did, too, so I did." Quentin's eyes widened. "I worked the controls and we rose. Up. Up. Up. We waved to the last of the children." He looked like he was going to be sick. "That copter was attached to a crane. I never would have urged you to get in if I didn't believe it was safe."

Mia closed her eyes briefly, unable to wipe from her mind the memory of the sickening plunge from the top of the hangar-high building. "It's not your fault, Quentin."

Quentin studied his hands, turning them palm to topside as if he'd never seen them before. Or would never see them again. "But it is. I talked you into it. You never would have done it without me. But, no, Quentin wanted to play and he wanted you to keep him company!" He smashed a fist against his forehead, barely missing his glasses.

She grabbed his shoulders and shook hard. "Listen, you. I chose to get in that copter and I won't have you blaming yourself. If we're dead, we're dead."

"No!" Quentin shot his fists skyward. "We are not dead!"

To that, Mia said nothing. She could kick herself for agreeing to step foot in that crazy copter, but she'd wanted to show Quentin she wasn't so work-obsessed she couldn't have a little fun. But she wasn't one to argue with reality.

As a producer, she dealt in facts, budgets, actuality. Fantasy was Quentin's lifeblood, but at this moment, she couldn't see how fantasy could do them any good.

The door creaked outward and a white-haired man poked his face around the corner. "If you wasn't dead you wouldn't be waking me up at this

time of da night. Now make up your mind. Youse
coming in or staying out there?" He spat and Mia
jumped. "Don't make me no difference."

"Mr. Merona?"

"What of it? In or out?"

"You ran the corner market off Melrose?"

He shrugged. "Mebbe. Mebbe not. Who wants ta
know?"

Mia fell silent. If only she hadn't stolen that jar of
Noxzema, she could tell him her name with a clear
conscience.

"Let's go in," Quentin said suddenly and moved
toward the door.

Mia followed, wishing her mother hadn't been so
old-fashioned. Soap and water were good enough for
her so soap and water were good enough for Mia.
But her pimples had driven her to theft and now,
who knew what would happen to her. Could seeing
old man Merona be a sign . . . ?

From whom? From where? Out of habit long
dormant, Mia almost murmured a prayer to the
Virgin Mary, but caught herself. She'd left religion
behind, outgrown the Catholicism of her Irish mother and Sicilian father by the end of her first semester
at UCLA. Okay, so she was dead. So okay, the
church would say she had sinned. Big deal. Yet Mia
couldn't help but look over her shoulder, knowing in
her secret self she expected demons to pounce on her
at any moment and bear her off to hell.

The goosebumps returned full force and Mia
shifted her attention to her surroundings, reminding
herself she'd outgrown that superstitious bosh. She
blinked from the wattage blazing in the great hall
where they now stood. Merona had disappeared, but

all around them people bustled and loudspeakers blared.

"It's Grand Central," Quentin said. "Look at that clock over there, and the balconies framing the upper level. These archways are the exits to the trains."

Mia saw what he meant. The old benches were back in place. Some of them even had those old-timey televisions fastened to them at intervals. "It's brighter, though."

"Guess that makes sense," Quentin said, and chuckled. "You need a lot of light when you're dead. Oh, man, what a joke. Dead at twenty-six!" He ripped his ever-present Yankees cap off his head and dragged his fingers through his curly brown hair. Mia wanted to reach out and shush him, hold him to her and comfort him.

And have him comfort her, too.

She didn't want to be dead. She turned twenty-five only last month, and there was so much she hadn't experienced.

Oh, she'd had lots of adventures, especially for a girl from East Los Angeles. In the years during and after college when she served as Quentin's chief production assistant, she'd trekked with him to New Mexico where she slept in a tent and fought off snakes during Quentin's first low-budget shoot. Later, in Mexico, she endured thirteen days of Montezuma's revenge while Quentin put together his acclaimed short *Quetzalcoatl's Overcoat,* and during the frenzied production of *SlashDance,* she braved the gangs of South Central Los Angeles.

SlashDance won Quentin the Oscar for Best Director, for which he'd thanked his producer Mia

Tortelli in the star-packed Shrine Auditorium. In the wake of the Oscar success frenzy, Mia followed Quentin into a $70 million deal at MegaFilms with the title of co-producer, a corner office, and so much money she almost considered getting her hair done some place other than SuperCuts.

Oh, yes, she'd had adventures, achievements, triumphs.

But what she craved was love.

Glancing at Quentin's sorrowful face, she thought of her dreams of him waking one day and realizing Mia was the only woman for him. She ached for the number of times she wished for the courage to share her feelings with him. But Mia allowed only her good common sense to rule her life. And good common sense dictated that she not let silly emotion ruin a good thing. If Quentin was ever going to look at her as a woman he had to come to it on his own.

But oh how she wanted him!

"Mia, my friend, we may as well look around." Quentin offered her his hand. She accepted the offer of friendship and comfort as they set off to explore.

Smiling men and women manned brightly lit ticket windows. Orderly queues formed in front of the dozens of windows, but Mia couldn't help but think some of the people standing there looked quite stunned and lost. Others wore the air of old-timers.

"How long do you think people stay here?" she whispered to Quentin.

He shrugged. "You're the ex-Catholic. You tell me."

"Well, that was a long time ago."

He smiled and raised his brows. "You're an old lady of twenty-five, can't have been that long ago."

"Don't tease me, I'm dead."

His smile faded. "It doesn't matter how long people stay in Purgatory. Nothing matters once you're dead."

A fresh-faced youth on roller blades swooped up and executed an elaborate pirouette before stopping in their path. "Oh, but it does matter," he said, extending a white-gloved hand. "Welcome to Purgatory. I'm Brian, and I'm your tour guide."

"Disneyland lives on," Quentin said.

Mia smothered a smile and shook the boy's hand.

"Actually, sir," the boy said, "Mr. Disney never stopped in here."

"Oh, I didn't mean that," Quentin said. "I'm sure Walt must have gone straight to heaven."

"I wouldn't know about that, but this terminal serves only people who die by accident." Holding out a device that resembled a Nintendo Gameboy, he said, "I need to scan you into our system." He placed the unit over the center of Mia's forehead, then moved it to Quentin.

"The third eye," Quentin murmured, curiosity gleaming in his eyes.

Taking in the lively look that had replaced the earlier anger and denial, Mia knew Quentin was thinking of ways he'd use this experience in his work. She'd seen that look so many times before.

Reading from his hand-held unit, the boy whistled, then glanced up at Quentin as if he wanted to ask for his autograph. "Quentin Grandy," he breathed, suddenly exhibiting the gawkiness much more typical of a fifteen-year-old. "*SlashDance* was the most rad film!"

"You saw it?" Quentin glanced around the huge hall. "Here?"

The boy looked down and flexed his gloved hands.

"Oh, no, not here." He sighed then his faced brightened once again. "I haven't been here long."

"What are you doing here?" Quentin asked.

The boy studied his feet. "Er, blading accident. Didn't see the car."

"So you're dead." Quentin clearly continued to struggle with this reality.

"Oh, yes, Mr. Grandy, I'm dead." He toyed with the Welcome to Purgatory button on his lapel. "And so are you, if you don't mind me saying so."

"Hell, no!"

All sound and movement halted. Mia knew several thousand eyes were turned on Quentin. Tugging on his sleeve, she said, "Maybe you'd best let up on the profanity while you're here."

"Over my dead body."

The boy laughed. "You're so funny, Mr. Grandy." He slapped his knee, and around them sounds began again, as if someone had reopened the audio feed. Then, catching Quentin's thunderous scowl, the boy sobered. Reading from the display of his gadget, he said, "You and Miss Tortelli are to report to Room 111. That's quite an honor."

"Why is that?" Mia asked as they scurried to keep up with their guide, who was scooting off across the marble floor.

"It's the Second Chance Room," he called over his shoulder.

Her heart leapt at the words, but Mia knew she had to stick to the facts. But it did seem some sort of a good sign that she and Quentin remained aware of their surroundings. After all, if they were 100 percent dead, shouldn't they be six feet under and oblivious to everything? "What's the Second Chance Room?"

"Ooomph!" The boy clattered to the floor, spinning on his bottom as if performing a breakdance. An elderly woman hunched beneath a moth-eaten purple coat hurried by, frowning and muttering, "Clumsy no good children always getting in your way, always causing trouble. Lousy good for nothings . . ."

Brian gathered himself to his feet, his face flushed. "Excuse me," he called after the woman, then said under his breath, "Stupid old bag."

From the loudspeaker boomed a deep voice calling, "Brian Goldsmith, report to Room 666. Brian Goldsmith, report at once to Room 666."

He flushed even darker, and said, "Well that tears it."

"What's going to happen to you?" Mia asked, wishing instead he'd tell her about the Second Chance Room.

"Oh, detention again, no doubt. You see, you stay here until you learn from the errors of your ways." He executed another pirouette, obviously intending to ignore the voice behind the loudspeaker. "Most people stay here until they repeat their lives and get it right. I'm fifteen and I've been blading for five years, so I should have known better than to try to beat the traffic on Wilshire. But I thought I was hotter and tougher than any stupid car and driver. So I stay in Purgatory until I learn to integrate that lesson. That's what it's called here."

"I see," said Mia, but she wasn't sure she did. "So what is the Second Chance Room?"

"Oh, I'm not allowed in there." The boy glanced over his shoulder. Two older teens wearing identical red blazers were bearing down on them, making good time on their own in-line skates. "Oh, oh, I gotta go. It was really nice meeting both of you. Room 111 is just over there—" He pointed somewhere over his shoulder and sped off, the two other red coats swooping past in fast pursuit.

Another jacketed attendant was closing the doors of Room 111 when Quentin and Mia finally located it. He gave them a sharp look and blocked their entrance. Once he scanned their foreheads, though, he grudgingly let them enter.

Mia couldn't help but notice the attendant stepped outside and closed the doors behind him. So he wasn't allowed inside either. Hmm. With a shiver of excitement, she realized they were about to discover what went on behind the doors of Room 111.

Clamorous hordes lined the sidewalks of Hollywood Boulevard surrounding Mann's Chinese Theater. The April sunshine broke cleanly through, warming the sidewalks and toasting the rowdy crowd. From the direction of the Roosevelt Hotel a wave of cheering erupted, growing in scope and volume as the crowds closer to the theater began to chant, "She's coming. She's coming."

A cream-colored limousine inched forward, pelted by pink roses from the waiting fans. The crowd adored their high priestess and lined the streets to pay their respects. And to catch a glimpse of her unbelievable body.

Inside the car, however, all was not rosy.

"Oh my God, do I have to do this?" Chelsea Jordan restrained herself from tearing at the hair her stylist labored over for two hours. To what point, Chelsea questioned as she shook the blonde mass, knowing full well she looked as if she'd only now risen from her bed. With a sniff, she slammed shut the mirror built into the side of the limo and swiped the champagne bottle from the silver ice bucket.

At first her only answer was a sigh from the wisp of a woman sitting opposite her. Then Frances Rosen, her personal manager and the closest person she had to a friend, said, "We do what we must do."

"But I don't want to put my handprints in cement." Chelsea arranged a frown, careful not to crease her delicate skin. "I just want to be left alone."

Fran chuckled. "Leave that to Garbo, chickie. Your life isn't your own, and I don't suppose you'd ever want it any other way."

This time she frowned for real. "What do you know?"

"No need to be rude." Fran spoke softly, but there was iron behind her words.

Chelsea immediately despised herself for being so mean. Dropping the bottle back into the bucket, she flung her arms around Fran's bony knees and begged her forgiveness. "For I am truly a terrible person," she ended in a whisper.

The limousine ground to a halt. Fran said, "Sit up and act like the star you are."

At once, Chelsea composed her face and her bearing. She could hear so many echoes in her head of similar commands. Her father, before he'd betrayed her, letting her know she was a special girl, a star who owed the public a perfect performance and impeccable manners. Her dancing teacher, her voice coach, the Miss Manners clone brought in to tutor Chelsea at age five.

Chelsea lifted her chin. She'd sold her soul for stardom and now was no time to chicken out.

"Much better, chickie." Fran buzzed the driver,

who stopped the car and began to fight the hordes to ease himself around to open Chelsea's door.

She treated the crowd to the sight of one slim ankle, posed atop a spike heel designed to make balance impossible. Twirling her ankle slowly, she primed the spectators, working them into an uproar before sliding her pin-up legs from the limo. The strapless pink satin sheath she wore scarcely covered her crotch, but Chelsea didn't think about that as she flaunted the body millions loved to adore.

Fran handed her one trademark long stem pink rose and Chelsea stepped into full view, the stem nestled between her perfect white teeth.

Give 'em sex, Aldo had been fond of saying, and they'll never complain. Like all the men Chelsea had ever known, Aldo had been a two-timing skunk with his briefcase slung between his legs. But Aldo, bless his horny head, had launched Chelsea back into the world of the movies, the only world she'd ever called home.

Aldo was dead, but she was alive, the thousands here to watch her leave her handprints testimony to Aldo's smarts.

Handprints of a star.

Big fucking deal. So she was a star.

For the slightest of seconds, she considered rebelling, contemplated walking offstage forever.

But she did as she was programmed, dipping her chin in acknowledgement of the greetings of the bystanders and bending forward, teasing those lucky men up front with a glimpse of her cleavage.

She'd set out to become a star cum sex goddess to punish her parents, and her lowlife father cheated her out of satisfaction by getting himself killed before she arrived as Hollywood's latest successor to both Marilyn and Madonna.

Removing the rose from her teeth, she pouted a kiss at the crowd and beckoned to an old guy with a camera strung around his neck. He blushed and pointed to himself, as if she couldn't possibly intend to single him out.

Chelsea winked at him and he straightened, gaining at least an inch in height as the matronly woman by his side hid her surprise. The blushing man inched closer in the screaming crowd and Chelsea swayed atop her heels, straining forward until she managed to stroke the red-faced man on the lips with the petals of the rose. He stammered and grabbed hold of the rose as another man attempted to intercept it.

Well, she'd made one person happy.

Blocking out the fawning faces of the men and women who screamed her name, she turned to take the arm of Salvatino More, head of MegaFilms studio. As usual, Sal was sweating, his creased forehead drizzling like a windshield in a storm.

"Sugar," he said so that only she could hear, "remember what we agreed on."

Chelsea treated the crowd to a regal nod and a saucy wiggle of her hips, then said to Sal, "You mean what you and Fran agreed on."

"Chelsea! We love you!" A rain of pink blossoms fell upon them, tossed by some waving revelers from a window overlooking the sidewalk. She blew them a kiss and wondered if those people would adore her if they had one iota of the thoughts that dwelt in her heart and lurked in her mind. Like her latest fixation, her fear of turning thirty.

Or her even stronger determination to die before that birthday arrived.

The screams grew louder. A band struck up "God Save the Queen." Sal gripped her arm tightly as the rent-a-cops strained to hold back the swarming crowd.

"Image, sugar, image. Just do me a favor and pretend to be the lady your mother was." Sal practically had to shout into her ear, and as soon as he did so, he smoothed his Italian silk jacket, as if he were pretending nothing were amiss.

Why did he have to mention her mother? Any comparison to her mother brought out the rebel in her. Sonya Van Ness had always played the princess in public, but Chelsea had survived the truth behind the facade.

Image, hah! Chelsea dropped Sal's damp arm as if it were swathed in spittle rather than silk and stepped to the waiting bank of microphones. God only knew she could lead a university level class on the topic. Good old Chelsea, no substance, all image.

Somehow Sal and Fran had gotten it into their heads that the public was growing more conservative. They'd decided that her latest film opening in three days would benefit from Chelsea turning over a new leaf.

"*Pssst,*" whispered an all too familiar voice as Chelsea smiled and waved across the podium weighted with recording equipment.

Go away, she said to the voice in her head.

"I am so-o-o happy to be here today," she crooned into the microphones.

The crowd cheered. Pink rose petals floated down and Chelsea drove the fans to another wave of raucous exuberance when she stretched open the low bodice of her sheath and captured some of the blossoms, making it clear not a scrap of lace or satin covered her famous breasts.

Sal never should have mentioned her mother.

"That's right, babe. But you know how to fix him." Today the demon wasn't letting up.

"Today," Chelsea breathed, "is the most exciting day of my life." She fluttered her eyelids, and counted on one pink-tipped nail after another, "This day is absolutely more exciting than my very first Academy Award, and this day is divinely more exciting than the entire week at Cannes—" She waited while the crowd laughed at her joke.

"Okay, babe, sock it to them," whispered the voice.

"I promised to behave," she argued in her mind.

"To try to behave. Those aren't the same. Besides, he mentioned your mother."

Chelsea pretended a frown and tipping her head to one side, she said, "And this moment is infinitely more exciting and more long-lasting than sex with Arturio Grande." She named the box-office idol she was reported to have slept with once and discarded.

The crowd roared.

Chelsea laughed along with them, only she laughed at them for laughing at her.

Sal and Fran, beside and slightly behind her, managed smiles. Chelsea winked at them and stepped to the spot that had been roped off to protect the wet cement.

The voice didn't let up. *"They cast you as a sobersides in this new film because they're afraid you're losing it. You're almost thirty and you're not gonna keep those thighs thin forever. And those boobies."* The demon went off on a cackle. *"Gonna*

*sag to your waist, babe. Then whaddya gonna do with
your life?"*

She tried to silence it. She shook her head, almost
forgetting her surroundings. She couldn't grow old.
She was Chelsea, child star. Chelsea, teen soft-porn
princess. Chelsea, mega box-office draw.

"Tits, babe, don't last forever." The demon
pinched her on the nipple and flew away, still
cackling.

Chelsea held her hands forth to the waiting attendants and filmdom officials. They indicated the
placement, and she smiled into the cameras as only
an angel can smile.

She tipped forward, pretending to position her
hands this way and that. Then, as America and
much of the rest of the world watched, Chelsea
skimmed down the bosom of her dress and in the
wet cement immortalized her infamous 36Ds.

2

Anything for a second chance.

The thought tracked circles in Mia's mind as a wizened old man in a smoking jacket rapped on a podium placed in front of floor-to-ceiling red velvet drapes. The shabby upholstery of the chairs and the flocked wallpaper echoed the crimson color scheme.

Well, bad decorating wasn't her concern. Mia had seen *Heaven Can Wait*. She had more than one friend who claimed to be reincarnated. Maybe these things did happen. Though she'd reneged on her childhood Catholicism, right now Mia would say a Mass and believe in God if only . . .

If only she could live again.

"We're gathered here today," the old man began, then broke into a hack of a cough that set Mia's teeth on edge. Who was this guy? And why did he orate as if addressing a crowd? Quentin and Mia were his only audience.

"As some of you may know," as if he could read her mind, the old man glared at them from under a forest of gray eyebrows before continuing, "it has

17

been said that God does not play dice." He laughed,
the kind of laugh Mia never quite liked.

"However, I'm here to tell you that God does have
a sense of humor. And—" Another wave of cough-
ing interrupted him. "And, he likes to keep people
guessing."

"And you know why?" Now his voice rose, cre-
scendoing in a way that made Mia feel like she'd just
been called to the headmistress's office again.

Neither of them said a word.

Beside her, Quentin groaned and dropped his
head onto his knees. "This can't be happening to
me," he muttered. "I have a movie to make."

The speaker rapped on the podium. "Mr. Grandy,
if you do not wish to be present at this time, you may
be excused. Forever."

Quentin started to rise, and Mia, knowing full
well his allergic reaction to any voice of authority,
grabbed him by the hand. "Sit down and shut up,"
she whispered in a voice that would have done her
Sicilian grandpa proud.

The mulish look that claimed his face whenever he
set out to challenge authority flickered and faded.
Maybe, just maybe, Mia thought, watching Quentin
settle back into his chair, he was growing up. And
growing up for Quentin definitely meant choosing
which battles to fight.

Mia had told him more than once that jousting at
every windmill was a good way to develop tennis
elbow.

At least now he was pretending to pay attention,
which seemed to satisfy the speaker. After a long
moment, the old man said, "Since no one wants to
venture an answer, I'll tell you. You know why God
likes to keep people guessing? Because it makes them

more creative!" He laughed, then dragged a mono-grammed hanky from his robe and blew his nose.

Mia strained to read the single initial but in the dim room, she failed. She almost thought the man winked as he went on.

"Anyone allowed to enter this room is here for a reason. Because you have something many people lack. You have the ability to think, to challenge, to question, to design, to create. And you two schmucks had just brought a whole lot of happiness to a passel of children when you bit the dust!" The hanky went back into his pocket. "Do you get the picture?" he roared.

Mia leaned forward. Were they literally going to get a second chance? Turning to Quentin, she impul-sively caught his hand and said, "Something impor-tant is happening here."

Quentin patted her hand the way someone would to humor a daffy dog, pushed his glasses up on his nose, then planted both his hands in the pockets of his warm-up jacket. From the glum look on his face, Mia knew he was paying absolutely no attention. He'd retreated to the world within his mind, an ability that could be priceless in the right situation, and terribly irritating at moments like these.

She nudged him. He simply had to pay attention. Mia couldn't do this on her own.

"What?" he said sharply.

"Shh. You need to pay attention here."

Brows raised above the rims of his glasses showed that he was listening but thought otherwise.

"Wouldn't you do anything to be alive again?"

Quentin seemed to consider her question. "Hypo-thetically, yes," he said, but he kept his voice to a stage whisper.

"So pay attention and maybe, just maybe, we'll get another chance."

"You're the one who keeps insisting we're dead."

"Oh!" Mia slumped into the chair and half-turned from the man she loved, a man who could be most irritating when he wasn't being adorable.

"So," said the old man, "remember these rules. You may choose only one human being as your point of Intervention." He cackled. "So choose wisely. If you speak directly to the target assigned to you, the jig's up. And your assigned target must completely turn around his or her life. Half-hearted attempts at reform don't cut it." He rubbed his hands together. "Yessiree, I like to see *real* change."

Intervention? Target? Rules? Mia glanced around wildly, but no interpreter or convenient cue card carrier arrived to fill in what they'd missed while arguing. And somehow, she didn't think the old guy at the podium welcomed questions.

"You have been assigned—" The old man broke off and Mia could have sworn he glared straight at her. She shifted in her chair, ever ready to accept guilt.

"—a target"— at this his crinkly face split into a shit-eating grin —"specially selected with a great deal of thought."

Mia thought of Mr. Merona and wondered what demons from her past this old guy might let loose to haunt her.

He broke into a cough, then snapped his fingers. A little girl wearing old-fashioned buckle-on skates dashed in, carrying a plastic bag full of small envelopes that reminded Mia of the valentines the kids in her grade school used to exchange. The man smiled at the child as she skated up to him, then pointed toward Mia and Quentin.

The child zipped over and held out the bag. Mia hesitated and Quentin rolled his eyes.

"Don't make me sorry I chose you two," the old man snapped. "Don't make me regret being such a soft touch. I know people say I'm cold and angry but I tell you"— he slammed a fist on the podium and Mia jumped —"it just isn't true."

Mia snatched an envelope. Quentin practically ignored the scrap of paper that contained the key to their fate, but Mia began at once to open it with fingers that trembled.

"Hold it!" For such an old guy he had a voice that thundered.

She almost dropped the envelope.

"One more thing. I'm setting this timer"— he waved an egg timer in the air —"and you have until the last drop of sand has fallen to collect a second chance at life. So"— he grinned and Mia thought of the wolf in Little Red Riding Hood —"chop, chop!" Then he slipped through the velvet curtains.

Mia jumped up. Quentin remained rooted to his chair.

"Come on," Mia said, grabbing his sleeve. "We've got to figure out what to do. Try to understand these rules."

"Rules-shmules." Quentin rose from his chair and stretched like a cat waking from a satisfying nap in the sun.

"Don't you want to live again?"

"No question."

"Well, then, let's get going so we can get back to life." She tugged again at his sleeve.

Quentin gestured to their quaint and tattered surroundings. "Do you think any old coot who's crazy enough to engineer this cockeyed version of 'This Is Your Life' cares whether we follow rules?"

He pushed his glasses up on his nose. "Think about it, Mia. Let's take it as a given that we were chosen to be in this room. Okay. Why? The old guy said it was because we were creative. Any geek CPA with a calculator can follow rules."

Mia tapped her foot. "I do not believe you, Quentin Grandy. Of course creativity matters in the world you're used to, but this is Purgatory and any good Catholic can tell you—"

"Thou shalt follow the rules?" His voice was surprisingly free of sarcasm.

Mia stilled her foot. "Are you making fun of me?"

Quentin smiled and tickled her nose. "I would never do that." He pointed to the envelope she clutched in her hand. "Let's start by opening our valentine."

"Of course." Mia couldn't believe she'd been sidetracked. Holding her breath, she lifted the flap. Their lives depended on the person named within.

She stared at the typewritten letters.

She looked up at Quentin, her mouth sagging open.

He turned the plain white card around so he could read the name, then he whistled.

CHELSEA JORDAN.

Mia thought she'd be sick. Save the soul of Chelsea Jordan, the child star who'd turned into a soft-porn princess before maturing into a genuine movie-star bitch? "Oh, Quentin. This isn't fair."

From the front of the empty room, she thought she heard a cackle of laughter, an echo of her mother's voice reminding her life had never been fair.

"Think of this as a creative challenge, like the old guy suggested," Quentin said.

"You're the creative one."

"Just so." He was actually beginning to look happy for the first time since they'd found themselves in this mess.

"Do you have a plan?" she asked.

"A plan, no." He grinned. "Possibilities, yes. Come on, Mia." He draped an arm around her shoulders and they walked toward the door. "Let's begin with everything we know about Chelsea Jordan."

"Such as she's immoral, insufferable, unbearably spoiled—"

"You surprise me." And he did look surprised.

She at least had the grace to blush. "Oh, I guess I'm jealous. Look at her life, born with two silver spoons in her mouth, money, and an entree into the industry. My God, her father was Jack Jordan, tinseltown megastar. Her mother was Sonya Van Ness, sole heiress to the Van Ness fortune. Do you have any idea how much money that represents?"

Quent shrugged. "Money isn't everything."

"When you grow up poor it is."

He looked away and Mia knew he simply couldn't understand the strength of her feelings. He'd grown up comfortably well-off, the only child of professor parents both tenured at Stanford. No, Quentin couldn't relate to a dark-eyed teenager who filched a jar of Noxzema because she didn't have $1.29. To an adolescent who shoplifted out of boredom or rebellion, perhaps, but not from financial need.

"Anyway," Mia said, determined to deal with the present, "forget about my hang-up. I'm first and foremost a professional and how I feel about Chelsea

Jordan is immaterial. I can work with any talent in the industry, and for these stakes, I'll even force myself to like the woman."

"Bravo." Quentin applauded. "Of course, how you feel does matter, as it will ultimately affect your actions, but let's continue. What else do you know about Chelsea?"

"Child star. Worked steadily from age five to twelve. Did a lot of remakes of family-oriented films, most notably *Heidi* and *Rebecca of Sunnybrook Farm*. Now that I think of it, all her kiddie flicks were family oriented."

"Any rumors as to why?"

"Some say it had to do with Jack Jordan protecting his own image. One theory is he wanted to look ever-youthful, so he only let her portray young children. Some say he had visions of following Ronald Reagan into politics."

They rounded the end of the long corridor that led them back into the central terminal. The blast of loudspeakers and rush of gesturing, shouting passersby caught Mia off guard. The hallway had seemed almost soundproofed.

Quentin nodded toward the hubbub. "Makes me miss New York."

Fear clutched at Mia's heart. What if they never saw Earth again? No more Theater District, no more kite-flying at Venice Beach, no more agonizing yet life-sustaining hours spent together coaxing a film to life. They had to win. That meant she had to think. What else did she know about the infamous Chelsea Jordan?

"When did Jack Jordan die?" Quentin asked over the ruckus.

"Maybe ten years ago."

"When did Chelsea make that Italian porn pic?"

Mia made a move of distaste. "Not my area of expertise."

Quentin laughed. "Still the good little Catholic, aren't you?"

"It's like the color of your skin, it doesn't rub off." Mia surprised herself with that statement, but maybe it was true. In moments of anguish, she still tended to pray her rosary; a few times, driving past St. Basil's on Wilshire, the voices of the nuns stirred in her mind and she made the sign of the cross. And the first time she'd gone to be fitted for a diaphragm, she'd fled the Planned Parenthood office in confusion.

A month later she went back and carried through, determined to put the ghosts of the past behind her. Not, of course, that she'd ever had occasion to use the device, a bit of information she carefully hid from her sophisticated industry friends.

"Still with us?"

Mia blushed again. She was thinking that if she made it back to life, she'd make it a point to use the silly thing she'd gone to so much trouble to acquire. But she wanted to make love to Quent, not with just any bare-chested stranger spinning lines in a disco.

She glanced away, rather than face Quentin's scrutiny. "Oh, look." She pointed to a large glass-covered board in the center of the terminal. "That may be a directory of some sort. Let's see if it can help us make some sense of this place."

"You'd read the fine print if you were dying," Quentin said, but he followed along. "We're better off putting ourselves into Chelsea's emotional shoes and asking what she wants from her life. I mean, here's a woman you characterize as immoral and insufferable, yet she's a constant at B'nai B'rith fund-raisers. What does she believe in? What's missing from her life?"

Mia nodded as she scanned the board, but she wasn't really agreeing. The silly actress had everything anyone could ask for. "Her manager Fran Rosen probably forces her to appear at those functions. Fran was smuggled out of Germany as a baby. Everyone else in her family died there. So, let's not give Chelsea Jordan too much credit for that charity work, nor waste too much time on emotions. Remember, our time is limited."

"There's no guarantee we even have a fair chance," Quentin said. "Or that this is actually happening to us." He pinched his cheek. "I keep thinking we'll wake up from this dream and step out of the copter."

"Thinking that way won't help," Mia said. She pointed to the directory. "Room 111 is on here, as well as a Room 666." That number set off a superstitious shiver. Then she saw it. "Look, a CD ROM Library of Life on Earth. Second level. Let's go!"

"Hmm." Quentin made no move. He was reading over her shoulder, an easy thing for him to do as he was a good five inches taller. His breath ruffled the spikey top of her hair and his nearness, despite the platonic reality of their relationship, set up drum beats in her blood. "Didn't that old guy call this wild-goose chase an Intervention?"

"Yes." Maybe if she stepped closer to the board she'd escape the sweet torture of bodily contact. She inched forward till her nose pressed almost to the glass.

"Here's a listing for an Intervention Office," he

said, one finger trailing across her cheek as he pointed to the board.

"Oh, good. They'll probably have complete rules and explanations there." Mia sidestepped free of Quentin's unnerving touch. "Ground level. That must be here in the main terminal. But this directory isn't very helpful. It should indicate which direction at least."

"Organizing heaven, Mia?" Quentin sounded amused.

"I'm a producer for a reason."

"And a very good one you are. Let's find the Intervention Office, then hit the CD ROM room." Quentin's face had taken on that dreamy look he wore when his mind and imagination joined step and danced far away from mere mortals such as herself.

Mia allowed a moment of hope for their plight. "Do you have a plan?"

Quentin grinned his little boy grin. "Even better, I have an idea."

The bottle of vodka stayed maddeningly full.

Raising the jug to eye level, Chelsea took the measure again. For two hours now, she'd been forcing down swallows but the poison tasted so vile she could scarcely stand more than a sip at a time.

A damp something about the size of a cotton ball pressed against her ankle.

"How's my wuddle Toy-Toy?" Chelsea was surprised to find she tottered as she bent to collect her tiny toy poodle. She kissed his velvet button nose. "Don't you worry, Mama's taken care of you."

Cuddling her pet to breasts still scratchy from the

cement of only three days ago, Chelsea turned her attention back to the wet bar.

"These are Mama's wuddle pills," she said, pointing to the stash she'd been accumulating. Two hours ago, after she opened the vodka, she'd lined them up in rows, like extras patiently waiting to go on camera.

Toy-Toy tucked his head onto his paws and promptly went to sleep.

She attempted another sip of vodka. If only she could get drunk she could take those pills.

Disgusted as the thought made her feel, she knew she couldn't swallow them sober. Not only was she a useless human being who paraded like a cheap slut, she was lily-livered.

For three days she'd been locked behind the doors of her private suite, the precious rooms no outsiders were ever allowed to invade. Her famous pink palace, her oft-photographed rooms, were for show only. Chelsea had yet to spend one night in those quarters that took up an entire wing of her house.

Upstairs in her real rooms, she could escape.

Escape from her miserable existence.

She wrestled down another swallow and Toy-Toy stirred against her chest as she choked.

Sometimes she blamed her life on her father. Other days on her mother, a woman whom Chelsea always thought the state should have sterilized. No woman that self-centered should have been allowed to bear a child. On really bad days, when the demon descended upon her, she blamed it for her lack of happiness, for her life so many envied and not one human being understood.

But in her heart, she knew she alone was responsible.

She alone had started down the path of adolescent rebellion. Sure, she'd hated her father for shipping her off to Switzerland, yanking her away from the only life she knew—that of movie-making. The studio, the lot, the life on location, those were home to her in a way her parents' home in Beverly Hills had never been.

And because she had hated him, and wanted to punish him, she had set out to shame him.

At seventeen, she'd taken up with Aldo, the happy-go-lucky Italian pornographer. He'd introduced her to a lifestyle that stuck to her like dogshit on a tennis shoe.

She hadn't known who she was, a problem that plagued her still. And Aldo had taken advantage of that, casting her in that disgusting *FellatioNeighborhood*. With each new posture Aldo tortured her into, each new indignity he asked that she suffer, she did so with glee, saying to herself, "Take that, Daddy dearest, for sending me away. For wanting to keep me a child forever."

In a way, Aldo set her free. She returned to Hollywood an adult sensation, the press flocking eagerly around the Shirley Temple lookalike who'd metamorphosed into Deep Throat.

She made all the wrong choices, began to drown in the vultures who came to roost about her. It was Fran who saved her, Fran who pulled her free of the garbage that would have yanked her down the sewer of life. Muttering she owed Jack Jordan at least this much, she yanked Chelsea out of a casting call for a B film, drove her to Delores's on Melrose and lectured her on the way she would live her life from that day forward.

Funny enough, Chelsea listened. Craving, she supposed, the parent she'd never had. And Fran had come through, delivering a big budget film with major stars. The film opened to rave reviews, especially for Chelsea.

Only twenty-one, she'd arrived. Legitimate.

Too late to impress her father, though.

Fran came over the night after her first real film premiered. She held out her arms, told her Jack Jordan had died in a plane crash that afternoon. Private plane, only the pilot, Jack and—Chelsea could still remember Fran hesitating. She wouldn't have paused if the other passenger had been Chelsea's mother.

No, Jack Jordan died exactly as he'd lived.

Unfaithful to the end.

Ignorant of his daughter's triumph.

Chelsea forced another swig of vodka down her throat. Her father was gone to wherever bad fathers and mediocre actors go; her mother, the woman who'd never wanted the child she'd borne, died of a heart attack that same year. Because Fran had insisted, Chelsea appeared at the funeral, but her memories were as empty as her heart.

Only Chelsea carried on the Jordan name. Angry, rebellious, pathetic Chelsea.

She'd acted out for so long, she knew no other way to live. She just couldn't see how her life could ever be different. More movies, more money, more stunts like the one she'd pulled at Mann's. More men who wanted only to be seen with her or to brag to their friends they'd "had" her.

She shuddered and swayed out to her balcony, the train of her silk peignoir floating behind her in the gentle April breeze. A gloss of smog coated the hillsides across from her estate. No neighboring houses intruded upon the view.

After she first moved into her house, some enterprising photographer had captured her on a telephoto lens from the sole house perched impossibly on an outcropping across the hillside. Chelsea bought that house and had it boarded up.

The level in the bottle seemed to be inching downward.

She should have stuck to champagne, the only alcohol she ever touched. But swilling the bubbly preparatory to suicide seemed wrong.

It wasn't a celebration.

More like a resignation.

"Chicken," she said aloud.

Toy-Toy roused himself and yapped.

She headed inside and put Toy-Toy down on the wet bar while she searched for a champagne flute. Perhaps the vodka would taste better if she pretended.

Holding the glass, she tried to picture delicate bubbles floating skyward. She took a long swallow and promptly gagged. Toy-Toy coughed and began to choke.

She wiped her eyes and smiled at her pet imitating her.

Then she saw what her beloved poodle had done.

He'd eaten at least four of the pills she'd laid out.

"Oh-mi-God!" Grabbing him up, Chelsea made a beeline for her phone. She dialed 911 and screamed, "Overdose!"

Then, Toy-Toy in her arms, she raced from her suite shouting for help.

3 ⌐

Chelsea had had it with Vasquez Rocks. They'd been on location at this godforsaken jumble of boulders for two weeks now. She had to be up by four to be ready when the studio limo came to collect her for the more than hour-long drive.

How Fran talked her into this recurring role she'd never quite figured out. Chelsea hated the wailing wind that whipped through her hair and blew grit into her eyes, she loathed the production crew, and she despised the tourists who made the pilgrimage to ogle. If she heard one more half-wit explain that some episode of the original "Star Trek" had been shot there, she honestly thought she'd fling herself off the highest rock she could manage to climb in her shameful physical condition.

For a modern Hollywood celeb, she was in pitiful shape. She'd fired her personal trainer in a tiff several months ago and ever since she decided to kill herself, she figured her aerobic capacity didn't much matter.

Holed up in her trailer, miserable in a costume

that made Barbarella look like a nun, Chelsea grabbed the hairbrush from her stylist and threw it across the trailer.

"Don't you know anything? Where did you train, anyway, Trade Tech?"

The young man backed away. It was his first day on the job, his first shot on a union film. "Miss Jordan, simply tell me what you prefer—"

"You idiot, that's your job!" Chelsea knew she sounded like a five-year-old, but she didn't care. She wanted out of this trailer, out of the costume that wired her boobs up so high they bumped into her chin. "Scram, you worthless—"

The door opened without a knock and Chelsea whirled around. "Who—"

Fran stepped in, chatting with a man slung with cameras.

"Darling, the *Vanity Fair* photographer is here," Fran said in a bright voice that put Chelsea on alert.

"Lovely," she said, relaxing her shoulders and framing a smile topped with a pout. Out of the corner of her mouth she mumbled so that only the hair stylist could hear, "Get out and never come back."

Chelsea offered her hand to the photographer. She supposed he was someone famous if he'd been sent to shoot her, but she didn't bother asking his name. He would come and he would go. Because he was in the media, she wouldn't let him get to first base with her. Of course he would ask to take her to dinner, out to a club, back to the St. James Club, where he undoubtedly was staying. If he were gay, she'd say yes. Straight, no way. Not a reporter.

Fran said, "He wants to take some shots in your trailer. Is that okay with you?"

"Whatever you say," Chelsea said with a sweet smile. Fran had a decent sense as to how to handle the press. Or at least she had until she'd been bitten with this conservatism bug. The beating of tiny wings pushed into Chelsea's brain and she forced the damnable demon back into its box. Just this once she'd behave.

The photographer ignored her while he arranged his equipment. Why he wanted to shoot her in this cramped trailer was more than she could understand. But Fran must have a reason.

"Should I change?" Chelsea asked suddenly.

Fran studied her, scrunching her perennially sun-tanned face. Chelsea had told her more than once she ought to learn to relax her facial muscles and stay out of the sun. She couldn't be too many years past fifty, but in a strong light she looked more like seventy.

Then Fran nodded. "Put on a robe."

"Stop," said the photographer.

Chelsea rose. No one bossed her around. No one except Fran, anyway.

The photographer snapped away.

Chelsea stalked to where a sheer robe lay across a sofa. Holding it out, she said, "Were you objecting to me putting on a robe?"

The photographer nodded. "Natural. We want the natural you."

The demon snickered.

Chelsea tossed her head and stepped behind a dressing screen. "If I want to wear a robe, I most certainly will."

She fought her way out of the brief costume, knowing the results of the struggle would give the wardrobe girl fits. Then she bent forward and tossed her hair loose before donning the sheer pink peignoir. For good measure, she wet a finger and teased her nipples before loosely looping the single pink satin ribbon that held the concoction together.

As she stepped from behind the screen, the photographer went nuts, shooting frame after frame. He seemed to like it a lot when the ribbon came undone.

A bored look on her face, Chelsea dropped onto the sofa and spread her legs. "Would you like to get my pubic hair, too?"

The photographer grinned. "You're a real tease, aren't you?" But of course he took her up on it.

Fran was standing behind the photographer, gesturing frantically at Chelsea. Chelsea placed one cushion over her lap and one in front of her breasts, then grinned and winked. To Fran, she said, "This one's for the conservative public you're so worried about."

"When did *Vanity Fair* get into pornography?" Fran asked.

The photographer turned and looked at the agent, disappointment showing on his face. "Babe, this is art. A woman this beautiful, this open about her essential sexuality, she's like a Madonna. And I don't mean that slut from Michigan." He crossed himself. "I mean the real thing."

Chelsea stuck her tongue out at Fran and the photographer caught that, too. "Heaven, babe, this is heaven."

A knock sounded on the door. Fran cracked the door, said a few words, and then Chelsea saw her stuff an envelope into the pocket of her slacks.

"You may as well open it," Chelsea said.

Fran managed a look of embarrassment Chelsea

was sure she didn't feel as she pulled out the telegram.

The photographer took that moment to lean close to Chelsea. "Care to show me around town to-night?"

She took in his broad shoulders clothed in chic solid black, the muscled legs that probably never missed a day at the gym. She noted the lust in his dark brown eyes without giving it a second thought. That was the way all men looked at her. Gimme, gimme, gimme.

Puckering up, she said, "I am so sorry, but I already have plans." She caught his lapel between her fingers and played with it, just to torment the guy. Her face so close she knew he could feel her breath on his cheek, she reached down and fondled his crotch and whispered, "Maybe some other time."

He swallowed and she leaned back on the sofa, pulling her sheer robe demurely around her, teasing him with what he couldn't have. But the guy wouldn't remember she hadn't put out. He'd go back to Atlanta or wherever he was from and the legend would continue. Because she knew he'd be like all the rest; the story his friends would hear would be his version, the tale of how he'd balled Chelsea Jordan.

Fran cleared her throat. "It's from Ely Van Ness."

Chelsea rolled her eyes, then remembering the photographer, she sugar-coated her voice. "Yes?"

Fran walked over and handed her the telegram, then she turned to the photographer and hustled him out.

At that, Chelsea had to laugh. Fran knew her too well and feared a scene, which she didn't want to take place in front of a camera. Chelsea really ought to replace her, wean herself from Fran's teat, but what did it matter. Nothing mattered anymore. Except with the way Fran had been dogging her every step since poor Toy-Toy's accident, Chelsea wasn't having much opportunity to execute her plan.

The media had gone crazy over the overdose call to 911, and none of the press statements Fran issued killed the rumors. One tabloid ran a story comparing her to Marilyn Monroe, in which the reporter claimed Chelsea had slept with both Bill Clinton and his brother. That one made Chelsea laugh, then cry as she sympathized with poor Marilyn.

Since she held the telegram in her hand, she read it. "Come for a visit. Please. Your loving uncle, Ely Van Ness."

She stuffed the telegram under a sofa cushion. Fran had walked the photographer outside and for a brief moment she was alone. She looked down at herself, 99 percent naked, her pubes glistening through the robe. Honestly, how could she let any Tom, Dick, or Harry paw her with their eyes? She shook her head. It was only a body, only a tool. Hadn't she learned that from her earliest years?

The only part of her that mattered lived somewhere deep inside herself, and neither she nor anyone else had ever successfully excavated that soul.

She was afraid of what it might contain, afraid to look inside. And here was her great-uncle Ely, pestering her in telegram after telegram to come visit him. She shivered. It was one risk she couldn't take. The old guy was the only human being who had ever seemed to care about her, to listen, to ask questions about what she thought and felt. But now that she'd determined to take her own life, she was afraid to go visit him.

What if he changed her mind?

She rose from the sofa, let the sheer peignoir slip to the carpet, and pulled on a thick white terry robe. Tying the sash, she acknowledged her fears. If she went to Arkansas to see Ely, and had to go on living, she'd have to become a different person.

Mia sighed with relief when the American Eagle turbo-prop skidded to a halt with a rush of engine backwash. She could swear the wheels were hanging off the edge of the runway. Worrying about such things was unlike her; she understood the principles of flight and let matters take care of themselves. Yet for a dreadful moment, she'd feared they were going to crash.

"Silly me," she said, managing a weak smile for Quentin. "Can't die twice."

He answered with a grunt, and Mia knew he hadn't noticed a thing. Since the moment they found themselves the only passengers on this small plane, he'd been scanning the magazines. He clearly wanted to know how long they'd been in Purgatory.

More than that, Mia was certain he wanted to know the fate of the film he'd been directing. *Dino-Daddy,* pitched as *Jurassic Park* meets *The Flintstones,* was his first big studio mega-million-dollar project, appropriately enough financed by Mega-Films. Mia was concerned with the status, too, but in a practical way. If their mission in Arkansas failed, the question would be moot.

Mia bit her thumbnail as they waited for the steps to be rolled up to the plane. A year ago she'd broken herself of the nasty habit, but the pressure of this mission was too much for her self-control. Quentin had ultimate faith that the more creative a plan, the greater the chance of success. But Mia sure would have been a lot happier with all the *i*'s dotted and the *t*'s crossed.

She glanced sideways at Quentin, who continued to scan *People* as if his only concern in the world was catching up on the gossip about the beautiful people.

Quentin was so sure this Intervention plan was a stroke of genius. He wouldn't listen to reason, and only the plain fact that she had no better idea made her shut up and go along with him. Worst of all, Mia disliked that someone else had to die for Quentin's plan to work. That hardly seemed fair to her.

Before she could gnaw off the rest of her thumbnail, she thrust her hand into the pocket of her dress-length sweater. They disembarked on the tarmac, a hundred yards or so from the terminal. Quentin moved with his nose buried in *People,* the only magazine that hadn't pre-dated their last known date alive.

"Oh give me a break!" Quentin dashed the magazine against his forehead. "Listen to this—"

Mia darted a glance over her shoulder at the cabin attendant still standing in the doorway of the plane and jabbed Quentin in the ribs. "We're probably supposed to be anonymous," she said in a low voice.

"How can you worry about rules at a time like this?" He shoved the magazine into Mia's hands. "That idiot Salvatino More has replaced me with Russell Cruller." He spat on the ground. "Cruller! That two-bit yuppie couldn't direct his way out of a paper bag. He paid someone to do his final project at film school." He wove off onto the tarmac, carrying on about lunatic studio heads.

An attendant in overalls moved toward Quentin. Mia remained within the passenger walkway, trying simultaneously to focus on the printed words and keep an eye on Quentin.

Quentin clearly stood in an area passengers weren't supposed to go. But the attendant walked by Quentin as if he weren't even there and snatched at Mia's magazine. Quentin dashed over and grabbed it back, and the attendant backed away, a puzzled look on his face.

The small terminal seemed deserted except for one group gathered around an animal carrier. After the hurly-burly of Grand Central in Purgatory, the quiet settled Mia's senses. Several yards past the knot of travelers, she stopped to finish reading the reference that had set Quentin off, and when she did, uneasiness crept up on her like a shadow.

Quentin knocked his head against the wall. "Salvatino More has got to be the stupidest studio head I've ever dealt with."

"He's the only one you've done business with," Mia said without lifting her eyes from the page. If what she was reading were true . . .

"And the last one, the way things are going." He turned to her and gripped her shoulders. "You of all people must understand what this does to me. My film is like my baby. Would a mother turn her child over to a half-wit to raise? No! Would Einstein have taken on a moron for a lab partner? Absolutely not!" His voice grew louder with each statement.

Behind them, the dog's wails increased in volume. Mia placed a gentle hand over Quentin's mouth, wishing someone would do the same to the animal. "Quentin, Quentin. Calm down. Of course I agree that Russell Cruller is the worst possible choice to take over *DinoDaddy*. But you're missing the point of this article."

He tickled the palm of her hand with his tongue. She let go, confused by the tingles fanning out from where he touched her. She wished she could press her lips to his and let him tickle them with his tongue. Mmmm. She braced herself against the frisson of desire sweeping her. Stick to the facts, she reminded herself yet again.

Quent was looking at her as if she'd gone dumb. Which she guessed she had. His touch had a way of sending her common sense right out the door. Pointing to the magazine, she said, "The real point of this story is that you're not dead."

"I'm not?" Quentin snatched the magazine back and read aloud, "Due to the uncertain prognosis of Quentin Grandy's condition, Salvatino More announced last week that Russell Cruller would take over as director of the $70 million *DinoDaddy*. Grandy had announced only last December that the film would feature the latest in live action married with computer animation. Since a March 29 accident following a special effects demo for kids with cancer, Grandy has been in a coma at Cedars-Sinai Medical Center."

"My God, I'm not dead!" Quentin threw the magazine into the air and danced a jig.

The wails from the carrier turned to yelps. Mia's shoulders sagged as she watched Quent with a bittersweet smile, happy for him, happy that he quite likely could win a second chance at life.

But what about her?

Quent stopped still.

He turned and with a frown on his face, retrieved the magazine. He reread it, then turned to her and put an arm around her shoulders. "Mia, my friend, they didn't say what happened to you."

She knew at that moment why she loved him. Quent was brash and boisterous. But despite his self-centered ways, he always thought of her. They were a team, a man and a woman who belonged together.

He brushed a spike of hair from her cheek. "Just because they didn't mention you doesn't mean you're not in a coma, too. Hell, it's probably old news and you know *People* only prints the hot stuff."

She nodded, but a tear sneaked onto her cheek.

Quentin flicked it away with a touch of his finger. "Mia, I bet you a hundred bucks you're lying in a bed at Cedars-Sinai, hooked up to the same machines I am."

"A hundred dollars is a lot of money to wager."

He grinned. "Now you're back to yourself." He pointed to the door. "Come on, time's a-wasting."

She nodded, determined not to worry about her life-or-death status. She was a contestant the same as Quentin. Coma or no, if they won, she'd argue with God until he sent her back to Earth just to shut her up. For some reason, she patted the pocket of her sweater.

"Look," she said, holding forth a Visa card and an Arkansas driver's license in the name of Mary Joseph.

Quentin whistled. "Someone thinks of everything."

"Check your pockets."

His I.D. was in the name of Joseph Carpenter.

"Someone also has a sense of humor," Mia said.

"What do you mean?"

"Don't you know anything about religion?" Mia asked.

"Nope," Quentin answered, not at all concerned with his ignorance. "But if God or whoever has a sense of humor, that makes him less likely to care about rules."

"Maybe so, but the lady at the Intervention Office said time was definitely of the essence, so we'd better get a move on." She steered them toward the Avis counter she had spotted earlier. "Though if God was in such a hurry, why didn't he set us down in Hill Springs at Ely Van Ness's front door?"

"Maybe his compass was off," Quentin said and laughed at his own joke.

Mia frowned and stepped up behind a man being waited on at the Avis counter.

"How are you doing today?" The female clerk flashed a smile at the customer in front of Mia. The woman's eyes were bright and her voice cheery, but Mia couldn't help but wince at the teeth revealed by the smile. Molars had encroached on incisors which in turn threatened to squeeze the young woman's front teeth out of her mouth.

Mia locked her hands in the corners of her cardigan while the friendly clerk took her time assisting the man in front of them. She was trying to be patient, but patience was hard to come by.

Who knew how long they really had? And with only their hare-brained plan standing between them and forever never more. Against her will, one hand rose from her pocket, and she chewed on the thumbnail like a dog reclaiming a long-lost bone.

Just then the customer ahead snapped his briefcase shut and strode away from the counter.

"Hello," Mia said, stepping forward with a friendly smile to match that of the Avis woman. After all, they were in the country now, might as well be neighborly.

The woman turned her back on Mia and Quent and bent to tug at her nylons.

What bad manners. "Excuse me," Mia said.

Quentin leaned forward and drummed his fingers on the counter. The beginnings of a smile were forming on his lips. "Yoohoo, we have a reservation."

Mia looked at him sideways. Of course they didn't have a reservation. Not that it would matter if this woman continued to ignore them.

Mia could tell Quentin was suppressing a grin. He turned to her and said, "Put the magazine onto the counter."

"Why?"

His only answer was a grin and a nod.

Mia did as he asked.

The clerk finished her toilette by adjusting her bra straps. Then her face brightened and Mia smothered her irritation. Finally.

The woman pulled the magazine onto her working space and began flipping the pages.

Quentin laughed. Mia considered slapping a fist against the counter, but suddenly the light went on. "Oh, brother," she said, "we're invisible."

"Bingo."

She sighed. "So I guess God does have a sense of humor."

He nodded and winked at her. Then he strolled around the counter and surveyed the two reservations on the board. "I think I'll take the one marked Carpenter," he said, and helped himself to the rental agreement and keys while the clerk continued to turn the pages of *People*.

"We'd better scram," Mia said.

"Didn't you ever play any pranks when you were a teenager?"

Mia thought of the Noxzema and knew her face showed her guilt. "I wasn't into pranks."

"No time like the present to learn." Quentin began whistling, and Mia just knew he was thinking up pranks he could play as Mr. Invisible. Why, oh, why couldn't he take this a little more seriously?

A few minutes later they were standing outside in front of a red Ford Probe, the key dangling from Quentin's fingers. They were laughing, Quentin naturally and Mia despite herself.

The sunny mood remained with them as they found their way out of town and headed northwest. The glove compartment held a handy Welcome to Fayetteville map that included on the reverse a map detailing the northwest quadrant of the state, where Hill Springs was located.

They were careful not to linger too long at stop signs or red lights, where curious passersby might notice one red Probe moving under its own power. Though, as Quentin the car buff pointed out, someone had conveniently tinted the windows especially dark on this rental car.

A city girl always, Mia felt like a traveler in a foreign country. Quentin drove and she made use of the brief time she knew she'd have before dropping off to sleep. Riding in a car always made her sleepy. But at least if she were sleeping she wouldn't be worrying.

She checked the map, smiling as she read names like Little Flock and Healing Springs and Viney

Grove. This place was a far cry from West Hollywood. She could almost believe they were on vacation, or off scouting locations, not on an expedition
that would determine forevermore.

They made swift time, slowing only for the small
towns they passed. The road curved gently and
tracked up and down swelling hills. Cattle grazed in
the fields. Every so often they passed an enormous
metal shedlike building.

"I wonder what those are," Mia said after they'd
passed at least five of them in a row.

"Breeding houses."

"Breeding what?"

Quentin glanced at her. "For the chickens. You
know, the chickens that play a role in our plan. They
have to come from somewhere and that's where
they're bred and raised."

"Oh," said Mia, feeling stupid. She'd only thought
of the slaughterhouse end when they'd framed their
plans for Chelsea's intervention. "Imagine living
your life bred to die." She shivered. "I'm glad I only
eat free-range chicken."

"You and everyone else in L.A." Quentin sounded
amused. "The animal still lives only to die. So what
if it gets to see the sunshine first?"

"It's better for you. And it's a nicer life for the
animal."

"But in the end it makes no difference to the
bird."

He had a point. "If you're so concerned, why do
you eat meat?"

"There's a food chain and I'm on top." An old
school bus painted white chugged out from a side
road and Quentin slowed the car. "Now there's a
sight you don't see in L.A."

One feather, then another landed on their windshield. Unbelievably, the bus was loaded with caged chickens, layer upon layer stuffed with birds so close together Mia didn't see how the ones on the inside could still be alive.

"To market. To market," Quentin said.

"Ugh." Mia sighed as Quentin sped past. "I'm glad we only designed this Intervention and don't have to live through it."

Quentin nodded, a grim set to his jaw. "For your sake and mine, let's just hope Miss Chelsea Jordan is up to the challenge."

Finally alone in her mansion, Chelsea kicked the oven that took up at least ten feet of the massive kitchen designed by the former owner to make any catering company salivate with envy.

"Dammit," she cried, her frustration overwhelming her. As soon as Fran had gone home to nurse a cold, Chelsea had ordered her limousine, raced back to Bel Air, and given the entire staff the night off.

After kissing Toy-Toy good-bye, she'd found her way to the kitchen, a room she had entered only once, when the real estate broker insisted on showing it to her.

For an hour, she'd been trying to figure out how to work the stove. She was positive there was a way to commit suicide with an oven. After all, hadn't Sylvia Plath done it that way? But she couldn't figure out one button from the next and try as she might, she could make nothing that smelled like gas appear.

She kicked the door again, wincing at the pain it set up in her toes.

Then she heard someone open a door.

"Who is it?" she called.

A maid entered.

Chelsea narrowed her eyes at the Hispanic girl. She'd ordered everyone to take the night off or be fired.

"What are you doing here?"

"Miss, I'm picking up my purse." The woman scurried to a pantry room.

"And you couldn't get that tomorrow?"

The woman ducked her head and said, "I need my bus pass to get home."

"That's a sorry excuse. You're fired."

The woman's mouth fell open. "Oh, please, Miss Jordan."

"Shut up and get out."

She backed from the room.

"Stop." Chelsea thought she might as well get some use out of the maid's presence. "Come here and turn this oven on before you leave."

"Yes, Miss Jordan."

The woman hurried forward, turned two knobs on the front of the range and stepped back.

"Please, Miss Jordan, I have three kids—"

Chelsea glared at the woman. "Out." Then seeing the tears welling up in her eyes, she considered relenting. After all, this woman had started the oven for her. "Give me a piece of paper and a pen."

"Yes, Miss Jordan."

"And quit calling me that."

The woman handed her a memo pad from a drawer and Chelsea scrawled on it, "Pay this woman a hundred dollars."

She signed it and said, "Give this to Fran Rosen tomorrow."

"Yes, Miss—"

"And don't come back here."

The woman was almost out the kitchen door when Chelsea said, "Tell me why this doesn't smell like gas."

The woman looked puzzled, then a faint smile dawned on her face. "Because, Miss Jordan, that's an electric oven."

4 ～

Of all the escapades in which he'd gotten himself entangled, this journey to Arkansas had to be the strangest. Continuing to zip along the tranquil two-lane road, Quentin pushed his glasses up and contemplated the power of naming.

For instance, by thinking of this experience as a trip to Arkansas, he kept the whole thing in perspective. Mia, little worry-wart that she was, insisted on highlighting the life and death significance of this improbable challenge.

He glanced over to where she lay curled against the side of the seat and window, her head cushioned by his fleece warm-up jacket. It was hard to realize they weren't actually alive, so normal was the sight of her sleeping as he drove. Since their college days, she'd napped every time they'd made a trip together. For Mia, napping seemed to be a release valve from the pressure she constantly applied to herself and those around her.

Quentin slowed to negotiate a sharp curve, which reminded him of the contrast between this rental and his own growing stable of sports cars. Only the day before the accident, he'd taken delivery of a new Maserati. He jabbed at his glasses again and smothered a sigh. So much to live for.

Mia stirred and murmured something in a soft whisper. Quentin inclined his head to try to catch her words. A smile appeared on her face and Quentin couldn't help but notice the soft pout of her lips. Couldn't help but think there were matters far more inspiring than a car collection to make him risk all to win a second chance at life.

Mia looked like a woman aching to be kissed. He tightened his grip on the wheel, surprised at the thought. He glanced again, deciding he was right. Damn. Little Miss Mia, who mastered the overview as well as the details of a big budget film as easily as someone double her age, her experience, looked at this moment exactly like a princess awaiting her prince's kiss.

He smiled a bit at the incongruous picture. Mia, though only a year younger, was the kid sister he'd never had. Princess! No wonder he was famous for his ability to weave tales of fantasy.

He slid another look in her direction, in time to catch her blinking her eyes like a cat in the sun.

"Hey, sleepyhead," he said, dismissing his run of imagination. This was Mia, his friend, his partner, the woman who solved his business problems and rescued him from bad romances with dumb blondes.

"Hey yourself," she said, poking at the spikey top of her hair and sitting up to look out the window. "Are we there yet?"

"You know you always ask that question?"

"Do I?" She smiled. "I guess I'm happy being a creature of routine. So are we?"

"Only a few more miles. We'll zip in, see old Ely,

spring the plan on him, and get ourselves back to the airport and wait to be zapped back to wherever the hell we were."

Mia frowned and Quentin, seeing her starting to worry, said, "Don't ball up like a porcupine on me. Just give our plan a chance." He smiled. "Trust me."

She laughed and shook her head.

Quentin laughed with her. "Remember when you made the 'trust me' rule?"

"Yes, I do, and I've never regretted it. Anyone in the film business who says 'trust me' is not to be trusted." She frowned again.

"What?" Quentin slowed the car as they approached the outskirts of a town that had to be Hill Springs.

"Oh, I was thinking about Salvatino More."

"Yeah, he's as close to a 'trust me' guy as we've ever gotten, and now look what he's done to *Dino-Daddy*."

Mia leaned over and patted his hand. "Don't think about the film, Quentin. Just concentrate on this plan and getting back to life."

"Yeah, right." Don't name death and it can't name you. Quentin pointed out the window to a sign announcing Hill Springs, Home of the Proud Bird.

Mia nodded, and Quentin saw she'd started chewing on her thumbnail again. It was typical of Mia to comfort him while she worried herself sick.

They turned onto what looked like it must be Main Street, a supposition soon confirmed by a sign. Baskets of pansies hung from light posts along the three-block stretch of one- and two-story buildings. Quentin was thankful for the dark-tinted windows as a few people on the street stopped to watch the progress of their bright red car.

Quentin pulled into a corner gas station, parked next to a phone booth, and hopped out to check Ely Van Ness's address. The booth was remarkably clean and graffiti-free. So it seemed there were some benefits to small-town living. Not that Quentin would ever leave L.A., the city of stars that had taken him so generously to its milk-and-honey breast.

He lifted the thin plastic-encased book that served as the telephone directory for Hill Springs. The back-cover ad proclaimed Hill Springs home to thirty-five churches. Quentin whistled. What a place for an agnostic like himself to end up in this weird walkway between life and death. Thank goodness Mia knew something of religion. In a town with thirty-five churches, her religious background might come in handy dealing with old man Van Ness.

Search as he might, he found no listing for Ely Van Ness. He checked under both the N's and the V's. He repositioned his glasses and let his mind drift toward a solution.

A honk of a horn cut his thinking time short. He slid the phone book back onto the shelf (no chaining things down in Hill Springs) and turned back to the car.

A gas station attendant leaned against the passenger side of the car, picking his teeth and eyeing the results before wiping the toothpick on his sleeve and trying again.

Quentin made a face and wished he had a spare toothpick. The guy looked like he would be a lot of fun to play a prank on. But then the guy lowered the toothpick and peered into the passenger window.

Opening the driver's door, Quentin dove in and raced out of the station before the attendant even realized he'd lost his leaning post.

"Where does he live?" Mia asked.

Quentin glanced in the rearview mirror. The attendant had gone back to picking his teeth. "Don't know."

"He doesn't have a phone?"

"Guess not. Hard to imagine, isn't it, living without a telephone." Quentin pulled a U-turn and headed back to the thick of Main Street. People in a small town always knew everyone else's business. Ely should be easy to find.

"I feel lost without mine." Mia patted her left ear. "Some days I've felt as if I've grown a new body part." She stretched her arms over her head and Quentin was surprised to notice how the movement swelled her breasts.

He narrowed his eyes and took a second look. Just for reference, he told himself. Had Mia had an operation? Or had he simply never looked at her before? "What new body part?" he asked.

"You know, a phone attached to my ear." She frowned. "What did you think I meant?"

"Oh, that. Right."

"Are you paying attention to me?"

"Uh-huh." He pulled into a parking spot. No meter. Hmm, another luxury the people of Hill Springs enjoyed. "Look, why don't you pop into this store and see if you can discover Van Ness's whereabouts?"

"Why me?"

"Look at the name." Quentin pointed to the Mode O' Day sign. The display window featured what a costumer doing a fifties' retro film would probably call house dresses.

"You stopped here on purpose."

Quentin nodded. "Can't deny it." He threw a grin

at her. "Come on, Mia, my friend. If you want me to learn to play by the rules, the least you can do is take the plunge into living by your wits."

He watched as she thrust her right hand under her thigh and turned to study the shop front. Thata girl, he wanted to say, but he held his comments. He knew she hated her nail-chewing habit as much as he did, but in the past whenever he'd bugged her to stop, she'd grown worse. Then, suddenly, about a year ago, she stopped completely. Until . . . until whatever this was they were experiencing.

"Okay," she said, causing him to jump. "Off I go."

Mia managed an imitation of a confident smile and slammed the car door shut behind her. Talking to strangers never bothered her, something Quentin knew quite well. But getting information from a person who couldn't see her . . . now that was a hurdle.

Nevertheless, Mia stepped into the Mode O' Day with her chin held high, and almost ran headfirst into a rack of floral and pastel dresses. A daintily scripted sign read, "See What the Bunny Brought For Our After-Easter Sale."

Mia surveyed the small shop. Evidently the women of Hill Springs weren't interested in the bunny's leftovers. Only two women, both rather stout and sporting that funny purplish-white hair that sprouted on older women, were in the store, and they were positioned on either side of the cash register counter. Each wore a name tag, though Mia was willing to bet everyone in town knew the salesladies' names.

Moving closer, one careful step at a time, Mia was relieved that neither woman glanced her way. Whew! Being invisible wasn't an easy state to adjust to. Any moment she expected the women to turn on her, rulers cocked, much as Sister Marie had done the one day Mia wet her pants in the first grade. Then they'd toss her in the stockroom and make her write a hundred times, "I will not pretend to be invisible."

"Well, I think it's perfectly shameful the way that woman is throwing herself at Pastor Miller," the woman behind the counter said.

Mia thrust her Catholic schoolgirl fears into the memory box and turned her attention to the conversation.

She remembered from the Purgatory library that Pastor Miller was the name of the minister at Ely Van Ness's church.

"Of course," said her cohort, "it's not as if you can really blame the woman. It's a good thing the pastor's a man of the cloth," she added, hiding a girlish giggle behind her hand, "because he is the most devilishly handsome man I've ever laid eyes on."

Mia raised her brows at that news, but studying the woman whose bosom hung from her breastbone to her waistline, she wondered at the lady's definition of handsome.

"That you're right about," said the woman behind the counter with what sounded like a sigh, "but mark my words, Pastor Miller won't marry another schoolteacher."

"Oh, Hennie, how can you be so sure?"

"Because," she beckoned her co-gossiper closer, "I have it on good authority from his own mother, his mother mind you, that he vowed after Jenny's funeral the only way he'd marry again would be for love."

The woman on the outside of the counter pushed away with a frown on her face. "Oh, I declare, Hennie

Cobbs, that is the dumbest thing you've said in a month of Sundays. He married for love the first time and you're trying to make it sound like he didn't."

"Well, he didn't."

"Did too."

"Did not."

The outer woman, as Mia now thought of her, drew herself up and sucked in her bosom. "Are you forgetting that Jenny Miller was my third cousin once removed?"

"No, I am not. And don't go and get yourself het up like an old pea hen. I know Jenny thought the sun rose and set on Luke Miller but if truth be told he married her because he was a dutiful son and needed a wife so's he could—"

The door to the shop opened and Mia looked around with annoyance. Really, the interruption was worse than a commercial in a good television movie. Why had Luke Miller married if not for love? Stay tuned, after this word from Joy, the dishwashing liquid that you can see yourself in.

Another purply-haired woman walked in, clomping on a walking stick. This woman was very old, Mia could tell on closer inspection. Her skin was white and full of folds like stiff cake batter poured into a pan. Hefting the stick she waved it like a pointer at the women, then leaned on it as she drew a sheet of paper from the folds of her long brown skirt that stopped an inch above the black high-top shoes. Granny shoes, exactly like Mia's own grandmother had worn. One Sunday after Mass, Mia made fun of them and her granny locked her in the closet all afternoon.

"Now what was it I wanted?" muttered the old woman, peering through half-rim glasses at the paper.

From another fold she produced a pencil and Mia smiled as the woman scratched an item off what appeared to be a to-do list.

Moving quickly this time, Mia nabbed a pen from the checkout counter where the woman had fallen silent and turned to the customer with the cane. When the woman paused to scratch her head and mutter again, Mia inched the paper from her clutch and wrote near the top:

#1 today: Ask Hennie how to get to Ely Van Ness's house.

#2 today: Ask Hennie how to get to Pastor Miller's church.

The second point she added out of curiosity, or as she sometimes thought of it, woman's intuition.

The old woman patted her pockets and Mia slipped the list back into her hand.

"Oh, there you are," she said.

Mia jumped, guilt-stricken. How had the woman detected her?

But the old woman smiled and lifted the list closer to her face. Mia sighed with relief and crossed her fingers.

Obligingly, the woman advanced on the counter with a shuffle-clomp, and barked, "Hennie, good morning." To the other woman, she spared only a slight nod.

Hennie, the woman behind the counter, said with a smile on her face, if not in her voice, "Well, Miss Eulalie, what a pleasant surprise."

"No, I don't suppose it is," the old woman responded, peering over her glasses. "You misbehaved in my class fifty years ago and if I recognize the signs, you were up to no good when I walked in this door."

"Whatever you say, Miss Eulalie." Hennie folded her arms and looked cross-eyed at the old lady.

Mia smiled at the tableau of small town life, wondering if Hennie were biting her tongue. She sure hoped Miss Eulalie, tyrant that she seemed to be, was a creature of habit and remembered to read her list.

"I wanted something today, but I can't for the life of me remember what it was." She tapped her cane against the floor.

"Why don't you check your list?" asked the other saleslady.

"I guess you're not as dumb as I always thought," Miss Eulalie said to her, then cackled. Then she thumped the floor, hard, with her cane and read, "'Number one today: Ask Hennie how to get to Ely Van Ness's house.'"

"Why," said Hennie, "you know as well as I do where Ely lives."

Mia held her breath.

"Then why did I write it on my list?"

"I don't know." Hennie started to turn away.

"Young lady, answer me when I ask you a question."

Hennie kept her arms crossed over her chest and stuck out her lower lip.

The other woman said, "Take a left at the four-way, that'll put you driving south of town. Go two miles and turn right on Blueberry Lane."

"Thank you," said Miss Eulalie.

Thank you. Thank you. Thank you. Mia echoed as she jumped up and down.

Hennie leaned over the counter. "Is there anything you wanted to *purchase* today?"

"Let me see." The old woman studied her list. "Hmmm. 'Number two today. Ask Hennie how to get to Pastor Miller's church.' Now why would I ask you that?"

"Search me," said Hennie, picking up a feather duster.

"Respect your elders," Eulalie said with a thump of her cane. "Answer the question."

The other woman spoke up again. "Turn right at the four-way instead of left and the church is half a mile down the road. On the left."

"Very good." The old woman peered over her glasses. "It's too bad you had to go and get yourself knocked up your senior year. You could have gone to college and made something of yourself."

The woman turned ten shades of red and Hennie whooped. Eulalie must have let a town secret out of the bag. Mia felt sorry for the woman exposed, and as much as she wanted to watch the next episode, her sense of urgency kept her from sticking around to watch the fallout.

She had what she needed.

Pretty clever of her, too, if she did say so herself.

Quentin had almost drummed a hole in the dash by the time Mia slid back into the car, a wide grin dancing on her face.

Turning the ignition key, he said, "Where to?"

"How did you know I got the address?"

Quentin leaned over and tousled the spikes of her hair. "Mia, me darlin', you may be invisible to others, but to me, you're transparent."

The grin fled. "Go to the four-way and turn left." Then, her lips pursed, she said, "How transparent?"

He pulled another U-turn. "Very. When you're happy, it shows all over your face. For instance, when you're sad, it shows here"— he brushed a finger by the side of her mouth —"and here"— and continued with a gentle sweep across her forehead. Funny how he knew exactly how to answer her. He dropped his hand.

"I didn't know you paid that much attention to me."

He hadn't known it, either, but he didn't think admitting it was too smart.

"Just because you think I'm so easily read doesn't mean you know what I'm thinking, though," she said.

Mia sounded surprisingly obstinate. Why, he wasn't sure. He hedged a bit. "I'm talking about feelings, not thoughts."

"Oh," she said, and turned her face toward the side window.

She was in a funny mood. Maybe she'd wanted to surprise him with the fact that she'd obtained the address. The business facades of Main Street were behind them now and the street broadened out and evolved into what looked like the industrial strip. Signs sprouting from rather ugly masonry buildings hawked everything from fertilizer to hatchery chicks. A farm equipment store stretched out over two blocks. Ahead, Quentin spotted a blinking red light hanging from wires across an upcoming intersection.

"That's the four-way," Mia said. "And just for your information, I don't separate my feelings from my good common sense."

Quentin chuckled. "How did a Sicilian–Irish Catholic girl turn into such a Puritan?"

She flushed slightly and Quentin found himself wishing he could read her mind. Surely Mia had no
secrets. She was the most open woman he'd

ever known. His favorite person to deal with in the ego-bloated industry of moviemaking. His pal, his sidekick.

Her only response was, "Check your speedometer."

"Odometer."

"Whatever."

"For a precise individual such as yourself, I think you'd want to use the correct term."

She wrinkled her nose. "I've just never cared about cars."

"That's obvious from that junker you've been driving since college." Quentin thought of his own collection of glorious automobile chrome and steel and massed horsepower and experienced a pang of longing. "It's no wonder that old piece of junk finally gave up the ghost."

"Watch your tongue. I loved that VW bus. And if it hadn't refused to start the day of our crazy accident and you hadn't come to pick me up, it might have died on the road and I never would have made it to the lot, and you'd be caught in this pickle by yourself."

Quentin could have sworn hairs prickled on the back of his neck, an action he would have scorned as clichéd in any script presented to him.

Mia was staring ahead, nibbling once again on her thumb. She removed it long enough to say, "Do you suppose—"

"No!"

"I'm only speculating."

"Forget it. No way. Talk about convoluted reasoning!" Quentin gripped the steering wheel. "What you're speculating is that somehow we were supposed to be in that accident together, as if this whole thing is planned, our lives predestined or whatever the hell the phrase is."

"You don't have to shout."

"Sorry."

"Shouting won't change things, you know."

"That's easy for you to say," he said, shouting again. "I don't want to be dead. I have things to do, and I refuse to believe one bit of this ridiculous charade, and I especially refuse to believe I was meant to die." So why was he shouting?

Mia's quiet stare was asking him the same question.

He let out a breath and gave her a sheepish smile. "Sorry. My life has always been so straightforward. School, college, film school, movies, success, $70 million deal for *DinoDaddy*. There's no room in my life for this sort of superstition."

"Maybe it's real, just as real as *DinoDaddy*." She'd tucked her thumb back under her knee.

"Okay, Mia, if life is prearranged and we're 'meant' to be here"— he formed quotes around the word *meant* —"then are we meant to receive a second chance at life?"

"Well, a contest is only a contest if the outcome isn't prearranged."

"In a perfect world, yes. But remember the quiz shows? And what about boxing? Wrestling?"

"It wouldn't be fair for God—or whomever—to offer us a challenge and not let it be possible to win. Or lose."

Quentin raised his brows. He let scenes from his history lessons flash through his minds. He thought of Auschwitz and Hiroshima, just for starters. "Fair?"

"Well, I'm taking the point of view that this is a contest in the true sense of the word."

"Let's test it." Quentin applied the brakes, not at all gently, and pulled the car to the side of the road. Sitting back, he folded his arms across his chest.

"What are you doing?"

"If we're meant to win, we'll win whether we act or not. So let's sit here and see what happens."

"Are you crazy? This is life or death!"

As much as Quentin hated to sit still for even five minutes, he was prepared to stick it out all day to prove his point. He said nothing.

Mia shook his shoulder, fire blazing in her dark eyes. "You idiot, if it's not prearranged, then we'll lose."

He started to answer, but the only thought that came to his mind was how cute she looked when she was perturbed. But Mia hated comments like that. However, the women he dated cooed over the very same lines. He itched to tell her, wishing she'd then turn to him, softening the expression on her now-simmering face.

But if Mia reacted like that, she wouldn't be Mia.

He wanted her exactly the way she was, not as an auburn copy of the blondes he romanced.

Wanted her?

He must have fallen on his head in that accident. What had gotten into him, thinking about Mia this way was crazy, not like him at all. The two of them were always so busy working, he'd never had time to notice her as a woman. But he definitely noticed her now, his body responding to her in a most unbrotherly, unbusinesslike way.

"Mia," he said in a low voice, reaching to take her hand in his.

Mia jerked open the car door.

"What are you doing?" Quentin asked, startled from his reverie.

"One member of this team is going to do the right thing."

"Don't get out." Not now! Not when his eyes had been opened. "Please?"

"Will you get moving if I get back in?" She stayed half-in and half-out of the car.

"Hey, I was only presenting the other side of the argument. But, yes, I'll drive." What a schmuck! Posturing to prove a point, with Mia so worried. Especially when she could be right. After all, she only argued in support of his belief that the entire crazy mess hadn't been prearranged.

She kept one foot out of the car. "Cross your heart and hope to . . ."

He flashed her his boy scout salute as her voice trailed off at her choice of words. "Promise."

She settled back into her seat. "What do you think we should say to Mr. Van Ness first?"

"Let's just float in and write a message on his mirror with shaving cream."

"Very funny. You want to have fun being invisible, but this is serious business."

"But I am serious." He turned toward her. At this moment, watching her huge eyes filled with concern, he felt more serious than he had in a long time, possibly ever in his life. He didn't want to die when he'd only begun to awaken to this woman. "Look, we're invisible. He's an old man. We persuade him through supernatural means to change his will, and then—"

"That is the stupidest thing you've ever said." This time she looked really, really angry. "Why?"

"For one, you're insinuating he'll be so freaked he'll die from a heart attack and then his last will and testament can be put into effect. But it just isn't fair he has to die for our—your—plan to work."

"I don't want him to die." Quentin thought how much happier he'd be back in his screening room, happily reviewing dailies, or out on the set, bringing to life yet another fantastically terrific scene. "I don't want anyone to die. But, Mia, old people die. Young people, too. All four of my grandparents died in their sixties. Van Ness is eighty. That's ancient."

"I can't come back to life in good conscience knowing it'll be because I caused someone else to die."

"Why didn't you say this earlier when we were making our intervention plans?" Dammit, but she could be difficult.

"You said you'd thought of everything."

"Come on, give me a break. I didn't exactly have time to draft a storyboard on this scheme. One moment we're alive, the next we're dead, the very next we're in a room with some crazy coot, then poof, we're in Arkansas!"

"I will not do it your way."

He sighed and pushed his glasses back up his nose. "All right, let's long and short it."

Mia stared at him open-mouthed. "For something this serious?"

"Got a better idea?"

When she didn't answer, he opened his door and cast around on the ground till he found a suitable stick. He broke the twig in two pieces and, evening the tops, shielded them with his hand.

"Do you remember the first time we did this?" Mia asked.

"Yep." Quentin smiled and shifted in his seat as Mia leaned closer to study the twigs. Her knit dress clung sexily to her curves, seducing his mind from the matter at hand. But he answered calmly enough, "You wanted Chinese and I wanted Vietnamese."

"Right. And the next time it was which movie to see. Nice, simple, minor decisions."

"We also used it to decide the name for *Quetzal-coatl's Overcoat.*"

Mia smiled. "That's true. And you thanked me when you won the AFI award, too."

"So pick one." Quentin wiggled the twigs. "Long stick gets to go to Van Ness's house first and try it his way."

"Her way."

"Whatever you say."

"Okay, but if you win, you have to promise me you won't frighten the old man."

Quentin admired her tenacity on the point. Of course he didn't want to scare an old man into his grave. He'd only been trying to explain that death, for an old man, came naturally and his plan took simple advantage of that process.

But Mia was a caretaker, and her persistence on the point fit the woman who remembered the birthdays of the crew, sent flowers to those in the hospital, and ordered baby booties for new arrivals.

Softly, he said, "I give you my word."

"Thank you." Apparently satisfied, she turned her attention to the twigs. As she studied the tips, she ran her tongue over her lips. Quentin fixated on that entrancing gesture. When had Mia turned into such a little minx? His body stirred in a way that left no doubt he was more alive than dead and he considered for just a moment flinging the sticks out the window and running his own tongue over her delicious lips.

Then she grasped one twig and pulled.

The look of dismay on her face when he flashed the longer twig in his palm was worth a thousand words, and pretty much as effective as a cold shower on his amorous thoughts. "Gotcha," he said, but the victory felt pretty hollow. He wanted to stay right where he was and explore these reactions with a woman he'd regarded as a sister for so many years. He was an only child, but he knew he sure as hell wasn't thinking of Mia as a sister right this moment.

Mia swallowed, lowered the window and dropped the short twig on the ground. She said nothing, but Quentin wanted to ease the troubled look from her face.

"Remember I gave you my word," he said.

"Yes, I know, and I value that. Turn when you see Blueberry Lane."

He started the car and within another five hundred feet they came to a dirt road with a white marker reading Blueberry Lane. He swung in.

"Wait," Mia said. "While you're having your go at this, there's something I want to do."

"You know you can't contact anyone but Ely."

She gave him an impish grin. "Now who's worrying about the rules? Don't worry, I only want to check out a hunch. I'll be back in an hour to pick you up, okay?"

He gave her a thumbs up. "Take the car. I'll jog down the lane. A little exercise will feel great." And maybe he wouldn't feel quite so horny by the time she came to collect him.

Mia smiled a secret little smile and he suddenly

wondered what she intended to explore. But she climbed into the driver's seat without enlightening him and sped off, coating him in a cloud of dust.

5 ～

Following Hennie's directions, Mia passed at least five churches, all made of red brick and primly steepled. None of the signs bore the name of Pastor Miller. Just when she wondered if she'd misread the speedometer, as she preferred to think of the gauge despite Quentin's correction, she spotted a white clapboard building that looked more like a home than a church.

But sure enough, in tiny letters under Hill Springs Community Church, Mia found her confirmation. Luke Miller, Pastor. The pastors' names on the other church signs had been almost as large as the procession of First, Second, and Freewill Baptist church names. Funny how the only thing Protestants could agree on was how wrong Catholics were.

Leaving the car parked a few yards down the road, she then walked around the side of the church. A covered walkway connected a second building and behind the church, Mia spied a graveyard.

She skipped toward the tiny cemetery, drawn by the honeysuckle and wildly blooming iris. A white picket fence surrounded the graves. If she and Quentin failed, this pastoral setting was exactly where she'd want to be buried.

Then she pictured the Hollywood Mausoleum where her family would no doubt inter her. The only music there was the rush and roar of traffic, the decorations tag marks of gang members on better terms with death than life.

Another glance at the flowers and the scrubbed headstones and Mia balled her fists in her pockets and was surprised to hear herself saying aloud, "Please, God, don't let me be dead."

A mockingbird trilled above her. Mia looked up and the bird cocked its gray head, beaming a steady eye at her. He seemed satisfied by what he saw, and sang forth with another few measures.

Unsure of what had taken place, assigning most of it to an overactive imagination she hadn't known she had, Mia pushed open the gate to the graveyard. She was positive that bird could see her.

And if so, surely she wasn't dead.

So perhaps God did listen.

At that she shivered slightly. And retreated to good common sense, such as it was in this unreal existence, in the form of following her hunch.

She began methodically to study the gravestones. After finishing the first row, which appeared to be from the 1950's, she skipped to the back row, assuming those would be the most recent.

The mockingbird joined her, alighting with sure feet on the head of a marker three graves away and once again pinning her with a steady gaze.

"What is it? You want me to read that one or are you mocking me?" Mia laughed without humor at her own joke, but skipped to the headstone where the bird perched.

She blanched. The bird gave a merry cry and flew away.

Jenny Poole Miller, Loving Mother of Timmy, Devoted Wife of Luke.

By the dates on the stone, Mia calculated that the pastor's wife had died at the age of thirty-one, only a little over a year ago.

So chances were Luke Miller would be the right age to interest Chelsea Jordan. She'd love to know Timmy's age, too. What woman could resist a bright-eyed toddler without a mummy? Mia sighed, wishing she were performing this heavenly match-making for a woman she liked. But then, the idea wasn't for Chelsea to get the guy, only to want him badly enough to try to be a better person.

Mia turned her attention to the side building where two windows stood open. A narrow-shouldered guy sat in one windowsill, his back to her.

Pastor Miller?

She checked her watch. She had to know what Hennie and her sidekick thought of as "devilishly handsome." Somehow, she doubted anyone in this neck of the woods could measure up to the men Chelsea chewed up and spat out daily.

The man in the window shifted his body. The profile that met Mia's gaze was . . . she searched for a word . . . average. Nondescript brown hair fell across a high forehead, his nose leaned to one side, thick lips angled down at the corners.

Ooh, Hennie. What bad taste in men you have.

Mia checked again, wondering if she hadn't leapt

to conclusions. This man looked more like a teenager than a thirty-something widower.

"I still don't see why I hafta stay inside on a day like today," the guy in the window said.

"Your break," came a deep voice.

Mia perked up. The kid in the window wasn't her man.

The window emptied.

Mia tiptoed over and cleared the sill with her eyes. She wasn't trusting this invisible stuff around a preacher. At one time she would have believed a priest would know if a spirit were present.

The kid leaned over a pool table, setting up the rack. Against the opposite wall ranged a man clad in a faded denim shirt with jeans to match. The sleeves rolled back to highlight muscular forearms warmed to ginger by the sun. The jeans, Mia was positive, hid equally impressive attributes.

Daring finally to glance at his face, she gasped. Blue eyes that held both light and steel met hers under a wide brow. This man had brown hair, too, but it was the brown of mink, and swept back from his forehead in a shining drop to his collar. A collar, Mia noted, that was the only mark of the cleric on the man who had to be Pastor Miller. All right, Hennie!

She inched away from the window, fearful that he could and had seen her. The last thing she could afford to do was break one of the rules.

He was saying to the kid, "You're inside today, Darren, because it's a better place to be than county jail."

"Yeah, I guess so."

"Want to go back there?" He said this in a voice of inquiry, not threatening, as Mia would have expected from the context of the conversation and from most authority figures.

"Nah."

"When you're finished with your afternoons with me, you'll be able to play pool and hold your own."

"Yeah, I guess that's cooler than breaking inta the pool hall to get my money."

"That's the spirit." The crack of ball smacking ball rang out. "Nice break."

Mia crept away until she was out of sight of the windows, then bolted for the car, her heart racing faster than her legs.

How could Chelsea Jordan ignore a man like that?

How could any woman?

Mia found Quentin stretching his hamstrings beside the Blueberry Lane sign, a glum expression on his face.

Leaning out the car window, she said, "How'd it go?"

He shook his head and got into the passenger seat. "Remember *Sew-Sew and the Hand Grenade?*"

"Oops," Mia said, covering her mouth to hide the grin that threatened to break through. Back in their early college days, Quentin wrote and directed *Sew-Sew* as an anti-nuclear protest, his one attempt at serious drama. But he couldn't help himself; he kept throwing in laugh lines. And the title! Mia had known him only a few months, but she quickly advised him to rename the project.

Quentin hadn't listened. The show closed after one performance.

"So," Mia said, "Mr. Van Ness tossed you out?"

He laughed. "No, I hate to admit it, but I didn't even make it in the front door."

"What happened?" Not one to waste time, she put the car into gear and started slowly down the dirt road.

"He has a dog."

She waited, knowing Quentin would tell her at his own speed. He hated to fail. And with all the applause and acclaim he'd been receiving, failure wasn't something he was on a first-name basis with.

"Well, the damn dog wouldn't let me set foot on the porch."

Mia frowned. Had he really tried? "How did the dog know you were there?"

Quentin tapped out some rhythm only he heard on his knees. "I've been thinking that if I were directing this journey of ours as a film, I'd do something corny and go one step further on this invisible schtick."

"And?"

"And animals would be able to see us."

She laughed, then bit out a groan as the car hit a rut. "That's silly."

A mockingbird flew low across the windshield.

"Maybe it's not so silly."

"Which is it, Mia?"

"Oh, I was thinking of just now, back at the church. I could have sworn there was a bird there who saw me, and even knew what I wanted to find. But"— she grabbed his knee—"something even better happened. I met the most gorgeous man!"

"You *met* someone?" Quentin actually sounded alarmed.

"Oh, not in person." Mia waved a hand. "I peeked through the window at this charming Hill Springs Community Church. And I have got to tell you, the preacher there is one hunk of a man. If he ever gives up the ministry, you could make him a male sex symbol overnight."

Quentin popped his knuckles. "Sex symbol, huh? Since when have you been interested in hunks?"

She couldn't resist batting her lashes. Did her eager heart deceive her, or did Quentin sound jealous? "I am a woman, you know." She tried for a flounce, but she knew her hair did nothing but bob a bit atop her head.

Quentin frowned. "Why'd you go see this guy, anyway?"

"Female intuition." She wanted him to stew; she wanted him to be jealous. Yes!

The house came into view. One-story, built of what looked like some sort of local fieldstone, with broad steps leading to a nice-size porch under a sweeping roof. From her early stoop years in immigrant-crowded Los Angeles apartment buildings, Mia had always appreciated a comfortable place to sit outside. To the far side of the house sat a vintage pickup truck restored to a state of lacquered glory. Leafy trees sheltered the house.

"It's lovely," Mia said. "But it's an odd house for a man as rich as Ely Van Ness."

"That fits in with the story of him turning his back on his life of wealth and privilege."

"Mmm. I bet there's a woman involved in that story."

His brows shot up. "Why do you say that?"

She gave him a saucy grin. "More female intuition."

From around the back cantered a black and white dog.

"Oh, look. A border collie," Mia said, admiring the perky yet purposeful step. "They're very smart, you know."

"So why wouldn't the pooch let me in?"

"I'm sure it's nothing personal," Mia said, thinking of the mockingbird picking out Jenny Miller's headstone. "Lots of things seem to be happening for a reason."

"Oh, no, not that predestination crap again." Quentin jerked open the car door, but before he could get one foot out, the dog rounded the car, effectively herding Quentin back into his seat.

Mia opened her car door. The dog came to her side and sat back on its haunches, head tipped to one side, yellow eyes friendly. She flashed a smile at Quentin, then said, "I'll give you the all-clear as soon as the doggie lets me know it's okay."

The collie accompanied Mia to the steps, then raced back to the car, cutting short another attempt by Quentin to gain his freedom.

Mia tapped on the screen door and peered into the house, trying to calm herself with a few deep breaths, the way she'd been instructed in her Relax with Yoga class before she dropped out after the second session. She just wasn't comfortable with mellow.

She could see a comfy-looking sofa and chair, a coffee table piled with books, a plaid flannel dog bed, and built-in shelves crammed with more books. Despite his advanced age, Mr. Van Ness apparently had good eyesight.

Behind her, the car roared to life and Mia turned in time to see Quentin drive off in a shower of reddish dust.

The border collie approached the steps. Mia thought his black and white face, divided half and half vertically like a mask, adorable. She held out her hand and greeted him with "Hi there."

The dog cocked his head to one side as if he were analyzing her words, then sniffed her hand, but seemed too dignified to lick it.

"There you are," boomed a voice as a silver-haired man in a jogging suit rounded the corner of the house.

Mia jumped. Wasn't she still invisible?

"Macduff, sit."

Of course, the dog.

"And who do we have here?" The man bounded up the steps and held out a hand to Mia.

She automatically extended her hand, which he grasped and pumped. "Mia Tortelli," she said, forgetting all about her fake identification.

"Pleased to meet you. Won't you come in?" The man's eyes sparkled. He had the beginnings of a suntan, an upright bearing that went hand in hand with the jogging suit and his brisk stride.

"Uh, I'm looking for a Mr. Ely Van Ness."

"Yes?" He peered at her over raised brows and reached for the screen door, which he held open for her.

"Does he live here?"

The man nodded, and indicated she should enter. Never, ever, take a ride with a man your parents don't know ran through Mia's mind, but what did she have to lose? And this nice-looking older man certainly didn't look like her idea of a rapist or murderer. She stepped into the house. Man and dog followed.

"Now, what can I get you? I have carrot juice, fresh squeezed this morning, or apple, from the orchard down the road."

Juice. Health food. Exercise. Mia's mouth dropped open. Quentin's two sets of deceased grandparents must have been overweight, overstressed couch potatoes who smoked like chimney stacks. Weakly, she said, "You're Mr. Van Ness, aren't you?"

He looked surprised at her question. "Yes, of course. That's what I'm doing here in Mr. Van Ness's home." Then he smiled, as if to take the bark out of his words. "Carrot or apple?"

"Carrot, please." Actually, she detested carrot juice, but if drinking the stuff would make her look like Mr. Van Ness at eighty, she'd gulp it down. Of course right at this moment she wouldn't give too much for her chance of reaching twenty-six, let alone her eighth decade.

"Have a seat and I'll be right back." He stepped away, crossed a small dining room with that spring in his every move and disappeared. The house was so small Mia could hear him humming in the kitchen. What a shock Chelsea Jordan would have when she saw this place—if she could convince this robust-looking man to leave a will that would change his grandniece's life forever.

And hers.

And Quentin's.

She dried her palms on her sweater dress and reached out to accept the glass of what looked like orange milk. "Thank you, Mr. Van Ness," she said.

He settled onto the sofa opposite where she'd perched on the edge of the only chair. "Call me Ely. Now, what can I do for you?"

"That's a very good question, Mr., um, Ely." Mia pleated the hem of her sweater dress. Well, there was nothing to do but start with the story and let the chips fall where they may. "I'm here, but I'm not really here, if I can explain . . .

". . . so you see—" Twenty minutes later Mia wrapped up her tale of how she and Quentin arrived on his doorstep, relieved that Ely seemed to be listening with serious attention. He hadn't ordered her out of his house, or even once guffawed. "—my friend and I studied what was recorded about Chelsea's life and read about you and we thought you were our key. So that's why we picked you for our Intervention point."

Ely drank the last of his carrot juice and sat the glass on a coaster on the coffee table. "And how do I figure into this plan?"

Mia blushed. Looking at the man sitting erect across from her, she couldn't bring herself to say he was supposed to change his will and conveniently, like an old dog, lie down and die.

"Well," she began, "Quentin thought you could be very creative with your will." She took a deep breath and said all at once, "You fix it to say that Chelsea has to come here and live in your house and work at the poultry plant for a month or all your money goes to that fanatical neo-Nazi group that's headquartered around here. Quentin says Chelsea is quite committed to fund raising for B'nai B'rith and would do whatever it takes to keep hatemongers from getting your money."

She took a breath and added before he could comment, "Plus, I want to add that she has to go to Pastor Miller's church for the four Sundays she's here."

Ely raised one brow at that, the strongest reaction he'd shown so far. "Why Luke Miller's church?"

"Because he's gorgeous and single and has a son."

Ely shook his head slowly.

"You think I'm insane, don't you?" Mia asked. Suddenly, she couldn't stand it, being there or having said so many crazy things to this nice old man. Leaning forward, she said, "Oh, I know you can't want to believe me, but all this is true. And I know what Chelsea Jordan is like. She's your relative, so I'll watch my tongue, but the woman is impossible! She needs to learn to live like the rest of the world, understand what it's like to go without and have to work and work hard. Plus, if for once she met a man she couldn't have . . ."

"Oh, so that's it." Ely laughed. "Not really matchmaking at all, are you?" He stood and stretched, then regained his seat. "All right, Miss Mia Tortelli, let me assure you I don't think you're insane."

"You don't?" A spear of hope took form.

He shook his head. "But I do see one teeny little hitch in the getalong of your plan."

Mia nodded. She saw one big enough to drive a Mack truck through. But she'd let him say it. It seemed only proper to let him chastise her for stereotyping him with one foot in the grave.

"The good Lord doesn't tell us what the days of our lives will be. I could go to sleep and not wake up tomorrow. However"— he grinned —"longevity is a well-guarded gene in my family. So I don't think having me change my will is going to help you meet your challenge in a hurry." He rubbed a hand across his chin, then smiled. "But I have to say I think you've an ingenious plan for changing Ms. Chelsea. One of which I heartily approve."

"Well, that's something." At least he hadn't read her the riot act, for which she was thankful. He must have been a good father, patient when his kids messed up. And what a wonderful grandfather he must be. But in her glance around, she hadn't seen any family pictures or scattered toys. "Don't you have children of your own?"

"My wife Rebecca and I were never able to have children." He sighed and Mia regretted asking the question. "That's one of the reasons I've wanted to reach out to Chelsea. She was such a special child."

Mia swallowed, but didn't comment. From the stories she'd heard, the only thing special about Chelsea's childhood was the way every adult kow-towed to her every command, dependent as they were on the moneymaking power of the child star.

"So," said Ely, clapping his hands together, "let's see. What shall we do about this quandary?"

The dog raised its head from the flannel bed at the sound of Ely clapping. Mia reached down and stroked his head.

"Macduff wouldn't let your friend up the steps," Ely said.

"You *saw* Quentin?"

He nodded.

"And you can see me, too, can't you?"

"Yes." He was clearly waiting for her to explain her question.

"But you see," Mia said, "Quentin and I are invisible to everyone else we've come across since we arrived from Purgatory. Except you and Macduff." She didn't mention the bird; he would think she was tetched.

"Ah." He smiled again. "The Lord does work in mysterious ways, doesn't He?"

"I really wouldn't know," Mia answered, somewhat uncomfortable with Ely so easily expressing what she herself had wanted to think.

"Are you religious?"

"I was raised Catholic."

"Episcopalian myself, but I must say I prefer Luke Miller's commonsense brand of theology."

"Are you and he friends?" Mia was curious about the minister with the knock-em-dead looks.

"For years, and with his father before him. His house is the one you pass coming down the lane." Ely rose and walked to the door, where he stood gazing out the screen door. "I think I hear your friend returning." He reclaimed his seat and with a small smile said, "That's a rough road to drive so fast."

"Quentin doesn't know any other way."

"Ah." Ely toyed with his juice glass. "A man who lives his life in a hurry?"

"Absolutely." Mia wondered if that sounded critical. "That's not necessarily a bad thing. I mean, Quentin's always accomplishing things."

"And what about you, Miss Mia? Are you in a hurry, too?" He asked the question in a gentle voice, almost drowned out by the slamming of a car door outside and bounding footsteps.

Quentin knocked on the door, too sharply to be polite, but right at that moment, he didn't care. He'd driven around town until he'd located Hill Springs Community Church. After one sighting of that angel-faced preacher, the only thing he wanted to do was get Mia out of town. Fast. Before she got another look at Mr. Perfection.

The dog answered the door, then turned back as a man's voice called "Stay" then "Come in."

He opened the screen door and stepped into a patch of a living room. A quick glance told him there was no way Chelsea Jordan would last an hour in this house, let alone a month.

"Hi, Quentin," Mia said, "meet Mr. Van Ness." With a funny sort of smile, she pointed to a silver-haired man in jogging sweats.

The man rose, and Quentin looked up into a lively pair of blue eyes that looked nowhere near graveside.

"Call me Ely," he said, shaking hands with a firm grip.

"Ely," Quentin said with a nod, then performed a fast pace of the floor area.

"He's a quick study," Mia said.

Ely chuckled. "Despite the circumstances, it's a pleasure to meet you, Quentin Grandy."

Quentin stopped and forced his body onto the sofa. He'd been taught to respect his elders and just because both his life and his death were messed up beyond belief didn't mean he should disregard his rearing. "Thank you, sir," he said, pushing his glasses back up on his nose and wondering whether they were allowed to change Intervention plans in mid-stream.

"Ely and I were just discussing the pickle we're in," Mia said.

Drumming his fingers on his knees, Quentin nodded. "Time to re-think." He peered at Mia, wondering whether she was still picturing—what had she called him—that sexy hunk? He straightened his posture, lifting his chest. Think fast and with luck they'd be out of Arkansas in another couple of hours. Funny how none of the pretty boys in Hollywood had ever made him feel this way about Mia. Why, Arturio Grande was playing the lead in *Dino-Daddy* and never once had it occurred to him to be jealous.

Of course, not until today had he noticed Mia was . . .

A woman. Quentin shifted on the sofa, glancing to where she sat, a precious porcelain doll wrapped in that soft sweater dress that suggested curves that cried out to be explored.

"Don't worry, Ely, he seems like he's in a trance, but that's what he looks like when he's thinking," Mia was saying.

"Thinking," Quentin muttered, shifting his body. How could he think when Mia filled his mind? "We simply have to let nature take its course."

Ely raised his brows. "Meaning I agree to change my will and we sit back and wait?"

"Couldn't you just send Chelsea a telegram and tell her there's an emergency and she has to come here?" Mia was looking excited and Quentin admired the way the color rose in her cheeks and the way her freckles danced.

The roar of a motorbike interrupted them. Ely walked to the door.

"Afternoon, Ely," called a man climbing off a Harley.

"Afternoon, Duke." Over his shoulder, Ely said, "Duke's the Western Union man."

From the porch, the messenger said, "This here message says a Mr. Joseph Carpenter and his wife will be arriving soon, to stay longer than they figured on. You expectin' company, Ely?"

Ely started to shake his head, and Quentin said,

"Say yes. That's my Earth-alias." Jeez, where had that term popped up from? He'd fire the writer, that's what he'd do.

"As a matter of fact, I am," Ely obligingly answered.

"Does he always read people's mail?" Quentin held his tongue in check. He normally would have shouted, "What the fuck is that message supposed to mean?" Somehow, sitting in the living room of the patriarchal Ely Van Ness didn't seem the time and place.

Mia looked at him in alarm. "Are we stuck here?"

Quentin could only shrug. For once, he had no answer.

Ely took the telegram and tapped it against his palm. "Duke, send one for me when you get back to the station."

"Sure thing. Another one to your grandniece?"

Ely nodded.

"What's this one to say?" Duke pulled a small spiral notebook from his jean's pocket.

"Very ill. Please come at once."

"You don't look so sick."

"Well, Duke, when you've lived as long as I have, you'll learn things aren't always the way they seem."

"Right." The messenger put the notebook away and waved away Ely's cash.

"No, Ely, it wouldn't be right to take your money, not as you're sick and all. This one's on the house."

"Thank you, Duke," Ely said to the man's back.

The Harley roared to life.

Quentin studied Ely closely. "You're not at all sick, are you?"

"Afraid not." Ely smiled. "Let me get you some carrot juice."

6 ⌒

Chelsea kept her gaze fixed on the crumpled bit of yellow paper Fran had forced her to read.

Pulling her silk robe close as if it could ward off the chill overtaking her, she turned from Fran's assessing eyes.

Fran saw too much, and Chelsea wanted to be alone with her guilt.

She'd ignored all her great-uncle's telegrams. Even the one before this, the one that read "Very ill. Please come at once."

Now that didn't matter.

Nothing did.

Except that she was a shit. Chelsea blinked her heavily coated eyelashes. When that gesture only blurred her vision further, she swiped at her eyes with the hem of her thousand-dollar negligee, selfish bitch that she was.

She hadn't meant to be so bad.

Once upon a time, in a world far lovelier than the one she inhabited now, a kindly old relative had been her only friend.

She sank onto a loveseat and pictured the Santa

Monica Pier that long ago day, the day that was to be his last visit. Just the two of them, Chelsea dressed in white, the way her father insisted, with that silly hat with the blue ribbon that Uncle Ely let her toss into the Pacific. "They need that hat in China more than you do here," he'd said with a chuckle, and applauded as she threw it to the waves.

"I'm ten, you know," Chelsea said, chasing with her tongue a blob of chocolate ice cream about to escape the cone. "And I'm a movie star."

Ely nodded. "Which makes you happier? Chocolate ice cream or being a movie star?"

She kicked her heels against the back of the wooden bench, giggling behind her hand. The ice cream, thick and cold, tingled all the way down her throat. Her mother and father never let her eat ice cream. Especially not chocolate.

"Ice cream," she answered, taking another bite to prove her point.

"Ah," said her wise old uncle. "And how much do you like being a movie star?"

"It's okay, I guess. But I'd rather go to school and have friends. Mother says all the money I make is better than friends, but I think she's wrong." She scowled.

"What is it, chipmunk?"

"Mother doesn't like me."

"Why do you say that?"

"I can tell."

He looked at her with eyes that told her he understood.

"I'm sorry, because I know Mother is your family, but she's really not a nice person." Chelsea bit off another chunk of ice cream and for a few minutes her mouth was too deliciously cold and full to speak.

"Perhaps your mother is unhappy?"

She glanced up at her uncle. His face looked sad, and he was staring down at the oily water that lapped the wooden legs that held the pier in place. "My father, too."

"Ah," he said once more. "I thought they married for love."

"Love!" Chelsea spit out a precious bit of ice cream. "My father loves himself, my mother loves herself, and together, they love my being a movie star."

"And you're only ten years old?"

She shrugged. "You grow up fast in this business."

"Oh, little one, you're too young for that sort of knowledge."

With a sigh, she said, "Then I've been too young for a long time. Daddy praises me when I'm finished with a film. Mother ignores me. My tutors try to teach me, but they at least are easy to ignore." She crunched into the cone, but it didn't taste nearly as good as the ice cream, so she tossed it to the gulls.

One squawking bird beat out another, snatching it from mid-air with a shrill cry of victory that cost it its prize. Chelsea laughed. "Look at that. That gull could have had the cone if it hadn't wanted to brag about it."

Ely smiled at her. "You're a wise little girl, aren't you?"

"I'm just me," she said.

So many years later, Chelsea sighed and stared at the telegram in her hand. "I'm just me," she whispered. The little girl who'd gone home that day with sunburn, and been yelled at by both her parents. Ely had been sent away in disgrace, branded a bad influence and every time after when she asked when he was coming back to visit, her mother would say, "Ely isn't welcome here anymore."

Just like that.

And now Ely was dead.

Fran cleared her throat. "You'll go to the funeral. That will help."

"What good will that do?" Chelsea let her head loll against the back of the couch. Felt the stretching of the tendons or whatever they were in her neck. Hanging. She hadn't thought to try hanging herself.

From the corner of her eye, Chelsea watched Fran scoot her wiry body onto the same sofa, the look that said "mothering" set clearly on her sun-browned face. Funny how a consummate businesswoman like Fran could convert to such a role. She could strike a multimillion-dollar deal, then swap cold remedies. Knowing she was in for a lecture, Chelsea set her expression on automatic pilot and struggled not to remember Ely.

To remember was to agonize.

Fran gathered her hands in her own. Chelsea allowed the gesture, neither fingers nor wrists offering resistance.

"I'll see to your schedule. They'll shoot around you. I'll even call the minister"—the telegram rustled as Fran eased it away from Chelsea —"Pastor Miller, it is, to ascertain the details."

Chelsea felt the pressure in her shoulders shift from side to side as she rolled her head to express "Leave me alone, the last thing I'm going to do is attend a funeral."

Fran smacked her lips, a habit she had that annoyed Chelsea to no end. Smack. "Well, attending this funeral is the only way to make yourself feel better for ignoring him." Smack. Smack.

"Forget it."

"Chelsea, my dear, when you're my age, you'll come to understand the value of a funeral."

"You mean when I'm dead?"

Smack. Smack. "I don't need you as a client, you know that, don't you?"

"What?" For the first time, Chelsea lifted her head. She studied Fran through narrowed eyes. What was the woman talking about? Of course she needed her. Fran was an agent and personal manager and without a star—a star like Chelsea Jordan—Fran was nothing. Zippo. History in Hollywood.

"Now, sit up and tell me you're going to your great-uncle's funeral."

"Leave me alone."

"Enough people have left you alone for too long."

"Screw you."

Fran laughed.

At that, Chelsea sat up, pulling her silk robe tightly around her. "And what's so funny?"

"It's a good thing you're an actress, not a writer, because 'screw you' certainly doesn't take any statuettes for originality."

"My, my, we are on a bit of a high horse today, aren't we?" Chelsea wasn't sure what game Fran was playing, but she damn sure wasn't going to be caught in her net. Ely was dead and as he was the only person who mattered to her one whit in the state of Arkansas, there was no way she was going to attend a funeral where people would gawk at her, and others would doubtless approach her at the graveside for a frigging autograph.

Fran had let go of Chelsea's hands. Now she leaned close, hands planted on her bony knees. "Chelsea, please go. Please give yourself the forgiveness your great-uncle no doubt would have given you."

"Why would he do that?"

"Because, it seems that he loved you." Fran said these words in a soft voice, and something about the way she shielded her eyes from Chelsea caught her attention.

"Why does this mean so much to you? Why does it matter?"

Fran, hard-boiled old trooper that she was, showed evidence of a tear or two on her lashes.

"Nothing is more important than family," Fran said after a long pause.

Chelsea snapped her mouth shut, stopped short in her budding tirade. Her manager rarely mentioned her family, and only once had she told Chelsea their story of hiding safely until early spring 1945. Only three months old, covered by a pile of rags, too weak to cry, Fran had been overlooked by the SS.

Fran blinked her eyes again.

Chelsea patted her bony shoulder. "It's all right, Fran. I'll go." She rose from the sofa and after a moment, Fran did, too.

"I'm pleased," Fran said, swiping at her eyes.

Chelsea thought of Ely, dying alone, without any family, and experienced another pang of guilt. Her only consolation was that he was dead, and couldn't know she wasn't coming to his funeral. Dead, unknowing.

But she knew, knew she was beyond redemption. "Don't you worry about the arrangements," Chelsea said, summoning a smile worthy of an angel. "I'll call Pastor Miller and have my secretary make the flight plans. Just take care of the shooting schedule."

In one fluid stride, she caught Fran at the door and took her gently by the shoulders. "Thank you for caring about me," she whispered, then ushered her crotchety interfering manager out of the trailer.

Alone, she sat at her dressing table and forced herself to look into the mirror. It wasn't her eyes or nose or lips or cheekbones she studied. Those had been photographed, described, emulated all too often.

No, she tried to look through the face in the mirror to see if anything lay beneath. To see whether any fragment of the child Ely had once called wise still existed.

She kept staring and finally she caught a glimmer. Because she knew, as surely as she sat there, that no longer could she try to take her life. For better or worse, her only way to make amends for ignoring Uncle Ely was to live.

Curious George's latest adventure safely concluded, Luke Miller closed Timmy's favorite book of the moment after reading it for the third time that night. He smoothed a hand over his son's tousled hair, thinking he should have brushed the tangles out before coaxing Timmy to bed. Tomorrow the thick curls would be a matted mess worthy of a pigeon's nest.

Jenny never would have put Timmy to bed in such a state. Luke thought he detected a smear of chocolate on one earlobe, but decided not to look closer. Boys were made, as his mother used to say, of frogs and snails and puppy dog tails. A little chocolate wouldn't hurt.

Jenny would have thought otherwise. He pictured

her bending over the bed, a damp washcloth in hand, ministering to the spot Timmy missed. He saw her finishing off the spot cleaning with a tender kiss.

His eyes misted, and he smoothed his hand once again over his son's forehead. "Your mommy loves you," he whispered, and eased off the side of the bed. He'd already said the same for himself, before tucking Timmy in bed. But every night Luke ended their bedtime routine on behalf of a mother he didn't know how long Timmy would remember.

That goodnight amounted to only a pittance of the ways in which he tried to make up for his son's loss.

But no matter how he tried, he knew his son needed his mother.

The mother Luke had taken from him.

Blocking his mind from traveling that careworn path, Luke added the book to the stack leaning perilously on the overflowing bookcase, stretched his arms over his head, and with one last glance at his son, moved from the room. He left the door ajar and headed down the stairs.

The time-buffed stairs of the old farmhouse creaked in all the familiar places, keeping him company, lightening the silence of his solitude. The yawn he'd attempted to stifle arrived, full-fledged.

What he'd like to do was sack out on the couch in front of ESPN, remote in one hand, bowl of popcorn cradled against his chest. What he needed to do was prepare for next morning's meeting with the Ladies' Guild. They were finishing their plans for Vacation Bible School and the Summer Fair fund-raiser. He'd meant to read the reports earlier, but one of his hogs had taken ill.

Crossing past the archway to the living room, he

eyed the blank face of the television with longing, but managed to turn his back and march into the kitchen.

There his resolve almost withered. Dinner dishes littered the table; lunch and breakfast remains lined the counter next to the sink. The ham carcass, one of the many delivered so thoughtfully by the women of his church, glistened where the pineapple slices had clung before Timmy picked them off.

He stretched again, scratched his stomach, and set to the task of straightening up the mess. As he plunged his hands into the sink of soapy water, his sister Imogene's voice rolled around in his head. Only yesterday she'd cornered him out at the barn when she'd dropped Timmy off from his visit with his cousins. Concerned over the holes she found in Timmy's socks and what she called his "scrawny little chest," she launched into her favorite theme.

"You need a wife, Luke."

He'd raised his head a fraction from where he had squatted, mixing feed for his pigs.

She narrowed her eyes and assessed him the way he would a Poland White on the auction block. "You need a woman's touch. Look at that stubble, and those shadows under your eyes. Timmy's a mess, your house is a disaster zone, and, besides that, it isn't right for a preacher not to have a wife."

He had clenched his jaw at that line, but let her go on.

"You need someone to keep that old house from falling apart. Until you married Jenny, it looked like it should have been condemned, and now it pretty much resembles its old self. She's been gone more than a year now. No one will talk if you remarry."

The feed poured, he straightened. He towered over his sister, who'd never made it past five feet three. "And just whom should I marry?"

Imogene had the grace to blush just a bit. "If you looked around, you'd find plenty of women wanting to marry you."

"And what about a woman *I* want?"

"You didn't seem too shy towards Bridget Nolan in high school."

"High school." Luke turned away, his hands on his hips. When he turned back to his sister, he forced himself to speak in a calm voice. "Listen, Imogene, I appreciate your help with Timmy, everything you've done, I really do. But I don't want Bridget. I don't want Sally or Susie or whoever else is the flavor of the week. I don't want a wife for the sake of having a wife. Everyone said a preacher needed a wife, and that's exactly why I married Jenny." He cleared his throat, wondering if his sister had ever guessed the truth.

She looked at him, her brown eyes bright with what he suspected were unshed tears. She'd been Jenny's best friend. She'd been Jenny's matron of honor at their wedding. And here he was telling his own sister he hadn't ever really loved his wife.

He dropped his clenched fists and walked to the barn door, where the bright sun cast a sharp line of shadow. Standing in the dark, he said, "I tried to make her happy, but after she died, all I could think about was she'd never truly known what it was to be loved."

Luke turned back around. "I stole that from her, and I promised God and myself I'd never marry without love again."

Imogene walked toward him, her arms open.

"Little brother, it's okay." She reached up and took him in her embrace and patted his back as if he were Timmy. "Jenny loved you, and it made her world complete to be your wife. So don't kick yourself."

Luke squeezed his sister gently on her shoulder and wiped away a tear he spotted on her cheek. "Thanks, sis. Sometimes I think the only way I'll be free from this burden is to fall completely and helplessly in love with a woman who will have absolutely nothing to do with me."

Imogene fished a tissue from a pocket and smiled at him. "Well, if you're not out dating, you won't be able to find that peculiar form of punishment." She put away the tissue, then said, "So you won't mind coming to dinner a week from Sunday, will you?"

Luke groaned. "Who is it this time?"

"I don't think I'm going to tell you in advance," Imogene said with a touch of mischief lighting her face.

"You don't play fair. You know I wouldn't turn down one of your dinners, so you know I'll show up even though I know you're matchmaking."

She smiled. "Precisely."

Luke smiled now, despite the greasy scum floating atop his dishwater. He loved his sister. And while the last thing he needed was a wife, Imogene had one thing right. His house was a mess. Looking into the water, frustrated that he hadn't made time to call the dishwasher repairman, he promised he'd check into a cleaning service first thing tomorrow.

He'd meant to replace the dishwasher more than a year ago, had even picked one out that Jenny had admired in the Maytag store in Fayetteville.

The chime of the doorbell broke into that thought. With a smothered sigh, Luke checked his

kitchen clock. After nine-thirty. Doubtless a parishioner with a problem. Reaching for a dish towel, he
dried his hands and wished for his father's infinite
patience in dealing with the parade of problems
brought to his door.

Infidelity, alcoholism, teen pregnancy, marital
strife, unemployment and the fear of welfare—Luke
never knew what crisis would come next. But he
remembered his father going to the door many a
night, sitting up late into the evening in his study in
the church rectory where his mother still lived.

As he forced his weary body to the door, Luke
glanced at his size-twelve Adidas, wondering whether he'd ever fill his father's shoes, asking himself for
the umpteenth time how his father expected him to
live up to the obligations he'd imposed with the
deathbed request for Luke to take over the church.

A request made possible because years earlier, his
father, gentle Machiavellian that he'd been, had
agreed to Luke's request to try for a baseball career
in exchange for his promise to attend a seminary
after he finished college.

Thinking what would it hurt to please his Dad as
long as he got what he wanted, too, Luke had done
the seminary courses part-time, making straight A's
as a gift to his Dad.

At the same time, he'd batted .300 and been
scouted for a farm team in Birmingham.

The door bell rang again, just as Luke reached for
the knob.

"Hold your horses, I'm coming," he muttered,
then composed his face to an expression passable as
serene and caring.

When he saw who stood under the glow of his

porch light, he smiled with relief. He unhooked the screen door, beckoned his friend Ely inside, and led him to his favorite corner of Luke's worn sofa, a sofa he'd refused to let Jenny replace.

Ely settled in, then said, "I'm sorry to barge in this late, but I need your help."

Luke took the opposite corner of the battered rust-colored sofa. His butt fit comfortably into the sagging cushion. "Shoot. You know I'd do anything to help you."

Ely appeared fascinated by the hem of his pants. "Anything?"

Luke thought of his wife's funeral, when Timmy would accept comfort only from Ely. He thought of how kind and generous Ely'd been, not just to himself over the years, but especially to Timmy during the year since Jenny's death. He'd given Timmy a job feeding his chickens and never tired of him playing with Macduff. "For you, yes."

"Then let me tell you a story," Ely said, "a most unusual story."

"And just what do you suggest we do now?" Mia tossed the useless flashlight into the trunk. Dead batteries.

Not much help for changing a flat tire after dark.

Quentin's grin surprised her. "Relax, Mia. Cars are my second hobby. I'll have this puppy changed in no time." Leaning into the trunk, he lifted the spare cover and, with no apparent effort, hefted the tire onto the ground.

"You can do that?" She stepped farther from the road as a big truck clattered into view and swept by, not slowing at all for the curve marked 45 m.p.h.

Rubbing her upper arms, though the evening wasn't cold, she said, "Well, hurry and do it, then. It's spooky out here."

Quentin made some noise that she interpreted as "silly girl" and continued fishing in the trunk. When he straightened, she could tell even in the dark that his face bore a look of disgust. "No jack," he said.

"Ah." What she refrained from saying was I told you so. Mia interpreted the telegram as a message for them to stay with Ely. Quentin insisted they'd done what they had to do and should return to the airport.

She'd drawn the short twig.

And here they were, stuck on the side of the road.

Another truck swooped by.

She would have bitten her nail but face it, no nail remained. Not after this hair-curling day. Not after the dead-end of the hale and hearty Ely Van Ness. Not after the hours they'd sat and talked with Ely, sipping glass after glass of carrot juice. Mia rubbed her cheek, wondering whether it had turned orange. The time seemed well spent, listening to his family tale and trying for some insight into another avenue of intervention.

But try as he had to assist them, they'd come up with no other ideas. In the end, Ely agreed to change his will as they requested. Since they weren't sure of how long they really had to make this miracle work, they had no way to know whether his offer would help.

But it was certainly an offer better accepted than rejected. They had nothing to lose for trying it.

"Yeah, what do we have to lose?" Quentin muttered the very words Mia was thinking and she jumped.

He waved a wandlike object and said, "Oh, boy, do I have an idea."

She knew that tone of voice only too well. "What kind of idea?"

"We'll hitchhike."

"Is it safe?"

Quentin only looked at her sideways, and she supposed she was grateful he hadn't laughed at her stupid comment. "Well, we can't stay here, but I do think we should reconsider and go back to Hill Springs. I can't help but think the rules—"

"Mia, will you please quit worrying about rules?" Quentin's voice sounded very stern all of a sudden. "If—and I'm only saying if—you accept the improbable reality of our situation, then it's perfectly ridiculous to think some Calvinist archangel is sitting around Heaven or Purgatory or whatever the hell it's called—"

Just then an eighteen-wheeler raced by, the driver leaning on the horn. Mia jumped. "Watch your tongue," she said.

"Anyway," Quentin went on as if she hadn't spoken, "if you accept we've been challenged to earn another chance at life, then you've just got to believe that it's a contest of wits. Creativity will always win out. Face it, babe, rules are for accountants." He seemed to think he needed to soften his words, because he leaned close and brushed his fingertips over her lips.

Mia's blood stirred at the contact, confusing and derailing the words of debate that leapt to her tongue. She moved her lips softly against his touch, only to be met with disappointment. He'd anchored his hand safely back in his pocket. Very well. She was woman enough to accept a platonic gesture of comfort for what it was. Cramming her wanting heart back into its safety net, she took a deep breath and said, "How does one hitchhike?"

"Normally," Quentin said in a voice that now sounded a little breathless, "you raise your thumb and look plaintive."

"Or you wiggle your leg and look sexy?"

Quentin grinned. She could make out his white teeth against the black of the night. "As in *It Happened One Night?*"

"Now that was a movie."

"Frank Capra, 1934. . . ."

"The walls of Jericho."

"Jericho?"

"Don't you remember? Clark Gable and Claudette Colbert have to share a room and they have this blanket between them and there's this bit about how she's safe because he doesn't have a trumpet . . ." Mia heard her voice trail off. She'd vowed long ago never ever to throw herself at Quentin. But right now that's the only thing she wanted to do.

"Of course I remember. That just isn't the first scene that comes to mind." He worked on the object he'd pulled from the trunk earlier.

"That's because you're a man."

He waved the wand. "Good thing, too. Here's the plan. I'll light this flare. Someone's bound to stop. You're always hearing how friendly the South is."

"And then we ask them for a ride?" Mia couldn't keep the sarcasm from her voice. Surely Quentin hadn't managed to forget they were invisible.

"No, silly." Quentin twisted the flare and the light showcased the look of anticipation on his face. "We steal their car."

7 ⌔

"**I** have a real bad feeling about this scene." Quentin downshifted the gears of the pickup truck they'd "borrowed" from two shit-faced good old boys who stopped to pop another cold one and inspect the emergency flare.

He studied the darkened airport through narrowed eyes, wondering again about that telegram. Perhaps he should have listened to Mia.

Beside him, Mia slept. Before she'd drifted off, she'd collected and crunched the wealth of beer cans clattering around in the truck, announcing they should drop them in a recycling bin.

Despite his misgivings at the airport's shuttered look, Quentin smiled. No one but Mia Tortelli would worry about the environment when she herself had one foot on Earth and the other somewhere south of Heaven.

She sighed and shifted slightly, her head tipping toward him. Reaching over, he ventured a tentative finger toward her freckly cheek.

Smooth.

Soft.

Warm.

He continued his exploration, outlining the pucker of her lips with the barest whisper of a touch. He didn't want her to awaken and find him studying her with the same intensity he scrutinized a camera angle.

That was business.

This was . . .

Pleasure?

Nah. Quentin discarded that notion. In the film biz, he and Mia worked together as powerfully as the V-8 in his Ferrari 348. But they argued as often as they agreed. She was stubborn and fussy and besides, she simply wasn't his type.

Not blonde. Nor busty. And definitely not a bimbo.

She moved just enough that her cheek caressed his fingertips. He warmed to her unconscious gesture and lifted his hand to stroke her pugnacious nose ever so lightly.

Not his type?

Then why did the sight of her sleeping next to him, responding to his touch, make him randier than any of the Hollywood starlets eager to hang on his arm in public and pleasure him in private?

"What are you doing?"

Quentin jerked his hand back.

Wide awake, Mia glared at him.

"Nothing."

"Oh." She wiggled closer to the passenger door. "I was having such a strange dream." She blew out a breath and said, "I suppose nothing's the way we're used to it being right now, is it?"

He wanted to ask her about the dream, but

thought better of it. Never once had she expressed an interest in him as a member of the opposite sex and he wasn't into rejection. "As a matter of fact, I was trying to wake you."

Quentin pointed toward the airport terminal and drove slowly to the main building. "If I were a betting man, I'd say this airport is shut down for the night."

Mia sat straighter and peered through the windshield.

Quentin pulled over in a no stopping zone.

"What are you doing?"

"Stopping."

"Here?"

"Do you have a problem with that?"

She pointed to the sign.

Quentin smiled. Easing the truck into the passenger loading zone, he said, "Mia, I confess I only did that to get your goat."

"At a time like this?"

"Okay, okay. Let's think." He drummed on the steering wheel. "Think about all that's happened tonight." He ticked off on his fingers, wishing Mia hadn't awakened, wishing that he were continuing his exploration of her face with those same fingers.

"Ely wasn't one foot from the grave."

"I mean what happened after that." Quentin didn't like being reminded of that blunder.

"Our car wouldn't start."

"Right, and then we had a flat."

"And no jack."

"And we made it back here only to find it shut down."

Mia nibbled on a thumbnail. Quentin leaned over and tugged on her hand.

"Sorry," she said, looking embarrassed.

"Only trying to help."

"You're saying we're not meant to be here, aren't you, Quentin?"

He drummed harder. "I don't think I'd choose those words, but yeah, it seems that way."

"We should have stayed in Hill Springs."

"Yep, you were right."

Mia smiled, but at least she didn't say I told you so. "Back to Ely's then?"

He nodded.

"What about the truck? We can't exactly keep it."

"Serve those boys right if we did."

"Now, Quentin, that wouldn't be—"

"Right."

"However, they did come along just in the nick of time, so maybe it's meant to be that we use their truck."

Quentin grinned. "That's good enough for me."

"Until we get back to Ely's."

He pointed the truck toward the airport exit, whistling. He'd long ago learned to enjoy life a moment at a time. For now, he wasn't all-the-way dead, and he had Mia beside him. That gave him time. Time to win Mia.

Luke knew who Chelsea Jordan was, of course.

Even if the celebrity hadn't been his friend's great-niece, he would have known of her.

During his brief career in the minor leagues, half his teammates had sported posters of her in their lockers. Betty Grable, move over. Madonna, go home to Michigan. Chelsea, who managed to combine vamp with virgin, ruled their hearts.

Or at least their gonads.

She wasn't his type, though. The girls who giggled in the bleachers and followed the teams never appealed to him. And despite his respect for Ely, he'd never thought of the man's grandniece as any better than a camp follower.

Jenny in her own gentle way had urged him to be less judgmental. Chelsea's childhood movies had all been so sweet, and Jenny, who always found something good in a person, said that it was probably only Hollywood hype that made Chelsea Jordan out to be a world-class slut.

Only Jenny hadn't said slut.

Not his sweet, innocent, wistful Jenny.

Sweet, innocent, wistful—and dead for just over a year.

Dead because Luke hadn't finished his sermon for the next morning and Jenny had volunteered to run into town to collect Timmy from a cousin's birthday party, a duty that should have been Luke's.

Luke turned the circle of his wedding band. The doctor had kept telling him Jenny died instantly when the semi crossed the center line. As if that were a comfort.

With a sigh, he forced his mind to consider the situation Ely had set into motion with his evening visit. Only a friend as true as Ely could have persuaded Luke to act as he'd done. Ely had even sworn on his dead wife's memory that what he was up to was a matter of "life and death." There was no doubting Ely's sincerity and as he was the sanest man Luke knew, he'd done as his friend requested and sent the telegram to Chelsea Jordan. He'd even stood in the pulpit of his church and struggled through the announcement that Ely, absent from town on a brief visit east, had succumbed and now

rested in the heavenly comfort of our Lord and
Christ Jesus.

Luke rubbed his eyes and rose from his office in
the back of the church. Since sending the telegram,
he'd kept a vigil within earshot of his phone. But
now the Colson kid was due for his pool lesson; Luke
would wait no longer for a phone call that obviously
would not come.

He barely suppressed his grimace of disgust. Not
to acknowledge a death in one's family. Not to call,
or wire, or appear. The heartless woman probably
had a private plane at her beck and call. And she
could certainly travel first class, not being bothered
with the inconveniences suffered by most air passengers. If she wanted to pay her respects. If she wanted
to honor Ely.

If.

What had Ely said? If, not when.

Luke rose, stretched his arms over his head and
sighed. He'd missed his morning run and his body
yearned for the release his five-mile course provided.
But Timmy had been crankier than usual, refusing
even to respond to the treat of having Ely staying in
the house with them.

Subscribing to a theory about anniversaries of
emotionally linked events, Luke suspected Timmy
unconsciously associated this month with his
mother's death. Only two weeks had passed since the
anniversary of Jenny's death, and for those entire
two weeks Timmy had been what Luke's own mother described as "quite a pill."

And Luke himself hadn't been much more
cheerful.

A knock sounded at the door and Luke went to
answer it. Perhaps . . .

He opened the door to the Colson kid's bored
face.

No telegram.

Forget it, Miller. The woman was beyond contempt.

"So like I'm here like I'm uh, s'posed to be."

Luke managed a smile of welcome. "Good,
Darren. Go on over to the rec room. I'll be with you
in a second."

Regretting the need for the action, Luke reached
for the phone and punched in the number he'd
looked up earlier.

Hornbsy Smallwood, Esquire, knew wherein his
duty lay.

He had been, after all, a member of the Arkansas
state bar for seven years now, a feat he'd accomplished on his fourth attempt. The first failure his
father had taken in stride, the second had brought on
a bleeding ulcer, and after his third failure, his father
had locked him in an attic room of his Victorian
mansion and sentenced him to life without partying
until such time that he passed the exam.

His father, J. Oscar Smallwood, was at that time a
lawyer of distinction, a man held in respect by not
only those residents of Hill Springs who sought his
services, but a lawyer respected in Little Rock and in
surrounding cities of much larger size and jurispru-
dential prestige.

Hornsby grew up in the shadow of his father.

Wanting his father to admire him, fearing he never
would.

Hornsby did as his father wished, and became, on
his fourth attempt at passing the bar, a man licensed
by the state of Arkansas to practice law.

Sadly, though, even Hornsby could admit he was no lawyer.

As luck would have it, his father passed on soon after, leaving his practice and his considerable estate in the hands of his only son, his dearly beloved wife having died sometime during Hornsby's second attempt at the bar and Hornsby's first divorce.

But, Hornsby reflected, lazing about in his silk robe mid-morning, popping another porn video into his state-of-the-art VCR and preparing to salivate as he watched on his sixty-four-inch projection TV, all that had nothing to do with his duty as a lawyer.

To the one client he had left.

The only client of his father's he hadn't driven off, what with missing all those goddamn ridiculous statute of limitations and with pissing off the clients and the opposing counsel, well, never mind that. Hornsby pressed the Play button of Chelsea Jordan's infamous Italian flick *FellatioNeighborhood* and prepared to enjoy it for the *n*th time.

His robe fell open and he absently stroked his already interested dick.

Who needed a third Mrs. Smallwood, when he had video?

And Chelsea.

Her face swam into focus.

Then those tits.

He panted.

Poised his hand.

Fuck that shit about knowing wherein his duty lay.

Ely Van Ness had two things going for him. One: he was either too stupid or too naive to fire Smallwood. Two: he was related to this cunt who sucked dick on film like she was doing it in real life and maybe, just maybe, if Smallwood hung on to Van

Ness, he'd get to meet the only woman who made him feel like a man.

Not every guy could find this flick. Smallwood had paid a handsome amount of his old man's money for a pirated copy of this Italian masterpiece to add to his collection. Supposedly they'd all been withdrawn—hah, hah, no pun intended—from the market when Chelsea went legit after her return to Hollywood.

He groaned and flicked the Volume Up button with his free hand. Then he applied both hands to his immediate pleasure as a shimmeringly naked Chelsea lowered herself from a trapeze bar, head down, deepthroating the engorged actor who was probably too stupid and ungrateful to recognize the gift he'd been given.

Gift.

The very word caused Smallwood's equipment to stop in mid-motion.

Goddammit.

Ely Van Ness had screwed with his will and all of Smallwood's careful attentions had been blown to hell in a handbasket.

Oh, Hornsby was too crafty to skirt too close to the line of undue influence, but the old geezer's prior will had certainly left to Smallwood a considerable sum. Plus the fees he'd take in as executor of a $10 million estate.

He pumped. He stared at the screen and willed himself to think only of the smut-assed blonde with a mouthful of meat.

Willed his mind not to dwell on what the cunt's great-uncle had done only a few days ago.

Shafted him.

Royally.

Except the old guy was in such good health, all it would take would be an unselfish visit from Hornsby Smallwood, legal advice for free, and the old man would see the error of his ways. Not quite sure this new will would hold up in court, you see, he'd say. Explain that he'd done some research (research—egads, what was that? First year law school drudgery??) and discovered the types of conditions Van Ness had set forth wouldn't stand in court, and that would mean his fortune would pass intestate. Wouldn't want that, now would he? Intestate had always been synonymous in Smallwood's mind with impotent.

Ah, the life surged back in his body, the blood rose in his dick.

He pumped again. Anything but impotent. Testate testes. He laughed.

He responded.

The cunt on the screen had turned, offering to his view the incredible virgin peach of her ass.

His pulse raced.

His hand surged.

The phone rang.

Goddammit motherfucking phone!!!!

He cussed Alexander Graham Bell. He cussed the operator. He swore at the film maker who at that moment decided Chelsea should turn, face the camera, make a great OOOH of her perfect lips (the ones on her face that still shone from her honeyed attack on the actor's dick), and skip toward a field of daisies.

Ah, erotic film making lifted to a whole new state.

Offer it and yank it away? Oh, yeah, it only made him want her more.

The phone shrilled again.

Smallwood freed one hand and grabbed at the phone that sat beside him.

"Whaddya want?"

"Luke Miller here. Sorry if I'm disturbing you."

"Oh, Reverend. No, no, not at all. Just, uh, getting ready to visit my maiden aunt." Fuck! He grabbed for the remote, but instead of finding the Volume Down button, he hit the Up.

"Wanna fuck me? You'll have to catch me." Chelsea's voice rang out.

Hornsby slapped at the remote.

"If this is a bad time, I can call back."

"No, no, not at all." Smallwood batted the quisling of a remote control and finally found the mute button. The romp on-screen continued, with Chelsea leading her pursuing man . . . er, now in the plural, through a field of daisies. Her boobs danced above the swaying grasses and every so often he caught a glimpse of dark hair between her thighs. "Always have time for a man of the cloth." He closed his eyes and concentrated on the telephone. He'd rewind when the goody-two-shoes hung up.

"Good a time as any," Smallwood rattled on. He didn't give a flying fuck about religion, but he did know Ely attended Miller's church. He also knew, courtesy of Van Ness's blabbermouth accountant, just how much money the old guy lavished on the Hill Springs Community Church. He'd paid for the recreation center, he'd sprung for team uniforms and supplies, for both guys' and girls' softball, and the blunt he dropped in the plate every Sunday wasn't to be sneezed at.

"Just thinking about you and all the good folks

over at your church, as it was." Smallwood prided himself on his small talk. His father might have been a man of few words, but Smallwood had never found himself at a loss for cocktail chatter. He'd perfected it at the frat house in Tuscaloosa.

"Is that so?"

Smallwood normally would have bristled at the tone of Miller's voice. Skeptical, to say the least. The punk had been nothing better than a ball player during high school. Two years behind Smallwood, if he remembered correctly. Of course, Smallwood had run in a different crowd. A superior crowd, with his family being so much better off and all. Who could countenance a preacher's kid putting on the airs Luke Miller did? Acting like he was so goddamn special after playing for that Birmingham stringer team for all of a year. Acting like he was the equal of a Smallwood, for God's sake.

Nah, never had there been love lost between a Smallwood and a Miller.

But who the fuck cared? All he wanted to do was get rid of the pesky phone call and get on with Chelsea.

Get it on with Chelsea.

He gripped the receiver. "Something on your mind, Reverend? Everything going fine on your side of town?"

A long silence followed.

Just when Smallwood would have broken in with another quip, Miller said, "You mean you haven't heard?"

"Heard what? About who?"

Across town, Luke grimaced at the receiver. Whom, he corrected silently, thinking that gaffe was the least of Smallwood's sins. But right at that moment, Ely ranked higher on his blacklist than the sleazy lawyer.

He let Smallwood wait for the news while he railed in his mind at his friend. *Dammit, Ely. How could you put me in this position? You'd better be damn sure whatever you have up your sleeve is a matter of life and death, because you've got me swearing and you know what the hell that does to my conscience.*

Luke cleared his throat. He needed to get on with the lie he had promised to tell. Go ahead, lie to the lawyer. Tell him Ely is dead. The Colson kid was waiting for his pool lesson. At least he appeared to be redeemable. He showed when he was due, grumbled only slightly, and played the game with a fair hand. He seemed to have seen the foolhardiness of breaking and entering.

Tell this scum lawyer Ely is dead and tell him what he's supposed to do about it.

"What is it I haven't heard?"

"That Ely Van Ness is dead."

A groan. A gagging noise. A gasp.

"I'm so sorry, to tell you like this over the phone." Luke dug his fingers into the receiver and thought of Ely, only that morning, cooking buckwheat pancakes for Timmy and coaxing a laugh out of him. "He died in Connecticut, over the weekend. At least he was with his family."

"Holy shit."

"Again, I am really sorry—"

"Of all the fucked timing."

"I'm sure you are as distressed as the rest of his friends."

"Distressed? What kind of a pansy-assed word is that? I'm fucked! *Fucked, do you hear!* Do you know what that senile old goat did only a few days ago? He came in here and made out the most motherfucking ass-backward will I have ever seen in all my years of practice as a lawyer."

Luke held back a groan. Perhaps Ely was going over the edge. Had Luke missed all the signs? Had he failed to help his friend? His parishioner?

"Motherfucker wanted to die."

"Well, he may have had a premonition of his death. I say that only because he left me a letter asking me to contact you to handle something for him in the event of his death."

"Handle something?" More sputters flew over the phone. "I should think so. I'm the goddamn executor of his will. In charge of his estate. All $10 million of it!"

"You're his lawyer. I'm sure you're right about all of that. All I know"— Luke rubbed his temples and found the place in Ely's instructions that pertained to Smallwood— "is I'm supposed to read this note to you."

"Hurry up and read it, then."

The man had never had any manners. Luke had never understood Ely's decision to retain Smallwood just because his father had been Ely's attorney for years and years. The elder Smallwood—now he'd been a real man. A good lawyer. A pillar of Hill Springs. With a sigh, Luke realized the irony implicit in his comparison. Did people say that about him and his father?

In a clipped voice, he read: "I want you to ask Hornsby Smallwood to fly to California (with expenses to be charged to my estate, naturally) and inform Miss Chelsea Jordan in person that unless she returns with him to Hill Springs within twenty-four hours the will cannot be read. Her inaction will result in $10 million dollars falling into undesirable hands. If Smallwood accomplishes this task, he is to be paid the fee of ten thousand dollars. If he fails, he is no longer executor of my will."

Luke expected more gagging noises as soon as he finished that last line. Smallwood, however, sounded pleased.

"Oh, is that all I have to do? For ten grand?" He laughed, a sound that turned Luke's stomach.

The man defined arrogance. "Do you know who Chelsea Jordan is?"

Smallwood laughed, a sound that oozed over the line and contaminated Luke's ear. "Do I know who she is? Hah. What man doesn't know that tw—"

"And you think it will be a simple matter to convince Miss Jordan to leave California?"

"No sweat. I'll simply inform her, as her great-uncle's attorney, of the issues involved, and impress on her all that is at stake. Her only concern will be what to wear."

"Oh, is that so?"

"What's the matter, Miller? Van Ness leave you a letter asking you to help and you already failed to charm her?" He snorted. "Talk about apples and oranges. You wouldn't know what to do with Chelsea Jordan if she were spread-eagle in the—"

"I've read you the note."

"What's the matter, Reverend, can't take a joke? Too righteous to haul ass over here and take a swing at me?"

Luke loosened his grip on the phone. Letting Smallwood get his goat accomplished nothing. He'd done what he'd promised Ely. "I really don't think, in the light of Ely's, er, death, any of these differences matter."

"Of course, of course." Smallwood toned his voice down. "Poor old man."

"She lives in Bel Air." Luke read the street address Ely had provided. "I get the impression he wants this done right away."

"And done properly." Smallwood chuckled. "I'm the man for this job."

Somehow Luke doubted that. He also didn't trust Smallwood as far as he could throw him. "Remember something, Smallwood. Remember Ely is my friend and I'll be watching out for his interests."

"Don't you mean *was* your friend?"

"I can't think of him as dead." No wonder there.

"Well, once you're dead you're gone. But what the hell, there's a lot of living to be done for those of us lucky to still be around. If you want me, Miller, I'll be at the Beverly Hills Hotel."

Click.

Down went the phone. Luke imagined Smallwood dancing around his dead daddy's house, making plans to spend ten thousand dollars Luke would be willing to bet he'd never see.

But Smallwood wasn't dancing.

He was kicking himself.

Hard.

"You stupid fucking idiot!"

He beat at his chest. No one else in the world knew what was in that new will. The witnesses knew only that Ely had written a will. They hadn't read it, only attested to the signature. If not for his own tongue, he'd be home free. He could have produced a copy of the prior will and destroyed the new one and who the hell would have known the difference? But he had to go and scream to a preacher—a golden-boy preacher everyone in town would believe—that Ely had changed his will only days ago.

His daddy had been right.

A one-hundred-percent fuckup. That's what he was.

He faced the mirror over his wet bar.

Didn't like what he saw. Not at all.

Bleary-eyed motherfucking idiot.

He raised his fist and smashed the glass.

8

Mia had almost decided to stop worrying over their predicament when their stolen truck coughed and sputtered, then like a crew member on a union-decreed break, refused to budge. Dead in the road.

She laughed. Quentin swore.

At least it died on the crest of a rise, so they were able to push the pickup to the side of the road.

"This is the longest night of my life," Quentin said, lifting the hood of the truck. "But dammit, I've never met an engine I couldn't fix."

Searching the truck for a flashlight, Mia held her tongue at Quentin's comment. She thought of reminding him of their abandoned rental car, but there didn't seem to be any point. Perhaps if he'd had tools he could have repaired it.

So she quietly and dutifully held the flashlight the good old boys conveniently carried while Quentin explored under the hood with an air of purpose that quickly degenerated to frustration. But no matter how hard he cursed the worthless piece of Detroit junk, the engine refused to turn over.

Ever the realist, Mia handed the torch to Quentin

and set about preparing a bed for them by moonlight. Fields covered with hay surrounded the road on both sides. A sheltering tree, branches spread wide, offered a canopy for the beach towels she rummaged from the truck. She couldn't imagine where the former occupants of the truck went to the beach, but thanked them for lugging around the towels. Those two were probably still sleeping it off beside the stranded rental car.

To her surprise, she actually found herself humming happily as she gathered dried grasses and leaves and fashioned them into a semblance of a bed. City girl always, her camping experiences were limited to roughing it on location on Quentin's early films.

By the time Quentin kicked the fender for the last time, Mia had a cozy nest prepared for them, topped off with the beach towels.

"So where do I sleep?" Quentin asked, tossing the flashlight into the truck and smothering a yawn.

She pointed to the nest.

"And you?" She thought Quentin's stare more intense than usual. She pointed again. "Here."

"You want us to sleep together?"

She glared at him, wanting to tell him yes, you fool, in every sense of the word. But he looked so incredulous, as if she carried the bubonic plague or had never had her teeth straightened.

"Of course I don't *want* to." She delivered her response full scorn ahead. "But the seats in the truck don't recline, the back of that truck is full of junk, and the truth of the matter is sometimes you just have to rough it." There, that should show him. He didn't have to act so disgusted over lying down next to her. "We'll keep our clothes on," she added.

"I should think so," Quentin said.

She blushed, realizing she'd blurted her last words aloud.

"Well, whatever. I'm bushed." Quentin dropped to the towels and patted the spare inches beside him. "Come to bed, Mia, my love. We've got a lot of walking to do in the morning."

Mia, my love. How wonderful those words sounded. Even though he didn't mean them, she hugged the effect of them to her heart as she lowered her body cautiously to the ground.

"I don't bite, you know," Quentin said from behind the bill of his Yankees cap that he'd propped over his forehead.

"I'm far more concerned with snoring than biting."

He laughed. "Have no fear. I never snore."

"Thank God for small favors." As soon as Mia uttered those words, she reminded herself she had a lot more than small favors to be thankful for. Like for being alive, or whatever state they were experiencing. Like getting a second chance at life. Not to mention the secret pleasure of lying next to Quentin.

But as she lay back on the pallet, she decided she could scratch that last item from her bedtime prayers. Forget pleasure.

More like torture.

Quentin lay back with his arms raised over his head, his head pillowed in his hands, his cap and glasses abandoned. His T-shirt had drifted free from the band of his jogging sweats. When she peeked, she saw curly hairs on a hard stomach that looked like an advertisement for Body By Jake.

He gazed at the night sky, an unusually calm and quiet look on his face. How she longed for the right to touch him, to explore the thick brows over eyes dark and always inquisitive. She wanted to trace a line from jaw to chin to chest, rest her hand over his heart, then slip lower, following the trail of that curly hair to—

"Look at those stars," he whispered.

Mia tore her thoughts from the only star in her firmament and looked heavenward.

"The stars never look like this in the city," he said.

Even through the covering of the tree, she could see the winking stars lighting the dark blue sky like bulbs on a Christmas tree. "They are beautiful. Growing up in L.A., I never saw things like this."

"We forget. We get all wrapped up in the artificial stars and we look down rather than up."

Mia looked at Quentin in surprise. "Being out here is turning you into a philosopher."

"Perhaps it is." A shadow passed over his face. "Mia, we don't even know where we are, whether we're alive or dead or both having the same crazy-assed dream."

"Now that's impossible. How could we both be having the same dream?"

"Please, Mia, not tonight." He smiled and touched a finger to the tip of her nose.

She heard his plea not to be practical. Not tonight, in their magical bed under the stars. She snuggled into their bed of nature, and whispered, "Okay."

They lay there in companionable silence.

Mia turned on her side, clearing another few inches between their bodies. Even though the evening had cooled, she needed no covering. Heated by Quentin's nearness, her blood danced in her veins, causing incredible sensations low in her pelvis. She knew that anatomical term wasn't accurate, but it was as close as she could get to describing to herself what her body couldn't deny. She wanted this man.

This man whom she had loved since the beginning of time. This time, or real time.

She stole another glance at his face and caught him staring at her. She colored, positive he could read her mind. But no, to the part of her that wanted him, Quentin had always been oblivious. Softly, she asked, "If this experience is a dream, how do you want it to end?"

Quentin lowered his arms and stared at the stars that shone with such amazing clarity, echoing a clarity he now felt in his heart. He turned on his side facing the woman he knew he wanted, absorbing her beauty, her nearness.

How did he want this dream to end? He smiled in a way that he knew lifted the corner of his lips in a sexy come-on quirk. It was a smile guaranteed to drive a woman crazy wanting to please him, make her whisper, what are you thinking?

Mia said nothing.

He clenched his teeth in frustration and tried the smile again.

"Don't you know how you want it to end?" she repeated.

Quentin considered coming right out with the truth, his dawning realization that Mia was the only woman for him. But he'd only scare her off. He had to show her he was worthy of her, that he wasn't the feckless playboy she thought him to be. "Happily?" he asked, angling for safety in his response.

"For a world-famous director, that's a very unimaginative answer."

"So replace me." He groaned as he remembered

that's exactly what Salvatino More had done to him. "Hire what's-his-name like Sal did."

"I can't replace you."

"No?" That sounded hopeful. He gazed into her dark eyes that glimmered in the starlight. The shifting shadows from the slight breeze that ruffled the branches above them cast her face alternately in dark and light. Her breasts rose and fell as she breathed and he wanted to pillow his face between them. No, face it, Quentin, that wasn't what he wanted to do with those breasts. He pictured her wriggling beneath him as he sucked first one nipple until she screamed, raising her to heights of passion with his kiss. A kiss that would be only the beginning.

"I can't replace you because you and I are the only two people on heaven or earth in this predicament," Mia said.

"Oh." Even those damping words didn't lessen his incredible hard-on. He crossed his top leg farther over the bottom, hiding his groin. Damn, but he'd never get any sleep.

"Which, if you think about it," Mia said in a small voice, "is pretty scary."

"Why is that?" He tried to summon to mind the animation device he'd been tinkering with before their accident. All that appeared was the image of Mia panting and begging him to suck her other nipple, and of him lowering his tongue, and slipping his hand between her hot thighs.

"Aren't you scared, Quentin?"

"Scared?" Yeah, that he'd come just fantasizing over her. But far more important and far more frightening, he was scared he'd lose her before he could even win her.

"You know, about whether we're dead?" Her brow puckered and Quentin reached out to smooth it.

He didn't want to face that question. He didn't want her worrying over it either, frightening herself. But he knew her so well, the despair in her question came through loud and clear.

Hoping the darkness hid his erection, he shifted onto his back and reached out with a gentle arm to shelter Mia against his chest. "Mia, I don't have any answers, but for what it's worth, I'm here with you. And if it helps, I'll always be your friend." He wished he'd said more than friend. But he held back on the other offers he'd like to make.

Mia had always been there for him, had stood shoulder to shoulder with him for the years before he hit the big time in Hollywood. The least he could do at this moment was forget his needs and offer her comfort.

She lay her head on the curve of his shoulder, somewhat stiffly, he thought, but at least she turned to him for reassurance. With her religious background, she couldn't help but be beset with all sorts of nightmarish scenarios Quentin the lifelong agnostic couldn't conjure.

He had only two nightmare scenarios: Mia would remain only his friend, only his producer, and never his love.

The second, of course, was that Russell Cruller would ruin *DinoDaddy*.

But at this moment in time, he'd sacrifice even *DinoDaddy* if Mia came to love him.

He smoothed the top of her hair. "Go to sleep, Mia, my friend."

* * *

Not another interruption!

Chelsea scowled at the door of her location trailer and snapped, "Whatever it is had better be important!"

The knocking stopped.

That meant whoever it was didn't belong or had enough sense to go away and come again another day.

Not, thankfully, that there'd be another day on this miserable location. One last scene left to do, for Chelsea anyway, and then she'd be off tomorrow for a well-deserved vacation. She'd told no one her plans, especially not Fran, who thought she was going to Ely's funeral. Since she had decided she didn't have the right to kill herself, she had opted for a recuperative two weeks at an exclusive and secluded Virginia bed and breakfast where she could contemplate her pitiful existence.

Satisfied the intruder had disappeared, Chelsea lay back on her chaise, picking up where she'd left off in the medieval romance. Alexandrena was about to achieve what existed only between the covers of a book—undying, committed, virtuous love. With a very sexy guy who looked nothing like the long-haired pretty boy on the cover.

The book she was reading could be made into a movie she'd enjoy doing. No matter what obstacles came her way, the heroine pluckily and cleverly outwitted and overcame them. Plus she found a guy who loved her for her true self, despite her image as a trouble-making vixen.

Chelsea sighed and turned the page. If only—

Rap-a-rap-rap.

"What the hell do you want?" she screamed.

Through the door, a voice as oily as the streets in

the once-a-winter rain, said, "Miss Jordan, Security here. Sorry to disturb you, but we need to speak with you. Only for a moment. The briefest of moments."

"Then come in!" Stuffing the book under a cushion, she snagged a *Variety* from the coffee table. Not that she was ashamed of reading romances. But when her own life was supposed to be the stuff from whence legends are made, well, she couldn't afford to get caught fantasizing by some schmuck who might sell the story to the tabloids.

"Sergeant Jones, ma'am," said the security officer, tipping his hat and flicking a greedy eye around her trailer.

His name was one of millions to hit her ears since she could toddle, for Chrissake. Lifting her brows, she tapped a cherry red nail against the slick paper of the trade rag.

"Not that I would have bothered you, you understand, knowing your desire for privacy"— at that he finished his survey of the trailer and turned his eyes on her —"no, I would have sent the man packing, for all he claims to be a lawyer. But Ms. Rosen insisted I check with you."

"Oh she did?" Fran had been getting far too bossy. Acting like a parent, the last thing Chelsea needed in her life. "Whoever it is, throw him out." She snapped the *Variety*.

"But Ms. Rosen said—"

She leveled her gaze at him. "If you are not out of my trailer before I finish this sentence, I'll have you—"

He backed out, lips flapping words she didn't bother to acknowledge.

"—fired!" She threw the *Variety* at the door, then retrieved her book from under the cushions.

But the magical spell had been broken.

With a sigh, she rose from the couch and paced the floor, thinking the words "Five minutes, Miss Jordan" couldn't come soon enough. She wanted this travesty of a movie behind her, once and for all.

The scene required her to ask an alien for help when her costume caught on a rock and started to rip apart.

Why the moron director had left this scene for last she couldn't fathom. Of course movies weren't shot from beginning to end, but leaving till last the scene where she met the alien who fell in love with her, which influenced his actions for the rest of the film, made no sense at all to her.

But plainly Russell Cruller hadn't the talent to direct a real movie, a story with heart. She'd vowed early on to never, ever make another picture with that man behind the camera. She could scarcely credit the rumor that as soon as they wrapped, he was taking over the interrupted production of *Dino-Daddy*. If Quentin Grandy ever came out of his coma, he'd kill Russell Cruller.

From the beginning Cruller had leered, set up her scenes so that she wore less and less. And in this last scene, she'd be surprised if he didn't have the damn rock stripping her naked before it was all over.

She shuddered and glanced at what passed as a costume. Shimmery breastplate cut to her belly button, wisp of a skirt covering only a silver thong slicing her ass. If Fran Rosen was so worried about her image off-camera, why did she keep putting her in these sex and shoot-em-up flicks?

She could be a virgin off camera and no one who saw any of her movies would ever invite *her* to Sunday School. Or *oneg shabbat*.

The door opened, no knock.

Chelsea groaned.

"No need to be rude to Sergeant Jones, you know," Fran said, stepping in and shutting the door behind her.

A gust of the ever-present wind slipped in with her, and Chelsea comforted herself with the reminder that after today she'd be free.

Free.

What a delicious word. Perhaps she'd never return. She'd settle in some town far from Hollywood and all its madness. She'd shave her head and forgo designer dresses and sacrifice her daily massage.

The only people who would miss her would be the ones who lived to exploit her.

"You're not feeling well today, are you?" Fran settled on the sofa. "Say the word and we'll halt production."

"No!"

"All right, all right." She made one of her smacky noises that drove Chelsea crazy. "As soon as you finish this last scene, I want you to meet someone."

"Forget it."

"Don't you even want to ask who it is?"

Chelsea made a face and yanked at the breastplate that pinched into her ribs. "Why should I? You're going to tell me anyway."

Fran smiled. "That's true. Well, this story does sound a trifle odd, but there's a man here who says he's a lawyer from Arkansas."

Arkansas. Great-uncle Ely. Chelsea kept her face perfectly expressionless, defying Fran to make her show she cared. "So?"

"It seems he is your late great-uncle's lawyer."

"Don't you mean *was* his lawyer? He's dead, you

know." She delivered the statement with all the apathy of a sixties' Haight-Ashbury inhabitant.

Fran frowned.

"That will wrinkle your face prematurely."

"And so will your acid tongue." Fran chuckled. "Anyway, he says he has instructions to speak with you."

Chelsea whirled around from where she stood near the door. "How long have you been in this godforsaken business? Of course he's going to say something like that. What a crock!"

"You know, Chelsea, exactly how long I've been running interference for you. And this business is only godforsaken if you insist on living that way." Fran touched the miniature silver mezuzah she wore on a chain around her neck. "I don't just sit around looking pretty. I've checked this man out with the Arkansas state bar and the Hill Springs police. He's exactly who he says he is."

"So what does he want?"

"To deliver a message to you."

She manufactured a yawn. "Well, I guess that wouldn't hurt."

Knock-knock. Chelsea's instant frown vanished as her call sounded. "Five minutes, Miss Jordan!"

"Have him wait in Security. I'll speak with him after we wrap."

"He'll be on the set. Given that he is your relative's lawyer, I saw no harm in letting him watch a little Hollywood up-close."

"You did what?" Chelsea picked up the first thing she saw, a jar of face powder, and flung it across the room. "The indignities I have to endure! You know I don't want some potbellied country lawyer gawking at me. This scene is bad enough with only professionals on the set." She felt bad for covering Fran in a cloud of beige powder, but she refused to apologize. "You're fired!"

Fran brushed her arms and legs and rose from the couch.

"Keep this up, Chelsea, and I just may quit." Then she stalked from the trailer, her head held high.

"Witch," Chelsea muttered, then sneezed as some of the dust blew across the room. "I'll show you and this geek lawyer a thing or two."

She knew exactly how to do it, too. Fran could issue press releases to control the damage until she turned blue in the face, but when Chelsea finished with the country bumpkin, he'd go back home to Arkansas and tell everyone who'd listen just what a slut Chelsea Jordan was.

9 ~

Hornsby Smallwood wore Brooks Brothers suits and Ralph Lauren ties. He drove a Mercedes, one of the few in Hill Springs, the other three belonging to the CEO of All Right Foods, the company that owned the town.

He vacationed twice a year, dividing his time between Cancun and the Bahamas. On his first honeymoon, he and the airhead he'd been shackled to spent five days in Paris.

No, Hornsby Smallwood didn't consider himself the product of small-town barbarism.

But he'd never been to Hollywood.

Never before bluffed his way onto a movie location.

Never, despite his wildest fantasies, ever imagined he'd be standing face to face with Chelsea Jordan.

The goddess of his favorite porn flick waved a tiny hand in his direction and smiled in such a way that Hornsby suspected all she wanted to do was take him back to her trailer and fuck him.

He gulped. Trying for casual, he waved a hand.

She said something to Ms. Rosen, the woman who'd cleared him through security, and walked straight toward him.

Her breasts didn't look as large as he thought they would. Even in the scant costume she wore, they looked less full than the images he panted over on his big screen.

Despite that disappointment, he had to admit to being impressed. Tiny waist, rounded hips that swiveled with every step, legs that didn't stop.

He managed to keep from licking his lips. People milling about eyed him with looks he didn't appreciate. Probably wondering who the hell he was. He swaggered and threw a smile at Chelsea as she stepped up to him.

"So you wanted to see me?" she said, a pout on her lips and sex gleaming in her eyes.

"Right. That's right." His dick strained at his zipper like a randy dog smelling a pack of bitches.

"And I suppose you like what you see."

"Absolutely."

A slightest hint of displeasure flitted across her perfect face. "Well, then, big boy, you help me out and I'll listen to your message."

"Help you?" What could she want from him? Then he smirked. Oh, Hornsby, you haven't lost your sex appeal.

She pouted and scratched a pointed fingernail across his chest. "I'm having just a little bitty bit of trouble getting into this scene and I thought you might like to help me get in the mood."

"Smallwood's your man. Just tell me what you need." For dramatic effect, he added a wink.

Moving so quickly she caught him off-guard, she

ground her body against his, catching his cock standing at the ready.

"Ooh," she breathed, "you are just the one to help me."

"Just what do you think you're doing?" Ms. Rosen barked.

Smallwood would have jumped back from Chelsea but she had one hand wrapped around his balls.

"Getting in the mood for this scene."

"I'm not sure Mr. Smallwood is the best person to use for this."

"No?" Chelsea wrapped her other hand around his erection. "I think he's happy to help."

"Let him go."

She tugged again.

"Into pain, big guy?" she whispered.

As a matter of fact he was but it didn't really seem the time and place to discuss his preferences for big-breasted women who wielded whips.

"Poor baby," she cooed without waiting for an answer. "Why don't we stroll over to that rock and get you comfortable?" Scrunched against him, Chelsea half-tugged, half-dragged him through the people standing about.

He thought he caught a flash of a camera and in a corresponding flash of vanity wondered if he'd make the tabloids. Hornsby Smallwood, Hollywood lover.

Emboldened by the image, he drew an arm around Chelsea's shoulder and pinched her breast.

She giggled and he repeated his action.

"So what's this scene about?" Hey, what could there be to this acting stuff? Maybe he'd give up law and move west.

Chelsea sat cross-legged atop a large boulder and

patted the spot beside her. His eyes popped as he saw she wore nothing under the brief skirt.

"Sit real close and I'll tell you."

He settled facing her and she waved down at the crew. "Give me five minutes then get ready to roll."

A man in a Panama hat standing next to Ms. Rosen shook his head and called up, "I'm the director here, and I'll thank you to remember that."

Chelsea stuck her tongue out at the guy. To Smallwood she said, "Russell Cruller couldn't direct his way out of a paper bag. Now, what I want you to do—" She beckoned him closer, a naughty look dancing on her face, and whispered in his ear.

"What?" He almost yelled as he processed her words. "Up here? With all those people watching?"

She pouted. "Chelsea wants you," she said.

Hell, he wanted her, too, but foreplay in front of a crowd wasn't his game.

"If you do it," she said, "I'll do whatever it is you want me to do. Whatever it is you came here to ask me, I'll tell you."

His fingers itched to touch her. Damn, she'd probably drip on him before he even got inside. Still, that really wasn't his style. He'd far prefer the quiet of her trailer and her on her knees, taking care of him. Now that was Smallwood's idea of the perfect moment.

"You want me, don't you," she whispered, then before he could answer, she drew his face to hers and sucked his tongue halfway down her throat.

When he came up for air, he gasped, "Yes, I want you, you cunt."

She laughed, a gurgle deep in her throat, exactly where he wanted to be.

As quickly as she'd pounced to kiss him, she

scooted away, turned her back to him, and spread her legs wide. He licked his lips, wondering if she seriously expected him to do as she had asked.

She let her head fall back and her hair tossed wildly about her head as the wind danced around her. She looked, Hornsby thought, as if she were being screwed at that very moment.

How did she do that?

He hadn't even touched her yet.

From behind those sultry lips, she said, "Get off the rock."

"What?"

She lifted one finger and pointed, not even bothering to look at him.

Then he understood. He'd played his role. He'd helped her get into the mood she wanted. The cunt hadn't meant a word she said, probably would have slapped him if he'd touched her twat. Backing away slowly, humiliated beyond belief, he slipped from the rock and into the sidelines.

"Action," called the director, who wore a huge smirk on his pansy-assed face.

Smallwood wanted to sink through the earth. He felt like a discarded plaything. Of course he dismissed entirely that she'd asked him for help in getting into the scene. He'd taken that as any guy would have, as a come-on line.

He smarted. He burned. His dick throbbed.

A bronzed and muscled actor dropped onto the rock where Chelsea thrashed about. The man leaned over her and with one brutal slash, ripped the breastplate from the top of her costume. Her breasts heaving, Chelsea stared up at him, her mouth a perfect oval of fear.

And titillation, too.

Smallwood stared in spite of his humiliation. If he were home alone, viewing this movie, he knew which role he'd play. He'd stand above her on the rock, wielding his weapon, until she satisfied him.

"Cut," called a voice and Smallwood jerked back to his surroundings.

Thank God, they were done. He'd deliver his message and be gone. He refused to let this woman use him in front of these people again. When a woman wanted Smallwood, she got him only on his terms.

Chelsea strolled off the rock and back to her trailer. Smallwood started to follow her, but Ms. Rosen materialized and caught him.

"She's changing costumes for the next camera set up. You may speak with her when she's done for the day, not before."

So they weren't finished. Embarrassed again by his display of ignorance, Smallwood nodded, mumbled, "Of course," and suffered through another three hours of endless retakes.

Suffered in more ways than one. Each time the bronzed actor stood over her, he pictured himself taking Chelsea Jordan. By the time the crew wrapped, he was quite worn out. If he didn't get back to his hotel room and relieve his pent-up sexual tension he feared permanent damage.

Chelsea climbed down from the boulder for the last time to the polite applause of the crowd. She flicked a hand, the princess dismissing her subjects, and flounced off to her trailer.

Smallwood scowled. Even if she came panting after him on her knees, she'd go begging. Hornsby Smallwood alone knew the contents of that will awaiting them in Arkansas. By humiliating him,

Chelsea Jordan stood to lose a lot more than the best sex she'd ever had.

Ms. Rosen interrupted his thoughts with a tap on the shoulder.

"You may speak with Ms. Jordan now."

"Thank you," he said in his most dignified voice and walked with her toward a row of trailers.

"You musn't take anything she does personally, you know," said the woman.

"Is that so?" He knew he blushed.

The wiry woman nodded and gave him a sad-faced smile. "She's a bit of a spoiled child."

"A child who is almost thirty should learn to respect her elders."

"My, my, Mr. Smallwood. Take that tone with Chelsea and the last place she'll go is Arkansas."

"Thank you, but I know how to handle clients."

She lifted her brows and paused in front of the largest trailer. After knocking once, she opened the door and stepped in, motioning him to follow.

When he saw her standing there swathed in a robe that could only be called translucent he forgot all about his intention to spurn her. With a swagger in his step and a gleam in his eye, he stepped into the trailer and advanced on her. "Shall we talk over dinner?" he said in his most suave voice.

"Do I look like I'm dressed for dinner?"

He chuckled and nodded, hating himself for swooning over her, but quite overcome with lust. He could just make out that her pubes were trimmed but not completely shaven, exactly like in *FellatioNeighborhood*. "I'll bring the meat," he said with a suggestive lift of his brows.

"Oh my God. Fran, get this creep out of here."

Ms. Rosen darted between them, thick terry robe

in hand. "Try to remember not everyone walks around half-naked and maybe you wouldn't attract such talk if you adhered to that idea," she said, drawing Chelsea's arms through the sleeves and tying the robe.

Chelsea sat down in front of her dressing table, a petulant look on her face. "So what does he want?"

Smallwood had never, ever in his life been knocked down twice by the same woman, and certainly not two times in one afternoon. His cheeks flaming, his blood pressure threatening to blow his carotid, he said, "I have a message from your great-uncle Ely Van Ness." To himself, he said, "Be cool, this is a ten-thousand-dollar mission for you."

"So?" said Miss Prick Tease with a twirl of her brush.

"You are requested to attend the reading of his will tomorrow at noon."

"No can do." She dropped the hairbrush and began dabbing cold cream on her face.

"Do you have some prior engagement that interferes?"

She slapped the lid onto the table. "That's none of your business, Mr. Country Casanova."

Oooh. Smallwood narrowed his eyes and fixated on the ten grand in cash. "Your great-uncle was quite fond of you and instructed me, decisively, that his will may only be read in your presence."

"So read it now." She faced him, glop masking her face.

She really wasn't going to like this part. Smallwood took a quick breath and said, "The will may only be read in my office in Hill Springs."

"Arkansas!"

He nodded, pleased; triumphant actually. She

didn't need to speak the name of his home state as if it were some strain of the Ebola virus.

She wiped the cream from her face and despite his anger he watched in amazement as her perfect nose and high cheekbones reappeared. Her lips shone rosy and plump.

His dick, unable to process the message that he considered this bitch beneath contempt, continued to throb.

Only the thought of his refuge at the Beverly Hills Hotel and the two telephone calls he couldn't wait to make kept him in check.

Swabbing on moisturizer, she turned to Ms. Rosen and said, "Get rid of him."

"No can do," she mimicked.

Smallwood choked back a laugh.

Chelsea tossed her brush across the room.

Fran leaned forward and spoke very slowly. "We'll take the MegaFilms jet first thing in the morning, stop in Arkansas, and then you can continue on to your vacation. I'll fly back domestic."

"Oh what a sacrifice. Besides, why are you going?"

"Because I don't trust you not to don a parachute and exit some place over Santa Fe."

"Well, that's about the last civilized place between here and the East Coast."

Smallwood cleared his throat. "Then it's settled."

"Yes," Ms. Rosen said.

"No," Chelsea said.

"It's the least you can do for your relative. You skipped the funeral, after all."

Chelsea's face clouded over. She dropped her head into her hands and when after a long moment she moved her hands, her face looked older. In that briefest passage of time, she had aged.

And with that change, Smallwood knew the matter was settled. The bitch at least had a concept of conscience.

But not much sense of social grace. Without another word, she rose, walked toward the back room of the trailer and slammed the door behind her.

As he promised, Quentin did not snore. Mia, whose father snored so loudly her mother wore a Walkman to bed, was impressed.

Not that it made much difference to that night's rest. She shifted on the bed of leaves, scooting away from Quentin each time he changed position. Soon he had most of the bed and she lay on her side on the very edge.

Not that she didn't want to be close to him. But when his hand flopped over against her rib cage her heart raced and she longed to take his hand and press it to her breast. So she lay awake watching his face, admiring the way the play of shadow and light would highlight first one feature, then another.

She finally decided his eyes, even closed in sleep, were her favorite feature. Craggy brows with thick hairs framed his deep-set eyes. Lashes thick and long lined his shuttered lids. Once she felt brave enough to reach over and touch them and trace a finger oh-so-lightly over his brows.

When Quentin was awake, those same eyes flashed with light and humor. They were dark brown and shone like her grandmother's prized and polished mahogany highboy. His energy flowed through and lit his face from the eyes outward.

Her gaze fixated on those closed eyes must have

served to hypnotize her into sleep, because the next thing Mia knew the stars and moon had been replaced by a silvery gray dawn.

Her head lay pillowed on Quentin's chest, her upper body rested in the curve of one of his arms. Quickly, before he woke up, she slipped out of his embrace. He'd objected so strenuously to sharing the small nest she didn't want to be embarrassed by him waking to think she'd come on to him during the night.

"Hey, what are you doing?" Quentin's voice didn't sound like him; it came out croaky.

"It's time to get up," Mia said and rose to her knees, brushing her dress and shaking off her long cardigan which she'd used to cover herself.

"Can't be." Quentin groped around on the ground till his hand reached his Yankees cap. He propped it over his face.

"It's morning, it's time to get moving." Mia stood and stretched.

Quentin slid a hand around her ankle and tugged. "Come back to bed."

This, from the man who hadn't wanted to sleep next to her? "Why?" She didn't move. Her ankle tingled where his fingers made contact.

"I like to wake up slowly. Ease into the day."

"Oh, you're one of those, aren't you? I wondered why our calls were always so much later than other crews." Mia looked at him, lying stock still, his face hidden. She guessed it wouldn't hurt to give him a few minutes to awaken. She sat down beside him, legs stretched in front of her, crossed at the ankles.

He patted the empty spot by his head. "Come on, lie down. It's too early to be so energetic."

"We have a lot to do today."

He grunted.

His breathing slowed again.

"Are you going back to sleep?"

No answer.

Well, she wasn't going anywhere without him. She lay down on her side, propping her head on her elbow, and watched his chest rise and fall. Around them, the field was coming to life. Birds chirruped and sang in the trees, darting down for the occasional worm. A few cows grazed in the distance. A crescent of sun broke through on the eastern horizon.

Feeling surprisingly refreshed, as if she'd slept for days and days, she stretched her arms over her head and nestled into the bed.

"Now isn't that better," Quentin said, flicking the cap from his face. "You don't gun a cold engine. You let it idle, let the oil warm the crankcase."

Quentin closed his eyes even as he finished that sentence. His own oil had already warmed his crankcase. His groin throbbed. Damn. He wanted her just as bad this morning as he had last night. Sleep hadn't cured his hard-on. No, sleep had made it worse.

He sat upright. "All right, we'll do it your way."

"But I'm just getting the hang of this." She pouted and stretched her arms over her head again, lifting her breasts to peaks he ached to explore with his tongue. Quentin bit on his thumb to hold back a yelp of torment. Didn't she know what she did to a man?

What the hell. Maybe she did know and she was signaling him. Now that was a thought.

Still sitting, he said, "So you always bolt out of bed wide awake?"

She nodded. Her eyes were half-closed and she looked entirely too kissable.

"Well, since we're here together, I'll give you a lesson on the pleasures of waking nice and slow."

"You will?"

This time he nodded. "Close your eyes and roll your head to the left, then over to the right. Take a deep breath and let it out all the way."

She did as he instructed while he admired the plump rise and fall of her breasts with every breath she took. Though he'd never thought of her as busty, that motion was causing him to reconsider his assessment. The cotton knit of her dress left little to the imagination.

"Now," he said, speaking in a low, measured voice, "roll over on your tummy and I'll teach your muscles a nice slow wake-up routine."

She hesitated for a fraction of a moment while Quentin held his breath. Then she turned over and wiggled around getting comfortable on the leaf bed. The wiggling almost put him over the edge, but Quentin prided himself on his control.

Stroking with the lightest of touches the back of her neck, he said, "Let your mind drift to a most pleasant place." He glanced around them. "Imagine yourself in a peaceful field of hay with a man who's—"

"—my friend?" Mia murmured from the side of her cheek.

"Your best friend." He moved his hands to her shoulders and circled the firm flesh of her back. So many times he'd performed these ministrations on women technically more beautiful than Mia. On women who looked like cover models upon first sight in the morning. Mia's hair looked even spikier than usual and a cowlick in the back kinked her hair upwards. He touched her hair with a wayward stroke and Mia murmured something he couldn't interpret.

Probably keep your hands to yourself.

But none of those other women made him feel the way Mia did. Her skin was silken olive, her muscles toned and lithe. Of course, none of his past lovers were what any man would call bowsers. Most of them had been starlets seeking an entree and he, insecure as to his own attractiveness quotient, used them to prove his sex appeal.

Mia stirred and settled into the nest. "This feels wonderful," she said.

"And much better than rushing into the day willy-nilly?"

"That's a funny word."

"Hey, I'm a funny guy," he said lightly, then moved his hands to her upper thighs.

She stiffened slightly, and he said, "If one part of you is out of sorts, that zaps it for the rest of you."

"Oh."

He took that as assent and kneaded gently, counting to a hundred in his head to keep from thinking of the massage he wanted her to give him.

Ooh. Mia squirmed as Quentin's fingers stroked her thighs through her dress. She hoped he couldn't tell exactly how good he made all her body parts feel. Her insides had long since passed from relaxed to liquid.

Hot, sticky liquid.

She buried her head against the beach towel as he moved to her bare calves. She avoided stockings, blessed with skin dark enough to make them unnecessary.

Where he touched her skin her flesh sizzled. The fire started on her calves and then licked up her legs, to the backs of her knees, to the tender skin on the insides of her thighs.

Warm and tender and strong, his fingers spoke directly to her body. Her dress hiked upward as he made his way in slow killer strokes to her panties, a scrap of lace and satin that were among Mia's few vanities. She shopped the catalog, of course. Buying in person at Victoria's Secret violated the element of fantasy Mia enjoyed, one of the few nonpractical treats she allowed herself.

She thought for the most fleeting of moments of stopping him. Of turning over and saying in her starchiest voice what do you think you're doing? But she wanted him to want her, to possess her, to ravish her. Who knew what would happen in their lives? Quentin making love to her here in this improbably invisible world might be as close to heaven as she ever came.

Ahh! Quentin felt his breath coming in rushes, the need in his groin threatening to overwhelm his brain. Mia's firm cheeks begged his touch. The way she wriggled set him on fire. Perhaps his brain had been expecting some barrier. Knowing Mia as he did, he'd anticipated a wall of sensible white cotton with firm elastic bands.

But the sight of Mia's flesh playing peek-a-boo through the lace of a dainty bikini bottom flamed his desires. He let his finger follow the scrap of lace around her hip and down to where he encountered a triangle of satin covering her patch of curls.

His finger skimmed the satin with an ease that begged him to slip beneath it. The panty was warm, the crotch damp. Quentin knew his expression wavered between a groan and a grin as he opened her with a teasing dance of his finger.

She gasped and he found the control to still his hand. Then she wriggled against him and half-turned her upper body to face him.

His finger embedded in her nest, he tried for his sexiest smile.

"What are you doing?" she asked in a breathy voice.

"Massage?"

She nodded, the little half-jog of her chin she did when she was thinking something through. Then she tightened her muscles around his finger, pulling him in deeper, and rolled onto her back. "Please proceed," she whispered.

He groaned and worked her dress clear of her hips and waist, bunching it under her breasts. Then he lowered his head. His breath hot against the scrap of satin, he whispered, "For you, Mia, a full body massage." Then he slipped the scrap of panty down her legs.

Eyes still half-closed, she lay her head back, offering herself to him with a lift of her hips. He accepted the gift, delving for the honey of her sex, probing and tasting and tantalizing her until she writhed and with a great look of wonder on her face, cried out, "Oh, Quentin, I'm dying!"

She shuddered and with a great smile on his face, he drank of her passion. My hot little Mia, who would have guessed it?

He untied the drawstring of his sweats and began to lower his pants, craving the warmth of her sheath for his own release.

She looked up at him, a glow in her eyes and

Quentin paused to lean over her and kiss her belly button. Then he said, "My God, you're hot. And what a body. You've kept this hidden all these years." Reaching beneath her bunched-up dress, he sought her breasts and released the catch of her bra. More lace and satin. He grinned.

The earlier glow in her face seemed to have dimmed. Well, he'd take care of that. He shed his shoes and pants.

A car swept by on the road. He'd forgotten all about the rest of the world. Well, when you were invisible, you could do whatever you wanted. No one could see them making love in this meadow.

He turned to Mia, easing himself over her. "My angel, you are lovely," he whispered, and captured her lips.

She kissed him with a fierceness that startled him. But by now he should have known his Mia was all tiger. Nudging her legs apart, he prepared to enter her. He didn't think he could do without dessert much longer.

Mia pressed a hand against his shoulder, a look of worry flitting across her face.

Suddenly he comprehended. She might be a tiger but she was still Ms. Practical. "No, Mia, I don't have a condom."

She laughed.

"You think that's funny?"

"Quentin, that's the last thing on my mind. We don't know whether we're alive or dead, so why worry about birth control?"

Quentin hated to talk during sex. "So what's the problem?"

Mia looked up at Quentin hovering above her. His erection burned against her thigh and nudged against her still throbbing sex. How could she tell him at this moment the truth about herself? Should she? Shouldn't she? "Well, it's rather awkward, but—"

"MOOOOOO!" A cow bellowed close by.

"What's awkward?" Quentin was starting to look belligerent. "We're a man and a woman attracted to one another, making love." He kissed her and said, "Now can we get on with it?"

Mia closed her eyes and decided for once, not to worry. Why tell him? He'd discover for himself soon enough. Lifting her hips, she pressed up against him as the tip of his penis teased her sticky warmth.

"MOOOOOOOO!"

Mia opened one eye and glanced over Quentin's shoulder in the direction of that animal sound.

Not fifty yards away loomed one of the biggest cows she'd ever seen, watching them with lowered head and unwavering gaze.

Quentin was beginning to enter her, still only the head of his shaft teasing her, then withdrawing, then dipping again. She tried to catch her breath as the sensations he set off in the moist folds of her sex spread through her veins.

Tapping him on the shoulder, she whispered, "Quentin, what's the difference between a cow and a bull?"

He groaned and writhed. God but she was tight. He hadn't even buried himself within her and he was ready to launch his missile. And she was talking about cows! "Is this a riddle?" From behind clenched teeth, he added, "Now?"

"Not exactly." She tilted her hips and he tried to inch inward.

He managed to answer, "Think of it this way. A bull has horns and a cow doesn't."

"And a bull is more dangerous?" She was panting and performing delicious dance steps with her hips.

"Yeah, because we guys are always horny." He laughed at his own stupid joke. But how could she talk when he was in the throes of the buildup of what was promising to be the most incredible orgasm of his life.

"You have to stop," Mia said, pushing against his shoulders.

"What?!" The cry came from deep within him. Yeah, all the way from his testicles to his throat.

"I'm serious, Quentin. There's a bull in this field and he's starting to paw the ground."

Quentin glanced behind him just as the bull began to charge.

Leaping up, he grabbed for Mia's hand and their clothing and raced for the road. The ground thundered as the bull gained momentum behind them. Mia screamed as she hurtled the fence. Right behind her, Quentin vaulted over, seconds before the bull tore at the fence with his horns.

Yanking his pants on over his throbbing erection, Quentin turned and glared at the animal as it stood pawing the ground and raising and lowering its head. "Dammit, go find your own cow."

10 ⌒

By the time the MegaFilms jet circled to touch down at a small private landing field near the Arkansas-Oklahoma border, Chelsea wished she'd never heard the name Hornsby Smallwood.

Fran had cozied up to the ghastly lawyer like an out-of-work starlet to a producer holding a network commitment. Toy-Toy, who hated to fly, had refused his tranquilizer and an hour into the trip had yapped until he'd made himself sick. All over the seat.

Instead of strolling into the shelter of her Virginia bed and breakfast where the staff was trained to politely refrain from commenting on one's celebrity status, she was about to endure God-only-knew-what inconveniences at the hands of this hick lawyer.

Why Ely retained him she couldn't fathom. Maybe there weren't any other attorneys in Hill Springs. She remembered Ely telling her about his small town. When she'd been a young girl starved for companionship, his stories of friendly people, of neighbors who stopped to inquire after a sick child or an expectant mother, charmed her. Where she lived, both as a child and now, all lives played themselves out behind tall fences. And many of those fences, including hers, were electrified.

But now, impatient to escape to her long-promised solitary retreat and reluctant to be reminded how she had failed the one member of her family she had honestly loved, she closed her mind to Ely's tales.

Half an hour.

She'd endure the will-reading, and be gone. She'd sent her luggage on to Virginia the day before, thinking nothing of jetting it across country to be ready for her upon her arrival. With what she put up with at the hands of Salvatino More and MegaFilms, she more than deserved every one of their jets at her beck and call.

At least the stop would be quick. Smallwood had told Fran only his secretary knew of his mission and she had always been the soul of discretion. A relief to Chelsea, who had instantly regretted giving in and would indeed have refused to make the trip had Fran not camped out at her house and taken Toy-Toy hostage until Chelsea climbed into the limo to drive to the airport. Now that Fran knew Chelsea had blown off the funeral, she was acting bossier than ever.

Honestly, the indignities she suffered.

She bussed Toy-Toy's topknot. He rolled his scared little eyes and whimpered. "We're almost there, my wuddle puppy love," she crooned, promising herself she'd stuff that tranquilizer down his throat before they took off for Virginia.

The plane glided to a flawless landing. The lawyer rose, stretching and looking so pleased with himself that Chelsea wanted to grab his balls and yank really, really hard. But what did it matter? He'd go on with his miserable existence and so would she.

She remained in her seat until Fran prodded her. Collecting Toy-Toy, Chelsea moved to the door of the plane, her mind closed to everything except enduring the next hour. Dark glasses perched firmly on her face, she stepped onto the stairs that had been moved into place.

And right into a swarm of screaming men and women, back-lit by an aurora of camera flashes.

During the hike to Hill Springs from the hayfield, Mia was careful not to let her hurt feelings show. Quentin had introduced her to the most marvelous sensations she'd ever known. And then called her a cow.

But under the circumstances, considering he had been speaking to a bull, she could overlook that slight.

What she couldn't overlook was what he hadn't said while they'd been wrapped in the throes of passion.

"You're hot" didn't equal "I love you."

Not even close.

And she, craven fool that she was, had let him make love to her, started to surrender herself completely, totally, blissfully.

As only a woman in love could do.

If that bull hadn't come along when he did, she would have given herself completely to him.

Then he would have discovered that she was the last virgin left in Hollywood. Mia knew that she was neither prudish nor promiscuous. She saw things simply. To her the equation worked. Sex belonged with love and she'd never loved anyone but Quentin.

So she'd gone without other experiences, smiling knowingly when other women spoke of multiple orgasms. Now that she'd had a taste, though, she could scarcely stand being locked out of the candy store.

But until Quentin unlocked the door to his heart or she learned to get over him, she'd continue on her path. With that thought, Mia stiffened her spine and her resolve to stick to business. During their long walk, she'd come up with Plan B, which Quentin had pronounced as inspired. But it, too, depended on Ely's willingness to help them.

"I wished I'd thought of this solution before." Mia hop-skipped to keep pace with Quentin. They'd reached Ely's place only to find him gone, but he'd left them a note saying he was down the lane at Luke Miller's house.

"So why didn't you?"

"I guess I was so dazzled by your convoluted plan I couldn't think in terms of feminine duplicity."

"Now don't blame me. You agreed to it. You even acted like you thought it was brilliant."

"It was brilliant, it just needed some fine-tuning."

"Look, I think I see Ely. He's outside the house." Mia squinted.

"Is there a reason we're walking so fast?" Quentin asked.

"I'm walking exactly as fast as you are." With the spell of their morning lovemaking broken, he was back to being impossible. "You probably feel the same sense of urgency I do."

He looked sideways at her but said nothing.

So, he did feel it. Mia smiled in triumph and called out to Ely, "We're back!"

At a trot, they moved onto the sweep of lawn in front of a quaint blue farmhouse trimmed in pert white. She could picture Sally Field and James Garner stepping out onto the porch, frosty glasses of homemade lemonade in hand. It was that kind of place.

"Well, this is a surprise," Ely said.

"Why? You left us a note."

"When you didn't turn up for days," Ely said, turning the hose to a different bed of flowers, "I figured you'd gone back to Heaven."

"We never were in Heaven," Quentin said.

"Purgatory," Mia added. Then she said, "What do you mean it's not the next day? We left your place last night, the car died, we had to uh—borrow a truck—"

"Mia, none of that matters. Tell him your plan." Quentin's face held none of its usual light-heartedness.

Ely glanced sharply at him and Mia did, too. If they had lost time, Quentin was right. "I, that is we, have a new idea."

Turning the knob on the end of the hose, Ely cut the water. "I'm listening," he said with a twinkle in his eye.

Mia almost asked why Ely was watering Luke's flowers. Instead, she took a deep breath then said, "All you need to do is change your will and *pretend* to be dead." She watched his face for a reaction. Surely he would at least consider the possibility.

Ely smiled, a big grin that lit his face. "Do you ever think some things are just meant to be?"

"Is that a 'yes'?" Mia asked.

"Plan A is already underway," Ely said.

"That doesn't mean you're dead too, does it?" Mia couldn't stand it if they'd caused this nice man's death.

Quentin started to smile, then broke into a laugh. "That's why you're not at your house, isn't it?"

Mia shot him a puzzled look, then suddenly she understood. Impulsively, she stood on tiptoe and kissed Ely on the cheek.

"Thank you, my dear. I paid a visit to my lawyer, then I had the pastor announce I'd died on a visit to my East Coast relatives. Had him set the other necessary wheels in motion." He grimaced. "But it still remains to be seen whether the plan will hold up."

"She hasn't responded, has she?" Even though Mia knew how spoiled and selfish Chelsea was, her heart sank.

"Don't give up yet, my dear." He switched the water back on and gave a planter of petunias a drink. "I've sent my lawyer after her and I have faith in him."

"Persuasive, eh?" Quentin asked.

"No, greedy. I left instructions if he brought her back for the reading of the will he'd get ten thousand dollars."

Quentin reached out and shared a high-five with the old man.

Mia started chewing the sorry remnant of her thumbnail.

"Who's that Uncle Ely is talking to?" Timmy asked from behind a mouthful of cereal. Milk dribbled down both sides of his chin, making him look like a high-calcium Dracula.

Luke smiled at his son and said, "Don't talk with your mouth full."

Timmy swallowed and promptly repeated his question.

"I don't know," Luke answered, thinking Timmy looked much happier this morning. Having Ely around the house could prove to be the right tonic to bring Timmy out of his sulks. To satisfy his son, he glanced out the window. "He's outside by himself, watering the cannas."

Timmy shook his head emphatically. Droplets of milk flew. "He's talking to a man and a woman. And the woman looks like my mommy."

For the briefest of moments, Luke closed his eyes and prayed for the wisdom to guide his son. Maybe letting him pretend helped him. "And what does the man look like?"

His son wrinkled his nose and rose to his knees in his chair to better see out the window. Pressing a hand over his mouth, he giggled. "He looks funny. But he is wearing a baseball cap."

Luke smiled, despite his dismay that Timmy had invented yet another imaginary playmate. Normally he saw no harm in make-believe for children, but he'd worried about Timmy's drawing back from the world around him in the year since his mother had died. "Which team?"

"Yankees."

"And who is the most famous Yankee of all?" Luke carried his cereal bowl to the sink. He'd forgotten to call the dishwasher repair place yet again.

"George Steinbrenner." He giggled again.

Luke smiled. What a marvel his son was! If only

Jenny—he cut the thought at the root. Uneasily, he glanced again out the window. Ely stood where he'd been earlier, but he seemed to have forgotten he'd already watered the peonies. The water gushed on as he stared at the horizon.

His friend sure had been acting strange lately. Faking his death, forgetting what he was doing. Luke grimaced at the thought of watching such a vibrant man slowly unravel. His own father had gone so quickly, lingering only long enough to exact the death-bed promise from Luke that had changed his life and brought him back to Hill Springs.

Luke swung around from the sink. So many thoughts he kept himself from thinking.

"I'm going outside to see the lady who looks like my mommy. Maybe she's an angel from heaven," Timmy said.

"Later, okay? Go wash up now or you'll be late for kindergarten."

Timmy made a face, but climbed up the stairs. He despised kindergarten, and often came home in tears, accompanied by notes from his teacher explaining he wasn't adjusting to group activities.

Luke thought of his sister's advice.

Maybe he didn't need a wife, but Timmy sure could use a mother.

11

Trapped!

Behind her, Chelsea heard the door of the plane slam shut. Below her, covering the tarmac like the swarm from a tipped-over beehive, milled her least favorite people: reporters.

Fran was fond of saying Chelsea ought to be thankful to the tabloid press since they'd made her far richer than she could have become on talent alone. Fran liked to say a lot of mean things like that, claiming someone had to keep Chelsea's head down to size.

Yet, Chelsea thought as she stalled on the stairs, it wasn't like Fran to call a press event and not fuss in advance over Chelsea's wardrobe, hair, and choice of language. During the flight, Fran had paid little attention to Chelsea.

Just then her manager stepped backwards up to the stair below Chelsea's. Out of the side of her mouth, she said, "The darling vultures are here and I didn't even scatter the bread crumbs."

"You swear you're not responsible for this?"

Fran nodded. "Had to be Smallwood. But that doesn't mean I won't make the most of it." She tugged at Chelsea's elbow. Toy-Toy muttered a tiny growl.

"Come on, give 'em a smile."

Fury ripped through Chelsea. Lousy, double-dealing lawyer, lying about only telling his secretary. "I will not give them a smile. I'm here to visit the town where my great-uncle lived his last days and I'm too overcome with grief to speak. So do your job, hustle me through the crowd, then go back and make a nice little speech about family values."

Fran smiled. "Sometimes, Chelsea dear, you remind me of your father. He always did have a quick tongue."

Chelsea ducked her head as Fran and the two plane attendants cleared a path, sweeping her through the twenty or so people all calling out her name and snapping photos.

Toy-Toy yapped and tried to fling himself from Chelsea's clutch. She held on, using his body as a muff to protect her face. Bad enough that she had to stop in Arkansas without the press turning it into a feeding frenzy. She didn't want to be reminded of this detour—ever.

The entourage rushed through the small terminal building, the press following like hounds scenting the fox.

Normally, despite her dislike of the game, Chelsea played them to the hilt. But these guys couldn't be any of the regulars. Not out here in the boondocks. And she didn't want to banter. She wanted to be left alone.

A Mercedes stood in front of the building, the

passenger doors open. Smallwood sat behind the wheel, looking very pleased with himself. Hating to accept rescue from him, Chelsea hopped in the back of his car. Maybe she could persuade Toy-Toy to get carsick.

Fran jumped in the front. The plane attendants slammed the doors and Smallwood peeled away from the building.

"Aren't you going to stay and talk to them?" Chelsea asked.

"I think I'll save that until after the will is read."

"If Ely was foolish enough to leave me any money, please keep it quiet. My mother's family despises me as it is."

Smallwood laughed, a rather nasty sound. "Shouldn't think you cared whether anyone liked you or not."

"Shut up and drive," Fran said, before Chelsea could swing in with her own retort.

Chelsea looked out the window at a vista of green fields merging into softly rolling hills. The sky, unlike a typical southern California sky, glowed a clear blue, no pollution in sight. White clouds fluffed above the trees.

She took a breath and Toy-Toy sighed and nestled his nose on her thighs. It was pretty here, in a rustic sort of way.

The fields gave way abruptly to a strip of road as ugly as the fields were pretty. Chelsea stared at concrete buildings and parking lots with pickup trucks and crumbling billboard-size signs advertising farm equipment and a gas station with the ridiculous sign of EAT spelled in a crossword with GAS.

Smallwood turned and the street metamorphosed to a wide avenue with restored wooden buildings on either side. Striped awnings decorated most of the building fronts. Cheesy, but a step up from that poverty row.

He parked and said, "Here we are. Offices of Hornsby Smallwood, II." He smirked and added, "Better hurry unless you want to meet the press."

Too bad Toy-Toy hadn't barfed. Well, there was still the ride back to the airport. She jiggled him a bit as she left the car. He looked at her with reproach in his eyes.

"I'm sorry, wuddle one," she whispered.

"I have a dog," Smallwood said, holding open the door.

"Oh?"

Good thing Fran answered, because Chelsea had no conversational tidbits to scatter before this skunk.

"A Doberman. This little rat wouldn't even make an appetizer for him."

"His name is probably Adolph," Chelsea said.

"How'd you know?" Smallwood actually looked surprised.

Fran looked nauseated.

"Let's just read this will." Chelsea marched across the reception area and through a door marked with a brass sign that read "The Boss." She settled Toy-Toy onto a red leather sofa and snapped her fingers. "Don't try to run up your bill."

Smallwood glared, then walked to a wall safe, opened it, and pulled out a sheaf of papers.

Fran remained standing, a sour look on her face as she studied the lawyer.

Smallwood took a seat behind the ornate antique desk and shuffled the papers.

"Start," Chelsea said. "I'm late for my vacation."

Hornsby laughed under his breath, a wheezy sound that set the hairs on the back of her neck on edge. "Vacation, eh? St. Moritz? Palm Beach? Why not stay here in Hill Springs and breathe the fresh air?"

"Never."

He broke the seal on a large envelope and said, "He who laughs last laughs the loudest."

Chelsea tapped her foot. She'd worn spikes, a foolish thing indeed for traveling, but they did set off the line of her tangerine silk pants and tunic. Flats just didn't work with flowing pants. Toy-Toy looked up at her as Smallwood began to read, and she stroked her puppy's ears.

It didn't take Smallwood long.

To ruin her life.

He looked up when he finished reading the document, a gleam of anticipation oh-so-evident in his eyes.

Chelsea refused to be had, refused to be made the butt of some joke, especially in front of this creep. She gathered Toy-Toy and stood. "Coming, Fran? I'm sure we can catch a cab to the airport."

Fran didn't answer.

"I said—"

"You're seriously thinking of leaving? Of walking out that door?" Fran looked at her like she was some sort of bug.

"What else?"

Fran pointed a finger towards Smallwood.

"Oh, that." Chelsea shrugged. "This will is obvi-

ously a joke. Some sort of hoax perp—perptr"—
she stumbled over the word, her composure more
disturbed than she cared to reveal —"penetrated by
this disgrace to the legal profession."

"What makes you say that?" Fran asked.

"Come on! Uncle Ely would never, ever ask me to
do any of those disgusting things."

"Why not?" This time Smallwood asked the question.

"Because he had to have known I couldn't. I'd
never be able to do any of those things." She tugged
on Toy-Toy's ears a mite too fiercely. He wiggled
away and jumped onto the carpet.

"Can you imagine me—me—living in this lousy
town for a month? Working in some factory? Surviv-
ing on minimum wage? Going to church on Sunday?" Her voice crescendoed and out of the corner
of her eye she saw Toy-Toy tremble and lift his leg
against the edge of Smallwood's leather sofa.

Smallwood snickered.

Obviously he hadn't seen the dog.

Fran said, "Did you listen to the entire reading?"

"I got the gist of it."

"Including the part about what happens to his ten-
million-dollar estate if you walk out that door and
carry on with your own miserable, petty existence?"

"There's no need to speak to me like I'm five years
old. Or to be insulting. I know the answer. The
money goes to some local group."

"Am/Am." Ice chipped from Fran's voice.

"So?"

"That stands, my dear self-centered friend and
client, for Americans for America. It's a white su-
premacist, neo-Nazi group that's been linked to at
least three synagogue bombings. They hate Jews,

blacks, and ninety-nine percent of politicians, pretty much in that order."

"Oh." Chelsea rose and walked to the window, her brow furrowed. She'd never heard of that group and couldn't believe Ely supported them. She didn't care about much, but the work she did for Jewish causes did matter to her. Even though her father had taken her to temple only a few times in her life, she appreciated, in her own vague and selfish way, the relation to something larger than herself. She didn't care that people thought she only did it for Fran.

At last, she turned back around. Advancing on Smallwood's desk, she said, "Why did Ely choose that group?"

"Oh, rest assured, I helped him in the selection of an alternative beneficiary." Smallwood looked as pleased as a rat in a granary. "Not of course that as his counsel I selected a group to whose credo I conform. Simply suggested a cause any Hollywood liberal was apt to despise."

"Very clever of you," Fran said. "So Ely only chose Am/Am because of your suggestion, and then you did this will up fair and square."

"Right before he died." Smallwood merely looked pleased; Fran's insinuation of misconduct obviously went right over his head.

"That's it!" Chelsea snapped her fingers. "He'd gone off his rocker. Old people do that. Fran, call my lawyers and have them get me out of this mess. And out of this town."

Smallwood pushed his telephone toward Chelsea. Before lifting his hand from it, he said, "Must tell you if any attempt is made to contest the will the money goes straight to Am/Am."

"I don't believe you."

The evil glint in his eyes kept her hand from the telephone.

"That's not a chance you can take, Chelsea." Fran pushed her hair back from her face and rubbed her eyes with hands that trembled. "It's not just a question of your image and what the press will say. It's a matter of personal integrity."

Chelsea stuck her lip out and refused to concur, even though she agreed and could see she was doomed. Even if she wasn't half-Jewish, she couldn't let ten million dollars fall into the hands of a group ruled by hate. She might be considered obnoxious by her staff, by every hairdresser in Hollywood, and by her personal manager, but somewhere beneath the glitz and cleavage lay a real heart.

A heart that wouldn't let her walk away.

Smallwood started to whoop, a ruckus as out of place in his leather and mahogany office as a hyena at a black-tie affair.

"Just what is so funny?" Fran asked with a frown that should have warned Smallwood to shut up.

"I'm sorry. I can't help it. But the joke's just too good."

"What joke?" Chelsea asked, knowing she was being insulted yet again at the hands of this yokel.

He wiped at his eyes. "I knew you'd never do it. From the first moment I laid eyes on you in that ridiculous costume, I knew you were nothing more than a prick tease with no backbone." Smallwood began gathering his papers.

"And you find this humorous?" Chelsea took a step toward his desk.

He nodded. "My friends at Am/Am are going to be mighty pleased."

"Your friends?"

"Well, I mean the uh, the alternate beneficiaries will be pleasantly surprised at this windfall."

"And they'll use the money to buy lots of guns and bombs, won't they?" she asked sweetly.

"Oh, I wouldn't know about that. As a matter of fact, I picked this group out of the phone book. Totally at random." He wiped his brow. This time he dabbed at beads of sweat, not tears of laughter.

Inside, Chelsea was dying. She knew not a flicker of emotion showed on her face. Thirty days in this burg! She cursed Ely, all the while withering Smallwood with a gaze lethal enough to strip paint off a stage backdrop.

She turned, looked at Fran who had a hand wrapped around her silver mezuzah.

Well, she wasn't doing this for Fran.

The issue went beyond one person's life, one person's losses.

Therefore, she had no choice. And to throw in a minor reason, she didn't like a creep like Smallwood assuming she'd fail. Yeah, she'd do this thing.

But she didn't have to like it.

She yawned and bent down to retrieve Toy-Toy. Affecting a look of nonchalance, she said, "What the hell. I'm in between films, and I've got nothing better to do."

"What did you say?" Smallwood croaked.

Chelsea snatched a copy of the will from his desk. She looked him straight in his weak gray eyes and winked. "He who laughs last laughs loudest."

Then she stalked toward the door.

"Before you go," Smallwood said, "I need your credit cards and any money over $125 you're carrying."

"Whatever for?"

"You have to live on your wage, and your wage is $4.25 an hour for forty hours a week, minus taxes. I've gone easy on the tax estimate."

Chelsea jutted her jaw and clutched her Chanel bag.

Fran said, "Go ahead and give him the money while I'm here to witness."

"No."

Smallwood gave her a nasty grin and began walking to where she stood. "Then you lose and Am/Am wins."

"Motherfucker," she said.

Fran lifted her brows. "My, my, maybe a month of church on Sundays will improve your manners."

Chelsea opened her purse, knowing this must be what it felt like to be mugged. She held out her wallet. Fran took it from her and counted out $1500 in hundred-dollar bills, then gave her back $125. She also robbed her of her Nieman-Marcus and American Express cards.

"Cheer up, Chelsea," Fran said, "there's probably no Nieman-Marcus within a hundred miles of here, anyway."

"And most places here prefer the Discover card," Smallwood added.

She knew the geek was laughing at her, so she froze her face and pretended not to care. "I won't be needing anything from your crummy stores."

She made sure Fran stood over Smallwood as he put her money and cards into an envelope and sealed and signed over the flap. Furious at Fran for not agreeing to call the lawyers and get her out of the situation, Chelsea refused even to look her manager in the eye.

What the woman ought to do was fly back to L.A.

and huddle with that expensive firm she retained. Even though Smallwood said the will couldn't be contested, Chelsea didn't believe that for a minute. Lawyers had a way to get around everything. She might have dropped out of that stupid Swiss boarding school her father had shipped her off to, but she wasn't ignorant.

Without saying good-bye to Fran, Chelsea left by the back door. To avoid the press, Smallwood offered to drive her to Ely's house in his secretary's car.

The lawyer drove her out of town, whistling under his breath, a tuneless number that irritated her more than the worst of Fran's bad habits. She stared out the window, resting her chin in Toy-Toy's coat, counting the seconds until she found a way out of this fix. Screw Fran. She'd call her lawyers herself.

A short way out of town Smallwood turned down an unpaved road marked Blueberry Lane. The name was cute but the road needed a lot of work. Chelsea held onto Toy-Toy as they bumped down it in the secretary's rattly old car.

Smallwood slowed in front of a winsome blue two-story house with white shutters and an inviting front porch. For a moment, Chelsea experienced a flare of optimism. The car kept going, extinguishing her hope.

The lane dead-ended into a gravel turn-around in front of a small one-story building that looked like some farmer had thrown rocks together to build it. It, too, had a porch, but not one as pretty as the house down the road. A pickup truck sat in the gravel area.

Smallwood halted and swept an arm toward the house. "Your castle, Princess."

Ignoring him, Chelsea climbed from the horrid car, clasping her poodle as if he were a life jacket. He looked around with his bright little eyes and Chelsea expected him to hide his head in her armpit. Instead, he scrabbled to jump down.

She held on tighter. "No, Toy-Toy." God only knew what horrors lurked. "Not safe, wuddle one."

"I'll pick you up tomorrow morning and drive you to work, to make sure you know where it is. After that, babe, you're on your own, except for your first day at church. Be ready at 6:15 sharp." He turned away.

"Wait, where's the key?"

Smallwood laughed. "We hicks don't have to lock our doors."

He drove off. Dust blew back on Chelsea. She stamped a foot and coughed and held on to a rebelliously wiggling Toy-Toy.

Filled with misgivings, raving against a world that had conspired to ruin her, she walked toward the house.

Sure enough, the front door opened with the turn of the knob. She stepped in and let her poodle down on the carpet. Little light filtered into the room, but from what she could see the room appeared cluttered with books and papers. Moving into the next room, she found a dining table, three-fourths covered in books. Beyond that, a kitchen and tiny back porch.

A hall led off the dining room to a bedroom and bath.

That was it.

The entire house would fit in the entry area of her Bel Air estate.

Unbelievable.

Ely had been a rich man, a man who could afford any home anywhere. And this is where he had lived.

Chelsea shook her head and wondered if her relative hadn't been deranged. Well, this pint-size pigpen strengthened her argument that the will should be set aside due to insanity.

The first order of operations was to call her lawyers. She looked around for the telephone. Funny, but it wasn't in the living room or the bedroom. Stepping into the kitchen, she wrinkled her nose. Smelled as if the maid hadn't taken out the garbage.

Then she laughed. Crazy old Ely probably hadn't even had a housekeeper. She'd have to take care of that. Surely there were enough poor people in this town who could use some decent wages.

She couldn't find a phone anywhere. Beginning to lose her temper, she flung stuff off the dining table. Newspapers, scientific journals, musty volumes of history books with no pictures, all these she dumped onto the floor.

Hah! Suddenly she realized what the old man must have done. Taken it out to torture her. She'd pop into town and call.

Collecting Toy-Toy, she said, "Let's get out of here, wuddle one." He barked and wagged his tail. The moment she stepped outside, he flung himself free and scampered down the steps and into the side yard.

"Toy-Toy!" Chelsea ran after him. Two steps into the grass her spike heels sank and refused to budge. "Goddamn old man. Probably in hell laughing at me right this minute!" She wanted to take back the words the minute she said them. Tears formed in her eyes but she refused to give in to them. She had to be strong to rescue Toy-Toy.

Leaning down, she unfastened her shoes and left them in the grass. Tiptoeing across the yard, refusing to let herself think about spiders and ants, she moved off in the direction he'd fled.

"Come to Mommy, wuddle one. Don't be frightened. I'll make everything okay-wokay for you."

At the back of the house stood a row of low buildings enclosed by a wire fence. A smell worse than the garbage in the kitchen wafted from the building. Toy-Toy stood yapping at the fence, stretching up on his little hind legs.

"I'm coming, Toy-Toy."

Holding her nose, she ran to him.

He yipped and took off.

"What in the hell is wrong with you?" Chelsea forgot all about baby talk and screamed after her fleeing pet. Toy-Toy was the only link she had to her real life. She couldn't afford to lose him.

"Baawk-bawk-bawk!"

Chelsea jumped and stifled a scream. She looked up to where the sound came from. On a wire strung between two poles sat a very large bird.

"Bawwk!"

Toy-Toy danced around underneath the bird.

"You're no bird," Chelsea said, feeling quite foolish. "You're nothing but a chicken."

The chicken hopped off the wire and soared back into the fenced pen.

Toy-Toy looked disappointed.

Catching him off-guard, she picked him up. "That's enough adventures for one day."

Panting, he cocked his head. His precious little violet bows had come undone in his racing about.

She carried him to the pickup truck and retied the bows. Fortunately, a key gleamed in the ignition.

She slid behind the wheel. Surely anyone could drive a truck. She understood they were easier than cars. Just get in and point.

Barefooted, she pressed the accelerator and turned the key. The truck leapt forward a foot or so. She caught her breath and tried to start it again.

Then she realized there was something other than a gas pedal and brake at her feet.

A clutch.

She knew then and there she was in trouble. Aldo had taught her how to drive a stick shift, but right now she was far too distraught to remember how to make the thing go. Momentarily defeated, she pulled Toy-Toy away from where he was happily looking out the passenger window and climbed out of the truck.

The sky shone bright and blue above her. Birds sang in the trees surrounding the house. She lugged a reluctant Toy-Toy back into the house. He took up a station at the door, standing on his legs, his nose pressed against the screen.

Chelsea was too upset to be hungry but she knew her baby would be hungry soon. She checked in the cramped kitchen, relieved to find a bag of dog food. It certainly didn't look like what Toy-Toy was used to, but under the circumstances her poor poodle would have to rough it.

Even though Smallwood had robbed her of almost all of her money, he hadn't taken her travel supply of sleeping pills. Chelsea reached in her bag and spilled the pills into her hand. A bird swooped past the door, trilling a cheerful song. Toy-Toy yapped happily. Chelsea studied the palmful, then shook most of them back into the bottle, leaving only two in her hand.

"After all," she said to Toy-Toy, "Mummy doesn't want to be late for her first day at work."

"Believe me, we don't have a thing to worry about." Smallwood finished mixing himself a bourbon and water, then juggled the phone between ear and shoulder while he capped the bottle.

"Yeah, when you called me from California and let me in on this little windfall you said she'd never get this far."

"I don't know what you're complaining about. You won a thousand-dollar bet the moment the bitch decided to stay in town."

"This ain't about chicken feed, it's about the big money."

Smallwood sipped his drink and smiled. "In a way it is about chicken feed. Once she sets foot in that plant tomorrow, we're in like flynn."

A grunt traveled over the line.

"I delivered the letter of instructions to the plant manager after I dropped off Chelsea at Van Ness's place. I'm telling you, Pi—"

"No names, for chrissakes."

"Oh, sorry." Smallwood took another sip. This cloak and dagger stuff really wasn't his sort of thing. He should stick to theory and let the good old boys handle the rough stuff.

"I gotta go."

The line went dead.

Just as well. Smallwood needed to relax. He strolled to the VCR and slid in his movie of choice. As he straightened, his silk robe slipped open.

God, but Chelsea Jordan was a bitch.

Her image, tongue at the ready, swam into focus on the screen. Setting his drink on the coffee table, he hit the Pause button and pictured her groveling at his feet, begging him to let her suck his dick.

He let that image overlay the picture of his own stupidity, of his letting his association with Am/Am slip. He'd pushed the wrong buttons on that little cunt or she'd be well on her way back to California. Of that fact he was sure, but since he alone possessed that guilty knowledge, he saw no need to confuse his cohorts with the facts.

He did, however, want to punish her.

Hah! His hand, cool from the glass, shocked him as he wrapped it around his erection. He'd let little Miss Prick Tease suffer a day in that chicken plant and as soon as she cried off, he'd offer to drive her to the airport.

And then he'd take what he wanted from her.

Even if he had to get a little rough.

With his free hand, he hit the Play button.

12 〜

The manager of All Right Foods thought of himself as a good man. In thirteen years, he hadn't missed a day at the plant. Every Sunday found him at the First Baptist Church, helping fill the collection plate. Every few months or so he had relations with his wife.

He'd been born in Hill Springs and in another thirty or forty years he reckoned he'd be buried there, too.

He ran a tight ship. No slackers need apply at All Right Foods. The poultry processing plant rivaled the big boys in production and every so often they managed to snatch a contract for KFC or McDonald's from Tyson Foods and Sanderson Farms. All Right didn't qualify as a power player in the multi-billion-dollar chicken processing business, but they turned a fair enough profit for its majority shareholder to enjoy the good life.

The Chief, as he was known, flew his own private plane, taking off and landing from his own private strip behind his country compound. The Chief's wife shopped in Dallas, and lorded it over the small country club set. As a matter of fact, they owned the country club.

The plant manager didn't begrudge his boss his wealth. He saw no need to envy a lifestyle that held no appeal for him. He rather liked his three-bedroom ranch-style house with the above-ground pool. It sat on a corner lot and allowed easy access to the First Baptist Church and the corner market.

He wouldn't have known what to do with a private plane. He'd never flown in any plane, having lived his entire life in Hill Springs.

So he happily managed the plant, keeping a careful eye on the nigras who would slow the speed of the line if he didn't keep his supervisors circulating with eagle eyes. The best thing that had happened to the poultry business, in his opinion, had been the influx of Orientals, mostly Vietnamese refugees. Resettled to Fort Chaffee, then released into the countryside, they'd been eager to work.

The women were the best. Some of them could debone chicken faster than he could say spit. And they'd work for hours without complaining. No lazy-ass carpal tunnel complaints from them. He hated to admit it, but they put his own people to shame.

But most of the whites had bettered themselves. Moved up to working at Wal-Mart, leaving the dirtier jobs to the foreigners. And the nigras, of course.

Not that there were many of them. Hill Springs was God's country, pure and clean and simple. And there were plenty of people in town willing to work to keep it that way.

So he did his part, making sure only the best of the workers were kept on.

He did have one man, even if he was a nigra, worked harder than any man in his employ. The owner had questioned his judgment, but he'd stuck by his decision to promote Willie Sims to supervisor. Made sense; his people would listen to him and the Viets were afraid of him.

Some days the plant manager feared Willie, too, but he tried not to let it show. When six-foot-five Willie leaned over you, the light glinting off his gold front tooth, you paid attention.

Pretty much one day was the same as another, always had been, and up until last night, the manager would have assumed things would continue that way.

Sitting at his desk earlier than usual, he ran a finger between his neck and collar, and read again the letter Mr. Smallwood had delivered yesterday.

My grandniece will be coming to town soon and will need a job. I am asking that you put her to work for one month within your plant and treat her the way you'd treat any other employee. Mr. Smallwood will answer any questions you may have and you may bill her month's salary to my estate. It is imperative that she not be given special treatment, or put to work in the office. I want her in the back, sweating alongside the rest of your crew. Should she fail to perform and you find cause to fire her, please inform Mr. Smallwood at once. Thank you for your assistance. Please give my best to Mabel and the children.

ss/Ely Van Ness

Highly irregular. Most unusual.

But Ely Van Ness had been a good man. He used

his money to help others. Only two years ago, he'd donated the money to make over the employees' lunchroom, something the manager hadn't understood at the time. Still didn't. Who needed TV at work? But years earlier, he'd also provided a new playground for the town's grade school. The school all three of the manager's children attended.

He sighed, pulled at his tie, and checked his watch. Ten minutes of seven. The whistle for day shift blew in ten minutes. Mr. Smallwood said Miss Jordan was to report for seven.

If she ran late, he'd have to write her up. Even on her first day. Especially on her first day.

Might as well start her off on the right foot. Ely Van Ness was watching him from heaven and the least he could do for a man who remembered his wife's name and asked after her and the kids was this favor for him.

This morning, Timmy thought before he spoke. Even though his dad hadn't gotten mad yesterday, he could tell he wasn't happy about the make-believe friends Timmy had seen talking to Uncle Ely.

So he'd probably really get mad about the newest one.

"Who's living in your house, Uncle Ely?" he asked through his cereal. Darn, he'd forgotten again. Manners were such a drag.

"Timmy." His dad looked up from where he was ironing a shirt. "How many times do I have to tell you not to speak with your mouth full?"

"Sorry." He wiped his mouth with the back of his hand and gave his dad the smile he used when he wanted to get the kindergarten teacher off his back.

Ely buttered a piece of toast. "Why do you ask?"

Adults were like that. They couldn't just answer you, they had to ask another question. "Because."

"Did you see someone there when you went to feed the chickens last night?"

He shook his head and quickly shoveled in another bite of Cheerios.

"Well, there might be someone coming to live in my house."

"Who?" His dad asked the question, pulling the shirt from the ironing board and reaching for a hanger.

"Now that's a long story and I wouldn't want to make Timmy here late for school."

"And that's an evasive answer if I've ever heard one."

Timmy wrinkled his nose. "What's evasive?"

His dad hung the shirt on the doorknob and took a seat at the table. "Not answering directly."

"So it's not exactly a lie."

"True."

"But it's not too helpful, either." His dad looked at Ely with the look he usually reserved for Timmy when he got in trouble.

"I'm sorry, Luke. Please trust that when the time is right, I'll tell you what's going on."

"Is it a girl?"

"Is who a girl?"

Ely sat up straighter. He actually looked excited. "Are you sure you didn't see someone yesterday?"

Timmy thought of the shoe he'd hidden in the back of his toy chest. Silver, and covered in diamonds across the front. Most definitely it was the shoe of a princess, someone as special as Cinderella.

He didn't care much for girls, but princesses were altogether in a different category. Knowing his fairy tales, he'd taken only one of the shoes.

He shook his head. Out of the corner of his eye, he checked his dad's reaction. He seemed pretty upset, but he figured Uncle Ely was on the hot seat this time.

The telephone rang.

His dad got up and answered it.

The phone always seemed to ring when things were getting interesting. Pretty sure his dad couldn't see him, Timmy lifted his cereal bowl and drank the rest of his breakfast in one long slurp.

Then he burped and wiped his face with his hand.

"Those kind of manners won't get you invited to the White House," Uncle Ely said.

Timmy laughed and pushed back from the table, screeching the chair satisfactorily on the floor. "A good spy doesn't have to worry about silly things like manners. Neither does a baseball player."

"And you're going to be both?"

"Yeah."

His dad walked back to the table, a really funny look on his face.

"Go brush your teeth," he said.

"Who was that on the phone?" he asked, ignoring the order.

"None of your business. Now, go!"

He said it in That Voice, the voice that made Timmy miss his mom. She had never yelled at him to get him to do things. He stuck out his lip and started to refuse.

Uncle Ely said, "Timmy, your dad and I need to talk. Scoot."

His gentle voice reminded him of his mom.

"Okay," he said. Then glaring at his dad, he added, "Because Uncle Ely asked me to."

Once he cleared the doorway, he paused, as any good spy in training would do, and heard his father say, "That was Hennie Cobbs on the phone. I don't know how you're going to handle this, given that you're pretending to be dead, but your grandniece has come to town. According to Hennie, the word's all over town that Chelsea Jordan is in Hill Springs."

Pretending to be dead? Timmy's mouth dropped open. And he got in trouble for having make-believe friends.

He jerked his head up. Too late.

"Busted," his dad said. "Now go brush your teeth."

Timmy loped up the stairs, too amazed to argue.

Chelsea's mood couldn't get much more foul. She kissed Toy-Toy good-bye, worried sick what he'd do all day without her. Her head felt stuffed with cotton batting and if she hadn't had the sense to set the alarm, she probably would have slept at least another day and a half.

Outside, Smallwood kept honking his goddamn horn. She stomped to the door and yelled at him to stop. Then she continued her hunt for her shoes.

When he started honking again, she gave up and went outside.

And stumbled over one of her heels.

"You're already late," Smallwood said, leaning his head out the window of his Mercedes.

"Big deal," she muttered. She looked like hell, having had to wear the tangerine silk outfit two days in a row. Now she was supposed to limp along on only one shoe? "I can't find my other shoe," she said.

He tapped on his watch.

She tossed the thousand dollar shoe onto the porch. She was in the country; she'd go barefoot.

She got in the car.

"My, my, aren't we cheerful this morning," Smallwood said, starting to whistle under his breath again.

"Start that crap and I'll get out and walk."

He laughed. "Just to show you what a nice guy I am, I'll swing by my house and let you have a pair of shoes."

She looked sideways at him. "Into cross-dressing, are we?"

"Funny. When a man collects ex-wives, he sometimes finds himself with leftovers."

She could believe his wives were exes. Glancing out the window, she commented, "At least it's a nice day."

"Now that's more like it. A little cheerful morning conversation."

"So what kind of factory is this I'm supposed to help out?"

"Help out?"

"Did this Mercedes come with an echo or did you order it special?"

"That's quite a sense of humor you have there, Chelsea. The factory you're going to er—help out is a poultry processing plant. All Right Foods is the number-one employer in Hill Springs and the surrounding area. Yessirree, Hill Springs, Home of the Proud Bird."

"So they need some P.R. or some such?"

"P.R.?"

She frowned at him. "Public relations. What else could they want me for?"

He laughed so hard she thought he'd drive the car off the road. So she kept her mouth shut, refusing even to say thank you when he stopped at a decent enough old Victorian house and ran in to fetch a pair of shoes.

Flats, but she looked so dreadful already, she didn't complain.

About fifteen minutes later they pulled up at a guard shack in front of a sprawling windowless metal building. Smallwood showed some ID and pointed at her. The guard gave her the once over and she turned her head in the other direction. Why couldn't men keep their eyes to themselves?

Finally the car moved forward. Smallwood stopped before a garage-style door. "Showtime, babe," he said, and started whistling.

Chelsea got out, trying to maintain her balance, not to mention her composure in shoes that were half a size too big. Without her spike heels, the legs of her silk pants scuffed in the dirty tarmac of the parking lot.

She shuffled up the three stairs to the door Smallwood held open, thankful she was three thousand miles from her usual stomping grounds, and grateful the wolfpack of the press hadn't followed her. Fran must have worked some magic on them.

Feeling and looking as bad as she did, Chelsea couldn't possibly be of any use to any company. She'd simply explain to the manager she'd have to come back tomorrow.

A wide-eyed receptionist ushered them down a long narrow hallway and into an office with a door that proclaimed it the domicile of the plant manager. A man with thinning brown hair rose from behind the desk. He wore a short-sleeved white shirt and a skinny black tie. Chelsea thought he looked like Ward on "Leave it to Beaver" reruns, only not as intelligent.

Smallwood said, "As promised, here is Chelsea Jordan."

The man frowned. "You're late, young lady. Fifty-five minutes late. That's cause for a write-up. Three write-ups and you're fired." He jerked a hand across his throat.

"Excuse me?" Even though no one had offered her a seat, Chelsea took the chair opposite the desk. What was this mousy man raving about?

A knock sounded at the open door and a man wearing a blue smock over his clothes poked his head in. Tossing from hand to hand something that looked like a cross between a Tiny Tears doll and a Butterball turkey, the young Asian man said, "Hey, boss, I've got 'em to 2.9. How's that?"

The manager said, "I need them as close to 2.7 as possible."

"Okay, I try." Grinning, the man turned and left.

Chelsea realized, suddenly, that the man had been tossing a chicken carcass as casually as she would a tennis ball. She swallowed, positive that somewhere east of the Van Nuys Airport she'd fallen down a rabbit hole.

"Exactly what is going on here?" Chelsea said.

"Business." The manager tapped his watch. "And it's your business to be here on time." He buzzed an intercom box and said, "Tell Willie I need him in the office."

He shoved a piece of paper across the desk. "Sign this, Miss Jordan."

She signed it without reading it, a habit Fran had tried to break her of for years.

"Now remember, two more write-ups and you get your walking papers."

Another knock sounded and a hulking African-American man blocked the doorway. He smiled and Chelsea saw a gold front tooth. Tacky. She frowned and looked away. She wished the manager would get to the point about what he wanted her to do. She needed to call her lawyers and she needed to go shopping. This outfit was ready for the discard pile.

"This is Willie, the day-shift supervisor. He'll show you around and get you started."

Willie handed her a blue smock, a rubber apron so heavy she almost dropped it, a blue fabric shower cap, and a white paper hat, a dubious look on his face. "These'll help some, but that's a mighty nice outfit you've got on there."

Chelsea stared in horror at the smock. Her hairdressers wouldn't have dared use such a rag on her.

Smallwood looked to be choking. Chelsea knew, when she looked at his face, that he was enjoying himself far too much.

Once again, at her expense.

She turned to him. "I think you can go now."

"Sure, babe. Remember to call me when you need a ride to the airport."

He waved at the manager, walked past Willie without glancing at him, and disappeared down the hall.

Chelsea put on the smock, but balked at the rest of the gear.

Willie pointed to the identical covering he wore. "Believe me, miss, you're better off wearing it."

The manager tapped his watch again.

Willie glanced at Chelsea's purse. "Maybe we could leave this here in the office today, boss?"

The manager nodded, sat down behind his desk and started to shuffle some papers.

But Chelsea was sure she caught him staring at her, wetting his lips with his tongue. She donned the rubber apron, set the white cap on her head at a jaunty angle, then tossed the shower cap on the manager's desk. With a flounce, she followed Willie out the door.

13 ~

One step through the door took Chelsea from normalcy to hell.

Humid air, ripe with a stomach-churning stench, invaded Chelsea's nostrils and climbed down her throat. Liquid oozed from the cement floor straight into the flat slippers she'd borrowed. God only knew what splattered on her from the sludge collecting in troughs cut into that same disgusting floor.

It took her less than a minute to bolt.

But when she turned, she slipped. Only Willie's rock of an arm kept her from falling face forward in the unspeakable muck.

She saw his lips moving, but couldn't hear him over the chugging and whining of motors and a deafening clanging noise.

As she righted herself from her near-fall, she glanced overhead.

And screamed.

She stood gaping at an overhead assembly line filled with—she swallowed hard—dead, naked pinky chickens, hanging by their feet from metal hooks.

Hundreds of them, thousands, inched along as the line moved, paused, jerked, and moved ahead. With each jerk of the line, water, blood, and flecks of what couldn't possibly be but looked like feces flew through the air.

She grabbed at her hair with her hands. The white cap fell to the floor and wilted. "Oh, my God."

Willie shook his head. He appeared to be laughing. "Follow me," he shouted into her ear. "And watch your step."

She knew stuff she couldn't bear to describe was falling into her hair. Her perfect gorgeous beautiful hair, soiled by refuse from dead chickens. She forced back a sob.

The puddles on the floor had already seeped through the hem of her tangerine silk pants. Cursing Fran and her family and her mother for being related to a sick old man like Ely Van Ness, she kept her eyes fixated on Willie's calves and inched across the slippery floor, farther into hell.

The towering African-American stopped in front of a metal bin upon which chicken bodies dropped plunk-plunk-plunk at a methodical rate from a chute. They dumped haphazardly atop one another, then spread onto the bin where it bowed out. Overhead, the line of hooks clipped by. A Vietnamese woman, her mouth fixed in a grimace of concentration, grabbed the birds as they dumped into the bin and flicked them, leg-first, onto the waiting hooks.

Only the hooks didn't wait very long.

As Chelsea watched in horrified fascination, she saw that scarcely an empty hook passed the woman as she grabbed and flung with a quick snap of her wrist.

Willie tapped her on the shoulder. "Hoa will teach you what to do. This is your station."

"Are you crazy!" Chelsea screamed into the man's ear.

He winced.

"I'm here to do public relations. Tell me what you want me to say. Write me a cue card, for God's sake!"

He pointed to the line, motioned the woman to make room beside her. "Boss man said this is where you go, so this is where you go."

The woman made a jerky bow of her chin. Grabbing a bird, she motioned to Chelsea how to pick it up, then flung it expertly on the moving hooks.

Chelsea gaped.

The woman handed a bird to Chelsea.

The chilly damp flesh smacked against her hand like putty. "Ohmigod!"

She dropped the bird, staring at the luminescent slime left on her hand.

The woman tsk-tsk'd, a sound Chelsea could hear even over the demonic din.

The woman handed her another bird.

Chelsea managed not to drop it, but she couldn't get it onto the hooks to save her life. She hoisted it, then tried to hold the hook with her left hand while she wedged the feet—trying desperately not to think of them as feet—onto the hooks.

Finally, hanging by one foot, the bird moved down the line.

Not bad.

The woman stared at her.

Chelsea stared right back.

Meanwhile, the dead carcasses piled up in the bin.

"Hurry up the line," someone shouted. "The Colonel can't wait all day!"

The woman flicked three chickens onto hooks while Chelsea concentrated on picking up one of the lifeless animals. She closed her eyes and tried to do it without looking.

Without thinking.

Those Am/Am people had better be worse than Hitler's offspring, she swore to herself. Putting me through this humiliation! She started to throw the bird down, to walk out the door.

But she was afraid.

Afraid to let the other side win.

These birds hadn't had a chance.

Obviously they'd been meant to die.

And some people, the people she had to fight against, would just as soon do that to any human beings they disagreed with, disrespected, or despised.

She flung a bird onto the line.

The woman next to her grunted.

But sure as shit when lunchtime came, she was calling her lawyers. There was only so much she could do for any cause.

She was Chelsea Jordan, after all.

The woman kept hooking three or four birds to her every feeble attempt.

Pretty soon she sensed, as much as saw, Willie appear behind her.

"Kinda slow, aren't you?" he shouted.

She turned around. "You do it if you're such hot stuff."

Stepping up, he flipped the birds from the pile to the line even faster than the Vietnamese woman.

Chelsea's mouth dropped open. She swiped her

brow with the sleeve of the atrocious blue smock, not caring that her makeup melted onto the cloth. What did that matter when under the rubber apron her silk tunic stuck to her skin, plastered by the increasing heat and the unbearable humidity of the metal-roofed workroom. What did that matter when by now she smelled almost as bad as the room around her?

Willie smiled, pulled a fresh white paper cap from a pocket, plopped it on her head, then motioned for her to take her place again.

A whistle blew, a sound that pierced even the din. The line shuddered, like a train coming to a fast stop, and screamed to a halt.

"Ten minutes," the woman said, and disappeared.

Chelsea turned around.

Willie was gone, too.

She looked up at the cemetery of chickens. She looked down at her hands, smeared with slime and bits of blood. She shuddered and wiped them on her smock. Seeing the workers file toward a door at the far end of the area, she followed.

She needed a telephone.

Bad.

"I still say the least we can do is help her hang those chickens." Quentin's face was set in that mulish look of his.

With the workers on break, Mia let go of the death grip she'd locked on Quentin's arm to keep him from going to Chelsea's aid. "And I still say she should get through this on her own." From their perch on some sort of supply rack, they'd been watching Chelsea struggle, horrified by their surroundings.

"You and your rules." Quentin looked disgusted.

"We made up this part of her program and we can alter it if we choose."

Mia looked down at the abyss filled with chicken carcasses. "Quentin, I don't think I could have lasted as long as Chelsea has." She paused, marveling at Chelsea's pluck and her own newfound respect for the ditzy actress. Then she caught Quentin's hand. "My concern isn't for the rules, it's for Chelsea. If we help her, she'll never know whether she could have done it on her own."

Mia hoped Quentin didn't point out Chelsea was unlikely to know whether two invisible beings helped her hang chickens. Her reasoning might be a little bit off, but the principle of self-reliance was sound. She eyed Quentin, waiting to see if he'd understand.

The stubborn set to his jaw softened. "You're right, and I'm wrong," he said, gracing her with a smile that warmed her heart. "Let's stay with her at least until after lunch. The least we can do is provide moral support."

Mia wrinkled her nose, but she couldn't disagree.

The break room was hot and stuffy, but blessedly free of those awful machine noises. Voices chattered, some in languages Chelsea couldn't identify. But nothing could help the smell. The stench of blood and guts possessed her nose.

Right inside the room, she paused. The two women closest to her were drinking Cokes. Chelsea licked her lips. She had no money with her. Not even a few quarters to buy relief from the thirst built up in that steam room of a factory.

The women looked up at her, curiosity in their eyes.

But they didn't offer her a drink.

Or say hello.

Or act surprised to see Chelsea Jordan in their midst.

Shit, living in this backwater they probably didn't even know who she was.

But surely Uncle Ely had been proud of her, had told people . . .

She spotted a pay phone across the room and marched around the tables surrounded with workers chatting, smoking and snacking.

Clearly Uncle Ely hadn't harbored any of the fond memories she'd been kicking herself over. The old fart hated her!

Her mother always said Ely had been the black sheep of the Van Ness family since his tenth birthday. Even then he'd refused to attend private school where he belonged in the cradle of culture and privilege. "A renegade, a disgrace to the Van Ness name." Those were her mother's words.

Enamored of the attention he'd paid her, pleased to have been treated as a person rather than a doll, she'd built up image upon image of her great-uncle. As lonely and isolated as she'd been, the fantasies weren't surprising.

But right now they hurt.

Bad.

Chelsea tapped her soggy shoe on the floor and pointed to her diamond-studded watch, a watch worth more than these workers made in one year. The girl talking on the phone flashed a smile at her and kept on yakking.

Her back to the rest of the room, Chelsea considered her plight. She felt people staring at her, gawking rudely. But no one walked over, no one said a word to her. Just as well, she didn't want to speak to any of these people.

The girl laughed.

Chelsea frowned at her.

Again the girl waved a hand and smiled.

"You're hogging the phone," Chelsea said.

The chatter in the room dropped in volume.

The girl kept talking.

A whistle blew.

People moved rapidly from the room.

The girl hung up and walked away.

Chelsea grabbed for the phone and put through a collect call to the lawyers she paid so handsomely.

The operator told her there was no answer, only a message stating the office opened at nine o'clock.

"What the fuck time do you think it is!" Chelsea stared at her watch.

"Time to get back to work," Hoa said, tapping her on the shoulder.

The operator hung up on her.

She followed Hoa back into the bowels of hell.

Two hours later, when the whistle blew for lunch, Chelsea gave herself credit for trying. She'd pretended to be shooting a movie, playing some Norma Rae type. She only stopped the line six or seven times, while the chicken carcasses piled up and the workers jeered at her.

Following the others into the break room, she tried to push ahead to reach the phone.

To her disbelief, the same woman stood there, already talking and laughing.

Chelsea left the room and made her way to the front office.

"I need to use the phone," she said to the receptionist.

The young woman gave her an uneasy smile but said firmly enough, "There's a pay phone in the break room for employees."

"I am not an employee. I am—"

"If you're not an employee, I'll have to ask you to leave. No one without a security pass is allowed in here." The girl pressed a button.

The mousy manager appeared.

He must have been listening.

"This woman is refusing to let me use the telephone." Chelsea spoke in her most civilized voice, the voice she used only when making it a point to be polite.

"Of course she is." The manager huffed and puffed. He also wiped at his mouth. "Employees use the pay phone in the lunchroom. I suggest you go back there and wait your turn, or I'll have to write you up."

Never in her life had she been treated this way!

She drew herself up, looked down her nose at both of them, then turned on her heel, or what was left of it, and marched away. No one here treated her as if she were even human; no one here cared that she had no lunch and that she'd had no breakfast or even dinner the night before.

The bitch was still talking on the phone.

Chelsea took up her station next to the woman. Speaking loudly, she said to the faceless people sitting at the nearest table, "Some people are so inconsiderate. Such phone hogs."

The people shifted and looked at one another.

The woman continued to talk, smiling as she did so. Chelsea could hear her singing into the phone now, wasting even more time.

That was too much.

"Awfully rude, wouldn't you say?" she said to the person sitting at the end of the table.

The woman glared at her.

Another woman, across the table, said, "I'll tell you who the rude one is." She stood up, snapped her black metal lunch pail shut, and said, "You, that's who." She stalked away.

"My, my." Chelsea thought the woman's performance worthy of amateur theater. "Bravo." She clapped her hands together and turned to glare again at the woman on the phone.

Hoa walked over from the far end of the room. Pausing briefly, she said so only Chelsea could hear, "That woman's little boy is in the hospital. He has cancer. She calls him every break."

Hoa moved away, back to the end of the room.

Chelsea looked down at her shoes. She wanted to go through the floor. Everyone at the table watched her, none of their expressions friendly.

She shrugged and walked toward the door marked "Women." She'd die before she let these people see just how embarrassed she was by her behavior.

She slipped into one of the two stalls, locked herself in, and leaned her forehead against the cool metal of the door, unmindful of the guaranteed unsanitary state of the door. She'd scarcely had time for her tears of humiliation to form when someone rattled the door.

"Hey city girl. We got a message for you, bitch."

Chelsea pressed against the door, afraid to step back toward the toilet, frozen by the hostile voices.

"See, we gets paid bonuses for speed. But that means we all gotta be fast. And you, city girl, you're fucking slow. You get yo ass back out there—"

Shrill cries interrupted the tirade.

"Oh my Lord, a ghost! Run, girl! Eeek! Help!" Footsteps pounded away from the stall, racing for the door, which banged open then shut, cutting off the sound of the women's shrieks.

Doubly afraid, Chelsea clutched her smock. But whatever was out there had driven away her tormentors. Eyes screwed almost shut, fearful of what new nightmare awaited her, she peeked through a slit in the stall door.

But the only thing she saw amiss was a white smock lying in a heap on the concrete floor.

Dimly, she heard the whistle blow. She held her head and wished herself a million miles away. But by God, she wouldn't run away scared the way those pseudo-bullies had. How juvenile, waiting until she was in the john to threaten her. Squaring her shoulders, she opened the door and strode back to work.

She'd done her own stunts before. She might be out of shape, but she could be as tough as the next bitch.

Following Chelsea back to the processing line, Mia pictured again the look on those bullies' faces when she played Casper with that white smock. Quentin was right; being invisible could be fun.

That afternoon, Chelsea stopped the line only three times. Willie came by and told her he had to write her up for being too slow. She shrugged and threw another bird onto the line of hooks. Only three times—by her reckoning, that spelled progress.

"Three times write up and you're fired," Hoa said into her ear.

She only shrugged again. If it came down to that, her lawyers would handle it. That's what lawyers were for. And those sons of bitches had better answer their telephone when she called them after work.

Chelsea kept her head down, refusing to acknowledge the other workers or the macabre scenes playing around her. The sheer numbers of the dead birds overwhelmed her ability to imagine them as living creatures, strutting about in a barnyard the way that chicken had done only last night at Ely's house. How could they kill so many so fast? They just kept coming, dropping into the bin from the chute, chicken after chicken after chicken.

It wasn't real, she argued. She was playing a role, enduring torture as a means to an end. Unbidden, the memory of the days when she'd filmed that horrid porn flick flitted through her mind. Her hands almost numb from the constant grabbing and hoisting, she tried to work her mind into the same state.

That's how she'd survived the indignities of that movie. That's how she would survive this day. How she'd ignore her hunger.

They kept coming, carcass after carcass after carcass. Focused only on the animal flesh and the task of getting each one onto the hooks, Chelsea lost count of the time.

Hoa touched her arm gently. "That was the whistle. End of day."

"What?" Chelsea shook her head. She actually felt disoriented. No more chickens lay in the bin in front of her.

"You got faster," Hoa said, and walked out the door.

Oddly enough, it was Mia who decided not to worry. Once Ely told them Chelsea had swallowed the bait and arrived in Hill Springs, Quentin immediately began scheming on ways to help the process along. He'd insisted they accompany her to the poultry plant, only agreeing to leave after lunch when it seemed evident Chelsea didn't plan to bolt.

Mia spent the rest of the afternoon lazing in the hammock strung between two leafy trees in Luke Miller's back yard, thankful she wasn't the one at work at All Right Foods. Quentin kept jogging down the lane to Ely's house, checking for signs of Chelsea, then jogging back only to plop down on the grass beside her and fret over his lack of knowledge.

She could see him now, rounding the corner of the house, heading in her direction in an easy lope. His gait was perfectly fluid, every movement orchestrated smoothly. While Quentin ran, his body exhibited none of the jerkiness she associated with his constant flutter of activity. He jogged, she thought suddenly, the way a good dancer danced—muscle and fiber and energy synthesized.

Funny she'd never noticed that before. He'd run track his first year in college, before she'd met him. But he gave it up, choosing to devote his time to his first and only love, movie-making.

"Hey," he called and flopped down by her side, only to break into sit-ups. Between crunches, he said, "She's not back yet."

Mia yawned. Of course she wanted Chelsea to succeed. But she thought Quentin showed a little too

much interest in the whereabouts of the very blonde
and very seductive Chelsea Jordan, a woman who
epitomized his type.

Except he usually went for the starving starlets
and Chelsea's fortune could probably buy a studio.

Mia sat up in the hammock. "Next time you jog
down to check on her, I'll go with you."

Quentin paused in mid sit-up, his head held above
his shoulders, his stomach tucked into a tight flat
ball. He held his position and studied her for a long
moment. "Sure, she ought to be back from work by
then."

"We're not allowed to interact with her. How
many times do I have to remind you of that rule?"
Mia realized she was annoyed. The pleasure of the
sylvan afternoon had been shattered by visions of
Quentin falling for Chelsea.

"Hullo," said a cheerful young voice.

Mia jumped. Quentin scrambled to his feet. They
both turned around.

A small boy, maybe five or six, stood tossing a
baseball from hand to hand. He wore an oversized
baseball jersey with sleeves that hung to just above
his bony wrists. The shirt hung to his knees. Over a
head of curly dark hair, he sported a White Sox cap.

"Hi there," Mia said, her logical mind wondering
whether this adorable urchin was caught in the same
afterlife as they, or whether, like the animals and
Ely, he could see them.

"I saw you yesterday," he said, continuing to
throw the ball, "talking to my Uncle Ely. But I ran
out of time and my dad made me leave for school."

"So Ely's your uncle?" Quentin asked, squatting
and rendering himself level with the boy.

"Sort of. My dad said you weren't really there, but

I knew better. He doesn't understand make-believe."

That answered Mia's question. "My name's Mia and this is Quentin. What's yours?"

"Timmy."

"Is Mr. Miller your daddy?"

He nodded. "He's a preacher." He threw the ball high into the air, staggered around, then caught it as it dropped. "But he used to be a baseball player."

"And is that what you're going to be when you grow up?" Quentin asked.

Timmy scowled. "Grownups always ask that dumb question. How do I know what I'm going to be? How do I even know if I'll grow up?"

"Wow." Mia sat back in the hammock. Something about the intensity in the little boy's eyes tugged at her heart. Then she pieced together the tombstone in the churchyard with that look of loss. "Your mommy isn't with you anymore, is she?"

The boy shook his head, then he shrugged. "You look like her," he said in a small voice.

She started to drop from the hammock, intending to smother him in a hug, but she caught herself. He had a toughness about him that belied his tender age. Perhaps action would be better than sympathetic noises. "Did she play ball with you, Timmy?"

His look of scorn was universally male. "Are you kidding?"

Quentin grinned over at Mia and took up the slack. "But your dad does, doesn't he?"

"If he ever has time." Timmy scuffed a running shoe in the grass, then looked at Quentin with hope in his eyes.

Quentin tugged on his Yankees cap. "Want to see how your Sox do against my Yanks?"

The little boy grinned. "Let me get my glove." He raced toward the house, pausing to turn and call, "I'll get you one, too."

"What a sweetheart," Mia said.

Quentin nodded, but something about the way Mia said the words bothered him, especially when he remembered her raving over the preacher after her covert trip to the dude's church. "So you look like his mother?"

"That's odd, isn't it?" Mia flipped over onto her stomach, her small firm derriere displayed deliciously in the cotton dress.

Quentin's mouth watered. He'd been so close the other day in the hayfield. Ever since, she'd treated him like he'd been sprayed with repellent. Her asking to jog down the lane with him had surprised him, but she probably only asked so she could keep an eye on their chances.

She probably couldn't wait to get back to life, so she could visit this paragon of a preacher in person.

14 ~

Too worn out to argue with the driver over the fare, Chelsea eased her body out of Hill Springs' only cab and slammed the door.

"Cretin!" she shouted after him as he spun around, shooting gravel like shrapnel. He'd demanded twenty-five dollars to drive her home from that chicken hellhole, informing her with his nose in the air that as a rule he didn't let chicken plant workers in his cab.

"Oooh." She trembled all over, remembering the insult. He didn't deserve five dollars, let alone twenty-five of her $125 allotment. But at least she'd gotten home.

Home.

Lifting her eyes toward Ely's tiny house, she almost smiled at herself. Only yesterday the house had disgusted her. Now it looked like refuge.

She tiptoed on bare feet over the grass leading to the porch. She'd thrown Smallwood's shoes out the window of the cab. During the ride, she'd hacked her pants off with her fingernail scissors, desperate to keep the soiled silk from touching her body. Now the

211

expensive outfit fluttered in tatters around her calves.

Blood. Bits of chicken flesh. Her clothes reeked of that horrid musty smell which she knew had to be from the birds and the death. Unable to fathom what she'd endured that day, she sank to the steps.

"Yap! Yip!"

"Toy-Toy!" She crawled to the door and opened it. Her poodle dashed out, calling to her.

"My poor wuddle one, left all awone." Seeking comfort for herself, she gathered him to her breast and lay back on the hard surface of the porch.

He sniffed and wiggled and sniffed some more. Then without even giving her a nose kiss, he struggled and jumped from her arms.

"Toy-Toy!"

The poodle paused at the top porch step, cast her a look, then scampered down the steps and into the grass. Barking, he rolled on his back and waved his legs in the air.

She roused herself and moved off the porch. She had to save him from the dangers of the yard. But her precious one danced from her grasp and ran as fast as he could around the side of the house.

It was too much.

A day of rejection.

The first tear slid down her cheek. She tried to call it back with a sniff and failed. Her shoulders drooping, she made her way one heavy-footed step at a time back to the porch. There she leaned against the rail and studied her hands, battling the urge to cry.

Her nails looked like they'd been soaked in lye and water for a week. Polish practically gone, thumbnail split at the tip, one pinky nail hanging by the remnants of the adhesive.

A manicure. A massage first—no, a perfumed bath, then a massage and facial. The works.

Way back when, in another life, she'd read the script for *Steel Magnolias*. That hick town had a beauty parlor; surely so would Hill Springs.

She'd passed on that film, informing Fran haughtily that she wouldn't touch a "pink-collar" flick. But, within her secret heart she'd known the truth— she feared competing with so many talented women head to head.

If they could only see her now . . .

Something glittered through the moisture in her eyes. She cleared her vision and spotted one of her shoes.

Bending close to the bush beside the step to retrieve it, she thought she heard a gasp.

She looked up and around. Saw no one. Her imagination was working overtime. Probably a result of being alone in the middle of nowhere.

Nowhere. For the first time, she noticed the vibrant blueness of the sky. Beyond the lane, horses grazed in a pasture dotted here and there by a sheltering tree. Off to her left, she could see the other house on the lane, the pretty blue one that echoed the shade of the sky. To her right, only grassy fields, lined with tall, wavy flowers topped with lacy heads of white.

A bird swooped low across the front grass, spreading gray and white wings and hopping about in the grass. Another joined it, then quickly the two took flight, calling out.

After the noise and the smells of the chicken plant, the peace and freshness of the yard and fields helped steady her. She knew she had to get up, take a shower, and figure out a way back into town. She

probably should have made the cabbie wait while
she called her lawyers from town, but she wanted rid
of him as much as he wanted her out of his car.

She struggled to her feet. Her legs hurt, her arms
trembled, her wrists ached.

But she hadn't gotten fired. Dammit, that meant
something. She couldn't wait to shake the red dust of
Hill Springs off her feet, but she'd leave on her
terms, not because some half-wit plant manager
slapped her wrist three times.

Hobbling like a woman twice her age, but holding
her head high, Chelsea trudged into the house, too
exhausted to fret over Toy-Toy. He'd come in when
hunger struck.

"Wow," Quentin murmured as Chelsea disappeared into Ely's house.

"She's so pretty," Timmy said. "Like a princess."

Standing behind Timmy, Mia rolled her eyes.
Even after being run through the wringer, Chelsea
worked her magic. How did the woman do it? She
started to say she thought she looked like chicken
shit, but bit her tongue at the unkind words. She'd
seen for herself the hell Chelsea had endured that
day. Mia had never been a vindictive person, and
stuck here between life and death certainly seemed
no place to start picking up bad habits. "She looked
pretty worn out."

"I should think so!" Quentin stretched and
pushed his cap back on his head. As a precaution
they'd hidden in a clump of bushes nearby the
house, and even then the noise Timmy made when
Chelsea picked up a shoe had almost given him
away. "I can't even imagine how she toughed it out
today. What a woman."

"There were plenty of other women in that plant."

Mia heard the primness in her own voice, but couldn't help herself. She did admire Chelsea for not throwing in the towel, but Quentin's attentiveness rankled her. "It's a job, you know."

Quentin glared at her. The look hurt.

"My daddy says the workers aren't treated very well," Timmy said, starting once again to toss his ball.

"Is that right?" Quentin squatted down beside the boy. "What else does he say about the chicken plant?"

"There was this man, and he came to see my daddy and his hand was hurt"— Timmy stopped his ball tossing and motioned to his wrist —"he said he just couldn't go on any more."

"And what did your daddy say?" Quentin's voice was low and soft and it melted through to Mia's heart as she watched him speak with Timmy, man to man.

"He prayed with him."

"Oh."

Well, that stumped Quentin. Dear, dear agnostic Quentin.

"What did he pray for?"

Timmy tossed the ball in the air and shrugged his skinny shoulders. "Just prayed, I guess."

"Maybe he prayed for strength," Mia said.

Quentin glanced up at her, a wistful smile on his face. "That must be nice," he said, and stood.

"You wanna go with me to the chicken coop?" Timmy tucked the ball in his glove. "It's my job to feed Uncle Ely's chickens."

"You come here by yourself?" Mia asked.

He looked at her like she'd failed some basic I.Q. test. "I told you so already."

"Your daddy really doesn't worry about you here alone?"

"We're only the next house." Timmy held out a hand to Quentin. "Let's go, I'll show you my favorite. It's the rooster."

Male bonding in progress, the two of them moved off around the small house. Left behind, Mia tiptoed to a side window and peered inside. She'd gotten to be quite the peeping Thomasina.

Straining on tiptoe, she could see a dining table cluttered with junk. That looked pretty much as it had when she and Quentin had slurped down those quarts of carrot juice. Moving slowly, she edged around the house and checked the few other rooms. She figured the window with clouded glass must be the bathroom, a guess confirmed by the sound of running water.

Well, if she'd spent the day with a bunch of dead chickens, she'd be in the shower, too. Probably wouldn't come out for hours.

She'd spotted no luggage. Did Chelsea intend to stay?

Ely, bless his heart, had rewritten his will to Quentin's pie-in-the-sky specs. Work in the chicken plant, live in Ely's house, and per Mia's request, attend four Sundays at Hill Springs Community Church. Mia's real hope in Chelsea's redemption lay with Luke Miller. Redeeming Chelsea without throwing a man into the formula just seemed so improbable.

The water stopped. Mia raced back to the front of the house. She heard some squawking, then Quentin and Timmy rounded the corner of the house, a tiny poodle dogging their heels.

"What is that?" Mia said, pointing to the minuscule mutt sporting purple bows on his floppy ears.

"Chelsea's dog," Quentin said, bending to scoop up the animal.

It licked Quentin's chin with a tiny pink tongue. Quentin made a face but stood still for the treatment.

"How do you know it's Chelsea's?" Mia tapped her foot in the grass.

"She usually has the dog with her in her PR shots."

"And you make a habit of studying those?"

Quentin didn't quite meet her eyes. "I guess I haven't mentioned it, but I've been thinking of signing Chelsea on to our next project." He set the poodle down.

"For *Kriss-Kross?*"

He nodded, still not daring to look her in the face.

"Oh my God." Mia walked off a few feet. Her temper had raced from zero to boiling point.

"Are you two arguing?" Timmy asked in a fascinated-sounding voice.

Quentin knelt next to him. "What makes you ask that?"

"You sound a lot like my mom and dad." He kicked the grass again. "I mean, like they used to sound."

"Before your mommy went away?" Quentin asked in a low voice.

"Before she went to heaven." Timmy sighed and tucked his glove and ball under his armpit. "I think he's sorry now."

Mia dropped to the grass beside him, setting aside her desire to argue over *Kriss-Kross* with Quentin for her instinctive need to comfort Timmy. "I'm sure he misses your mommy," she said. "But all grownups argue, and afterwards, when they're alone, they make up."

"Always?" He stubbed his toe in the grass.

Mia nodded. "Mommys and Daddys who love one another always kiss and make up."

"Kiss! Yech!"

Mia reached out to offer Timmy a hug. He backed away a step, plucked his ball and glove from their storage beneath his arm, and tossed the ball skyward.

She dropped her arm, hoping she'd helped. Looking over at Quentin, she whispered, "*Kriss-Kross?* You'd offer that to Chelsea Jordan without consulting me?"

He bristled. He stubbed both his running shoes into the grass and tugged at his cap. "You're my producer. I would've discussed it first."

"Why is that woman right for our film?"

Quentin opened his arms, beseeching the heavens. Mia wanted to gag. *Kriss-Kross* was a script she and Quentin had written in college. They'd crafted the Hitchcock takeoff, her one foray into the creative side of the business, in the long-ago days before fame had touched Quentin with its golden scepter.

"Tell me," she said, her chin quivering. "If you can."

"It's the vulnerability," he said, flopping down to the ground. The poodle finally abandoned him, and raced toward the porch. Timmy dashed after it.

"Name one thing that's vulnerable about Chelsea I'll-Give-You-a-Blow-Job-Anytime Jordan."

Quentin rolled away from her. "Do you hear the hostility in your voice?"

"Yes, I do. Dammit! I put it there!" Mia wanted to cry. She wanted to shout. She hated Chelsea, hated any woman who knew how to wrap the man she wanted around her finger. "If you ask Chelsea to do that picture, we're finished."

Quentin said nothing. He lay on his back, watching the sky.

Mia waited, shaking inside. How could he want that woman in their movie?

Finally, he sat up. Leaning over, he took her hand in his. In the mildest of voices, he said, "I'm sorry if I upset you. Don't you think we ought to get back to life before we get into a major argument about the future?"

"Oh." Mia savored the contact, her susceptibility to Quentin's touch chasing off her wounded feelings. Still, she had to take a stand. She snatched her hand away and said, "If we get back to life where we belong, consider this issue up for further discussion."

"Toy-Toy, come!" Chelsea Jordan appeared on the front porch of the country cottage, attired in men's sweat pants and T-shirt. She looked gorgeous. Mia stifled a sigh of envy.

The little dog headed from around the house, chased by Timmy, and scampered up the steps, the child in pursuit.

Mia started to dart out to catch Timmy, then caught herself.

"Who are you?" she heard Chelsea ask.

"Timmy." The little boy stared at her wide-eyed. "Who are *you?*"

"My name's Chelsea." She held out a hand and they shook rather formally.

Timmy looked down at the ground. "You've got a nice dog," he said.

"Oh, thank you." Chelsea bent and collected the

dog. "He's my favorite wuddle poodle-woodle." She kissed his topknot and mussed his ears.

The dog squirmed and Timmy made a face.

"What's wrong?" Chelsea asked.

"That's a funny way to talk to a dog."

"Why?" She clutched the squirming poodle closer.

"My Uncle Ely has a dog and he doesn't talk to him that way."

"Oh?" Chelsea reared back from the boy, a puzzled look crossing her face. "How does this uncle of yours talk to his dog?"

"Come. Fetch. Round 'em up." Timmy started giggling.

"What's so funny?"

He pointed toward the poodle. "Can you see your dog rounding up cows?"

"Of course not." Chelsea kissed the poodle's nose. "He's not that kind of dog."

"But Uncle Ely's dog is." Timmy tossed his ball upward and caught it with a resounding *thunk* in the pocket of the glove.

"And what kind of dog does . . . your uncle have?"

"A border collie." Timmy danced about. "Most satisfactory. Smart."

Chelsea looked down at her tiny dog. "Doesn't mean he's any better than Toy-Toy."

"Sure." Timmy threw the ball up and caught it. "Wanna play ball?"

Mia drew in a sharp breath. Timmy hadn't asked *her.*

"Sometimes," Quentin said, "you shouldn't ask people what they think. Sometimes they up and tell you."

"And what is that supposed to mean?"

Quentin shrugged. "Most men want to be wanted." Then he sauntered off, moving toward Chelsea and Timmy.

Mia had barely registered her reaction when she heard Timmy say, "Hi, Quent."

"Hey," he said.

"Who are you talking to?" Chelsea asked.

"One of my friends," Timmy said. "You got any gum?"

"No." She shook her head. "Do you have imaginary playmates?"

Timmy nodded and checked her reaction with a quick tilt of his head.

"Oh, I always did, too!" Chelsea knelt down next to the boy. "Mine were called Sniggle and Snaggle and nobody but me could see them."

He smiled, then backed away and threw the ball toward her. She stuck her hands out.

And actually caught the ball.

She stared at it, looking amazed that she'd managed to snag it.

"Throw it back," Timmy said.

She scooped the ball underhand and it lost steam before making it halfway to the boy. Mia snorted. She'd played lot ball for years in the tough environs of East Los Angeles. Chelsea Jordan had probably never touched a baseball before in her pampered life.

Timmy ran and collected the ball. "That was pretty good," he said, and lobbed the ball back to Chelsea.

She caught it, then walked toward him, a frown worrying her forehead.

"Where do you live?" she asked.

"Down the road."

"Don't you think you ought to be getting home? I mean, won't your parents be worried about you?"

"Nah. My dad's busy and my mommy's in heaven."

"Heaven . . ." Chelsea murmured the word and gave the child a tender look. "Well, I have to go into town, so I can't play anymore," she said, and handed the ball back to him.

"Oh."

Oh, that was all he said, and Mia knew from that small voice and that brief reaction that Timmy was a kid who spent a lot of time by himself. Poor little tyke.

"Okay," Timmy finally said. "I'll see you tomorrow. Uncle Ely pays me to come over and feed his animals."

Chelsea nodded. Then, suddenly, she beckoned him over. "I thought the Uncle Ely who lived in this house died," she said.

"I gotta go." Looking troubled, he turned and dashed away, past Mia and Quentin and the poodle, down the road to his house.

Chelsea stared after him, then collected the dog, giving him a kiss on the nose. "Wuddle one, you're going to have to stay here. You know I'd take you with me, if only I didn't have to drive." She sighed and shoved the protesting dog into the house, then walked toward Ely's pickup truck.

"Poor little Timmy," Mia said. "It must be very confusing, knowing Ely's alive and hearing that he's dead."

"So he ran home to check on him."

The truck kicked to life and immediately bucked.

"Whoa," Quentin said. "Get her in gear, girl."

Mia frowned. "If she gets herself killed trying to drive that truck, I wonder what happens to us?"

"Wow, that doesn't sound like you. How can you be so selfish?" As the truck lurched forward, then stalled, Quentin said, "She doesn't know how to drive a stick."

"That's what happens when you're chauffeured everywhere."

"You know, Mia my dear, you're not at your best when you show your claws."

With that, Quentin walked toward the truck, a look of purpose on his face.

"What are you doing? You know we're not allowed to intervene directly."

"Hey, all the old guy said was we couldn't speak to the target." Quentin grinned and climbed into the truck through the open passenger window.

Mia ran after him. "You're crazy! Why are you doing this? You'll get us both—"

"—killed?"

Chelsea fiddled with the gearshift and the truck bucked.

Quentin blew Mia a kiss as the truck slowly moved forward.

"Hey, it's working!" Chelsea gripped the wheel and peered out the windshield.

What a ditz! Mia glowered at the cloud of dust that mushroomed from the truck as it moved down the lane. Yeah, ditz or no ditz, Chelsea Jordan fit Quentin's recipe for the perfect female to a T. And there they went, locked in that truck, snug as two bugs in a rug.

15 〜

Chelsea grasped the steering wheel and tried to visualize Aldo explaining to her the basics of driving a stick shift.

"You press the pedal in slowly, as a man makes love, as you shift the stick." Being Aldo, he'd leered at her, in case she'd missed his stupid innuendo. Seventeen, alone in Europe, and in shock at the movie she'd just wrapped, she gave him a smile back, thinking Aldo had served his purpose and it was just about time to ditch the jerk.

He must have taught her something, because the truck moved forward. Concentrating, she read the numbers on the knob and shoved the stick, none too gently.

And just like that, she was off.

Quentin tucked his body into the floorboard of the passenger side of the cab and snaked one hand over to the clutch pedal, resting the other on the gearshift.

The engine whined and strained, but Chelsea made no move toward the stick shift. Unable to bear an engine laboring in first gear, Quentin took matters into his own hands and slipped the truck into second. Chelsea seemed content to trundle along at that pace, seemingly unmindful of the other vehicles that whizzed by them once they turned onto the highway.

To Quentin, the fast-car aficionado, the ride was sheer torment.

To Quentin, the red-blooded male, the journey was a revelation.

He looked up the length of Chelsea's Grablesque legs, to the tiny waist and the breasts that did things to a Hanes T-shirt that should have been unlawful if not illegal.

He studied the pouty lips, the china-doll face, the notorious green gaze.

And felt nothing.

His heart and mind were filled with the forlorn, betrayed look on Mia's sweet face as he'd leapt into the truck. Dear Mia, whom he loved.

Now she'd be mad as hell at him when he got back. She'd probably give him the cold shoulder for the rest of the time they were in Purgatory. Not to mention once they made it back to life.

Tinseltown Times had called him America's newest creative genius. Some genius—he couldn't even come up with a way to win Mia's love.

Sitting tall behind the wheel, Chelsea chugged along in the truck. Only one or two cars honked as they sped by her on the highway. Pleased with her newfound skill, she drove down Main Street. Not seeing a pay phone, she rolled on through. At the light, she turned right, on a whim. Within three blocks she came to a large parking lot dotted with cars and a building with a sign that read "Safeway."

By the door, she spotted two telephone booths.

Gliding to a crawl, she swung the truck pretty much in line with the other parked cars. Looking around, her foot slipped from the pedal and the pickup bucked forward. She turned the key off.

She hopped from the truck, her spirits partially restored. She headed straight to the phone, requested the collect call, and glanced around. A fat woman in a shapeless cotton dress pushed a grocery cart overflowing with bags out the door. Chelsea made a face. That woman should take a good long look at herself. Chelsea might be horribly out of physical conditioning, but she'd never let herself go like that.

She tapped on the receiver, impatient to speak with a lawyer. Which one she didn't care. Any one of the overpaid yups and dinks should be able to get her out of this fix. If they couldn't, well, the first thing she'd do back in L.A. was fire the lot of them.

"Your call was refused," the operator said in a tinny voice.

"Excuse me?"

"Call refused. Would you like to place another one?"

"Would you like to fuck yourself?" Chelsea screamed into the phone. A woman with two small children made a horrified face and dashed past, dragging a child by each hand.

"I do not have to take this abuse," the operator said. The line went dead.

Chelsea hammered on the connection button. "Hello. Hello. Get back here and put this call through again."

When no one did as she demanded, she hung up

the phone and started to walk away. To her dismay, several people stood about, staring at her.

"What's the matter? You never see anybody talk on the phone before?" But she only muttered the words. Then she turned her back and reached for the receiver again.

This time the call she made went through.

"Fran Rosen," came the familiar clipped voice.

"It's me, Chelsea."

"Yes, I know, that's why I accepted the charges."

"Yeah, right." Chelsea clung to the phone and swallowed hard. "I'm coming home."

"Oh?"

"Tomorrow. Send the jet for me."

"I don't think so."

"You don't *think* so? If I may remind you—"

"Chelsea, cut the crap, okay?" Then Fran's voice softened. "I'm sure you're going through hell, but I've been doing some research on that Am/Am group and if you give up and let those bastards have ten million dollars, I will quit. You won't have to fire me."

Fran smacked her lips and Chelsea was surprised to realize she welcomed the familiar irritating sound. "If you knew what I had to endure today, you wouldn't ask me to go back in that place."

"People do it everyday."

"But not me!" Chelsea wailed and dug her fingers into the side of the scarred plastic that surrounded the pay phone.

"Find the strength."

"Hah!" Chelsea closed her eyes. The stench of the day still lingered in her nostrils, despite the long hot shower. "Get my lawyers to break the will."

"You'll have to ask them that yourself."

"I can't get through."

"Tch. Tch."

A suspicion bubbled up in Chelsea's mind. No, surely Fran wouldn't. "Did you tell them not to take my calls?"

Silence answered her.

A silence that condemned Fran.

"You're fired." Chelsea slammed the phone down, breaking the connection with her only friend. Leaning against the side of the phone stall, she gave in to feeling sorry for herself.

The sound of a barking dog finally broke through her miserable reverie. He sounded very close and very dangerous.

Chelsea feared any dog larger than Toy-Toy. She peeked around and saw a black and white dog with a brushy tail pawing the air and barking at nothing.

Crazy dog. No one was even nearby. What could he possibly be barking at?

She shrugged and entered the store. Poor wuddle Toy-Toy needed some decent food. And though she was feeling too irate, too abandoned, and too upset to be hungry, she had to eat something, what it was, though, she didn't care.

As long as it wasn't chicken.

When Chelsea headed to the phone, Quentin climbed out of the truck and stretched the kinks out of his body. While Chelsea made her call, he popped into the grocery to check the magazines for any mention of *DinoDaddy*.

Before he knew it, Chelsea was at the checkout. He dropped the magazine and left the store. He wanted to be ready to go before Chelsea tried to naviagate her way out of the parking lot.

He'd just put one hand on the door of the truck when he heard a low growl behind him.

"Aarf!"

Quentin looked around.

Ely's border collie met his gaze straight-on, fastening those remarkable yellow eyes on Quentin as if to examine what went on in his head.

"Nice doggie," Quentin said, inching open the passenger door.

The dog lunged at him, barking furiously. His attack drove Quentin away from the truck.

"Goddamn dog," Quentin said, doing a little growling himself.

The dog ran back and forth, back and forth, rounding Quentin like a sheep or cow.

"Would you look at that dog?" Quentin heard a man in overalls say before he scratched his head, spat something brown and vile on the ground, and climbed into his own pickup. "Looks like Ely Van Ness's hound. Thing musta gone crazy after old Ely died."

A gray-haired woman leaned out of the next car. "Yup, that's what happens sometimes. Reckon we oughter shoot him?"

The man spat again and shook his head. "Nah. That preacher'll take care of the dog."

The woman nodded and drove off.

From a few feet away, Quentin waved his hands, knowing even as he did so the pointlessness of the gesture.

"Macduff!" A man's voice, stern yet calm, called from nearby.

The dog quit barking.

Quentin spotted Chelsea climbing into the pickup. He had to get there before she pulled out—or clobbered someone lurching into gear. By the way she'd studied that gearshift knob, Quentin knew she'd never find reverse.

A tall man in worn blue jeans and work shirt, the one who'd called the dog, approached the truck parked behind Chelsea. He called again to the dog and the collie whimpered, looking back and forth from Quentin, to the man.

"Go on, scat," Quentin said. "You're ruining my life. Or what's left of it."

The dog whined.

"What is it, boy?" The man whistled a brief note of command, then opened the door of his truck.

Just in time to get slammed by Chelsea in a great grinding of metal against metal.

She had found reverse, all right. Quentin put his head in his hands and groaned.

Chelsea's head bounced back and forth like a yo-yo. She tried to guide the truck away from the one behind her and succeeded in ramming into it again.

Something snapped within her. First the lawyers refusing her call, then Fran chiding her. And in the store, the clerk had laughed at her when she'd asked for the chilled avocado burger she normally fed Toy-Toy for a bedtime snack. Laughed, and called the request over to the next checkout girl, who'd laughed along with her.

Chelsea flung open the door and stormed from the truck. How dare this hick park his truck so close to hers. If he hadn't stopped so near, this accident never would have happened.

Rounding the corner of her truck, she saw the door of the other cab was already open.

"You lughead," she cried, "can't you watch where you're going? Most people know how to park a truck and now look what the hell you've done to mine. And it isn't even my truck!"

Stopping for a breath, she glanced at the other driver. Scuffed cowboy boots, raggedy jeans showing lots of wear, a blue denim shirt washed soft and touchable . . . what was wrong with her? This man had rammed her truck.

"I'm surprised they give you people licenses." Chelsea looked up to the man's face, expecting to find yet another man either leering or laughing at her. It wouldn't have surprised her if the guy's cheek stuck out with a wad of chewing tobacco. Hicks! All alike.

"Don't you have anything to say for yourself?" she added crossly, before looking directly at the man. She'd kept her head down, wanting to avoid any chance of recognition. All those people gawking at her on the phone, the clerks laughing at her, it was all too much. If this geek happened to know her identity, and sold the story—she shuddered in disgust at the prospect.

When he said nothing, she looked up.

And had to smother a gasp.

He watched her with a curious glint in his eyes, but not the kind of look men usually gave her. He seemed to be adding up the bits and parts, assessing what he heard and saw. And not judging.

Not yet anyway.

"What's the matter with you? Cat got your tongue?"

He didn't even nod, just took off his cowboy hat.

She kicked the front tire of his truck. "You're lucky I wasn't hurt."

He nodded at that, just a brief movement of his head.

He had blue eyes, bluer even than Paul Newman's, and sleek brown hair that glinted in the sunlight like polished mahogany and curled a little as it reached the top of the shirt collar.

Not wanting to acknowledge he was more handsome than any man she'd ever met, she gave a little stamp of her foot. Handsome! The guy was a cowboy.

And she was a city girl, stuck here through no fault of her own. "I've got to go," she said, with a little sniff. "Isn't there anything you'd like to say?" Like an apology, she added to herself.

He inclined his head, settled his hat back on his head, and called to the black and white dog that had started barking and prancing around again. "Well, ma'am," he said in a low voice, absent of any particular accent, "if I were you, I'd learn how to drive that truck."

"Oh!" She flounced away, and flung over her shoulder, "I know perfectly well how to drive, thank you!"

Holding her breath, she gripped the wheel, determined to show that cowpoke she could handle any old truck. She shifted and moved forward, triumphant.

"Take that, you cowboy," she said, pulling out of the lot in front of a station wagon that honked and veered into the other lane.

Back at his post on the floorboard, Quentin screwed his eyes shut and clung to the clutch pedal for dear life.

Of course Luke knew who she was.

He'd seen her picture at Ely's; he'd seen several of her movies. The guys in Birmingham during his

brief stint in the minor leagues had drooled over her
and screened *FellatioNeighborhood* at stag parties.

Even if he hadn't known her identity, he could
have pegged her as someone from out of town. She
swore like a sailor, swaggered like a bantam rooster,
and—

Luke caught his thoughts. He knew how he'd been
about to finish that sentence. And looked at him
with eyes that any man would kill to watch soften
and glow and darken at his approach.

Strike that last image. The woman ignored her
great-uncle, didn't bother to show up for his supposed funeral, and couldn't go five minutes without
needing to wash her mouth out with soap.

He backed toward the door of his truck, happy
Macduff's barks had tamped down to an occasional
woof. What had gotten into the superbly trained dog
he couldn't fathom.

The dog jumped in the truck and Luke reached
over and fastened Macduff's collar to the safety
harness. Even though he'd grown up in this corner of
Arkansas, he'd never become inured to the number
of dead animals that littered the roadsides. So many
people didn't seem to care about the well-being of
their animals.

After settling into his truck seat, he fastened his
own seatbelt, a habit he'd never bothered with until
after Jenny's death.

If only . . .

If only . . .

Whew. Luke experienced a moment of disorienta-
tion as the image of Chelsea Jordan, petite and
blonde and angrily beautiful crossed with that of
sweet, innocent Jenny. He really shouldn't have

skipped lunch. His mind definitely played tricks on him.

As he headed out of town toward home, he mulled over the woman his friend Ely Van Ness bothered so much about. Why hide out? Why go through these machinations for a woman who'd probably never say thanks? Ely had always been a most sensible man. A trifle unusual by Hill Springs' standards, to be sure, but sensible. The story of how he'd met his wife Rebecca, wooed and eventually won the Hill Springs native, then renounced his wealthy but disapproving family was legend in Hill Springs.

Ely also had a record of picking more than one long-shot winner, whether it be the horses in Hot Springs or the stock market. But given the evidence thus far, aside from giving a man a testosterone rush, Chelsea Jordan didn't appear to be worth the effort.

Chelsea couldn't concentrate on the shoes she needed to buy. At Wal-Mart, she closed her eyes to the ignominy of the cheap goods they carried and plunked down thirty-nine dollars on a pair of leather athletic shoes that came up to the ankle.

While she shopped, she kept thinking of the parking lot hick. What blue eyes! But more than that, the way he'd stood there, so quiet. Like he'd been taking her measure. She hadn't noticed his hands, didn't know whether he wore a ring or not.

Not that it mattered. Chelsea wondered at herself for even giving that a second thought. The type of man who chased her didn't bother over a detail like a wedding vow. Somehow, she thought this man might be different.

She drove home slowly, snacking on the animal

crackers she'd bought. Grocery stores were foreign turf to her. She'd purchased fruit, the crackers, and an armload of StarKist's clever Charlie's Lunch kits. Tuna fish didn't live up to the caviar to which she was accustomed, but she and Toy-Toy could share it.

Almost sleepwalking by the time she made it home, she parked, fed them, and fell into bed.

Punching her pillow, she thought again of the blue-eyed man. If she crooked her finger, he'd come a-panting. It might help pass the time to break a local yokel's heart.

His voice, rich, controlled, fluid, echoed in her ears.

Would he come running?

This man might be different.

She found herself hoping so.

Sleep came quickly without pills. She drifted off, one hand on Toy-Toy's soft little ears, the image in her mind that of a blue-eyed man standing tall and silent and strong.

Friday four o'clock arrived, and the shrill of the whistle stopped the line, freeing Chelsea from the incessant motions of hand and wrist. She stood frozen, unable to comprehend that she'd survived the week.

Her lawyers had continued to refuse her calls.

She didn't even try calling Fran again, knowing the stone wall she'd encounter.

She simply endured the days of horror. Eight-hour days embroiled in heat. Days marked by moisture that trickled inside the gloves that were supposed to protect her hands, leaving them soggy and raw. Days in which the cloying odors crawled into her nose and buried themselves in her throat. Endless hours with workers who wouldn't meet her gaze, who swore when she bungled too many birds in a row and caused the line to shudder to a halt.

No more write-ups, though, since the two the first day.

Not bad for someone who'd never worked a day in her life.

Worked. Hah. Chelsea stripped off her soggy gloves and let them fall to the cement floor. She walked toward the door with Hoa, the one worker who had befriended her.

Each morning she waited for Chelsea at the end of Blueberry Lane and gave her a ride in a rather flashy black Camaro. Her son's, she'd explained, only that morning.

Hoa didn't talk much, and for that Chelsea found herself grateful. Had she been a chatterbox, Chelsea would have braved driving the truck every day rather than accept the ride.

Communication with a woman so different from herself seemed impossible. Hoa accepted the drudgery all day in the factory, then waited on her family half the night.

Home, Hoa had remarked in an offhand fashion, was a two-story house in which dwelled three Vietnamese families: seven adults and eight children. Many families shared denser quarters, Chelsea came to realize as she listened to Hoa's brief description. Still, she found that hard to believe, impossible to comprehend. Her mind flitted to her own estate in Bel Air, where she kept one suite of rooms for show, another for private life.

All for her. And Toy-Toy, of course.

Chelsea frowned, thinking of her pet as she climbed into the Camaro. Her poodle had taken to such strange behavior. It was almost as if the countryside had affected his brain, transforming him into some sort of country hound. A hound that preferred prancing around the chicken coop to cuddling up to Chelsea.

Hoa dropped her off at Blueberry Lane. Strolling in her Wal-Mart shoes, Chelsea rediscovered her leg muscles. She actually found herself enjoying the walk up the lane.

Without any car traffic, the lane was peaceful, sylvan. Her quiet steps didn't disturb the red clay the way the vehicles did. The sky remained that solid gorgeous blue blanket, today showing only a few glimpses of fluffy white.

In a very funny way, she felt at peace with her world.

Turning into Ely's front yard, she cocked an ear for Toy-Toy's yapping through the door.

Oddly enough, she heard nothing.

Concerned, she jogged forward, gasping for breath as she pushed herself beyond the new limits of her meager endurance.

Shoving open the front door, which as usual she hadn't locked, she called, "Toy-Toy, Mommy's home."

Nothing.

Silence.

Chelsea sagged against the door.

Then she ran out and around the house, toward the chicken coop.

She pulled up short, gagging at what she saw hanging from the clothesline.

"OhmiGod!"

But it wasn't her precious poodle. Squinting

against the reality of what she saw, she edged forward.

A chicken, feathers sagging groundward, hung by its feet from the clothesline. Stepping closer, fearing to do so yet driven to it, Chelsea saw what looked like a business card stuck through the chicken's beak.

Bending close, holding her nose, she read the card.

"Go Home, Chelsea-Jewess, Before You Get Hurt. America is for Americans Only."

She shuddered and dropped her hand.

Terrified lest she turn around and find her poodle subjected to the same treatment as the fowl, she started to close her eyes and sob.

Then she stopped, quite abruptly.

"You bastards," she said aloud. "Just try and scare me off. Filthy motherfucking prejudiced sons-of-bitches." She screamed more loudly as she finished the sentiment. "Just try to drive me away!" She shook her fist, then turned to circle the house, calling for Toy-Toy.

16 ～

On Saturday morning, Chelsea cracked open one eye to find Toy-Toy standing by her shoulder, tugging at the pillowcase with his tiny teeth. Poor wuddle tyke. Last night she'd found him cowering behind the chicken coop. The bullies who killed that chicken must have scared him half to death. But he'd cleverly eluded them.

"Grrr. Grrr."

Chelsea smiled at his miniature growl. "What's my wuddle one want?"

He pawed at the pillow.

Chelsea groaned. Out. He wanted to go out. Back in Bel Air, when Toy-Toy needed to be walked, she simply rang for a maid. Within minutes, a servant appeared to take care of her wuddle one's needs.

Here, dammit, she had to get out of bed and do it herself.

She reached to tousle his topknot but he jumped from the bed and yapped. Throwing back the covers of Ely's lumpy old bed, she frowned and looked about for the pink silk dressing gown she'd found in the back of the one closet. Imagine, only one closet!

Ely, for all his miserly ways and moral posturing, must have kept a lady friend.

Following Toy-Toy to the back door, she yawned and rubbed her eyes. Thank God for Saturday. She had the weekend to figure a way out of this backwater.

Outside, bright sunshine ravaged her sleepy eyes. She stumbled on the uneven boards of the back porch. Without a backward glance, Toy-Toy hop-skipped down the steps and scampered down the path that led to the chicken house.

Thinking of chickens, she shivered, wishing she'd only dreamed last night's horror.

She rose and peered toward the line where she'd found the strangled chicken, shielding her eyes as if to protect her from the harsh reality. If she couldn't see it, it couldn't be there.

Dead.

Swinging with each puff of breeze.

Attracting a swarm of buzzing flies.

Retreating to the steps, she choked back the bile that rose in her throat. What was she supposed to do about that mess?

She certainly wasn't touching it.

Perhaps she could contact the local ASPCA.

Well, for now it would have to hang there. She'd give Toy-Toy another two minutes, then retrieve him and retreat to bed.

Through another yawn, she heard a creaking noise and looked up to see the boy Timmy emerging from the chicken coop carrying a bucket. He closed the gate to the fenced-in area carefully and walked toward her, a shy smile on his face. Toy-Toy ran to greet him with a yap and a lick to each ankle.

Together they moved in her direction.

"Hello again," she said.

"Hi," he said, and fixed her with brilliant blue eyes fringed with lashes even longer than her own. "You've got five eggs this morning."

She tightened the sash on her robe and leaned forward to glance in the bucket. Sure enough, five oval globes lay in a mound. "What do you do with those?"

Timmy set the bucket down and started picking at a Flintstones bandage on his left elbow. "I dunno. I used to give them to Uncle Ely."

That gave Chelsea the opening she needed. "Timmy, was Uncle Ely actually your uncle?"

He glanced up from his methodic attack on the Band-Aid. "I guess so."

"What was his last name?"

"Van Ness. Everyone knows that."

Chelsea was definitely confused. To her knowledge, Ely had had no children. And certainly none of the rest of the Van Ness family ever stepped foot in Arkansas. "You know, I had an Uncle Ely, too."

"You mean we're related?" His eyes shone.

Now she'd done it. "Would you like to be?"

He quit picking at the scab he'd uncovered and nodded.

"Then let's say that we are."

"Okay." Timmy sat beside her on the steps and fingered the hem of her robe with a hand that hadn't seen soap and water in awhile. "So soft."

He gazed up at her and Chelsea was struck by what she could only call adoration glowing in his expression.

"You're very pretty," he said, dropping the edge of the silk.

"Thank you," Chelsea said, feeling for the first

time in a long time she'd received a genuinely
heartfelt compliment. "Where's your ball and
glove?"

He made a face of disgust. "My dad took it away
from me today."

"Why?"

He lifted his hands in a dramatic "Who can
know?" gesture.

"Were you naughty?" Chelsea suspected this wide-
eyed imp could be as mischievous as he was
charming.

"He just doesn't understand me."

"Well, I certainly know what that feels like."

"Do you?" His eyes lit up again. "You see, I have
these two new friends and when I try to tell my dad
about them he gets mad at me."

"He doesn't approve of your friends?"

He frowned—a fierce look indeed. "He says"—
disgust dripped in his tone —"they're not real. Only
imaginary."

"What's wrong with that?"

"Oh I know you understand, 'cause you had your
own imaginary friends." He propped his chin on his
hand, then dropped it quickly. "Hey, why don't you
come home with me and explain to my dad? Grownups always listen to other grownups."

Chelsea smiled at the innocence of Timmy's suggestion. His father wasn't likely to approve of his son
hanging out with a former porn star. "Just give your
dad some time," she said. "In the meantime, you
can still enjoy playing with your friends."

"And just not tell him?"

Oops. Some mother she'd be. That did sound like
bad advice. "Sometimes people aren't ready to hear
things. There's a time and a place."

"You're pretty smart, too." He jumped up and Toy-Toy did the same, dancing around the boy's feet. "I guess I should give you the eggs."

"Oh." What would happen to those chickens? Chelsea knew she'd never set foot in their pen. "Did Uncle Ely pay you to do those chores?"

"Yep."

"How much?"

"A dollar a day."

"That's seven dollars a week!" To pick up a few eggs and scatter some feed? Ely had been a wealthy man and she had to get by on slave wages.

"That's right. You're good at math, too, aren't you?"

She smiled despite herself. "Okay. A dollar a day."

He grinned and pulled a small spiral notebook from the back pocket of his shorts. He pulled a miniature pencil from the spiral binding and wrote a note in the book.

"How old are you?" Chelsea asked.

"Almost six."

"And you know how to write and do all these chores?"

This time he looked at her like she'd said something really stupid. " 'Course. Who doesn't?"

He put the notebook away and handed her the bucket. "I gotta go. If you change your mind about coming over to explain to my dad, we're the next house down the road."

Bending down, he rubbed Toy-Toy on the tummy. The dog yapped happily and Timmy flopped down on the grass and let him lick his face. Then with a wave, and one last wide-eyed look at Chelsea, he ran off toward the blue house in the distance.

* * *

Lying in the hammock, turning the pages of *Lady Chatterley's Lover,* Mia squirmed and denied the sensual images floating to the surface of her mind. She also wondered at Ely's choice of reading material, books he'd borrowed from Luke Miller's shelves.

When he handed her the D. H. Lawrence novel, along with *Jane Eyre* and *Pride and Prejudice,* Mia raised her brows. Interesting reading material for a country preacher.

Ely, with that thought-reading ability he mastered so well, said with a mild smile, "His wife Jenny taught English literature."

Oh.

Mia accepted the books gratefully and settled in to reacquaint herself with Lady Melton and the gameskeeper.

But unlike the first time, when she'd read it under the covers in high school, giggling but not understanding the nuances of sexual attraction, the book bothered her.

A lot.

She kept staring off across the lovely tree-shaded backyard of the preacher's farmhouse, picturing herself lying with Quentin in a secluded cabin protected by a thatch of woods.

They'd be exactly as they had been the other day in the hayfield. Only this time, no contrary bull would interrupt them.

Mia smiled as the juvenile phrase "go all the way" popped into her mind.

Oh, yeah, she'd saved herself long enough.

What if they lost this crazy challenge? What if Chelsea Jordan hopped back on a plane and holed up in Bel Air, as selfish and irredeemable as ever?

Whoosh! Into the black hole of forever-after

they'd go. She hoped not to hell; she said a swift silent prayer. Back to Purgatory, and then . . .

God only knew.

Mia closed the book. She had to do something physical, get her mind off heaven and hell and sex. The nuns at her grade school had taught her better than to think of the hereafter and lust in the same brainwave.

Mia rose and stretched her arms over her head, trying to dispel the confusion and desire. She really didn't know what she believed anymore, but she didn't feel like taking risks.

Which meant she ought to quit thinking of Quentin lying next to her, Quentin looking down at her, aroused and flushed with loving—

That thought stopped her.

In the hayfield, he'd said not one word about love. Then he'd chased after Chelsea like a racing greyhound after a rabbit. Every day he found an excuse to go check on her.

The sun leaned toward the west. Ely had mentioned a creek toward the back of the farm property. A good cold dip would cleanse her mind and her body. What she'd do for a towel she didn't know, but being invisible, drip-dry didn't seem a bad option.

This in-between life and death state had some advantages. Mia still wore the same dress. It never soiled; she never had to bathe. She could eat if she wished, but hunger never came knocking.

Her most constant emotional companions were her feelings for Quentin. She'd even begun to relax over their predicament, an attitude that drove Quentin crazy.

There she went, thinking of Quentin again.

She kicked off her shoes and headed for the creek.

Mia passed through a leafy copse of trees that blocked Luke's house from view and on the other side she saw the creek. Clear water lapped against a shallow bank. Stones worn smooth by passing water lined the edges. Overhead in the leafy trees, birds kept up a musical chatter.

What a sight for a woman born and raised in a neighborhood bounded by concrete, rushing automobiles, and smog-haunted skies. What a symphony for a woman reared with background music courtesy of ghetto blasters and shrill-voiced men and women angry at a world that fenced them in and thereby fenced them out.

Mia took a deep breath and hugged the moment of tranquility to her heart.

Through a lot of sweat, effort, and good fortune, she'd escaped the world of her childhood, and as she stood on the bank of this pristine stream, she promised herself if she ever made it back to life, she'd appreciate every blessing she had.

Even if Quentin never came to love her.

Standing as close to the water as she could without falling in, feeling very daring, she slipped out of her cardigan. Then, after a careful visual survey of her surroundings, she pulled her dress over her head and folded it nice and neat. Her logical mind told her that her invisible status nullified the need for such a check, but that same logic decreed the precaution necessary.

Wearing only her lacy Victoria's Secret panties and bra, Mia dipped a toe into the stream.

Delicious.

Cool and wet and invigorating. She threw her head back and smiled up at the sky.

And laughed aloud at her own crazy thought.

Ah, to allow herself the freedom . . .

Then Mia stopped laughing. Why not? Why not strip to the skin and swim in the nude? A product of crowded city pools, she'd never had the opportunity to indulge a secret fantasy of savoring the water lapping her breasts, of swimming free like a fish.

Bending forward, Mia undid the clasp of her bra and liberated her breasts. Stroking the delicate skin below her breasts, she eased the stresses of the underwire. Her nipples perked up and Mia experienced a moment of longing for Quentin.

A longing she tried to extinguish, but as she shimmied free of her bikini panties, the only image in her mind was that of Quentin slipping them off her, his eyes dark with desire, his mouth warmed with her kisses.

Deep within, she tightened and suppressed a longing pant. Thankful the water ran on the cool side, she waded out and plunged in.

From his hiding place behind a wide-barreled oak tree, Quentin bit back a groan. He'd come to the creek to swim, Ely having mentioned it to him only a few minutes earlier back at the house.

He hadn't meant to intrude on Mia's private dip, hadn't meant to peek. But once Mia started that heart-stopping slow-motion striptease, his feet refused to retreat, and he couldn't bear to call out to warn her of his presence. Revealing himself would stop the poetry of her movements, inhibit the freedom she rarely allowed herself, a freedom he could see she relished.

Quentin watched her dive beneath the water and reemerge, shaking droplets from her face and smiling like a kid in a candy store. He'd forgotten how much Mia loved to swim. A true Pisces, she had told him early on, mated with the water.

And what he wouldn't give to be that water. Lapping her, loving her.

He thought of stripping and diving in with her.

Pictured her turning, pleased to see him, opening her arms to him.

Quentin dropped the hand that had involuntarily reached for the drawstring of his sweats.

Who was he fooling? Mia welcoming him when she'd scarcely spoken to him all week? Each time he attempted to talk to her, she faced him with steel in her glare.

He'd only gone off in the truck to help Chelsea, a woman in need of help if he'd ever seen one. Mia didn't understand, being so capable, how good it made a man feel to rescue a woman. If Mia had been the one behind the wheel having trouble, he would have hopped in even faster.

But Mia just wasn't the helpless type.

Which he appreciated, Quentin reflected, pursing his lips and dropping to the padded mat of leaves beneath the oak tree. Most of the time.

He admired her prowess, had profited by it professionally. But she didn't need him for anything. And apart from his work, she seemed to think of him as nothing but an indiscriminate skirt-chaser.

So how was he to win her heart?

Because he knew now that his most important mission in life was to do just that. He wanted Mia.

Not for only this moment, not for his doll-of-the-week, but by his side, arm-in-arm, forging ahead, conquering the world together and retreating in tandem to the haven of their own private world.

His head spun for a moment.

A mockingbird swooped down, performing a quick fly-by of his Yankees cap. Quentin quickly dismissed the notion, but he thought the bird sang, "Serves you right. Serves you right!"

Mia had been there with him, for all these years. His pal, his friend, his co-creator, his producer. He'd been blind.

Blind.

What if it were too late?

What if they died and were buried and that was that?

Mia broke the surface of the water near the bank. Looking every bit the mermaid, she stood, half-in, half-out of the water.

Droplets sparkled on her rounded breasts. She swept her hair back from her face and lifted her face to the sun.

Quentin's heart caught in mid-beat.

The mockingbird returned, circled round him, then flew in a straight path to where Mia was now emerging from the creek.

"Qu-ent! Qu-ent!"

Mia shook water from her hair and smiled at her imagination. For a moment she thought the gray and white bird had called Quentin's name.

Small wonder, considering he was so much on her mind. Stepping onto the bank, she stretched her arms above her hand and danced in a circle to dry her body.

Her body sang from the swim in the refreshing stream. Mia couldn't remember when she'd felt so good. The image of Quentin leaning over her flittered to her mind, and she smiled.

A rock skipped against another one and Mia

glanced quickly toward the clump of trees. Feeling silly, she grabbed her dress and clasped it in front of her. No one could see her but Quentin.

And Timmy.

She hadn't even thought of the child. That omission was so unlike her. There, she'd forgotten for once to be responsible, and overlooked the good of an innocent child. Still, Mia reflected, she'd enjoyed her first ever skinny-dip.

"Who's there?" she called.

"Just me," Quentin said.

"Quentin!" Not Timmy, after all. A smile lifted the corner of her lips.

A man.

A woman.

A man this woman really, really wanted.

And nobody else around.

"What a surprise," she murmured, her heart racing.

What the heck. She'd played it proper all her life. Mia had sat back and watched Quentin go off with every dumb blonde in Hollywood. And all week she'd suffered as he'd fussed over Chelsea Jordan's welfare.

Maybe it was time to play by their rules.

He stepped from behind a tree. "Yes, quite a surprise."

"Did you come for a swim?" she said, holding her breath as she let her dress slide to the ground, the most daring act she'd ever performed. Quentin stayed where he was, open-mouthed.

She lifted her hands to fluff her damp hair and batted her lashes at Quentin. Raising her arms thrust her breasts higher. She did have good breasts, full and round and tipped with nipples that puckered at the naughty ideas racing in her mind. Sitting back and waiting for Quentin to notice her hadn't worked, so what did she have to lose?

Watch out Chelsea Jordan and Bimbos of the World. Here comes Mia Tortelli.

She could have sworn Quentin gulped.

Hiding a smile, she said, "Why don't you go for a swim? The water's lovely. Perhaps I'll dip in again."

Quentin rushed forward and grasped her hand. "No, no, it's getting late. I think we ought to go for a walk instead. Maybe check on Timmy, or Ely. Yeah, get some carrot juice."

She narrowed her eyes. Quentin was ignoring her offer. "What's the matter, big boy? Don't you see something you like?"

"Oh, Mia, cut it out." Quentin scooped up her dress and held it in front of her. "What's gotten into you?"

A tear, an object foreign to Mia, wrestled with the corner of her eye. "Don't you want me, Quentin?" she whispered.

He rolled his eyes, reached down, and picked up her dress. Leaning forward, he placed a quick kiss on the top of the spiky crown of her hair. "More than you know, Mia, my dear. But not like this. I want *you,* not someone you think you have to pretend to be in order to interest me."

"Oh." Mia didn't know which thought held predominance in her mind. That she was pretending, or that Quentin actually wanted her.

"Quentin." She tugged the dress from his hand and tossed it over her shoulder. She slid her hands around his neck, and said, "Say that again. Say you want me."

He caught her by the hips and pulled her tight

against him. "Oh, yes, I want you. I want the Mia Tortelli who makes me smile and laugh and see the world as a beautiful place."

Running a hand over the spiky top of her hair, he said, "I want the Mia Tortelli who's been my friend for years, my constant companion, my soul mate." Tipping her chin up, he gazed into her eyes, eyes he could see glimmered with unshed tears. Holding her tight, afraid she'd come to her senses and warn him off, he lowered his lips to hers.

The kiss he gave her came from his soul, born of the truth of his love for her.

Mia crushed her naked body even closer to Quentin, savoring his kisses. She inched her hands upward to his hair and stroked the back of his head as his tongue plundered her hungry mouth.

She held on as Quentin eased her to the soft sweet grass, smiled as he pillowed her head with his T-shirt and stripped off the rest of his clothes.

Quentin kissed her again, then lowered his lips to her breasts.

Mia sighed. She was in heaven.

"Don't ever think," Quentin said, circling a nipple with a heated tongue, "that I don't want you." He trailed a hand down her tummy, placing a palm over her throbbing sex. "But just in case, let me show you just how much I want you." He scooted lower, and with swirling kisses, teased her legs wide. With a deliciously wicked gleam in his eyes, he parted her heated lips with his tongue.

Mia moaned. Quentin reached up, placed one of her hands on her breast and circled her hand in a gentle and tantalizing massage. Then he kissed his way down her quivering tummy again. Amazed at how good it felt to caress her flesh as she watched him sucking her, Mia gave herself up to the waves of pleasure mounting within.

Quentin drank greedily as she came and Mia experienced a surge of power, sheer timeless feminine power. "Oh, Quent," she murmured, reaching to stroke his hair.

He rested his head above her pelvis for just a moment, then blew softly on her belly button. "Before we go any further," he said, "there's something I have to tell you."

The words surprised Mia. If anyone had a secret to share, surely it was she. She still hadn't told him she was a virgin.

"What is it?" she asked.

His erection nudging against her, Quentin lay above her, most of his weight on his elbows. Looking more serious than she'd ever seen him, he said, "I love you."

"What?"

"I didn't expect you to jump for joy, but I had to tell you. This isn't some quickie in the grass for me, Mia. This is life-and-death serious."

She captured the words and hugged them to her heart. "If you knew how long I've waited to hear you say those words," she whispered.

"You mean it?" Now he looked as excited as a kid on Christmas morning.

"I love you," she said, her heart spilling over. "For better or for worse, I've loved you for a long, long time."

Quentin kissed her on the lips, a gentle kiss that promised love and affection and respect. "Let me make love to you," he said, his voice asking her permission.

"Oh, please!"

He grinned and positioned himself over her. He began to enter her, setting off frissons of the most delicious feelings she'd ever known.

"Wow," she said.

He paused. "We're only just beginning, Mia me darling."

She smiled and lifted her hips.

He eased in, then stopped, a funny look flickering across his face.

"I should probably tell you—" Mia said.

"Shh, I think I know what you're going to say." He kissed her lightly and inched inwards.

"You don't mind?"

"Mind!"

Mia could tell from his smile how pleased he was. She thrust her hips, drawing him in. He hurt her only the tiniest bit, a hurt that disappeared from memory as he filled her body and they began to move as one.

17 ～

Luke had wrestled late into the night with his Sunday sermon. *Let he who is without sin cast the first stone.* He mulled over that phrase, considered the example of Christ chastising the scribes and Pharisees for the way they would punish the woman taken in adultery. Yet he felt unable within his own heart to refrain from judging Chelsea Jordan.

Surely, then, his father would tell him a message existed in that inability to forgive, to forgo a judgment that was not his to make.

Only he was not the man, nor the preacher, his father had always been.

When the first rooster of morning crowed, Luke woke with a start from the sofa where he'd fallen into a disturbed sleep.

The cock will crow three times before you deny me. . . . came to mind and he wanted to curse, to throw off the yoke of his ministry.

So much simpler to turn his back on this life, to pick up the scraps of his baseball career and beg, borrow or steal his way back into the minors, work his way up again.

But who was he kidding?

He had a child.

Responsibilities.

A church.

Parishioners.

Bleary-eyed and wishing Ely had kept his cock-and-bull plot to himself instead of letting him in on one of the craziest stories he'd yet to hear, he rose from the sofa and went to brew a pot of strong coffee.

Jenny used to do that, slip out of bed even when snow hugged the eaves of their house, pad down to the kitchen and put the coffee on. She'd return to wake him with a kiss and a mug of steaming, aromatic coffee. And many mornings the coffee cooled, long forgotten, as she slipped back under the covers.

Luke groaned and rubbed his eyes and made himself think of the scene at dinner last night.

Timmy had rattled on again about the man and woman living in their backyard, a woman who looked like his mommy. Luke finally told his son not to say it again, and Timmy stormed from the table.

Defeated, he'd put his head in his hands. Jenny would have known what to do. He had no clue.

He'd felt a gentle hand on his shoulder, followed by Ely telling him he should have told him all along, but had been afraid to risk any "rule violation." Then he'd jumped right into his story.

The coffee pot hissed. Luke rubbed his eyes again and wondered whether he'd been dreaming. Invisible people. Second chance at life challenges. Purgatory.

Maybe the whole story was true, or maybe Ely had flipped.

Whether it was or wasn't true, he owed Timmy an apology. He poured a cup of coffee and headed up the stairs to his son's room.

In the doorway, he paused. Timmy still slept, unusual for such a fireball of energy. His eyes looked puffy, and Luke experienced a stab of guilt as he realized his son must have cried throughout the night.

Tucked against his chest was his Curious George doll.

Luke moved to the bed and sat on the edge. Timmy opened his eyes a little at a time. When he focused on Luke, he grasped his doll more tightly.

"Hey, sleepyhead," Luke said, feeling incredibly incompetent at the task of parenting.

"Hey yourself." Timmy's mouth formed a mulish line.

"Look, champ, I came to say I'm sorry for yelling at you about your imaginary friends."

Timmy said nothing.

"I know it must get lonesome for you without other kids to play with."

"They're not imaginary."

Luke took a sip of coffee. If Ely had been telling a straight story, Timmy was right. "Okay." He set his cup on the bedside table. "What did you say their names were?"

"I didn't say."

He squelched a sigh. "What are their names?"

"Quentin. And Mia." He spoke to the wall and said the names as if they were being drawn from him by a torturer.

"What does Quentin look like?" He knew Timmy thought the woman looked like Jenny.

Timmy sat up against his pillows, still clutching Curious George. In a more animated voice, he said, "He's kinda tall, not as tall as you, and he wears a Yankees cap and he likes to play ball."

Luke nodded. The ideal imaginary playmate. Still, something about the description tickled some tucked away memory. "Does he have a job?"

"Not right now. But he used to make movies."

The memory blossomed. Luke stood up. "I'll be right back."

He headed swiftly down the stairs. Surely he was misremembering the picture, the name, something. In the living room, he scrabbled through the pile of magazines and books on the coffee table. Ely had a habit of reading the grocery-store tabloids—to keep up with his grandniece, he always said—and Luke had seen a front-page photo of—

He caught his breath as he pulled the issue from the stack. A bright-eyed young man looked back at him from the cover. A man wearing a Yankees cap. Next to him, a perky-looking woman with spiky brown hair and yes, indeed, a face that twisted his heart.

Jenny.

The same wise eyes, the same soft curve to her lips, the hint of the practical mixed with the day-dreamer.

He could see quite well why Timmy confused her with his mother.

The headline read: Biz Boy Wonder Hovers Near Death. Under the photo, the caption ran, "Director-producer team Quentin Grandy and Mia Tortelli both remain in a coma following a crane accident following a charity special-effects demonstration. All one hundred children from local children's hospitals had left the soundstage prior to the incident."

Luke dropped the paper. His hand shook. Too weird. Too weird by half.

Then he snatched the paper and took the stairs two at a time. But he forced himself to stroll casually back into the room. Showing the paper to his son, he said, "Do your friends look like these two people?"

"Yeah!" Curious George fell to the side of the bed. "Exactly." He sat back, a smug look on his face. "Now do you believe me?"

"Yes, son, I believe you." Luke mussed his son's hair and tossed the covers back. "Time to rise and shine and get ready for church." Timmy raced from the bed, whistling happily.

Luke collected his coffee cup, wondering what he did believe anymore, knowing he had no idea what words would come from his mouth when it was time for him to preach that morning's sermon.

Chelsea snuggled against the pillow and turned the page of the book she'd found at work on Friday. She'd read it twice before, but that never took away from *Something Wonderful*.

She'd gotten up once, to let Toy-Toy out. Her wuddle one had turned into an avid outdoor doggie, whining and yapping in such un-Toy-Toy-like fashion when she refused him time outside that she finally gave in and let him roam.

As soon as she turned the last page, she would rouse herself and call him in.

A knock sounded at the front door. In Ely's tiny house the sound seemed to come from beside the headboard of the bed.

Chelsea started and dropped the book.

She wrinkled her brow, wondering who it might be.

Then she checked the bedside clock.

Ten o'clock.

She wrapped the pink silk robe around her naked body and traipsed to the door, yet another job she'd never had to perform in Bel Air.

When she saw the man who stood on the porch, she was thankful she'd peeked out the window.

Smallwood. And all dressed up, too. Ugh.

Then she remembered. "Oh, my God. It's Sunday." He'd dropped her a note to remind her he'd drive her to church, per Ely's instructions. Through the door, she called in a saccharine voice, "Almost ready. Be right out." Then she raced to the bedroom.

What in the world did one wear to church? She'd find something decent in which to clothe herself. She'd be damned if she'd endure the torture of the chicken plant and screw up something so simple as sitting through some windbag mouthing a few platitudes.

Peering into Ely's closet, Chelsea spotted the makings of an outfit and yanked them on. If she hadn't spent yesterday afternoon curled up with her novel, she might have gone into town and either gotten herself out of this situation or at least picked up something to wear.

As it was, she had no choice but to make do with Ely's wardrobe.

Baggy trousers belted at the waist. A white undershirt from his dresser. The Cartier diamond studs she thankfully had been wearing the day she'd fallen into this strange state. A jacket, sleeves rolled back and collar turned up. A quick toss and fluff of her thick and unruly hair. Sunglasses.

Feeling as if she'd bested an adversary, Chelsea turned toward the door.

And stopped.

Barefoot.

She couldn't wear the Wal-Mart specials; they reeked of the chicken plant.

Am/Am. Call them Nazis. Call them neo-Nazis, there really was no difference. They couldn't win.

Her toenail polish still shone, free of chips.

Hadn't they gone barefoot in the Bible?

Surely Charlton Heston had been barefoot in *The Ten Commandments*.

Chelsea grabbed her Chanel purse and, walking with an attitude, went to meet Smallwood.

When she opened the door, she thought his mouth would drop to the floorboards of the porch.

He choked back whatever he had been going to say.

She stared him down through the dark glasses. "Time to go?"

"Not a minute too soon." He turned, then stopped. "Oh, this package was on the porch. I picked it up for you."

Chelsea reached for a small bundle wrapped in newspaper. A shiver of apprehension traveled her spine as she wondered whether the package contained another message from the same people who had hanged the chicken.

"Aren't you going to open it?" Smallwood asked.

Why did he care? Chelsea tossed her hair over her shoulder. "Sure." She undid the loosely tied string and to her surprise, saw both her high-heeled sandals.

"For Cinderella" was printed in crude, childish letters on a piece of white paper.

"That's an odd parcel to find at your door," Smallwood said.

Chelsea gave him a dazzling smile, giving no hint of her own puzzlement and said, "I sent them out to be cleaned." Then she slipped the shoes on and sailed ahead of him to his Mercedes.

During the drive into town, Chelsea maintained a prim silence. She neither liked nor trusted the lawyer. And, strangely enough, she realized the idea of going to church made her nervous.

She'd attended temple with her father a few times, but then only when Jack Jordan's mother had come to town to visit. She had only the scantest of memories of the cronelike old woman who spoke a funny language. Somehow, she didn't think her father liked having the old woman around, and by the time Chelsea was five and truly old enough to remember, Grandmother Rosenblum never came to their house again.

Her mother never bothered with church at all.

Walking into a small-town church filled with people who took the whole religious thing seriously unsettled her.

Possibly, she acknowledged, trying to ignore Smallwood's leering glances directed to where the thin T-shirt showed beneath Ely's open jacket, because she had no religious values of her own.

Religious values? She lacked values of any sort. A belief system. Ideals that made life worth living.

She swallowed and stared out the window at the cluster of reporters in front of the church. A few of the vultures had found her. "Damn it."

Smallwood smiled at her. "I would think a celebrity like you would be happy to see these maggots."

"Little you know."

He arched a brow. "I thought you'd appreciate me calling them up."

"Hardly." Without a look back, she yanked open the car door and stalked up the walk.

Of course they swooped down on her. She heard cries and questions and watched them ogle her outfit. God only knew what fashion trends would be set as a result of her being forced to wear Ely's things. That thought amused her, and she swept by without comment, a smile just lifting the corners of her mouth.

Not once did she turn to acknowledge Smallwood, left in her wake. Nor did she see the murderous look on his face.

A kindly-looking man in a suit opened the door to the entry area of the church, informed the journalists they'd simply have to wait outside unless they wanted to come in to worship, and motioned her in.

Bolstered by that protective act, she squared her shoulders, opened the interior door, and stepped into the church.

The music faltered and Chelsea knew that every single person on each side of the central aisle turned to stare at her.

She tried to lift her chin and keep her shoulders stiff. Who cared what these hillbillies thought? Out of the corner of her eye, she looked for a seat to duck into near the back.

Filled.

Every pew crammed to the edges.

She clicked one high heel after the other as she made her way up the aisle of the church. Everyone stared. No one made room for her.

Suddenly, she heard her name.

"Chelsea." Again, a young boy's voice called her name.

From the very front row of the church, Timmy waved to her, pointing to the place beside him.

Breaking into a smile, she strode forward, giving him a little wave as she reached his pew.

He offered her his small hand. Grateful, her eyes oddly damp, she took his hand in hers.

Timmy smiled up at her, and offered her an open book. She accepted it, not knowing what it was; then, as her eyes cleared, the music came into focus.

Hymns.

Trained to sing from her earliest years, she fell into musical step, holding the book low enough for Timmy to share. The song she didn't know, but the melody pleased her. Always a quick study, she gave herself to singing the lyrics, holding the last note to its fullest.

Longer than anyone in the church, she realized with a blush, as she felt all those eyes on her again. Everyone took their seats and she followed suit, determined to get through the morning without drawing any more attention to herself.

The person who'd been leading the music thanked everyone and announced Pastor Miller, then sat down in the front row on the other side of the aisle.

Chelsea let her mind drift, anywhere other than where she was, waiting for Pastor Miller, whoever he was, to do his thing and be done with it so she could go back to *Something Wonderful*.

A man approached the pulpit, black robes swinging against his legs. Tall legs, Chelsea noted. With a spring to their step, not at all like the old dragon she'd expected.

She lifted her face, up, up, and gasped at what she saw.

The man in the pickup truck.

The man she'd hit. And cursed.

"Good morning," the man was saying. "Today— today," he seemed to stumble and lose his place. "As most of you know"— here he grinned and Chelsea found her heart somewhere in her throat at the boyish look—"my father was known to use his children as examples in his sermons. I promised myself when my own son was born that I would never, ever, do such a thing."

Here his face grew almost grim. Chelsea clutched the lapels of her jacket. "But sometimes things happen for which we have no explanation. God does indeed work in mysterious ways. We human beings, too, work in ways most mysterious. Some good. Some not so good. But for all we must bear responsibility."

He gazed out over the congregation, making eye contact and nodding at several people.

"My son believes in imaginary playmates. For this, knowing how he grieves for his mother, I have chastised him, wanting him to deal squarely with reality. But from this experience with my son, my friends, I have a lesson to share, and relate to the Gospel."

He cleared his throat, leaned forward behind the podium and said, "What did Jesus mean when he said 'Unless you turn and become like children, you will never enter the kingdom of heaven'?"

He paused, letting his question sink in.

"Unless we consider our possibilities boundless, unless we are willing to comfort and aid strangers in our midst, in a way a small child will do, without scrutiny, without consideration of one's past or reputation, unless we are willing to step aside from our own preconceived notions and biases and obey the command 'Judge not,' we shall not enter the kingdom of heaven.

"My son told me of imaginary playmates. I scolded him. And for this action I was wrong.

"To him these friends are real. And perhaps they are indeed angels traveling this earth, angels in need. If Jesus Christ appeared to any one of us sitting in this room today, as a stranger in need, and we turned him away, what do you think would be our ultimate reward?"

The minister shook his head. His question was answer enough, and he was smart enough to know that. Chelsea marveled at the way he'd managed to shame the people for gawking at her.

For she had no doubt, even though he never once let his gaze settle for long on her, that he'd spoken off the cuff, spoken to protect her.

Even though she'd been such a bitch to him.

She felt small and unworthy. Hell, she was small and unworthy, and it felt good to say it to herself. She squirmed in her seat, thankful she hadn't removed the dark glasses.

Then her brain kicked into gear and she thought of Timmy's references to his make-believe friends. She looked from the child's blue eyes back to those of the man in the pulpit. Identical.

Timmy glanced up at her again, a happy expression on his face. Answering him with a smile, she reached over to tousle his hair.

His smile broadened.

She couldn't swear to it, but she thought the

pastor, in the middle of his sentence asking the congregation to rise for a closing hymn, choked.

Well, what was truth for the congregation was truth for the minister, she thought, rising and turning in the book to the song indicated.

Feeling curiously at peace, she joined the others in song.

18 ~

The music ended.

A moment of silence struck the church.

Chelsea knew without looking around that people were eyeing her. Maybe some of them were even thinking of the minister's words as they bored holes in her back, a back she kept carefully straight, chin high. She didn't know why but for once she cared what people thought of her.

The woman sitting on the other side of Timmy offered her a smile and a hand to shake. "Let me be the first to welcome you to Hill Springs Community Church. I'm Imogene Harris, the pastor's sister. What's your name?"

Chelsea lifted her own hand, accepting and shaking briefly. "Chelsea Jordan," she said in a low voice, wondering when the last time was she had to tell anyone her name.

"Chelsea's my friend," Timmy said.

"Is that right?" She smiled when she said it, but the look on her face said she didn't believe him.

"Yep." He tugged a pair of lime-green plastic

sunglasses out of his pants pocket, popped them onto his face, then began pawing the air as if he'd gone blind.

"Timmy, where are your manners?"

Chelsea touched her own dark lenses, still perched firmly on her nose. Disappearing behind them was second nature to her, but clearly she'd set a bad example for Timmy.

With a hesitant hand, she lifted them from her face and dropped them in the breast pocket of Ely's jacket. "Thank you," she said to Timmy, tapping him on the shoulder, "for reminding me I'd forgotten to remove my sunglasses."

Imogene Harris gave her an assessing look.

Timmy slipped the glasses from his face, rewarding Chelsea with an adoring smile.

Chelsea knew the minister had joined them even before he spoke. He moved lightly for such a tall man. He, too, offered her a hand in greeting.

She met his hand with hers, unaccountably pleased at the feeling of strength his touch communicated. Then she met his gaze.

Which pleased her a heck of a lot less.

He didn't stare or glare or condemn, not actively anyway. Evidently he attempted to practice what he preached. Still, something in his expression accused her.

"Miss Jordan," he said, "I'm Luke Miller. Welcome. I see you've met my son."

She looked from child to father, confirming what she'd figured out during the minister's talk. Same deep and dusky blue eyes, same ability to see through one with those eyes, same quirk of mischief lingering about the lips. More hidden on the father's face, of course, but Chelsea suspected the imp lived within him as well.

"I gather we're neighbors," she heard herself saying.

The Harris woman's eyebrows shot up.

The minister nodded. "You're staying in Ely Van Ness's house for awhile?"

"Not for long."

Timmy scuffed a foot on the floor. "You can't leave now. You just got here."

She smiled and resisted an urge to smooth his disheveled hair back from his face.

"Hey, Dad, can she come to dinner with us?"

The minister hesitated.

Chelsea knew she was not wanted. She wasn't their kind. Only Timmy, innocent child that he was, couldn't see that. "I'm sorry, Timmy, but I'm afraid today isn't a good day."

Timmy clouded over.

"Perhaps another Sunday," said Timmy's aunt, looking relieved.

Too relieved.

Chelsea rebelled.

The minister had said nothing. He stood and gazed at her and at his son, and the longer he looked at her, the more she wanted to ruffle him. She knew from years of practice how to cause trouble for a man. True, he'd been gracious enough not to mention the other day in the parking lot.

"Oh, now that you mention it," she said slowly, "dinner might be nice. If it wouldn't be an imposition," she said, widening her eyes and letting her lashes flutter.

The minister looked at his sister. "Imogene?"

"One o'clock." She smiled, and excused herself quickly.

He said softly, so that only Chelsea could hear, "My sister doesn't react well to last-minute changes, but I know she's more than happy to have you for dinner. Do you need a ride?"

She started to say no, but how else would she get home? Another twenty-five-dollar cab ride? She couldn't afford it, not on the wages she made. Humbling herself to produce a smile, she said, "Thank you. That would be nice."

People were milling around them. Chelsea had sensed them all along, watching her as she spoke with the minister. She supposed if he accepted her they'd all do the same. Not that she cared. She did find it odd the minister hadn't offered her condolences over her loss. Didn't they do that sort of thing?

Someone else walked up to claim the man's time. Timmy tugged on her hand. "Come on," he said, "I want you to meet Vicky. For a girl, she's pretty cool."

Chelsea, safe with the child, let herself be pulled off. As she passed the other adults still milling about in the church, she knew they watched her. They probably thought to keep an eye on her so she wouldn't corrupt the children.

Luke stared after her, not even hearing the tale of woe Mrs. Stivers relayed to him. As her life consisted of one predicament after another, though, he safely assumed it to be of minor importance and let his mind run to Chelsea Jordan.

A woman who'd turned her back on a family member in need, ignoring Ely's pleas for a visit and the telegram about the funeral.

A woman who filled out a plain old white undershirt in a way that made a man's blood burn.

A woman who made her way through life using her body the way a man strapped for cash used his credit cards. Wasteful, wanton, doomed to repeat the same destructive behavior. See something you want? Flutter those lashes, tease with a bit of cleavage, pucker those lips.

A woman he'd gone and invited to Imogene's, assuring himself of censure from his sister whom he full well knew had already invited her latest candidate for the second Mrs. Miller to Sunday dinner.

Murmuring a sympathetic "mmmm" to Mrs. Stivers, Luke caught sight of his sister's nominee across the church. Imogene stood next to her, whispering. Nan Wagner was a fine upstanding young woman, a schoolteacher, just like Jenny.

And as boring a woman as Luke had ever met.

Chelsea and Timmy swam into focus. Timmy, clearly taken with his new friend, was introducing Chelsea to his kindergarten classmates. She nodded to the Dodson girl, and when the shy youngster whispered something to her, Chelsea knelt on the floor next to her and let the child whisper in her ear.

Nan Wagner raised her brows.

Luke could almost hear her tch-tch. According to Imogene, Miss Wagner was of the old school of child rearing.

"Well, thank you so much, Pastor Miller. You always do make me feel so much better." Mrs. Stivers patted his arm. "Just like your daddy, you are."

He nodded, hearing once again the echo of a judgment that simply was not accurate. He didn't want to be his father. Yet, when his father had laid the responsibility at his feet, asking him to take over the church, he'd said yes.

Because he loved his father.

He hadn't turned away, shunned his duty.

The way Chelsea Jordan had.

With a slight shake of his head, Luke turned to the next parishioner awaiting his attention, unable to answer the question: Just why *had* he invited Chelsea Jordan to dinner?

Still unable to answer that question, he helped her avoid the media by escorting her out through the rector's office. Timmy sat between them in the truck on the short ride to Imogene's house. She lived on the opposite side of town from Luke, on a farm dedicated to breeding chickens for the local poultry business.

Thankfully, Timmy chattered, because Luke found he had nothing to say. Or rather, nothing that he could say in front of his son. He found he wanted to take her by the shoulders and watch those big green eyes of hers widen and look at him in wonder as he leaned down to kiss those puckery lips of hers.

Completely unthinkable.

He jerked the truck to a halt, wondering what the worldly-wise Ms. Jordan thought about being hauled around in a truck that on workdays carried pigs and feed. Surprised to feel embarrassment at a lifestyle that gave him pleasure, he got out of the truck. Only a lifetime of good breeding forced his feet quickly around to the passenger door to open it for her.

She looked down her nose at him when he swung the door open and offered her a hand.

"We do have manners in the country," he said.

"And I'm not helpless," she said, nudging his hand away and jumping down.

She stumbled and Luke reached out with a swift arm to catch her before she could tumble to the ground.

"Damn shoes," she muttered.

Timmy echoed, "Damn shoes," and went off into a peal of laughter.

"Timmy!" Luke called his son's name with iron in his voice.

Chelsea colored and Luke hoped she felt some remorse for swearing in front of a child who obviously thought she walked on water.

"Sorry," Timmy said, clapping a hand over his mouth.

Luke stared from his son to Chelsea, wondering what to do with either one of them. Thankfully, Imogene's husband stepped out onto the front porch and waved at them, breaking the moment.

"Howdoo," he called.

Chelsea tested her step, careful to protect the ankle she'd twisted, and limped in her four inch heels, silently cursing her great-uncle Ely as she tried to keep up with the long, lean strides of the minister.

Hurrying to be some place she didn't want to be, with people who didn't care for her.

The story of her life.

The sun passed behind a growing bulk of clouds. Luke paused to hold the door open for her and without glancing at him, Chelsea stepped into his sister's house.

Sunday night found Hornsby Smallwood with his back against the wall.

Soaking wet.

The storm clouds had built during the afternoon and let loose just as his phone rang at six P.M.

The message had been brief. "Meet me at nine. The usual place."

He'd been prompt, arriving precisely on the hour

at the old Wal-Mart long since bypassed for the shiny new one sprawling just outside the town limits.

At 9:01, he found himself slammed against the cinderblock wall framing the back of the lot.

"What the fuck?!" Smallwood tried to fight off the attacker, but the man held his wrists together with one meaty hand that might as well have been handcuffs.

"I'll ask the questions," said the man from behind a ski mask.

As soon as he heard the voice, Smallwood knew who his assailant was. "Pike, what the fuck is the meaning of this?"

"I told you no names. How dumb are you?" The man let go of Smallwood and pulled the mask off his head. "Damn thing is awful hot."

"As befits a hothead," Smallwood murmured, knowing the play on words would be lost on the thick-brained sheriff.

"The point," Presley Elvis Pike, sheriff of Hill Springs, said, poking Smallwood in the chest with a stubby finger, "is that you ain't doing your job. You tole us no problem, no problem, the bitch wouldn't get the money. We made plans for that money, big plans, and now it's like we can taste it."

"What exactly do you mean?"

"If you hadn't promised it to us, we wouldn't be missing it. But now if we don't get it, we ain't gonna be happy." Another jab to the chest followed this sentence.

"Well, don't forget," Smallwood said, giving the sheriff a taste of his own poke-in-the-chest routine, "if it hadn't been for me in the first place you never would have had a shot at the dough. So back up and fuck off."

Pike narrowed his eyes and wiped the raindrops from the bill of his Red Man cap. "Either you get the bitch to leave or we bring in the big guns."

"Well don't get crotchety. You know I'll come through for you."

Pike snorted. "Takin' your time, aren't you? We already helped you along oncet."

Smallwood didn't ask; he didn't want to know. "She'll give in. That woman won't last another week in the chicken plant." Though Smallwood still couldn't figure out how she'd made it through even one day. He hadn't bothered with any concrete plans to run her off, figuring between the plant and the crummy little house and having to attend a Christian church, she'd give in. "Remember she doesn't care about anyone but herself. That I can tell you for sure."

The sheriff laughed and spat out a wad of tobacco too close to Smallwood's shoes for his liking. "What's a matter, she turn you down?"

He didn't even answer the question. Jesus, how had he fallen in with such rabble? His goal had been lofty, idealistic. He intended to help stabilize America's white community. He was sick and tired of all the special treatment and excuses and goddamn talk of slavery reparations.

Smallwood straightened his shirt and said in his most dignified voice, "Chelsea Jordan will be out of town well before the month is over. And don't resort to violence that can be traced back to me or I'll turn you into the FBI myself."

"Is that so?" Pike patted his gunbelt and Smallwood fought off a shudder. "Well, I reckon we'll wait and see who's on first."

Then he turned and disappeared into the rainy

night, moving in surprising silence for such a lug of a man. But then, Smallwood hadn't heard him walk up, either. The shiver ran full force down his back. Hugging his arms to his damp chest, he hurried back to his car, locked the doors carefully, and watched to make sure no one followed him.

Chelsea lay in bed Sunday night, listening to the rain and comforting Toy-Toy, who hated thunder.

She'd finished her romance novel earlier. Ely had lots of books scattered everywhere, but none of them interested Chelsea. Philosophy and religion and health.

So with nothing good to read, she had nothing to buffer her mind against the reality of her own life.

She stroked Toy-Toy's trembling body and relived the disaster of Sunday dinner at the Harrises' house.

The women had gone to the kitchen, the men to the living room. If Imogene hadn't physically propelled her toward the kitchen, Chelsea would have gone outside with Timmy and his cousins.

She had more in common with them than Imogene and the other female guest, a prune-faced schoolteacher named Nan Wagner.

"Mean old dragon, too," Chelsea said to her dog. "Worse than the wicked witch of Oz."

Oh, yes, when it was clear Chelsea knew how to do nothing, not even slice bread, Nan had informed her with a sour and superior voice that she'd never catch a man without knowing her way around a kitchen. Having pieced together that Imogene was trying to set Nan up with her brother, Chelsea set her mind to flirting with Luke.

Just to teach the woman a lesson, of course.

By the end of the meal, Nan sat in silence, twin

roses of anger blooming on her cheeks. Imogene paled while her husband concentrated on chewing his pot roast.

Luke, though, seemed to enjoy her constant questions about life in Arkansas. Never once during her barrage did she give Nan a chance to get a word in edgewise. From the way Chelsea simpered and hung on his every word, no one could have guessed she didn't care for the man. Though she did like the way he agreed with her that something should be done about the oppressive conditions in the chicken plants.

But damn him and those deep eyes. He never once looked at her the way all other men did. Even when he and Timmy drove her down the lane, and she let her hand rest in his longer than necessary as she said good-bye, he didn't leer or smirk or gaze at her cleavage.

"So, wuddle one, there you have it. I throw myself at the man, and he doesn't even act like I'm a woman." She kissed his topknot and added, "I did do a good job of punishing Miss Priss, though."

She laughed but felt no joy. Stroking her pet's now-matted fur, she whispered, "Oh, Toy-Toy, I'm tired of being naughty." He wagged his tail, then another bass explosion of thunder rumbled over the house and he quivered. "It'll be okay, wuddle one," she said.

Wishing for someone to comfort her, she fell asleep.

Down the lane, Luke finished tucking Timmy into bed, said good-night to Ely, who was curled on the sofa reading, and retreated to his room.

To mull over the day.

So the woman could be charming. Converse intelligently. Speak eloquently of the conditions the chicken plant workers endured. And make a man feel as if he walked on water.

So what.

She meant nothing to his life. Soon she'd flit out of town, whisked away no doubt in the same private jet town gossip said she'd arrived in.

His clothes landed in a heap on the floor and he climbed into bed, sleeping nude as was his custom. And alone.

And tonight, in the big bed he'd bought when he and Jenny married, lonely. Lonelier than words could say.

He stuffed another pillow behind his head. Poor Nan. Imogene had chewed him out over the phone within minutes of his arrival back home that afternoon. According to her, he'd rudely ignored Nan, humiliating her beyond belief.

Luke regretted that, but he'd scarcely noticed her sitting at the table.

Next to Chelsea, other women faded into the background.

He tried to tell himself he was only reacting this way because his body ached from needing a woman.

In the past, in his ball-playing days, how easy it would have been to fix that need! Now he wore the yoke of the collar, the accountability of a servant of the church.

The burden of morality.

He groaned and knew he'd not sleep easily.

In many ways his meddlesome but well-meaning sister was right.

He needed a wife.

As St. Paul expressed it, "It is better for a man to marry than to burn."

But not Nan Wagner. Not some female who met the specs but didn't own his heart.

He'd vowed after Jenny died that he'd marry again only for love. A love so strong he could not live without the woman.

He punched his pillows and said aloud, "Now you tell me where I'm going to meet anybody like that around here."

Of course silence was his only answer.

Silence and thoughts of the way his body responded when Chelsea Jordan took his hand in hers to say good-bye, looking up at him as if he were the only man on the face of the earth.

"You fool," he whispered.

Chelsea Jordan was a self-proclaimed slut, a wealthy celebrity who had probably slept with half of Hollywood.

A woman who could have any man she wanted.

A woman who made his little boy smile and laugh in a way he hadn't in the past year. A woman who made one of Ely's old suits look like it belonged on the cover of *Vogue*. A spoiled, cosseted, and protected female who had managed to survive a week in a poultry processing plant, under conditions Luke knew were hellish.

He rubbed his chin and wished he could give himself relief. But tonight that wasn't the answer.

His mind overflowed with thoughts of Chelsea, but he didn't want those images driving him to the edge, delivering him to physical release.

With a sinking feeling, he realized he wanted more than that.

Luke Miller, country preacher and pig farmer, wanted Chelsea Jordan to want him.

And only him.

19 ～

When Hoa dropped Chelsea off after work on Monday, Chelsea said she didn't need a ride the next morning.

The Vietnamese woman said nothing, but fixed her eyes on Chelsea, making Chelsea feel some explanation was necessary. Hoa had been kind to her, and as she wondered how to tell her of her decision, Chelsea experienced a prick of guilt.

"I'm quitting," she finally said.

"Why?"

"Are you kidding?" Chelsea jerked at her sweat-stained hair and a chicken feather drifted past her face. She stank of blood and sweat and the horrible musty smell that she thought of as chicken death.

And human death, the slow demise the workers underwent by enduring such inhumane conditions day in and day out.

"Why? No new reason. I just can't stand it anymore." She'd fixated on the idea all day, thinking she'd leave and go see her lawyers in person. They might refuse her calls but they couldn't lock their doors.

Hoa kept staring.

"Oh," Chelsea finally mumbled, "I suppose that's rude of me when you can't quit."

"It's my job."

"But why can't you quit?" Chelsea liked that idea. "Why go back there? Can't you get a job doing something else?"

The woman didn't respond. Which gave Chelsea her answer.

"The people around here don't want to hire a foreigner, do they?"

"They don't even like us working in the poultry plants. Some say we take jobs away from real Americans."

"I say let 'em have them."

"Those same people want you to quit." Hoa had lowered her voice and Chelsea had to lean into the car to hear her.

"What people?"

"The story of why you are here has traveled. We know the Am/Am group will become rich if you go home now." She spoke straight ahead, as if she didn't want to interfere directly with Chelsea's decision.

But she damn sure wanted her to know what she thought.

"You're telling me if I quit they'll be happy."

"And that they will make life difficult for others."

"What can those creeps do?" She'd thought that through all day long, as she toiled in the stifling heat of the building, a heat not lessened at all by the few fans that beat away at the torpid air near the metal roof high above.

"Last year," Hoa said looking down at her hands, "many dogs disappeared in town. Dogs that were

loved by children and parents. These people, these
people that you will let win, posted papers saying
that we Vietnamese killed and ate the dogs and that
Am/Am was the only group that would tell this
truth."

"That's terrible."

"Even more terrible is that those people in
Am/Am killed the dogs so they could blame us."

Chelsea's stomach lurched at the heinous story.
What if someone had sacrificed her precious Toy-
Toy to some sick cause?

"They have done other things, much worse. So far
they have not killed any people, but they will."

Hoa put the car into gear. "Do you want me to
pick you up in the morning?"

"Yes," Chelsea whispered. "I'll be ready."

Barely able to lift one foot after the other, she
trudged to the house, sickened by the thought of
returning to that place of killing, but doubly sickened by the story Hoa had shared.

She'd just turned the doorknob with her bone-
tired hand when another car drove up.

With a nervous glance she checked to see who it
was. If those people wanted her gone, would they try
to help her along with her decision to quit?

A now-familiar blue pickup sat in the gravel turn-
around. The black and white dog from the grocery
store parking lot sat in the back, his head cocked to
one side, as if he, too, were studying her.

She made a face at the dog. Luke Miller emerged
from the driver's side and she made another face at
him. Pesky man. He tipped his cowboy hat and
strolled toward her.

Chelsea looked down at her blood-splattered
slacks. Slacks that the man walking towards her had

commandeered from his sister's castoff pile so she
could have some suitable clothes to wear to that
godawful plant.

Even the blue apron and the heavy rubber apron
and gross shower cap and revolting white paper cap
(with the slogan, All Right Foods, Home of the
Proud Bird, parading across each side) the workers
wore didn't protect them from the offal and splatters
of the birds.

So many birds.

Birds that kept coming, down the line, down the
line, no matter how fast she worked.

Chelsea gulped. Even if she didn't give a fig what
Luke Miller thought of her, she couldn't bear to have
anyone see her in this state.

She threw the door open and rushed inside, showing Luke only her backside, but before she could
slam the door, Toy-Toy hurtled past her and leapt
outside. When she heard the minister step onto the
porch, she cracked the door and said, "What do you
want?"

Not that she could be sure by the inch-wide
vantage point, but she thought he smiled. "To talk to
you," he said.

"This really isn't a good time."

He nodded. "Go ahead and get cleaned up. I'll
wait on the porch."

"It will be a while."

"I understand. Take all the time you need."

She eased the door closed, wondering at the kind-
ness in his voice. But the man was a minister, used
to tending to his flock. Still, he seemed remarkably
calm. Most men would demand her time, preen
before her, certainly not content themselves with
waiting on a porch on a humid afternoon.

Opening the door, she said, "Would you like to wait inside? It might be more comfortable."

He tipped his hat over his eyes, but he didn't answer.

"Well, don't feel that you have to," she said, and started to slam the door.

He stopped it with a swift hand. Stepping inside, he said, "Thank you."

Backing away, she entered the bathroom and barely checked herself before she slammed that door, too.

The man brought out the worst in her.

Luke settled on his favorite spot on Ely's comfortably worn sofa and whistled softly through his teeth, wondering what it was like for a queen of cinema, a woman who'd been a movie star since the age of five, to be caught by a man stinking, her face smeared with what Luke recognized as the slime wrought by a day on the line at All Right Foods.

Not a good feeling for Chelsea Jordan.

His whistling picked up.

Somehow the thought cheered him.

The woman could do with an education in the real world. How the other half, or seven-eighths, actually lived.

Maybe old Ely knew what he was about.

He found it odd she hadn't asked him about Ely. Didn't she grieve for him? Didn't she want to know about his last days? Under the circumstances, he was just as glad she hadn't bothered to ask.

He'd have to lie.

Though, listening to the shower flow from behind the closed bathroom door, he did think this time the end justified the means.

He heard Macduff bark in a warning tone and

moved to the door to check. Ely's dog was not prone to false alarms. Given what Timmy had told him that led him on this expedition to speak with Chelsea, his senses were on alert.

No other vehicle stood in the drive. No dust had been kicked up on the lane.

Macduff barked again, and Luke laughed as he saw the bit-of-fluff poodle charging the larger dog.

Luke whistled to Macduff and the dog sat on his haunches and quit barking. The poodle took advantage and ran full speed ahead to throw itself at Macduff.

"Toy-Toy, what's wrong, wuddle one?" Chelsea dashed to the door, pulling on a pink robe, a robe that clung to the curves of her body still damp from the shower.

"Is someone hurting him?" she cried, catching hold of Luke's arm.

"More the other way around," Luke said. He looked at her freshly-scrubbed face, her long wet hair streaming down her back. No makeup. No artifice. Just concern for her pet.

"Oh." Chelsea remained in the doorway with him, but her hand slipped free of his arm. "Come to mummy."

The dog ignored her, continuing his assault on the much larger border collie. Macduff, to his credit, scarcely batted an eye at the little pest.

Luke took advantage of her nearness to breathe in the scent of Chelsea. He expected exotic, but what he found was Head and Shoulders and Zest.

Ely's brands.

He suppressed a smile and marveled at how well Chelsea wore the basics. A bead of water dripped from her hair and trickled over her cheek. She reached up to brush it away and caught him staring.

"Oh!" She backed away from the door, pulling her robe more snugly around her. "Whatever am I thinking?"

"That your dog was in danger?"

"You are the oddest man." She lifted one hand to pick the weight of her damp hair from her shoulders and kept the other hand on guard at the front of the thin robe.

Luke tossed his hat onto the coffee table. "And what makes you say that?"

She didn't answer. She simply swept from the room, wet head held high.

Chelsea shut the bedroom door behind her and propped the wastebasket against it. Which was silly, because the last thing in the world she expected was Mr. Goody Goody to come after her.

But maybe she wanted him to.

The pink silk robe slithered to the floor and Chelsea asked herself where that silly idea had come from. But her nipples had peaked into a state of interest she couldn't deny. How long had it been since she'd wanted a man?

She touched one of the betraying nipples and whispered, "Forget it. He's too nice for you."

Then she jumped into a pair of Ely's sweats and another one of his undershirts, wishing she had a clean bra. Despite the heat of the afternoon, she pulled on a sweatshirt jacket and zipped it to cover her breasts. And she almost laughed at the picture she made—porn queen turns prim and proper for the preacher.

When she returned to the living room, Luke Miller

was sitting on the sofa reading one of Ely's boring books. When he saw her, he rose and waited for her to be seated before he resumed his place.

My, my, these country boys did have manners.

"Your dog seems to have calmed down," he said.

She ran to look out the door. Toy-Toy was curled between Macduff's front legs, sleeping.

"He's made a friend," Chelsea said with a smile. She sat down. "I suppose I should offer you something, but there's no one to prepare anything."

Luke seemed to choke.

"Are you okay? Let me get you a glass of water." She hurried to the kitchen, rummaged through the cupboards, and filled some sort of jar with water.

"Here you are," she said, feeling pleased with herself.

He sipped from the jar and seemed to feel better. "Thanks. Water's fine." He put the drink down and leaned forward, a very serious look on his face.

"I came to see you because of something Timmy said."

Chelsea's heart sank. Concerned parent warns slut away from innocent child. She supposed she couldn't blame him, but her fury flared at being judged without evidence against her. Always that damned reputation of hers. "I don't care what you say, if Timmy wants to be my friend I don't see why he shouldn't." She stuck her jaw out and waited for him to argue.

Luke looked shocked by her reaction. "That's not what I'm here to say. As far as I'm concerned, if Timmy doesn't drive you crazy, he can come over every day."

"You really mean that?"

"Why wouldn't I?"

"Well, um, lots of people wouldn't consider me the best influence . . ."

"Miss Jordan, many people don't consider *me* the best influence." He smiled and reached across the sofa to pat her hand.

She stared at his hand covering hers. She didn't jerk away, though.

Then he, too, stared at his hand. He willed it to draw back, to return properly to his side. Instead, he turned her hand over and traced a circle on the delicate skin.

He wasn't sure, but he thought maybe he was holding his breath.

As she seemed to be.

He saw, studying her hand, several reddish, puffy spots where the fingers joined the palm. "From the plant?" he asked.

She nodded.

"You're being very brave."

She snatched her hand away. "Fuck that. I'm not brave. I'm here because I'm trapped. And don't forget it. Now what do you need to tell me before you leave?"

Luke stared, shocked by the abrupt change in her behavior. Just when she seemed a vulnerable, approachable, naturally likeable woman, she turned into a street-mouthed tramp.

But as suddenly as she'd turned on him, he saw what she was doing. Chelsea Jordan, actress, was trying to scare him off.

He almost smiled, the thought made him feel so good.

Women didn't do that unless they were afraid they might care. Suppressing the urge to whistle a happy tune, he stuck to the reason for his visit.

"Timmy told me someone left a dead chicken on your clothesline."

Chelsea wondered if she'd heard him correctly. One minute he caressed her hand, stirring the craziest feelings of tenderness in her, and when she told him to get fucked, instead of slamming out the door, he expressed concern. Slowly, she said, "That did happen."

"What did you do with the note?"

"What makes you think there was a note?"

"I wasn't born yesterday," he said dryly.

"As far as I know, it's still out there. I certainly haven't gone to check."

"And the chicken's still there?" Luke looked like he was going to gag.

"I wasn't touching it!"

"Of course not. You stay here. I'll go out and take care of it."

He rose. Despite his command, she followed him out the door. Both dogs roused themselves and trailed after them.

The smell hit her even before they'd rounded the corner to the back. Funny she hadn't noticed it before. Maybe because it had been raining.

Luke stopped and Chelsea bumped into his back.

He turned and lifted a hand, resting it lightly on her shoulder. "You really don't want to see this. I'll get Ely's shovel and bury it."

She'd seen enough dead chickens. "Thank you," she finally said.

He dropped his hand and she felt strangely bereft.

Chelsea bent to collect Toy-Toy. When the other dog followed Luke, Toy-Toy yapped and struggled so she let him go. He trotted off through the grass that

stood to his chest, waving his little tail, happy to be a
country dog.

Returning to the house, she made her way to the
kitchen, realizing that after all the work she'd done
that day, her stomach rumbled with hunger.

Tired of her diet of tuna fish and fruit, she opened
the refrigerator. The only item she recognized as
food consisted of the growing mound of eggs Timmy
collected.

She wondered how to turn an egg into dinner.

Maybe she'd ask Luke before he left.

Then she heard the Wagner woman's whiny voice
warning she'd never catch a man without knowing
her way around the kitchen.

Maybe she wouldn't ask Luke.

Some things had to be easy to figure out.

Look how simple it had been to drive that truck.

Luke knocked at the front door. "All done," he
called.

Chelsea went to the door and opened it wide.

"I thought you wanted me to go," he said, fixing
her with those deep blue eyes as if he could see right
through to her soul.

Not that she had a soul.

"That's right," she said. "I do."

Luke leaned against the door frame, a smile playing along the line of his lips. He had beautiful lips,
well formed with a hint of a pucker in the top. "I
do," he repeated softly.

Irritated that he seemed to be making fun of her,
she stamped her foot. "Go home."

"Need my hat." He pointed toward the coffee
table.

"Well take your hat and go." She grabbed it and
thrust it through a wedge in the door.

He placed one large hand on the door, holding it open. Looking down at her, he said, "Listen to me. The card was gone, probably washed away in the rain. But if anything—anything—like that happens again, I want you to tell me right away. I'm going to report this to Sheriff Pike."

"Oh, please don't."

"Why not?"

"You don't know what it's like, living your life in bed with the press. They'll be all over the story. Just let it die."

He continued to look grim. "You're in a peculiar situation here. The way I understand the story, if you stick this thing out for a month, those fanatics miss out on quite a fortune."

She nodded and rubbed the goosebumps that had gathered on her arms.

"Are you sticking around?" he asked softly.

Jutting her chin toward him, she said, "What's it to you?"

Looking at her with an unreadable expression, he said, "That's a good question." Then he turned, gave a sharp whistle, and strode to the truck. The black and white dog bounded toward him and leapt into the back.

Toy-Toy raced into the front yard, yapping as Luke drove away.

Mia had been pumping Ely for hours about Luke's life story. Quentin thought he'd gag if he heard one more glowing account of how Luke had turned around so many of the young people in town, how he'd been a sports star, how he'd given up the majors as a result of his father's deathbed request to return to pastor the church.

Mia lapped it up, sighing. Her eyes shone.

Finally when he couldn't stand it a moment longer, he jumped up from where he'd been mending Timmy's glove beside the hammock and said, "Let's go check on Chelsea."

"Let's not," Mia said.

"And why not?"

"You know we're not allowed to intervene."

"I don't intervene when I go over there, I just scope things out."

"Oh?" Mia couldn't help herself from objecting. Even though since the day at the creek she believed Quentin loved her, she still wrestled with the demon of jealousy.

"Aw, come on, I'm not going to break the rules and speak to her. I won't do anything but watch."

"Watch?" Mia's voice turned to starch. "Don't you mean ogle?"

"Perhaps," he drawled. Quentin knew he shouldn't tease Mia. But he didn't want her thinking he'd fall by the wayside every time a gorgeous blonde crossed his path. He wanted her to trust him.

"All right, I'll go with you. To make sure you don't break any rules."

Ely smiled and Quentin wanted to ask him whose side he was on. But he continued to mind his P's and Q's with Ely, a man he'd come to respect, a man of integrity and imagination.

Ely pointed to a pickup careening into the drive. "I think Luke went down there earlier. Guess he's back now."

"Ooh, he went to see Chelsea?" Hope sounded in Mia's voice.

"You still think he's the magic ingredient in all this, don't you?" Quentin asked the question in a low voice, admiring the way Mia's eyes sparkled when she wore that look that said she believed with love all things were possible.

Mia nodded. "I will admit when I first came up with the idea of making Chelsea go to his church I wanted her to be spurned by him, but now"— she smiled at Quentin and reached over and squeezed his hand —"now, I want everyone to be as happy as we are."

His fear over her jealousy of Chelsea evaporated. He leaned over and kissed her, chastely enough considering Ely was there. "Me, too," he said, holding out a hand to help her from the hammock.

They strolled hand in hand down the lane. But as they neared the house, Quentin sensed Mia's hesitation.

He paused. "What's wrong, muffin?"

She started to speak, then stopped.

"Tell me," he whispered.

"I-I never thought of myself as a jealous person," she said at last.

"Me neither."

"But"— she turned her big eyes on him and he saw a tear or two sparkling on her lashes —"but before when I thought you'd never notice me, at least I didn't have something to lose." She dabbed at her eyes. "Does that make sense?"

"And now you're afraid you're going to lose me?" Quentin tugged at his Yankees cap. He didn't have the words to reassure her. Only time and his love could do that.

She kicked at the dusty gravel and nodded.

"What can I do to make you trust me?"

Mia nibbled on the inside of her cheek. She knew she was being insecure and ridiculous, but she wanted him to prove he put her first. She took a deep breath and said in a rush, "Not go check on Chelsea?"

"What?"

"You heard me," she said.

"Don't be ridiculous. You can't test love that way. It's not fair."

In her heart she agreed, but she'd made her statement and now clung to it.

Quentin started walking.

She caught at his arm. "What are you doing?"

"I'm going to make sure Chelsea Jordan is okay. You and I both know there are people, bad people, who want to see her fail. And I'm going to do everything within my power to make sure that doesn't happen."

Mia's lip trembled. She wished she'd never uttered the stupid challenge. Of course their second chance at life, which hinged on Chelsea's softening behavior, was the essential matter.

She hurried after him. She'd apologize as soon as they left the house. After all, she had her pride.

They walked the rest of the way in silence, Mia wishing she weren't so stubborn, knowing she had to learn to trust him. Love without trust—what was the point?

And if they did win a second chance at life, Quentin might press the point of offering Chelsea the *Kriss-Kross* role. Everyone in the industry knew Chelsea Jordan never made a film without sleeping with either the director, producer, or leading man—and sometimes combinations thereof. The woman's promiscuity was legend.

If Mia wanted Quentin, she'd have to trust him even in that situation.

Just thinking about the nightmare of Chelsea doing *Kriss-Kross* steamed Mia even more. She walked faster, absorbed in her dismal thoughts.

She and Quentin had dreamed for years of the day they could bring their co-written Hitchcock send-up to life. Now, with the clout of the studio and the promise of *DinoDaddy*'s success, Salvatino More would let them do any picture they wanted.

And Mia wanted to do *Kriss-Kross.*

She could argue against Chelsea for the lead. But if Quentin wanted Chelsea and the studio wanted her, Mia's vote would count for naught.

Besides, Chelsea was perfect for the film.

But, if Chelsea Jordan took the part, Mia vowed as she stomped into Ely's yard, it would be the first-ever Quentin Grandy film not produced by Mia Tortelli.

"Cat got your tongue?" Quentin asked softly, smiling at her.

Embroiled in her worrying, she didn't answer. If she couldn't believe that she mattered more than any other woman, why say anything?

Looking hurt, Quentin shrugged, walked to the back of the house, and peered inside a window. "Holy cow!" he shouted and bolted to the back door.

Her heart in her throat, Mia chased after him. Had something happened to Chelsea?

20 ⌒

Black smoke poured from the stovetop. Pops and crackles issued from a pan. The stench of sulfur filled the air. Mia covered her nose and wiped eyes that watered instantly.

Quentin grabbed a cloth.

Chelsea appeared in the doorway, flapping a paperback book she held in one hand. She wrinkled her nose and peered at the stove.

A sizzling sound erupted and Quentin made a dash for the saucepan just as a spark zapped Chelsea on the cheek.

"Oh my God! I'm hit!" Chelsea dropped the book, a look of horror on her face. Tears flowed immediately.

Mia marveled at the stupidity of the woman. What would she have done if Quentin hadn't been there? Let the house burn down?

A sick feeling hit her stomach. Mia remembered all too clearly the old guy in his raspy voice warning them, "If you speak directly to the target, the jig's up." What if . . . what would happen if Quentin in

301

his impetuous way ignored the rule and spoke to her?

She tugged at his arm. "Let's get out of here."

"Are you crazy? She needs help." He chucked the pan in the sink.

"My face, I'm ruined," Chelsea sobbed, standing in the kitchen like a lost child.

"But not from us. We shouldn't be here."

"You don't walk away from someone in need." Quentin pulled free, yanked open the refrigerator, found an ice cube, and held it to Chelsea's cheek.

"There, now, it'll be okay," he murmured, stroking her hair and letting the chill of the ice absorb the sting of the tiny cinder that had flown from the charred pot. "What were you cooking?"

Mia waved her arms. "Stop!"

With wide eyes, Chelsea looked up at Quentin and said, "Boiled"— she hiccuped —"eggs."

Quentin looked at Mia as if to say—see, it's okay. Nothing happened. To Chelsea, he said, "And they boiled dry?"

She looked puzzled. "What do you mean?"

"You left them on too long and all the water boiled out."

"Oh, I didn't put any water in. Just eggs." Then she seemed to focus. "Did you know you look exactly like Quentin Grandy?"

Quentin dropped the melting ice cube to the floor.

Mia said in her sternest voice, "We have to get out of here. Now."

"Will you relax? That old coot obviously didn't mean what he said."

"What are you doing in my kitchen?" Chelsea said.

"Quentin Grandy, at your service." Quentin smiled, and before Mia's eyes, disappeared.

Mia made the sign of the cross and stared at the spot where Quentin had been. Gone. Everything but his Yankees cap, which drifted down and landed with a soft plunk on the kitchen floor. She choked back a scream and dropped to the floor, clutching the cap.

Chelsea glanced around, obviously puzzled. "Hello," she called, looking right through Mia, which led her to assume she was still invisible. Chelsea must have been able to see and hear Quentin because he broke the rules and spoke to her. The actress walked into the front of the house, then returned. She locked the back door and, looking uneasy, surveyed the kitchen once again before collecting her book and leaving the room.

Mia doubled over in horror. Quentin had flaunted the rules and the power that had sent them back to earth. Calling him an old coot! What was he thinking? Quentin's problem—one of them, anyway—was that he wasn't afraid of anything or anyone.

And look what that had gotten him.

She shivered. What if he were dead?

Dead forever?

Mia crushed his Yankees cap to her lips. Oh, Quentin!

She'd been so mean to him, refusing even to speak as they approached Ely's house. And now he was gone.

She had let her insecurity ruin their last moments together. What if she never got to see him again? Feel his touch, hear his laughter, revel in the way he tantalized her into sweet sensuous exhaustion?

"I promise," she whispered, standing there in

Ely's kitchen, "if we're reunited, I'll never be jealous again."

Mia wiped her eyes and began to back from the room.

Then she realized no one had turned the burner off.

Fearful lest she too disappear in an instant, Mia tiptoed to the stove. She hesitated, but her nature wouldn't let her leave the room without correcting the problem. And if the mysterious power did whisk her away, maybe, just maybe, she'd end up with Quentin again.

With a shaking hand, she reached for the knob.

Chelsea survived several more days at the plant without incident. To endure the monotony and agonizing repetitive movements, she pretended to be elsewhere. She let her thoughts drift to her miserable days in boarding school, to recalling the months after the Italian porn flick when, to punish herself, she gave her body to every man she met.

Then the chicken plant didn't seem so bad.

She didn't think of the days that stretched ahead, didn't count the hours or minutes of the day. She simply stood, shifting from one aching foot to the other, hanging dead birds on hooks, existing within only that moment.

When breaktime came, she rushed out the door with the rest of them. The line formed quickly in the restroom and to cope with the oppressive heat and sweltering humidity of the metal-roofed building, she drank as much water in the morning and at break as she could stand.

She'd made it almost to the end of the second week when she once again found herself the only person in the women's room at the end of the afternoon break.

As she reached to flush the toilet, someone banged against the door.

"Hey girl, we're back to talk to you."

"That's right, child," another voice said.

Chelsea froze. She'd only stopped the line once that day. What did these people want from her?

"We doan want you to come out till we're gone. But we want to tell you for a white-ass honky you ain't so bad."

She let out the breath she'd been holding. "Th-thank you," she said.

"Yeah, girl, don't let those Ku-Klukkers get that money, ya hear?"

"You know about that?" She buttoned her pants and drew the spattered apron down over her clothing. Who would believe Chelsea Jordan was holding a conversation through a bathroom stall door? Wondering at what had happened to her life, she added, "How?"

"Ooh, child, people knows what happens."

She heard feet shuffling from the room. She yanked the door open and raced back to the line.

Tardiness was not excused.

The rest of the afternoon, Chelsea kept up with the mountains of birds but now she looked around her, studying the deadened expressions so common on the workers' faces. The line of birds moved at such a pace that no matter the job of the worker, constant attention and motion were demanded.

A woman across from her wielded a pair of scissors. Chelsea had no idea what part of the birds she snipped with them, but she noted that not once did the worker have the opportunity to shift the position of her hand, or stretch and ease the muscles that must surely be cramped.

Chelsea saw for the first time the woman with the stopwatch. Holding forth the timepiece, a clipboard tucked under one arm, the grim-faced woman stood behind the shoulder of a woman on the far side of the U of the line opposite Chelsea.

As she kept up with the birds she had to hang, Chelsea studied the woman being timed and finally realized that that worker's job consisted of pulling the guts from each chicken. To her right, a jolly-looking man in a white coat stood, nodding as each bird passed by at a rapid clip.

That man was the only person not wearing a blue worker's smock and rubber apron. He had to be some sort of inspector, but Chelsea found it hard to believe he could see anything about the condition of the chickens at the fast rate the birds moved past him.

The woman pulling the guts out kept glancing over her shoulder at the woman with the stopwatch. Her face got redder and redder and each time she checked behind her, she missed a bird.

A whistle blew and the line stopped.

Willie Sims appeared beside the stopwatch woman.

He spoke to the worker. Of course in the noise and tumult of the plant, Chelsea couldn't tell what was said.

But she did see the worker burst into tears.

Willie motioned to someone else to take the woman's spot and escorted the worker from the plant. The line resumed.

Hoa shook her head. "That is too bad," she said. "Did they fire her?"

Hoa nodded. "The girl is pregnant and they don't

want to pay her insurance. So they watch her, make her crazy, do badly, then they fire her."

Chelsea stared at her in horror. "They can't do that!"

"No?" Hoa turned her attention back to the chickens that were piling up.

Chelsea did the same.

But she knew that wasn't the last of the matter.

The time would come when this nightmare ended for her. But these workers, most of them women who apparently couldn't get other jobs, would still be trapped.

Chelsea had made it a point to support the Jewish groups she and Fran had adopted. She made appearances, donated money. But anyone with leisure time and spare cash could do that.

For the first time, she actually saw a situation where she—and she alone—could make a difference.

Surprisingly energized, she whipped those damn birds onto the hooks at a faster rate, mentally daring the witch with the stopwatch to toy with her.

Driving home with Hoa at the end of that week, Chelsea told her newfound friend what she planned to do.

The woman said nothing.

"Don't you want better conditions?"

Hoa fingered the steering wheel. "It is not the way of the world."

"That's a defeatist attitude. No wonder they take advantage of you."

Hoa merely looked straight ahead.

"I'm calling a meeting for next Thursday after work. I'd really like for you to come."

Hoa at last turned in her direction. "It has been tried before. But there are no unions in this business. At least not in All Right Foods. You saw what happened to that woman last week. They forced her from the job and replaced her like that." She snapped her fingers, uncharacteristically animated. "And you think you can change things overnight." She shook her head as if the sorrow weighted it.

"Well, I can try." Chelsea jumped from the car and slammed the door after her, furious not at Hoa, but at the plant management. Those ogres had these poor people so beaten down they couldn't see they could change things.

Hoa handed her a brown-paper–wrapped package through the car window. "This is for you."

"For me?"

"After your story about boiling eggs, I thought you might like this." She smiled slightly and drove away.

Walking up the lane, Chelsea unwrapped the package.

A red-and-white-checked book lay in the paper.

"*Better Homes and Gardens New Cook Book,*" she read aloud.

Looking down at her sticky, sweaty, dirty self, she started to laugh. If she could labor in a chicken plant, what could be so hard about cooking?

Maybe, she mused later, letting the water pour over her in the shower, she'd invite the preacher to dinner. He struck her as an unusual man to find beneath a clerical collar. Maybe, just maybe, he'd support her move to organize the workers.

On Saturday, she sent the invitation via Timmy, suddenly shy to ask him in person. For a week from Sunday. She needed time to practice.

But when she got in the truck to go to town, it wouldn't start. Almost in tears, she thought of Toy-Toy starving, not to mention herself, if she didn't get to the store. She had only one Charlie's Lunch Kit left in the house and she wasn't about to try cooking eggs again. That domestic disaster had had her hallucinating about Quentin Grandy, a terrific director she'd love to work with, but why she thought of him then she had no idea.

Stranded in the truck, feeling sorry for herself, she heard another vehicle approaching, swirling a cloud of dust in its wake.

Luke shuttled down the lane, wondering just when his life had started going to hell in a handbasket.

He now had an invisible woman sleeping on the sofa in his living room. The arrangement worked fine for Ely and Timmy, both of whom chattered on endlessly with the woman they called Mia.

According to Ely, a tragedy had befallen Mia's companion. Mia was so distraught Ely had thought it the Christian thing to do to take her into the house.

It seems, Luke learned, she'd been sleeping in his barn.

And now here he was hurtling down Blueberry Lane to check on a former porn star, just in case the local Klan sympathizers had paid another call.

Because he had a feeling, a very strong feeling, Chelsea wouldn't mention such a visit to him. For all her fluttering eyelashes, she struck him as one tough cookie.

It looked as if he'd come in the nick of time.

Chelsea sat behind the wheel of Ely's pickup truck, cursing more colorfully than the guys on his old ball team.

"My, my, my," he murmured, enjoying the flush on her cheeks and the way she bit her lip in concentration.

He parked, climbed out, and strolled toward the driver's side, giving a wide berth to the front of the truck. He'd seen firsthand how dangerous the woman could be.

"Afternoon," he called.

With a scowl, she glanced over at him. "Oh, hello."

"Here in Arkansas, we try to be friendly to our neighbors."

"Well, how-dee," she said with great sarcasm. "But can't you see I'm leaving?"

Luke chuckled despite himself. "Actually, it looks like you're not going anywhere."

"I intended to go to town," she said and tucked a wayward strand of hair over her shoulder. "But this d—this truck won't cooperate. But as soon as it does, move out of my way."

"Don't worry," he murmured. "Would you like me to check it out?"

She gave a half-shrug, but he noted the spark of interest in her eye.

He glanced into the cab, but all he could focus on were her shapely legs sunwarmed to a light gold, stretching beneath the shorts Imogene had loaned her. Her feet were bare and the pearly pink polish that tipped her toenails gave her small feet a sweetly feminine air.

Luke forced his attention back to Chelsea's face. Safer. Much safer.

"I can check under the hood."

"That would be nice." She said it as if she actually meant the words. Luke smiled at her, the thought foremost in his mind that he'd love to check under her hood.

"First, turn the key," he said. He'd better stick to the business at hand.

She did and he ran an eye over the gauges, zeroing in on the gas needle that didn't budge above empty. "When's the last time you filled up?"

Chelsea gave him a blank stare.

'With gasoline." He was pretty sure she was only playing dumb, and wondered why she did it so much. Perhaps she thought men liked dumb blondes. "You do know how to drive, don't you?"

She colored, and Luke likened the pink of her cheek to rose petals, a poetic comparison he wished he hadn't made. This woman was trouble, something he'd best remember.

"It's not something I do a lot." She looked away, as if seeing a vision many miles distant. "I guess I don't really do much of anything."

"Oh, no, you're only a movie star known around the world."

"You wouldn't think much of that if you knew what my life was really like." Then she seemed to realize she was talking to a man she barely knew, for she straightened her shoulders, and said, "I really have to get to the store."

"I'll grab my gas can." That would get him safely away. Working quickly, he snatched the red plastic can he carried in the back of his truck, poured in enough to get her to town, and said, "You're all set."

She was looking at him, those green eyes of hers surprisingly childlike. He set the can on the ground. "**So**mething else?"

"Well," Chelsea said, not quite meeting his eyes, "I have driven to town before." She blushed, obviously remembering their first meeting. "But I could benefit from a refresher."

"You mean you want a driving lesson?"

With a frosty voice, she said, "Not a lesson. Simply a review. It's possible I'm a bit rusty."

Chelsea heard the rudeness in her tone, but she felt helpless to soften her tongue. She didn't want to look stupid around this man, a man who led a church, was a great dad to Timmy, and had been Ely's friend. But she didn't want to risk hitting anyone again, and she wanted to figure out why all the other cars whizzed past the truck on the highway.

At least he didn't laugh at her. He simply opened the door and said, "Scoot over and I'll review the basics."

She wiggled over on the bench seat, but not before he swung behind the wheel. His thigh, warm and rock-firm beneath jeans faded almost white, grazed hers and she forgot to scoot farther.

Chelsea tipped her head toward the preacher's and looked at him, really studied his face. His lips curved upwards, telling her he was a man who enjoyed life despite his losses. His nose had a lean slope to it, adding distinction to his face. And his eyes—his eyes graced with those dusky lashes were wells of indigo blue that seemed to see straight through the facade that was Chelsea Jordan.

Luke pushed his cowboy hat back on his head and watched Chelsea gazing at him. The warmth of her sun-kissed thigh singed his leg and sent his blood pumping. She hadn't moved over very far. He asked himself, looking into eyes that sparkled, eyes the green of the lush fields of his home when the spring growth blossomed forth, whether he wanted her to move.

And what he would do if she parted her lips and offered her mouth to him.

She wet her lips with the tip of her tongue.

Luke figured he'd better resume the driving lesson.

Because he knew what he would do.

"Pressing down the clutch pedal," he said, nudging her over slightly so he could settle behind the wheel, "disengages the clutch. Releasing the pedal results in the flywheel driving the transmission shaft."

"Oh."

"Never mind all that," he said. "Just watch me. When I press in the pedal, then I can shift gears." He did so and moved the stick into first.

First. Like first base. Would he ever get to first base with a woman like Chelsea? Forget it, Miller, he told himself. If you'd stayed in baseball and made it big and were sitting here with a World Series ring on, maybe she'd let you play DiMaggio to her Marilyn.

"You start out in first, then shift from first to second to third to fourth as you pick up speed."

Speed. He'd been fast. Broken records. Set new ones.

What did that matter now?

"The location of the gears are marked on this knob." Luke pointed to the worn white lettering on the gearshift knob. Ely should have bought a new truck a long time ago, but he claimed it was wasteful to buy a new one when there was nothing wrong with his old reliable one.

"Give me your hand," Luke said.

She offered her left hand but he reached over and said, "It's better to use your right, to get the feel of the stick." He cradled her palm around the knob, placed his hand on top of hers, and shifted through the gears. "Do you feel each position?"

Chelsea nodded, unable to look him in the eye. This man in no way had come on to her, hadn't treated her like a disposable Barbie doll the way most men did. Yet at this moment, listening to his words and savoring the touch of his hand on hers, she felt desirable, sensual, and strangely enough, innocent.

This man who'd no more look at her kind of woman than he would a prostitute, made her feel good to be a woman.

"Let me see if I can do it on my own," she said, edging his hand from hers. Any more contact and she'd overheat.

He slipped from the truck, walked around to the other side, and got in. Pulling the hat farther down over his eyes, he said in a gruffer voice than he'd used before, "Remember to push the clutch pedal in when you shift, then let it out nice and slow."

"Nice and slow," Chelsea whispered.

The truck rolled a few feet. She gathered a bit of speed and shifted to second, much more smoothly than the other day she'd crawled into town. "I'm doing it," she cried, pleased with herself for conquering her incompetence.

"That's good," Luke said, enjoying the sparkle of unaffected pleasure in her eyes.

"Now, to stop," he said, deciding he'd best get back to his house ASAP, "downshift."

"Oh, do it in opposite order."

He nodded.

"Makes sense," she said, turning the full power of her smile on him. Luke ached to touch her when she looked at him like that, all little girl innocence, showing none of the tough-lady let-me-shock-you nonsense she'd exhibited before.

"I guess," he said, remembering the original purpose of his trip down the lane, "the Am/Am people haven't been back to bother you."

"Oh, no," she said, gliding to a halt without even a lurch. Then she took her foot off the clutch and the truck leapt forward.

"In gear, pedal down," she murmured. "Thanks for the lesson."

"My pleasure," he said, opening the door. Then a question, a question that had bothered him since Ely had gotten him involved in this escapade, popped out. "This probably isn't any of my business, but I'd like to know the answer anyway. Why didn't you call when I sent the telegram about Ely's death?"

She clouded over, reminding him of Timmy's expression before he threw a tantrum.

"Ely has always been my very good friend," Luke said gently. "I'm not asking just to be nosy." Which he hoped to be true. He wanted to believe Chelsea Jordan had a heart. A heart, a soul, and a conscience.

They sat in silence, Luke waiting to see if she would answer.

Finally, she lifted her eyes to his and whispered, "I was afraid."

"Of what?"

She shook her head, a frown troubling her brow. "My parents never had any use for me, except as a child star to parade about. My mother, Ely's niece, really despised me. She always said I ruined her life, being born." Chelsea sighed, and gave a little laugh. "You probably think this sounds like some poor little rich girl sob story, but you asked the question."

She toyed with the steering wheel, then said, "Ely came to visit me, the last time when I was ten. He was the only person in my family who accepted me, who seemed to love me."

"So why were you afraid to come to him?" When he needed you, he added silently; when he begged you to come.

Again, she moved her head slowly from side to side, but this time did not answer.

He saw the single tear appear on her cheek.

He captured it with a gentle touch. "It's okay to cry for those we love."

"But I should have come." Chelsea beat her hands against the wheel. "Now it's too late. I owed it to Ely, and I turned my back on him. What a selfish bitch."

He tipped her chin up, wiped away another tear. "You're here now."

"What good does that do Uncle Ely?" she cried.

"Oh," Luke said, "you'd be surprised."

"Yeah, like he's in heaven looking down at me and seeing me suffer. Well, if that's so, I guess it serves me right." She swiped at her eyes. "God only knows flying here to visit Uncle Ely would have been a whole lot easier than hanging dead birds for a month!"

Luke laughed along with her, pleased that when she forgot to maintain her dumb-blonde image, she had a lively sense of humor. Still smiling, he slipped from the truck, shut the door quietly behind him, and said, "God does work in mysterious ways, you know."

She nodded. He started to walk away, then rounded the truck. Stopping at the driver's door, he said, "Timmy and I are looking forward to dinner next week. Thank you for inviting us."

She smiled, answer enough for him. He walked to his truck whistling, wondering if she could learn to cook as easily as she picked up on the fine points of driving.

21 ⟶

The low turnout at the workers meeting disappointed Chelsea. Counting herself, and Hoa, they were twelve. Twelve! She'd learned from Hoa that including the processing plant where they worked, and the deboning and frozen foods plants next door, more than a thousand people toiled for All Right Foods.

So many people so badly treated.

Chelsea studied the small numbers who'd ventured to meet her in the park down the road from the gates of the plant complex. Perhaps she should have gone against Hoa's advice and held the meeting in the lunchroom, before the workers scattered for the evening.

She looked at the silent faces, mostly women and several men. Black, Asian, white, they looked back at her. Clearing her throat, she said, "Even though I'm a stranger here, I can't sit back and ignore the things I see. I saw a woman fired the other day, a pregnant woman, who I now know has three other children.

"Hoa has told me about chicken itch, and how the time she wanted to go to the hospital for it, the nurse

in the plant laughed at her. Nurse! Why, if I've ever
seen a management flunky, it's that woman in the
white uniform."

One older woman clapped two gnarled hands
together. "Yeah, that's right," she said.

Encouraged by the comment, Chelsea took a deep
breath.

"I know you've no reason to listen to me, and I'll
be gone soon, but I simply can't turn my back and
not try to help."

"And why is that?" drawled a tall black man,
wiping sweat from his brow.

"To be honest, it isn't like me at all."

The man cracked a smile, possibly pleased that
she'd answered him openly.

Hoa stepped forward. "Miss Jordan has worked
beside me for over two weeks now. At first she
whined like a baby. Then she got tough, like an old
hen." Hoa smiled and Chelsea figured the figure of
speech was meant as a compliment.

"She says that we can work to better our conditions, that we can call for a union election and have
longer breaks and not have to work when we are ill."

Hoa looked at every face in the small gathering.
Chelsea held her breath, knowing that they were
much more likely to listen to an insider. "They will
try to fire us if we stand up to them. They will send
the woman with the watch to torment us. But I have
known torment before in my life. I do not mind
doing an honest day's labor, but in this company,
they ask for more than that, they ask for our lives. I
say we make a stand."

Chelsea applauded.

The others joined in.

"That was brilliant," she said to Hoa.

Hoa smiled. "I rented *Norma Rae* last night. It is a good movie."

Chelsea smiled back. "The power of Hollywood," she said, and passed out a handful of flyers to each of the people. "This paper asks for a representative of the National Labor Relations Board to visit the plant. Do your best and get as many workers as you can to sign these papers. Return them to me by Monday."

One woman, standing to the side of the group, said, "Where are you going to be when I can't feed my family 'cause these people laid me off?"

"They can't fire you for organizing. It's your right."

"Humph, they won't say it's for that. It'll be something else." The woman turned away, obviously disgusted and discouraged.

"Anyone who's fired, I'll personally support until you get another job."

The woman laughed. "Right. You'll be gone from here and back in your mansion. You're not going to remember us."

Chelsea swallowed. What the woman said was probably true. She'd fired her own staff willy-nilly, without ever thinking of them, of what it meant for them to get by on domestic workers' wages, at the mercies of some rich bitch who never once considered the reality of their lives.

In less than two weeks she'd be back in Bel Air.

Would she remember?

Or would she drown this nightmare in a magnum of champagne, float in a bubble bath, work the toxins out of her system with a body wrap, and with a flick of her wrist and a trick of her mind, pretend the entire month never happened?

Two weeks ago the worker glaring at her would have been right.

But now, Chelsea Jordan, heartless bitch supreme, hoped she was wrong.

The woman trudged off down the street.

Chelsea ran after her. Touching her on the shoulder, she said, "Please take the flyers. Please help. You cared enough to come tonight, cared more than many of the others. Doesn't that mean something to you? I promise—I swear—I'll help you if these bastards retaliate."

The woman lifted her head, brushed a hank of damp gray hair from her face with a pudgy hand. She studied Chelsea for a long minute, then reached out and accepted a sheaf of flyers. "I'll give you a chance," she said, then walked away.

Drained of every fiber of energy after a day on the line and the emotions stirred by the meeting, Chelsea thanked Hoa for the ride and for her support and made her slow way to the door of Ely's house.

"Toy-Toy, I'm home," she called, slipping into the dusky interior.

No patter of feet wafted to her ears. No excited yelp, no begging of her once-citified dog demanding to be let outside to roam, sounded in the small house.

Her heart leaping to her throat, Chelsea flipped the living room light and called her pet again.

No response.

Clutching her throat, forgetful of her stinky clothing and the chicken muck in her hair, she ran to the kitchen, then to the bedroom.

Then the bathroom.

Where she gasped, then gagged.

Scrawled across the mirror, in what looked to her horrified eyes like blood, was the message, "We warned you, Jew-bitch. Go home or you'll never see your faggy dog again."

"Oh my precious Toy-Toy!" Chelsea sank to her knees on the bathroom rug, fighting back tears. What had the creeps done to him? Had they killed him? Tortured him? Her imagination filled her ears with the ringing cries of his tormented doggie self. She cupped her hands over her ears and struggled for sanity.

"Stop, stop," she whispered. "The threat implies he's okay now. If I leave, they'll give him back to me."

She struggled to her feet, ran to the front door.

Where she stopped.

Who could she tell she was leaving? To whom was she supposed to capitulate?

Some nameless, faceless enemy who dared steal her innocent poodle as a pawn.

Anger struck and with it, a ferocious determination. How dare those creeps take her dog. Let them come out and fight fair and square. Let them show themselves to her face.

She wasn't going to back down.

They might have killed Toy-Toy already, or dumped him in some wooded area, which to the pampered tiny toy would have been as good as leaving him for dead. A sob caught in her throat, but she refused to give in to the futile weakness of tears. As much as she hated to admit it, more was at stake than the life of a dog.

These people were vicious.

And must be stopped.

She forced her feet to carry her to the kitchen, found a sponge, wet it in the sink, and went to wipe away the threat on the mirror. She couldn't quite face it as she swiped at the sticky message. With bile in her throat and horror filling her mind, she cleaned a bathroom for the first time in her life.

And vowed they'd not defeat her.

When she finished, she threw the foul sponge in the trash, then showered off the stench of the day. Afterwards, her hair hanging in damp strands, she wandered around Ely's house. Arms hugged to her chest, she strained for any sounds of Toy-Toy and wished for company.

But not just any company.

He'd asked her to send for him, practically ordered her to.

She thought of the concern that had shown in Luke Miller's eyes, of how he'd buried the dead chicken, of the words that he both spoke from the pulpit and appeared to live by in his life.

Wishing she had the nerve to turn to him, to ask for comfort, she curled up on the sofa. She pictured Toy-Toy the first time she'd seen him, a tiny bundle of fluff. When she'd held out a finger to him, he licked it and looked up at her, so trusting.

She picked him over the girl puppy she'd intended to select, taking him home as soon as he'd been weaned.

Chelsea sniffed as a tear slid down her cheek. Another tear followed as she indulged in a healthy mix of grief and self-pity. Pity because she longed to go to Luke, the first man she'd ever met who she wanted to like her.

A man who would never look twice at her.

* * *

Mia didn't know what had happened to upset Chelsea, but peering in the window from the porch, she recognized all the earmarks of a woman in need of comfort.

Feeling melancholy herself, she'd wandered down the lane, remembering with sweet sorrow the eagerness with which Quentin had galloped back and forth. She remembered, too, chastising him for his concern over Chelsea.

Mia sighed and wished yet again she hadn't been so mean to Quentin before he disappeared. If she couldn't have solace, she'd arrange it for Chelsea. With a purposeful stride, she hopped off the porch, picked up her pace and headed to Luke Miller's house. She knew a word or two from Ely would send the preacher down the road. Mia smiled. These days Luke Miller didn't need much encouragement to "check on Chelsea."

A knock sounded at the door and Chelsea jumped.

Maybe someone had found Toy-Toy and brought him home. She leapt from the couch and ran to fling the door open.

"It's you," she said, tucking her hair still damp from the shower back from her face.

Luke Miller removed his cowboy hat and studied her with that searching way of his.

Chelsea dashed at her eyes. "Would you like to come in?"

He followed her into the living room and they sat on opposite ends of Ely's comfy old sofa.

"I came to see how your workers' meeting went," Luke said.

"You knew it was today?"

"Hill Springs is one small town."

Touched that he'd driven down to inquire, Chelsea said, "Thanks for asking. It went well enough, but not many people attended."

"That's to be expected. Give them a few days to consider the situation then hold another one."

"That's exactly what I'd planned to do," she said, feeling more spirited. Though she had planned to ask his advice for organizing the plant at dinner on Sunday.

"Do you want to tell me why you've been crying?" He spoke softly, leaning toward her, his eyes full of concern.

Chelsea wondered whether silent prayers of sobbing spoiled actresses were actually answered. "Toy-Toy's missing."

"Run off or missing?"

She shook her head, miserable. "Kidnapped."

"Another note?" He was looking grim.

"Sort of," she whispered.

He reached across the sofa and with a tender hand encircled her wrist. "Tell me."

"A message, written in blood. On the mirror," she managed to finish.

His lips turned downward and anger brewed in his gaze. "Lily-livered scumbags."

"How could they steal my helpless little Toy-Toy!" Suddenly it was all too much for her and she burst into tears.

Luke slid closer and gathered her in his arms. "It's okay to cry, little one," he said, stroking her hair. "He's your baby, of course you're upset."

She snuffled and nestled her cheek against his shoulder. "How can people be so horrible?"

Luke continued smoothing her hair, then his hand drifted lower, fashioning slow circles down the center of her back. "I don't know," he murmured against her hair, breathing in the fresh scent, torn between jumping up to start a search for the dog and staying to comfort Chelsea.

Her tears trailed off, but she made no move to lift her head. Instead, she uttered a small sigh, then said, "Toy-Toy is all I have to live for."

Luke studied the woman in his arms, a woman known around the world, a woman who could buy and sell all of Hill Springs several times over. "Why do you say that?"

She shifted in his arms and tilted her chin. He stared into her weepy emerald eyes, wanting to kiss away the tears. She didn't answer.

Holding her gaze, he said softly, "Are you sure that's true?"

She nibbled at her lip. "Maybe not anymore, but last month I would have said yes." She blinked, then glanced at his arms holding her. "Oh," she said, "thank you. I feel much better." She scooted a few inches away.

Her answer implied she'd changed since coming to Arkansas. In these surroundings, in her simple clothing, wearing no makeup, playing no roles, Luke believed she had changed. He wanted to take her back in his arms, tell her how he felt about her. But he wasn't a man to take advantage of a crying woman. Forcing himself not to reach for her, he said, "I hate to leave you, but I'm going to go see Sheriff Pike. This matter is too serious to ignore."

Eyes wide, lips utterly kissable, she smiled at him. "Thank you," she said.

Two simple words, but coming from Chelsea Jordan, they made Luke's night.

On the porch, Mia sighed and hugged her arms to her chest. "How romantic," she said, missing Quentin so much she ached. But if Chelsea Jordan had learned to say thank you, surely she and Quentin had a chance.

Chelsea tried hard to find some dish in Hoa's cookbook she could relate to, wanting to impress Luke after the way he had come to her rescue the night after the workers' meeting. He'd been so gentle and made her feel so comforted.

Made her feel like a woman, not just a sex symbol. A desirable woman with soft edges and a good heart. And to thank him for that, even if that's the only thing that ever happened between them, she wanted to create a special Sunday dinner.

But none of the recipes resembled the food she normally ate. A nominal vegetarian since her early teens, Chelsea flipped quickly past the sections on beef, pork, lamb, and even faster past the divider marked poultry.

She made a special trip into town late Saturday, proud of the way she bumped up the lane in the truck, hardly grinding the gears at all. Hoa had taught her that phrase, when Chelsea recounted for her friend the experience of her driving lesson.

Despair set in after one slow walk through the grocery store. She had no idea what to prepare. Only a loaf of bread and a jar of peanut butter sat in her cart. Those she'd selected out of a fond but distant memory of Ely. But for her dinner she had nothing.

Then the oddest thing happened. She'd turned to choose some toenail polish when her cart started rolling down the aisle. When she moved to catch it, it raced ahead of her, careened around a corner, and bumped into a back section of the market where she'd not looked earlier.

To her amazement, she found items there she recognized. Caviar! Pickled herring. Packets of dark pumpernickel squares. Delighted, she selected enough for a feast, forgetting all about her wayward grocery cart.

And now, after church, not having heard a word of the message, she fluttered about the kitchen, waiting for her company.

Not that it mattered what they thought of her entertaining skills, she consoled herself. One more week and Hill Springs was history. She'd be ten million or so dollars richer and never once would she set foot in this town again.

She'd already decided what to do with the money, had called Fran earlier in the week, telling her to instruct her brokers to begin buying shares in All Right Foods. The company was traded over NASDAQ, and Chelsea for once appreciated the times Fran had explained to her what happened to all the money she made. Within a conservatively short time, Chelsea Jordan would be the majority shareholder in All Right Foods.

There was more than one way to bring in a union.

But now, tweaking one last sprig of parsley around the caviar, her thoughts were of her dinner party, not the plant.

"We're here," she heard Timmy call, then pound across the porch. Smiling, she walked toward the front door, through Ely's dining room which she'd cleared of all its paraphernalia to set a fairly decent looking table.

Ely had lovely china, white with a blue floral design. China, Chelsea thought with surprise, that was now hers, or would be at the end of the next week.

The idea saddened her, reminding her of the sweet man who'd been so kind to her. Reminding her of how truly horrid she'd been to ignore him. She had learned from her co-workers how beloved Ely had been in Hill Springs. Perhaps her plans to help the townspeople would in some way redeem her past selfishness.

"Coming," she finally called in response to Timmy's exuberant greeting, and went to open the door.

"I brought Macduff," Timmy said, pointing to the border collie waiting politely at the bottom of the steps. "To help you not miss Toy-Toy so much."

Chelsea looked at the wide-eyed child, touched by his thoughtfulness. "That's so sweet," she said sincerely.

Then her attention centered on Luke as he smiled a greeting and stepped through the front door. He actually looked pleased to see her, a thought which made it hard to concentrate on Timmy's chatter.

"I hope you find him soon," Timmy said, patting her on the arm and gazing up at her with sweet blue eyes, eyes so like his father's.

"I'm sure he'll come back any time now." And she hoped those words came true.

Luke remained standing. He'd left on the dark suit he must have worn under his cleric's robe. In the summer wool trousers and jacket, with a crisp white shirt, he scarcely looked like the pig farmer she'd encountered that day at the grocery store. He looked, she thought with a tinge of amusement, like a little boy with his hair slicked back on school picture day.

"Please," she finally said, "take your coat off if you'll be more comfortable."

He did so immediately and handed it to her. She hesitated, unsure what to do with it. "I'll put it in the bedroom," she said. "Why don't you both have a seat?"

That way she escaped from the room. She was as stiff as a mannequin and as tongue-tied as a twelve-year-old. In the bedroom, she held the suit jacket in front of her, enjoying the texture of the wool. She fingered a lapel and thought of the fabric resting against his chest. On impulse, she lifted the jacket and breathed in the scent of Luke Miller.

Luke Miller, unobtainable male.

Oh, she could use her normal wiles on him, shake her boobs and invite him into her bed. Only the bed belonged to her great-uncle and the idea of playing the tramp to this man turned her stomach.

Even if she threw herself at him, walked naked back out of the bedroom, the way Chelsea Jordan wouldn't have hesitated to do a month ago, he'd probably raise his eyebrows and suggest she'd catch cold naked.

Of course with Timmy there she couldn't do any of those things. After one last delicious inhalation, she lay the jacket on the foot of the bed and returned to her guests. Guests who were probably wondering whether she'd fled out the window.

From the dining room, she said in an overly bright voice, "Dinner's all ready, so why don't we sit down?"

"Oh, boy, I'm starved," Timmy said and started to sprint to the table.

Luke reached out and stopped him by grabbing the back of his shirt. "Son, haven't we talked about manners before?"

Timmy nodded.

"So let's remember to bring our manners with us when we come visiting."

"Sure, Dad." Timmy flashed him a smile, then with a giggle, said, "Maybe I'll lose 'em before we get home."

Luke shook his head, but in a nice way that went with his rueful smile. Raising a child alone had to be a tough job.

Obviously bringing his manners with him, Luke drew a chair out for Chelsea and waited until she sat down before he took his chair.

"Where's the food?" Timmy said, wrinkling his nose at the culinary display on the table.

"Timothy James Miller!"

"Sorry." But Timmy rolled his eyes and rubbed his stomach.

Chelsea looked at the feast she'd managed to assemble. Caviar, with pumpernickel cocktail slices and sour cream. Herring. Baby and field greens with crumbles of goat cheese and whole mushrooms. Those packages of baby greens had been a real coup. For dessert, strawberries and blueberries nestled in a crystal bowl accompanied by mascarpone.

True, the dinner looked nothing like the mashed potatoes and pot roast Timmy's aunt had served at her house, but Chelsea felt quite proud of the first meal she'd ever made.

Luke watched the uncertainty flit across Chelsea's

face. Like a little girl presiding over a tea party, she wanted them to admire her efforts. And even though he couldn't help but echo his son's sentiments, wild horses wouldn't have dragged the words from him.

He knew from what his sister had told him that Chelsea didn't know a bread knife from a can opener. As Imogene had put it, "the girl looked like she'd never set foot in a kitchen before in her life!"

Reaching for the caviar, he said, "You've outdone yourself."

She brightened. "I hope it's okay," she murmured, her eyes on Timmy.

"You eat this stuff?" Timmy said, pointing to the glistening black caviar.

She nodded.

"You like it?"

"Yes."

He let Luke put some on his plate. Then Timmy said, "Did you eat it when you were a kid?"

Now that was a loaded question. Chelsea Jordan's childhood had absolutely nothing in common with his son's.

She'd probably been spoon-fed strained caviar and nursed on French champagne. Luke dished salad onto Timmy's plate while the boy's attention was distracted waiting for Chelsea's answer. Salad ranked right up there with having to wash behind his ears.

"Actually," Chelsea said, a slow smile forming on her famous pouty lips, "I did eat caviar when I was a kid, but there was something I liked a lot better."

"What?"

"Wait right here," she said and left the table, heading toward the kitchen.

Timmy whispered, "I hope it's real food."

Luke smiled despite himself and managed to swallow a slice of bread and caviar, heavily camouflaged by the sour cream.

Timmy made a face. He made one right back, much to his son's delight.

Luke covered a second piece of bread with the fish eggs, surprised that after the first shock to his taste buds, the stuff didn't taste all that bad. Caviar just wasn't something found on the baseball circuit, nor in the lifestyle of a country preacher.

After a third piece, he stopped in mid-swallow to consider the irony of this woman who'd landed in their midst introducing him to something new, something he liked. She and he were equally foreign to one another.

"This salad looks like grass," Timmy said, playing with the greens Luke had sneaked onto his plate.

"Just try it."

At that suggestion Timmy zipped his lips tight and crossed his arms across his chest. Thankfully, Chelsea reappeared, holding a small plate up in the air.

"This is just for you," she said, placing it in front of Timmy and removing his other plate.

"Wow!" Timmy took one look at the open-faced peanut butter sandwich fashioned into a Mickey Mouse head, then jumped up and smacked a sloppy kiss on Chelsea's cheek. "Thanks!"

She blushed faintly. "You're welcome."

Timmy gobbled his sandwich, drank the glass of juice at his place and asked to be excused. "Gotta go check on Macduff," he said, and dashed outside.

"That was very thoughtful," Luke said. "Where'd you learn how to do that?"

"Ely." Chelsea spooned a dainty morsel of caviar

onto a square of bread. "One of the times he visited, we sneaked down to the kitchen and he made me a snack."

"Sneaked?"

"I wasn't allowed to eat peanut butter."

"Why not?"

"Fattening. Bad for my complexion." Chelsea shrugged her shoulders. "You get used to it."

"To deprivation? You were a child."

She gave a little laugh. "Oh, no, I was a child star."

"Do you regret that?" He asked, wanting sincerely to know her answer. Again, he was struck by how nice she could be when she forgot to act like a celebrity bitch.

She took a bite of salad.

Luke waited.

"When I see Timmy, so free, so lively, so natural, running about, gathering eggs, playing with the dog, tossing his ball in the air without worrying whether he has dirt under his nails or his designer shirt is mussed—oh, yes I regret it."

"What was it like being five and famous?"

"Seriously?" Chelsea turned those emerald eyes of hers on him in full-watt skepticism. Clearly she'd been asked this question many times before.

"I'm asking because I'd like to know what it was like for you," he said calmly, preparing another caviar treat.

"Oh." Twirling the ends of a lush strand of hair, she said, "Lonely. My father used me as a pawn; my mother ignored my existence. I lived in a big house with lots of servants, always a party going on."

Luke nodded, but kept silent.

"Every so often I'd be dressed up like a Shirley

Temple doll and paraded for the grownups. Usually right before one of my movies came out."

"P.R.?"

She nodded.

"Why did your mother dislike you?" He worded the sentence carefully, because he didn't want to discount her version, but a mother despising her child! The thought chilled his blood, especially as an image of Jenny cradling Timmy in her arms, singing softly to lull him to sleep floated to the surface of his memory.

"You don't think that's possible, do you?"

"Not in my heart."

"One time I overheard my parents having an argument." She took a deep breath and Luke could see her chest quiver as she let it out. "And those two could fight. It seems my father felt my mother trapped him into marriage. She was an East Coast blueblood, could have married anyone in the New York Five Hundred, but who did she want to twist around her finger but Jack Jordan, born Jack Rosenblum. He'd just won an Oscar for Best Supporting Actor and he was hot." Chelsea gave a bitter laugh.

"So evidently she pretended she was pregnant and her father, my grandfather and Ely's brother, gave his begrudging blessing to the union."

"And your father? Did he love her?"

She shrugged. "Maybe once upon a time."

"So you were born sooner than nine months from the wedding?"

"Oh, no, that's the lovely spin on this happy family story." Her mouth twisted. "Evidently my mother lied just to get her way and when my father found out, he was so mad he raped her."

Luke didn't say a word. He knew what she would say next. If she could bring herself to say it.

"So, you see, my mother really did despise me."

"Why did they stay married?" Luke didn't follow the tabloids, but Ely had told him Chelsea parents hadn't divorced despite Jack Jordan's infamous philandering.

She waved a hand, evidently shoring up her defenses again. "Grandfather Van Ness told my mother he'd given her her choice of men and if she didn't stick with him, he'd disinherit her. You see, there's never been a divorce in the Van Ness dynasty."

What a life. "You've been angry at your parents for a long, long time, haven't you?"

Her eyes teared, and Luke regretted causing her the pain of that statement. But the truth of it seemed apparent.

"Oh, yes, I've been angry." Looking across the room, and seeming to see very far into the distance, she murmured, "And I've regretted my entire life for quite some time."

Luke heard the despair behind the words. Reaching a hand across the table, he nestled one of her hands beneath his. "It's okay to be angry."

She laughed. "Would you say that to Timmy if you caught him tying firecrackers to his toes and lighting them because his mother died?"

Luke grimaced. "What kind of analogy is that?"

"Damn accurate." Chelsea pushed back from the table and turned to face him, hands on her hips. "I don't know why I'm telling you all these things, unless it's simply time to confess and you're conveniently here to listen to me. I wanted to punish my father, so I made that *FellatioNeighborhood* flick. I don't suppose a man of your calling has ever heard of it, but it's quite famous in some circles."

"Porn," he said, intending to show her he wasn't entirely sheltered behind the collar.

"Sick, sick stuff, but it made me more famous than my roles as Heidi or Rebecca ever had. And then I went back to California and hit the big time. Only Jack Jordan got himself killed before I could thumb my nose at him."

"Do you miss your father?"

"Don't call him my father!" Chelsea screamed the words, then dropped back into her seat. She covered her eyes with her hands, and said, "I'm so sorry. I'm ruining your dinner with my histrionics."

"No, you're not. And you're being honest."

"That's a funny word."

Luke pushed his plate away. "It can be painful, but it's kind of like popping a blister. Afterwards you tend to feel better."

"Ah, country wisdom."

Luke shrugged. "I haven't always lived in the country."

She looked at him from behind her hands. "Are you trying to apologize to me for the way you live? For being relatively untroubled and content?"

"Is that how it looks to you? You fly in here in your private jet, dabble in the real world for thirty days and skip away with all of Ely's money, back to your meaningless, pointless existence? And I'm some slap-happy pig farmer who doesn't know enough about life to question his existence?" Anger burned in his words and in his blood.

"Ooh, the man has hidden fire."

Luke stood up so fast his chair hit the floor. In one swift stride he was around the table, grabbing Chelsea Jordan by the shoulders, claiming her lips with his mouth, branding her with his tongue.

He felt her stiffen, then as he pulled her up from her seat and deepened the kiss, she lifted her hands and dug into the back of his neck with nails that streaked a path of pain on his skin.

He punished her with his kisses, rebuking her for being so beautiful, so unobtainable, and so judgmental about who he was without ever bothering to ask. But most of all, he punished himself for wanting this woman.

Chelsea fought for breath as Luke clasped her to his chest, half-dragging her from her chair and stealing all rational thought from her as he forced her lips apart, his tongue delving into her mouth, driving her to a frenzy of passion.

At first Chelsea struggled against him. She didn't want him this way, like any other man she could use and discard. But something about the way his lips covered hers, crushing and tasting all at the same time told her Luke Miller wasn't like any other man.

For he seemed to punish himself as much as he did her.

She stretched her arms up, touched the hair that curled so unpreacherlike over his collar, and something about the satin of that hair urged her to barbarism. She scratched his neck, reveling in the idea she caused him pain, drove him wild.

Panting, kissing, writhing in the ecstasy of wanting him, she tried to pull him down to her, down to the chair, then to the floor.

His arms were like boulders. Unbudgeable. "Oh, no, you don't," he murmured, and with one last searing kiss, he let her go.

Completely unprepared, she fell back against the

chair, her lips bruised, her heart wanting, her body aching. Touching a finger to her lips, she said with a pout, "We're not stopping now, are we?"

Before he could answer, Timmy skipped into the room. "Got any more peanut butter?"

22 ~

Chelsea spent her last week in Arkansas reliving Luke's kiss and wondering what would have happened had Timmy not interrupted them. Luke wanted her, of that she was sure. But the fact that he stopped—said no to her even before Timmy burst in on them—made her feel better than any fleeting sexual pleasure would have.

The week passed, she went to work, went home. Luke didn't visit, but late each evening after she'd turned her lights out, she thought she heard his truck drive down the lane, circle the turnaround, and leave.

Thursday arrived, her next to last day at All Right Foods. The witch with the stopwatch had dogged her every move. Chelsea was only one write-up away from being fired, and some of the forces in the company had redoubled their efforts to see her fail.

Which meant Am/Am sympathizers worked alongside her on the line, or in the management.

Which goaded Chelsea to intensify her efforts.

As soon as the end-of-shift whistle blew on Thursday, Chelsea breathed a sigh of relief and raced to the restroom to wash up as best she could before her second workers' meeting.

Hoa believed they would have a larger group this time. She'd prepared lots of copies of the petition Chelsea had written, asking the National Labor Relations Board to come and investigate conditions and take the first steps in forming a union.

Hoa insisted the word was out that people could trust Chelsea. Still, she had no idea how many would come. She understood they feared losing their jobs; God only knew the management of this plant saw them as replaceable parts. Fire one, hire another.

Chelsea wiped her face, marveling at the woman who looked back at her in the warped mirror. No makeup, hair braided to keep the poultry dreck out of it, skin that had gone an entire month without a facial.

She noted, too, the sense of determination. A strength of purpose foreign to her in her past. Lifting her chin, she said, "They didn't stop me."

Even though Toy-Toy remained missing, and the sheriff had basically laughed at her worries, the bad guys hadn't stopped her. "Dogs run off all the time," he'd said, doodling a report when Luke had insisted. And when they'd walked from his office, Chelsea had heard him mutter, "Damn dog's probably road pizza by now."

No, they weren't going to win.

She strode from the plant, across the gravel lot, toward the park down the road.

A park filled with workers.

Cheering, shouting, applauding workers.

Clad in their grimy, stinking, blood- and dreck-spattered clothing.

She walked faster and as she reached them, knew

there must be at least four hundred people. The bulk of the day shift. She broke into a trot, and as she stepped into the park, she heard what they were chanting.

"Chelsea! Chelsea! Chelsea!"

None of the adulation of her film fans had ever sounded so sweet. Moved by their trust in her, Chelsea knew she wouldn't fail them. Smiling broadly, she greeted the crowd with a two-thumbs-up salute.

Smallwood jerked his hand and cursed as blood welled to the surface of his chin.

"Goddamnmotherfucking dog," he said, aiming a kick at the poodle who had pushed the bathroom door open and nipped at his bare ankle, causing him to cut his face.

"Grrrrrr," answered the poodle in his falsetto growl.

Smallwood dabbed at the cut, asking himself again whether he had the nerve to slice and dice the dog.

He considered it, then shook his head. "Nah." After a splash of water followed by Aqua Velva, he squatted down and faced off with the poodle that had been making his life a living hell.

"Look, you fuzzball," he said, shaking his finger. "If it weren't for me you'd be dead, so you ought to smarten up and think about who's buttering your dog biscuits."

"Yip!"

"That's better." Hornsby stood up and reached for his silk bathrobe. "The way I figure things, Chelsea Jordan is going to be collecting that ten million. But as I haven't been too pleased at the way those gorillas have acted toward me, I really don't care that they're losing."

He checked his chin for any fresh blood and winked at the dog. "But I do care about Hornsby Smallwood, and that's where you come in." He tried to pick up the poodle, but the stupid dog leapt backward from him.

"All right, be standoffish. See if I care. But I know that Hot Twat Jordan will pay big money to get you back alive."

"Grrrrrrr."

"Yeah, I don't know why either," Smallwood said, and skirting around the dog, went to watch his favorite video. After all that had occurred, he wanted to hate *FellatioNeighborhood,* but as much as he loathed to admit it, no other flick aroused him the way that one did.

And a man needed his release. Especially on Friday afternoon after a long, hard week.

Hornsby slipped into his den, his body stirring in anticipation. Moving across the room he knew so well, he failed to look in front of him. Just before he reached the coffee table where he'd left the video, he stumbled over something.

Down the hall in the bathroom, Toy-Toy, tiny head cocked, stood on his haunches, regarding the window Smallwood had cracked open following his shower. Summoning all his newfound strength developed rambling in the country with Macduff, he vaulted from the floor to the countertop.

He was eyeing the distance from there to the window ledge when a bloodcurdling scream rent the house.

Toy-Toy hurtled out the window.

Smallwood ran from the den, down the hall, clutching his copy of *FellatioNeighborhood* to his chest. Tiny teeth had chewed and chewed and chewed, breaking through the plastic case and dragging his precious film into a scrapheap of videotape. "I'll kill you, you motherfucking sorry excuse for an animal!" he screamed, bursting into the bathroom.

Only to find the damn dog gone.

Smallwood dropped to the shaggy white rug covering his bathroom floor; crushing his ruined tape to his chest, he began to cry.

Luke rang the doorbell to Hornsby Smallwood's overly elegant home for the third time. Clearly the sheriff wasn't going to do anything to protect Chelsea. After discussing the situation with Ely, Luke had decided to visit the lawyer, to see if the lawyer had followed Ely's specific instructions and warned the Am/Am people that the will would be void if they in any way harmed Chelsea.

Concerned over Chelsea's safety, Ely was ready to reappear and nullify the will. Luke had left his friend worrying over whether he'd done the right thing, a question that bothered Luke, too.

Paying a visit to Smallwood was the first step. If that didn't satisfy his fears, he was prepared to collect Chelsea and offer her the protection of his home for her last few days. With only the weekend left, they might try anything.

If anything happened to her, he wouldn't be able to forgive himself.

Luke pressed the doorbell again.

Chelsea affected him like no other woman he'd ever known. That kiss! He felt it again, reliving it as he'd done time after time since Sunday. But it was more than a kiss, so much more than desire. He wanted to romp through the woods with her, dance through the night, whisper his dreams to her and hold her while she shared the secrets of her heart with him.

After Jenny died, he'd sworn not to marry simply to have a wife, a preacher's helper to preside over the Women's Auxiliary and fill in for Sunday school classes.

He'd sworn only to marry for love.

That vow mocked him now.

He'd met a woman who possessed his thoughts, his dreams, his blood. A woman his son liked and admired. A woman who would be back in California in three more days. Two if she left after church on Sunday.

Giving up on the doorbell, he pounded on the door. Smallwood's secretary had assured him he'd find him at his house.

The guy didn't go to work, didn't stay at home. What did he do?

Frustrated, Luke turned to leave. Back at his truck, he saw Macduff was missing. As a treat, he'd let the dog ride in the cab as Ely often did, then left the window down for air when he parked. He whistled, and heard in answer a low bark from near the side of Smallwood's house.

Luke went to investigate.

And found Macduff standing over a trembling Toy-Toy, licking his face.

Relief and anger hit at the same time. Luke bent to pick up the poodle, realizing as he did that one of the front paws dangled uselessly. As he stood cradling the dog gently, he looked up and saw a frosted

window, the kind commonly found in bathrooms,
open a few inches.

So Smallwood was one of them. Luke felt no
surprise. Smallwood was exactly the kind of leech
Am/Am attracted.

Toy-Toy whimpered and Macduff barked in response.

Moving as quickly as he could without jarring the
poodle, Luke got himself and the dogs into his truck
and roared off to the vet. He'd get Toy-Toy patched
up, then deal with Smallwood.

Chelsea's last day at the plant sped by. When the
whistle blew at four o'clock, Chelsea couldn't believe
that she was no longer bound to All Right Foods. She
pulled off the rubber apron, snatched the blue shower cap from her head, stretched her aching fingers,
and looked around her.

Many of the other workers were doing the same,
and most of them were watching her.

The line was still, the place quieter than usual. She
looked down at the slippery floor, at the open trough
with its trickle of moving water carrying the drop-
pings of chicken flesh and fat and guts, residue that
Hoa had told her was collected and ground into the
makings of cat food. Nothing wasted. Oh, no, not at
All Right Foods.

She looked at the tired faces of the workers who
surrounded her and overhead at the hooks now
empty, hooks that bore down on all of them for eight
hours a day, demanding to be weighted with dead
birds passing down the line to burden the next
worker, and the next, and the next, until the birds,
now half breasts or thighs and legs, plopped into

boxes for the trips to the grocery stores or the deboning or frozen dinner processing plants.

A tall black woman approached her, followed by two other women. "You didn't do too bad, child." She winked and added, "Not for a white-ass honky."

Other workers lined up, all passing by and shaking Chelsea's damp and workworn hand. Tears formed quickly in her eyes as Chelsea said good-bye to the people who would wake again next Monday to return to this place.

The room began to empty, and Hoa touched her arm. "Time to go," she said with a quiet smile.

On the drive to Blueberry Lane, Chelsea filled Hoa in on her plans to hire the necessary lawyers and consultants and improve working conditions. As soon as Chelsea controlled the plant, she planned to name Hoa manager of employee relations. Anyone in plant management who hadn't worked the line would be given sixty days to find another job or be offered a spot on the line.

Chelsea would have liked to close the plant, but she'd learned enough about the local economy to know such a move would devastate too many people. From the chick hatcheries to the breeders and growers to the processing plants, the economy was fueled by the poultry business. She'd do what she could with Ely's money to retrain workers and sponsor new businesses while she ensured decent conditions for the plant workers.

When Hoa drove up and parked for the last time in front of Ely's house, Chelsea turned to her. "I can't thank you enough for all your help. And for your friendship."

"You know you are welcome." She smiled. "You are a most unusual lady."

"Well, I don't know about that." Chelsea started to open the door. "You know, this probably sounds funny, but you're the first woman I've ever been friends with."

The woman touched her fingers to her heart. "Go in peace," she said.

Knowing she was about to cry, Chelsea climbed out of the car. She was waving good-bye when she spotted Luke's pickup kicking up a cloud of dust, heading her way.

Drat. Here she was again, looking like a street urchin. Well, he'd seen her once like this. He could see her again. She sat down on the porch steps and waited for him.

She didn't have to wait long. He leapt from the truck and ran toward her.

Her heart leapt happily. He was coming for her!

Then she saw the grim look on his face.

"I found Toy-Toy. He's at the vet's and the doctor said—"

Chelsea jumped up. She forgot about her stinking clothes and her disheveled hair. "Take me to him."

They raced into town. Luke had hated to scare her that way, but the doctor had been blunt. Toy-Toy's broken leg had sent him into shock and the vet didn't know if the dog would survive the surgery needed to correct it.

As fast as he drove, Luke managed a few sideways glances at Chelsea as he filled her in on what had happened. She seemed oblivious that she smelled pretty rank and looked a sight. Funny. He'd learned to like caviar, and she'd grown used to conditions he wasn't sure he could tolerate.

He roared into the veterinary hospital lot and hustled Chelsea inside and straight to the back. The doctor was working over the poodle and she broke into a run when she saw him.

"Oh my wuddle one," she whispered, stroking his ears with trembling fingers. "You were so brave to escape that awful, awful man. We're going to give you a medal for bravery."

Toy-Toy lifted his tail once, then twice, then as the anesthesia took effect, he stilled.

Luke put an arm around Chelsea. "We'll have to wait outside now." The doctor nodded.

They settled in the waiting area. Only one other woman occupied the room, a matronly white-haired lady who wrinkled her nose and moved across the room from Chelsea.

"I knew Smallwood was a creep," Chelsea said.

"He's been a dickhead since he was five."

"Such language!" Chelsea actually looked shocked.

Luke made a face. "What you mean is such language for a preacher."

She bobbed her head. "True."

"I'm a man, a human being subject to the same likes and dislikes and strong feelings as anyone else. Putting on a collar doesn't change that."

"No . . ."

He wanted her to understand him. Even if she left Hill Springs and never once thought of him again, he wanted her to understand the choices he'd made in his life. "Chelsea," he said, leaning close to her, "pastoring a church wasn't my first choice of careers. It's a calling I struggle with day in and day out."

"What did you do before?" She asked as if she cared, as if she were more than simply curious.

"Baseball." He left it at that.

"Baseball?"

"You don't have to say it like sewer cleaner."

She settled her lips primly. "After what I've experienced this month, I'm the last one to criticize any occupation. I was simply surprised, that's all."

"Why?"

"It's such a strange change. From playing to preaching. What made you do it?"

Luke studied his hands. "My father," he began, "was a man sincerely called by God to preach. He led the church here for more than forty years. Everyone loved him. I'd just been called up to the majors when my mom phoned and said Dad was in the hospital." He glanced away, surprised at the moisture in his eyes.

"Heart attack. He came to before he died, and he asked me to take over his church."

"Don't you have to go to school or something to become a minister?"

"Oh, I'd done that, majored in theology to please him, and played ball for myself."

"So you came back to Hill Springs and gave up your career?"

He nodded.

"Because your father asked you to?" She whispered the words, and Luke wondered what she was thinking.

He didn't have to wonder long.

Chelsea sighed and rubbed a hand over her eyes. "Wow. You did that for your father and I didn't even come visit Uncle Ely. I didn't even call about his funeral and you sacrificed all your plans for your family."

Exactly what Luke had thought, but now, coming from her like a confession, hearing the words of a sinner stricken with contrition, he felt only comfort and forgiveness. Chelsea Jordan had learned a valuable lesson.

"I want you to do something for me," she said. "I want you to say a prayer for Toy-Toy." When she looked at him, her eyes were begging him not to laugh at her request.

Luke bowed his head, took her hands in his, and began to pray. And as he did, he felt his own burden lift, felt the grudge he'd nursed toward his beloved father lifting as forgiveness flowed into his heart.

As if in answer to his prayer, words from the Book of Romans filled his mind: "All things work together for good to them that love God."

23 ⌐

"**F**our sixes," said the old man with a crow of triumph. "And on the first roll, too."

Quentin lifted the dice cup, staring into it for the nth time since he'd found himself back in the red velvet cavern of the Second Chance Room. Then he looked across the table to the old guy who'd told Quentin he might as well call him "Mr. G," as it had a better ring than "old coot." "You actually like this game, don't you?"

"Yeah." Mr. G chuckled and wiped his mouth with his monogrammed hanky, the "G" embroidered in crimson thread. " 'Course, I only took it up to get Einstein's goat, but it does help pass the time."

"That and meddling in people's lives," Quentin muttered.

"Oh, come on, be a sport about that. What's an old man to do? Besides, if it weren't for me, you'd be dead."

Rattling the dice in the cup, Quentin considered that comment. He had no idea how much time had slipped away since he'd last seen Mia; as far as he could tell, since the moment he'd touched and spoken to Chelsea he'd been sitting in this chair playing a dice game Mr. G called Chicago. But he took hope in the comment that he wasn't dead.

All was not lost.

"No," the old man said, "all isn't lost, but I bet you can't throw better than four sixes."

"If I do, what do I win?"

"I already explained we only play for pleasure here."

"Pleasure!" Quentin tried to push away from the card table. But as with every other time he'd attempted to move, he could not budge. Disgusted, he slung the dice from the cup.

Four of the five dice landed on the table, three of them sixes. The last die skidded to the floor.

"It's a six! Beat you!"

"Not so fast. If it doesn't land on the table, it doesn't count."

"What do you do, make up the rules as you go along?"

"Hey, that's an age-old rule. Everybody knows, from craps to Monopoly, the dice have gotta land on the table." Mr. G chuckled under his breath and collected the dice.

"I can't stand this anymore," Quentin said. "What are we waiting for? What's the meaning of all this?"

"You think there might be some meaning? Some purpose?" The old guy fixed him with his birdlike eyes.

"I don't know." Quentin raised his hand to tug at his cap, only to remember he'd lost it. He sure hoped Mia had his cap. Of course, the way she'd been acting before he disappeared, she might have burnt it by now. And forgotten all about him.

"Well, whatdayathink?"

Reckoning his answer might decide his fate, Quentin took his time to marshall his thoughts. At last, he said, "I think there are many things I don't understand. I built my life on the rational. Which is odd, considering my career is based on fantasies." He paused, wondering why he'd never dwelt on that irony before.

"It's because you never slowed down," the old man said.

"Would you please quit reading my mind," Quentin snapped. "I like to figure things out for myself."

"Be my guest." Another wicked chuckle followed that line.

"I've always thought life consisted of the earthly present. You lived, you died. So best to live to the max. But, all this"— he waved an arm around the dimly lit room—"and everything that happened to Mia and me in Arkansas, makes me question whether I'm having a really weird dream or whether there are other planes of existence."

The old guy nodded and wiped his brow. "Uh-huh."

"But even though I don't know the answers to any of those speculations"—Quentin took a deep breath—"I do know that I love Mia. And finding that truth is the most important thing that's ever happened to me."

"Not a bad speech," Mr. G said. "But whaddya gonna do about it?"

Quentin pictured Mia's perky nose, her spiky hair, her precious freckles; he thought of all the adventures they'd shared together, of how he missed her sharp mind and clever tongue; he felt the memory of her body warm and hot against his skin. "I'm going

to get down on my knees and beg her to marry me,"
he said, whispering. Yet the words echoed around
the room, bouncing off the red curtains covering
some sort of stage at the front of the room. "Marry
me, marry me, marry me," he heard, echoing in his
head, his heart, his soul.

The old guy shook the dice in the cup. "Some days
are worth all the effort," he said, and poured them
out on the table.

Sunday morning found Chelsea lazing about in
bed, but this time instead of escaping into a histori-
cal romance novel, she contemplated her own life.

Tomorrow she'd return to California. She could
have booked her flight for Sunday afternoon, but
some part of her heart balked at the idea. She knew
she was being foolish, but she wanted to give Luke
Miller one more chance.

One more chance to do what, she wasn't sure.

To kiss her again?

No, she wanted more than that.

To make love to her?

No, she wanted more than that.

Just what she wanted she feared to put into
thoughts, let alone into words. Chelsea held a pillow
to her breasts and admitted she didn't want to go
home. Going home meant leaving Luke behind.

And Timmy, too.

She sighed, thinking of his visit yesterday. When
he collected the eggs, he'd been sulky and withdrawn. She paid him the money she owed him for
the week and even that didn't bring a smile to his
face.

He hovered over Toy-Toy, whom she'd brought
home from the pet hospital, his tiny front leg in a

cast. And Chelsea knew the child was crying when he jumped up and left without a word of farewell.

But she had to go home.

Chelsea Jordan belonged in Bel Air.

She glanced across Ely's cluttered bedroom, to the open closet door where a navy blue dress with white collar and buttons hung. A dress unlike any outfit she'd ever worn. It looked almost . . . Chelsea smiled as the words prim and proper came to mind.

Yesterday before she'd collected Toy-Toy, she gathered her courage and paid a visit to the Mode O' Day dress shop. A very talkative old lady who said her name was Hennie followed her around, asking her question after question about her life in Hollywood. When the woman told her Ely had been one of her dearest friends, Chelsea softened and answered her questions, and bought the dress Hennie suggested as "perfect for church."

Now lying in bed and gazing at the dress, Chelsea wondered why she'd bought it. More make-believe, more pretend? But the past month had been all too real. Despite all she endured during that month, not once had she thought of killing herself.

That thought surprised her, sending her bolt upright in the bed. Why, she'd actually been happy. And not once had her old constant companion the demon appeared to torment her.

She yawned and stretched. She heard a shuffle-tap noise as Toy-Toy came into the room. "Oh most ferocious doggie," she said, picking him up carefully, "you were very brave." She kissed the top of his head and put him back on the floor.

That's when she saw the clock.

Church started in twenty minutes!

Here she'd been daydreaming and if she missed church today, Am/Am would win.

Skipping the shower, she leapt into her clothes, whipped her hair into a bun, grabbed her shoes and purse, and, racing past a startled Toy-Toy, fled to the truck.

The engine came quickly to life, but when Chelsea put it into gear, nothing happened.

"Oh, please, please, move," she said, reviewing her movements, checking that she'd pressed the clutch in properly as Luke had taught her.

Still nothing happened.

She got out of the truck. And gasped. The tires, all four of them, had been slashed. Shreds of rubber hung from them. And stuck to the front left tire was a white business card. Scrawled on it were the words, "Gotcha, bitch!"

She crumpled the card in her hand. Tears welled to her eyes as she thought of the money going to those hatemongers. After all she'd been through, for them to win at the last minute!

Chelsea glanced down at her new dress, the proper pumps she'd bought to match. With tears wetting her cheeks, she turned and walked back into the house.

Toy-Toy cocked his head, as if asking her why she'd returned. Bending down to pat his head, she thought of the tiny dog jumping out of a window, doing whatever it took to outsmart his captor.

"Oh, Toy-Toy!" she cried and checked her watch and dried her eyes. She tore off her new clothes, shrugged into one of Ely's sweat suits, pulled on the Keds she'd gotten from Imogene and jogged out the door.

She made it about fifty yards down the lane before

the pain in her side forced her to stop. Huffing and puffing like the wolf at the house of the three little pigs, she shook a fist in frustration. Church would be over by the time she, in her pitiful physical condition, could even make it to the main road.

As late as it was, Luke and Timmy would be long gone from their house.

She heard a dog barking and looked in the field to the right of the lane. Macduff waved his brushy tail and barked again before racing off into the pasture.

Forcing herself to move, she began to jog again.

Another bark sounded and she began to laugh and cry all at the same time as she saw Macduff herding a horse in her direction. She might not know a stove from a refrigerator, but Chelsea Jordan knew horses.

Jack Jordan had escorted her to her first riding lesson at age four. Their father-daughter picture taken that day at the stables had been featured on the cover of *Life*.

She put her fingers to her mouth and whistled. The horse lifted his head and trotted to the fence as she dashed across the lane. Mounting from the fence, she shouted thanks to Macduff and took off at a gallop, the wind in her hair.

"What the fuck!" Sheriff Pike had plopped down on the front steps of Ely's house after coming out from his hiding place in the bushes. After watching Chelsea discover the slashed tires and go back into the house, tears on her cheeks, he'd been chuckling and grinning, counting the guns Am/Am could buy with all that money. To mark the occasion, he'd helped himself to a swig or two from the flask he carried in his hip pocket. Somehow, between celebrating and sipping, he'd missed her leaving the house, but as he sat on the porch, squinting into the

sun, he could swear that was Chelsea Jordan hopping on the back of old man Higgins's horse.

"Shit!" His car was parked on the road at the
Blueberry Lane turn-off. He grabbed for his radio
and his flask at the same time. He dropped the radio
and it broke open. "Shit," he said again and took a
consoling slug of whisky. This whole fuck-up was
Smallwood's fault. If he'd done his job earlier, they
never would have been forced to act at the last
minute. He and the boys would be paying Smallwood a long overdue visit.

"Oh, no, you big bully, you're not going anywhere," Mia said, charging over to where the sheriff
stomped down Ely's porch steps.

With great care, Mia eased the gun from the
sheriff's holster, then lifted his hip flask to his lips.
The dolt drank, then suddenly realized he hadn't
moved the container himself.

"What the devil?" He swung his head around
wildly and stumbled on the steps.

"Guard him," Mia said to Macduff.

With what sounded like a gleeful bark to Mia's
ears, the collie herded Pike back onto the porch. The
sheriff reached for his gun and looked stunned when
he didn't find it.

Satisfied Macduff could keep the bumbling bad
guy corralled, wishing she could ride a horse the way
Chelsea had, Mia raced yet again to Luke Miller's
house. Ely needed to find an officer they could trust
to collect Pike, or better yet, the FBI. Pike and his
cronies would pay for what they'd done.

Peering out from the pastor's office, Luke surveyed
the church. He'd yet to see Chelsea appear. And even

though Timmy had pronounced at breakfast Chelsea wasn't his friend any more or she wouldn't leave him, his son had saved the seat next to him.

A seat that remained empty.

The congregation sang the third hymn and the music director looked around. Luke checked his watch and signaled him to lead another one.

She couldn't screw up. Not now. Not the last day.

And she wouldn't either. He regretted even thinking that thought. If Chelsea were late, or not in church, it was because of something or someone beyond her control.

He should have offered her a ride, made sure she got safely to church. She'd turned down his offer to stay at his house, and even though he'd been driving down to check on her at night, he'd been trying to wean himself, get used to the idea she'd no longer be living down the lane.

"You idiot," he said, and ripped off his clerical robe. Dwelling on his own loss instead of ensuring her safety. He made it to the back door and to the truck in record time. The congregation would keep singing and singing and singing, because church couldn't start until he got back.

On the highway that led to his house, he met the sheriff's car, lights blazing and siren blasting. Flashing his lights and waving his arms out the window, Luke managed to get the officer's attention. After shrieking to a halt, the car backed up to where Luke had stopped.

A deputy leaned out the window. "What is it man, can't you see we're having an emergency?"

"What kind of emergency?" Luke asked, thinking of the way the sheriff had blown off every concern about Chelsea's safety.

"Stolen horse. That Jordan woman rode off on old man Higgins' horse. We've no choice but to arrest her."

"Why would she be riding a horse? And where's Pike?"

The deputy shrugged. The man sitting in the passenger seat laughed and said, "Maybe her truck warn't working."

Luke didn't recognize the man, but he identified the type. Without another word, he swung his pickup into reverse, heading back to town as fast as he could, the police car right on his tail.

Luke spotted the horse tied to the handrail of the church steps as he jumped from his truck and ran into the church. Motioning to a deacon, he said, "Lock the doors."

Then, as his astonished congregation stared, he walked up the center aisle of the church to the front row where Timmy always sat, gathered a sweating Chelsea Jordan in his arms, and kissed her.

The church broke into applause.

Luke said so only Chelsea could hear, "Thank God you're safe." Then he threw a salute to his son, strode to the pulpit, and thanked the music director.

Then he took a deep breath, looked out over his congregation, the church he loved, and began his sermon with the words, "Today, let us give thanks for the life God has given us. Let us turn to the book of Hebrews, where we read in chapter thirteen, 'Let brotherly love continue. Do not neglect to show hospitality to strangers, for thereby some have entertained angels unawares.' "

Chelsea heard the opening words, let her mind drift to his kiss, then paid sharp attention when

Luke continued reading from the passage and said with a smile in his eyes, "Let marriage be held in honor among all."

After that she stopped listening, caught up as she was in her swirl of emotions. He'd kissed her in front of his church. And the congregation had approved! Chelsea wasn't sure when the idea of wanting to marry Luke first crept into her mind, but she knew, sitting there in the pew next to Timmy, that was what she wanted. Nothing less would do.

As soon as the service ended, Chelsea started to rush from the building to tend to the poor horse she'd been forced to leave sweating and snorting.

Luke got to her before she cleared the pew.

"Are you okay?" he asked, concern showing in his eyes.

She nodded. "Someone slashed my tires, but they didn't stop me!"

He smiled. "They didn't know who they were dealing with." Then in a lower voice, he said, "I'd like you to come to my house after church. There's something important I'd like to share with you."

As silly as it was, she knew her heart flip-flopped. She nodded, then went to check on the horse.

As soon as she stepped outside, a deputy advanced on her. "Horse thief!" he cried, yanking at a pair of handcuffs on his belt.

Chelsea stared him down and started walking the horse. Timmy ran out of the church, leading a distinguished-looking man by the hand.

The man approached the blustering officer and said, "That's my horse. Now go away and catch some criminals and leave us to fellowship in peace."

To Chelsea, the man said, "Horse needed a good

workout. I'll have my yardman collect him." With that, he pulled a cellular phone from his suit pocket and strolled away.

The deputy slunk off with his tail between his legs and a few minutes later Chelsea joined Timmy and Luke in their truck.

Timmy remained sulkily quiet, but he clung to her hand. She couldn't think of any words that would help, so she rode in silence to Luke's house.

She'd never been there before. She rode past it every time she went into town, admiring the rambling blue house with its broad front porch dressed with inviting white rocking chairs.

They walked inside to a spacious living room, much larger than Ely's cramped one, though of course the entry alone of her Bel Air mansion dwarfed this room. Timmy disappeared into the house.

Looking strangely uncomfortable, especially considering he'd been moved to kiss her in front of his congregation, Luke said, "Please have a seat. I'll be back."

Then he too disappeared.

Chelsea wandered over to a sofa and glanced at the magazines on the coffee table. A chill touched her when she saw her own face looking up at her from a months-old tabloid. Did Luke only want to score with a movie star?

She rifled through the stack, counting all the papers with her pictures on the cover. Feeling sick, she turned over the last one in the stack.

It was more recent, and the cover belonged to Quentin Grandy and his producer. She knew they'd been injured in some freak accident on the set of

DinoDaddy. She'd only paid attention because one day she intended to star in a Grandy film. The man was a womanizer, but he had talent.

She looked more closely at the picture, thinking of the incident she'd imagined when she'd almost burned down Ely's kitchen. The man who had appeared . . .

Nah. Chelsea dropped the paper. She'd long since decided she'd hallucinated the image, probably from the shock of the spark zapping her face.

She heard footsteps but didn't look around. One way or another she would know what Luke Miller thought of her. What he wanted from her.

"Hello, my dear."

Chelsea whirled around. That voice didn't belong to Luke.

"Ely?" She backed away. "But you're dead."

He shook his head and took a step toward her. "I'm sorry we had to make you think that."

"Sorry?" She clutched at her throat, staring at the man she'd thought she'd lost forever. He looked very much as she remembered, the kindly old gentleman of her childhood memories. "I thought you were dead and all along you've been living here?" Her voice rose.

"We did it for the best." Ely held out a hand. "I know this is a shock—"

"We?" The pronoun finally registered with her and when it did, anger at being tricked negated her joy at seeing Ely alive. "So Luke Miller was in on the joke, too. Oh, you two must have had a bellyful of laughs planning this trick!" She'd begun to shake. "I thought you were dead, I've grieved over you, and all along you were faking it."

"Chelsea, my dear, it wasn't like that at all." Ely joined her on the sofa, or tried to, but she jumped up and ran toward the door. "Let me explain."

"Forget it! How do you think I feel, seeing you when I thought you were dead?" Chelsea stomped her foot, something she hadn't done in weeks now. "Keep your filthy money. I'm out of here!"

She whirled and ran back across the friendly porch where she'd longed to sit and rock with Luke and watch the sunset. He'd left the keys in the ignition of his truck, so she took it, roaring off down the lane, fighting back tears.

Of course she was happy Ely was alive, but dammit, they'd deceived her.

When she skidded to a halt in front of her house, she found a Lincoln Town Car in the drive and Fran camped on the front porch.

"I've never been so glad to see anyone in my life!" she cried and ran to hug her manager.

Fran hugged her back, then glanced up with her sharp eyes. Chelsea knew she spotted the tears, the newly acquired freckles and a line or two that had crept around her eyes.

"You just missed some men in blue suits hauling a guy off your porch. No lack of excitement here, is there?"

"Who cares? Let's get out of here," Chelsea said, tugging on Fran's hand. "I'll get Toy-Toy and we'll go to the airport."

Fran snapped shut the notebook computer she'd been using. "Fine by me, I've got the jet. You've got quite an itinerary the next few days."

"Itinerary?" Chelsea echoed, her heart sinking even further.

"How do you think I kept the press off your back

here as well as I did?" Fran followed her in the house. "Didn't you even notice they quit dogging you? Well, you have me to thank for that but now you'll have to pay the price. You're doing a 'Today' show remote, Regis and Kathie, and 'Good Morning America.' And that's just your first two days back."

Chelsea heard the patter of words, but none of them registered. Luke had known all along Ely wasn't dead. No wonder he hadn't comforted her, or offered his condolences. He knew it was all a sham.

She grabbed her purse from where she'd dropped it in the bedroom. Her new blue dress lay crumpled on the bed, the pumps discarded beside it. She gave a little kick to the shoes. "Take that," she said. What an idiot she'd been, thinking she might fit in here, when all along the whole thing had been some orchestrated joke.

Why, Ely's money never would have gone to Am/Am. He simply could have strolled into the lawyer's office and that alone would have nullified the will.

Goddammit! Toy-Toy whimpered as she picked him up. Chagrined, she kissed his paw and whispered, "Mummy's taking you home where you'll be safe."

"What happened to him?" Fran asked as they headed to her rental car.

"It's a long story," Chelsea said.

Ely found Timmy crying in the kitchen, his head drooping over his bowl of cereal. Luke had dashed after Chelsea on foot, only to see her pass by in a cloud of dust in a big sedan. He'd returned to the house, refusing to let Ely comfort him, changed into running clothes, and left again.

"All my friends are gone," Timmy blubbered as Ely gathered him in his lap.

"Chelsea had to go home. She lives in California."

"But Mia's gone, too. Why did she have to go at the same time?"

"Are you sure she isn't here?" Ely hadn't noticed, but as upset as he was over Chelsea's reaction, that didn't surprise him.

Timmy fished Quentin's Yankees cap from the pocket of his shorts. "I talked to her right after breakfast and when we got home I found Quentin's cap on my toy chest. She left it to say good-bye."

"Mmmm." In his childish wisdom, Timmy was doubtlessly correct. Since Quentin's disappearance, Mia had clutched that cap, carrying it with her constantly, as if the connection could bring him back to her.

Given the improbable logic of all that had taken place, and the rules governing their situation as related to him by Mia and Quentin, Ely was pretty sure why Mia was no longer with them.

Both Luke and Chelsea had come to realize what each meant to the other. And for Chelsea, that realization sealed the change in her behavior. Thus, Mia and Quentin had accomplished their Intervention.

The darn thing was, the way Ely bungled the news he was very much alive may have ruined it for them.

"And I thought I was some wise old man," Ely murmured.

"Aren't you?" Timmy said, looking more his usual self.

"I don't know, son." Ely glanced around the homey kitchen, the windows still graced with the blue and white checked curtains Jenny had hung, the large country pine table where he sat with Timmy, a table with room for several more children.

Decades ago he'd turned his back on the societal expectations of his family and his class and found happiness here in Hill Springs. But could his grand-niece do the same?

"I just don't know, Timmy," he said, settling the Yankees cap on the child's head.

Chelsea endured the interviews, the endless posturing. She told herself if she could stand a month hanging chickens, she could smile at Regis, volley witticisms with Bryant Gumbel, and patiently explain yet one more time how she'd survived privation in the hills of Arkansas.

Fran orchestrated the circus. Chelsea merely played the role of marionette. When prodded, she moved; when the right buttons went off, she spoke.

The numbness lasted four days. Four days during which her thoughts zigzagged from Luke and Timmy and waking to hear the neighboring rooster crow, only to be interrupted by bizarre images of herself dressed in the navy blue dress she purchased at Mode O' Day, very much alive yet laid out in a white velvet casket.

On the fifth day, she woke up in her king-size four-poster bed, swathed in satin, threw the covers to the floor and screamed, "What am I doing?"

Of course no one else could hear her, locked away as she was in her private suite.

But the question was meant for her.

Hadn't she learned anything?

Hadn't she changed at all?

She didn't want to die; she wanted to live.

Heedless of the hour, she marched to her phone

and called Western Union, ordering a telegram to be delivered to Ely's house ASAP. The text, as dictated, read:

DEAR ELY.

PLEASE FORGIVE MY ANGER. I UNDERSTAND WHAT YOU WERE TRYING TO DO. GLAD YOU ARE ALIVE. PLEASE CALL ME. I'LL WAIT IN MY ROOM UNTIL I HEAR FROM YOU (HOPE YOU'RE NOT AS STUBBORN AS I WAS).

LOVE, CHELSEA.

And she did refuse to budge. Even when Fran showed up and screamed through the door that she had to go on camera in thirty minutes and why was the door locked. Even when she heard someone pounding at the lock. To solve that problem, Chelsea called through the door, "I have a gun. If you try to break in, I'll shoot."

That won her some peace and quiet. While she waited for Ely to receive her telegram, praying he'd call soon, she made a list of resolutions. Just because Luke Miller had broken her heart was no reason to turn her back on the friends she'd made in Arkansas.

She ordered raises for her household staff, sliding the note under the door as she knew Fran and several others were milling around there, waiting for her to emerge.

And she paced, regretting anew the way she'd ignored her great-uncle's pleas. What if he did to her what she had done to him?

Finally, some four hours later, the phone rang. "Oh, Uncle Ely," she cried, "I'm so glad you called."

He told her a story she found hard to believe, a

tale about angels and a second chance at life. He told her he'd only been trying to reach her, to help her find her way. And he told her, gruffly, that he sure hoped she'd give Luke the same kind of second chance that Mia and Quentin had been offered.

"That's up to him," she whispered, clutching the phone so tightly her knuckles turned white. "A woman can only do so much."

Ely chuckled at that. "Come on, girl, you're the last female I'd expect to hear that from."

"I just can't go there and throw myself at him."

"Ever heard of the telephone?"

She shook her head. She had played the pursuer too many times in her life, the black widow who sucked a man dry and dropped him for dead.

"Will you come see me?" Ely finally asked as the silence drew on.

"Oh, yes," Chelsea said. "I most definitely will."

"When?"

She hesitated. Going to Arkansas, traveling down Blueberry Lane, meant driving past Luke Miller's house, possibly running into him. But even that she would do for Ely. After all, his crazy scheme, conceived in love, had given her a second chance at life. "I'll be there next Monday," she said.

"Thank you," Ely said, and said good-bye with a smile in his voice.

Luke streaked into the yard from his run, neglecting to cool down. The grueling pace he'd set for himself on that morning's five-mile run pleased him. If he couldn't feel good, at least he could punish himself.

At his back porch, he paused long enough to stretch his hamstrings before clambering into the kitchen. He had to wake Timmy, get him dressed to go to his cousins' house, and get ready for a meeting at church at nine.

To his surprise, Timmy was already at the table, dressed and eating cereal.

"Hey," Luke said, "You're up bright and early."

"Yes." Timmy kept chewing.

Luke knew something was wrong. He sat down at the table. "Timmy?"

His son clouded over. "Did Chelsea go away because I was bad?"

"Of course not." That question explained why Timmy was up and at 'em. "Sweetheart, Chelsea went away because she lives in California."

"I don't see why she can't live here. She did live here." He dropped his spoon with a clatter.

"But Ely's living in his house again now."

"She could live with us."

Oh, no. Luke uttered a silent prayer for wisdom. "She would only live with us if she were going to be your stepmother."

"Okay."

"It's not that simple." Luke wiped his sweaty forehead and pushed his hair back.

"If you like her and I like her, why can't she come live with us?" Timmy's face took on that mulish look that settled in before he threw a really big tantrum.

"What about Chelsea? Does she get a vote?"

"You can at least ask her!" Timmy shoved a large mailing envelope across the table toward him. "And give her this."

He got up and ran from the table.

With a sigh, Luke opened the envelope. Inside was a handmade valentine, cut out of red construction paper. In Timmy's careful printing was the message: Please be my Mommy.

His heart broke.

Timmy had never gotten over Jenny's death. And what little boy could? It was hard enough for Luke to deal with, as much as he knew that bad things simply happened, even to good people.

But life went on. Luke fingered the valentine, wishing for the impossible.

If you like her and I like her, why can't she come live with us? He slid the valentine back into the envelope and went in search of a suitcase.

24 ～

After Mia had raced to get Ely to phone the FBI, she walked up the stairs to Timmy's room. She smiled at the little-boy jumble of toys and books, then placed Quentin's Yankees cap on the chock-full toy chest.

The next thing she knew, she found herself sitting in a chair in what she recognized as the red velvet confines of the Second Chance Room.

She started to get up, her first thought to find Quentin, but no matter how she struggled, she couldn't rise. Peering across the dimly lit room, she saw two men at a card table.

"Yoo-hoo," she called, but could not hear her voice. That frightened her even more than being immobilized from the waist down. Was she dead? Had they lost their chance at life? Or through the grace of God and the clever cooperation of Ely Van Ness, had they succeeded?

Lights came up in the front of the room, revealing a floor-to-ceiling screen. Music burst forth from speakers in the ceiling and "Coming Attractions" appeared in script across the screen.

Then for the briefest of moments, a spotlight shone, illuminating the table. Quentin! He looked exactly as he had when she'd last seen him, sans his Yankees cap. Her heart bubbled with joy and relief. She waved and pointed to her legs.

The smile on Quentin's face was music to her soul as he, too, struggled and tried to leave his chair. He wanted to come to her!

The old man who'd sent them on their journey sat across from Quentin. And on the table rested the egg timer set so long ago in this very room, only a few grains of sand left to run.

The spotlight went to black, but no matter what happened next, Mia knew she and Quentin were together.

She also knew that just before darkness claimed the room, the old man winked at her.

Luke wound through the streets of Bel Air, grateful for the Map to the Stars' Homes he purchased on Sunset Boulevard.

On his flight to Los Angeles, he'd settled within his mind and heart that he was doing the right thing. To let pride and fear of rejection stand in the way of potential happiness would be to follow the path of the fool.

If Chelsea slammed the door on him or laughed—well, so be it.

Timmy's valentine lay on the seat beside him, along with a ring box bearing a simple gold band.

He passed yet another estate, this one done in modern Moorish, and curved right. In front of Chelsea's address, he pulled over and surveyed the six-foot-high pink stucco wall and massive iron gates. Picturing his own modest country house, he swallowed.

But he pulled up and rang the gate buzzer.

Back in the Second Chance Room, Mia gasped as the image on the screen came into focus. An aerial view of the Los Angeles Basin dissolved to a shot of Luke Miller driving through the gates of Chelsea Jordan's oft-photographed pink palace.

Then the picture cut to a close-up of Luke's face just before the front doors swung open. Mia identified anticipation, hope, and a hint of nerves.

She glanced over at Quentin. He was staring at the screen, but as if he sensed her looking at him, he smiled and waved and pointed at the cinéma vérité. She couldn't hear him, but she thought she lip-read the words, "Way to go, Mia. You put these two together!"

The old man watched the screen, too. The look on his time-worn face Mia could only describe as that of a cat licking the cream off its whiskers.

Chelsea checked the time on her treadmill timer. Only twenty minutes! She swiped at her brow with the back of her forearm and continued.

Today was her thirtieth birthday, and as a gift to herself, she'd determined to improve her aerobic conditioning. She had a lot of living yet to do, and an awful lot to live for.

Even without Luke.

That thought tugged at her heartstrings. She pictured him in the pulpit smiling down at her, felt his kisses again on her lips.

She strode faster and swung her arms more

briskly, thinking of all the things she had to accomplish. She had a plant to reorganize. And she had Fran searching out new film projects; from now on, she'd do only movies she believed in.

A timid knock sounded at the door.

"Yes?" Chelsea called.

"Excuse me, Miss Jordan," a maid said through the door.

"It's okay, you can come in." Chelsea kept walking.

A Hispanic maid stuck her head around the door, apparently unsure whether she'd be yelled at or not.

Chelsea looked closely at the woman, then beckoned her in. Sure enough, it was Maria, the woman she'd fired for returning to the house for her bus pass the night Chelsea tried to gas herself.

Thirty days ago, Chelsea hadn't even known the woman's name, but this week she'd had Fran track her down and offer her job back.

"There's a man to see you, Miss Jordan."

Old habits dying hard, Chelsea almost snapped at the woman. She'd instructed her staff not to disturb her in the gym. "I can't see anyone right now, Maria. Look at me, I'm a mess."

The door opened wider and Maria whirled around.

Luke stepped into the room. "No, you're not," he said.

Chelsea stopped in her tracks.

Maria backed from the room.

"Why is it," Chelsea asked, "you always catch me when I look a sight?"

Luke smiled and said, "To me you're always beautiful."

* * *

In Room 111, only a grain remained in the egg timer.

Mia found her voice. "Oh, Luke, don't waste time. Ask her to marry you!"

Then she heard Quentin call, "Kiss her, you fool!"

And back in Bel Air, Luke must have heard them. He covered the room in three strides and gathered a sweaty Chelsea Jordan in his arms, whispering a question to her as he held her close.

She whispered back.

"Yes, I'll be your wife," sang sweetly from the speakers in Room 111. The old man broke into applause and cried, *"Mazel tov."*

Then he looked around the Second Chance Room, now empty except for him. He wiped at his eyes with his hanky and muttered, "No rest for the weary. Time for another project."

Quentin awoke to the irritation of a steady beeping noise. He raised his hand to slap at the source, but his hand wouldn't move.

Funny, he'd been dreaming he couldn't move and now he woke up and found himself immobilized. He looked around and saw to his surprise he wasn't in his bed at home.

The door opened and a woman in white popped in. "Oh, my," she said, "you're awake!"

"Of course I am." Then he noticed all the wires and tubes hanging from his body. No wonder he'd dreamed he couldn't budge.

Dreaming—

No.

"Where's Mia?" Fear stood in his throat as he asked the question.

"Miss Tortelli is right next door."

"Get me out of here."

Silently, he said, "Thank you, Mr. G, you old coot."

"Mr. Grandy, you've been ill a long time. I can't let you get up. I have to call your doctor."

He fixed the nurse with his most compelling look and said, "Unhook me and I'll give you a role in my next movie."

Before he could say Academy Awards the nurse had the tubes and wires undone. He sprang up and raced to Mia's room.

Her precious eyes were open and she was struggling to sit up in the bed when Quentin dashed into the room. He grasped her hands and said, "Mia, my love, I want to spend this second chance at life with you. Only you. Will you marry me?"

Mia pulled him close, and a lively gleam in her eyes, whispered, "If you get in bed right this minute and remind me how to wake up nice and slow and easy, the answer's yes. Yes! Yes!"